ISLAND *of* SWEET PIES *and* SOLDIERS

SARA ACKERMAN

ISLAND *of* SWEET PIES *and* SOLDIERS

Recycling programs for this product may not exist in your area.

ISBN-13: 978-0-7783-1921-4

Island of Sweet Pies and Soldiers

For questions and comments about the quality of this book, please contact us at CustomerService@Harlequin.com.

MIRABooks.com

BookClubbish.com

Printed in U.S.A.

For my grandmother Helen, who never forgot.

And for the soldiers.

ISLAND *of* SWEET PIES *and* SOLDIERS

Prologue

MR. MACADANGDANG SHOWED UP WITH A truck full of coconuts this morning. The way his back fender scraped across the road, you'd think he was transporting barrels of lead. He knows that Mama and Jean are suckers for coconut pie, and he's been extra helpful since Papa disappeared.

There's only one problem with a mountain of coconuts in your front yard—someone has to husk them all. He taught me how once, using a cane knife that could have hacked off my hand with one slip. First you hold the coconut in your hand like a baseball. Then you crack it in half with one big hit. When the water pours out, you hold it above your head and swallow it down.

Mama put an end to that. "Macadangdang! What are you doing? Teach *me*, not Ella," she said.

It's been almost three years now since Pearl Harbor, one year since Papa vanished. Everyone else measures time from the moment those Japanese planes shot their torpedoes into our ships. I measure it from the last time I saw Papa. People say things get easier as time passes but not in my case. Even though we get *special treatment*, as Jean calls it, that doesn't make up for being fatherless in the middle of a war.

Mama and Jean are plotting to sell pies to the new soldiers in town. Mama says we need the money, Jean needs a distraction, and I'll get to eat the leftovers. So it works out for all of us.

But back to my papa disappearing. I was there. Mama thinks I was playing in the Codys' yard. That's not true. Don't ask me to tell because I'm sworn to secrecy. Lives depend on it.

There are days when I feel like the secret is growing inside of me, and wonder if I might explode like a popped balloon. But I have to keep Mama safe, and not let the words out. Words that could ruin everything and put us all in danger. At first all I wanted to do was run to her, screaming, to paint the story in giant red letters across the wall. But it was a year ago, and writing didn't come easily. I still got the *b* and the *d* mixed up.

Nowadays, I keep the cane knife close. But not for the coconuts.

Chapter One

Territory of Hawaii, 1944

ELLA

THE FIRST SOLDIERS ARRIVED LAST DECEMBER. More came last weekend. On the day the first group arrived, Mama and I were on our way to Hayashi store for a vanilla ice cream after school. Mama fanned her face and fought off rivers of sweat, but I didn't notice the heat. Growing up in Hawaii would do that to a child, everyone always said. We were halfway down the hill when the ground began to vibrate under our feet. I thought maybe the Japanese were back, this time coming for us by land.

Mama squeezed my hand. "Honey, not to worry. The sirens would be going off."

When we made it to the main road, we saw the first truck rolling in. In the sticky air, I could taste the diesel on my tongue. No matter what Mama said, my heart hummed along with those trucks, about one hundred beats per minute.

"That man has blood on his head," I said, worried about a soldier leaning on the edge of the truck bed. His eyes were closed like he was in silent conversation with himself, or maybe God, and he wore a red-soaked bandage.

"Blood happens when you're fighting a war, sweetie."

Until that moment, I had never seen real live wounded soldiers. The soldiers were propped up against each other, looking out with blank faces. Torn shirts, bandaged limbs and eyes that had lost all smile. Folks from town rushed out to throw fruit to them. A coconut struck one man in the stomach and he slumped over. I wanted to help, but there was nothing I could do. My eyes followed him until the truck went out of sight. But even then, the funny feeling in my stomach stayed.

"Where did they come from?" I yelled above the rumble.

Mama seemed lost in her own thoughts, her big blue eyes glossy. "Hilo, probably, but before that, who knows."

In the distance, I could see that the convoy continued on through town—past the school, the bank, the post office, following the late-afternoon sun. The last three trucks turned up the road toward Honoka'a School, where we live.

I imagined a whole new wave of war happening, and this scared the gobbledygook out of me. By now we were used to blackouts and air-raid drills. If they could so much as see the burner from your kitchen stove, you were in trouble. Big trouble, like they would arrest you and haul you off to jail, maybe forever. Saving metal scraps was also important. I used to rummage around school for any old paper clips or nails or tacks. You could turn them in for ration tickets. Rumors swirled around town, too. *Hilo will be taken over soon by the Japanese. Midway is the next target. So-and-so is a Japanese spy.* Everyone was affected.

"Where are they going?" I wanted to know.

Mama shrugged. "I don't know, but we'll find out."

In Honoka'a, if you really wanted to know something, all you had to do was ask Miss Irene Ferreira, the telephone operator. Why was it that some people had names that had to be said together? Mama was always Violet, and Jean was Jean. But Irene was never just Irene. She swore she never listened in, and still, somehow, secrets leaked and stories spread. Even though the military took over the phones after Pearl Harbor, for some reason they let her stay on.

Once the endless line of trucks passed, we walked across the street to the small red house where she worked. Irene Ferreira sat amid wires and plugs. She wore a headset that made her look very official.

"Any idea what this convoy is about?" Mama said.

Irene pinched her plump lips together and shook her head. "Mum's the word. You know how the military is."

"Come on. You must have heard something."

Irene Ferreira looked behind Mama and me, and then stood to peer outside the dusty windows. "I hear they're building a base in Waimea town. Marines."

Technically, Waimea wasn't a town. It was more a ranch with a handful of wooden houses and stores sprung up around it. A cold and windy place full of Hawaiian cowboys and more grass than you'd know what to do with.

"Why our school?" Mama said.

Irene didn't answer.

"Is there something we don't know?"

That got my attention. If the island was filling up with soldiers, did that mean we were going to be attacked? I have my own bunny suit, which is a dumb name for a gas-mask contraption, but I never thought I would really need it. My breath caught halfway up my throat and my chest started squeezing in. This happens a lot. Vexation, Mama says. Besides not knowing how to breathe, I gnaw my fingernails to the point where they bleed and I pick at freckles and turn them into scabs. The worst of all is the stomachache that never goes away. It all started happening when Papa disappeared.

Irene said, "That's all I know. I promise."

As tempting as it was to stay and pry the information out of her, we decided to follow the trucks up to the school. The soldiers drove straight onto the newly clipped field in front of the gym, their heavy trucks sinking into the mud. Mr. Nakata, the principal, must have been mad, watching from the side of the gym. A man in a green uniform spotted us approaching and marched right over.

"Excuse me, ma'am. This area is off-limits," he said.

"We live here," Mama said, pointing toward our house.

"You don't live in the gym, do you? Please step away."

There was nothing Mama hated worse than being ordered around, especially by a newcomer. I sometimes point out that she was once a newcomer—here they call them *malihini*—but she believes it's more about how you behave and what's in your heart than where you come from.

Still curious, she dragged me over to the administration building, where the men unrolled strands of barbed wire and posts. Another group unloaded cots and stacks of green metal boxes. With no spare movements, they went about their business of taking over a part of our school. The war had finally arrived in our own backyard.

But for Mama and me, the war was not the worst thing that had happened lately. The worst had already come.

Chapter Two

VIOLET

THE KITCHEN WAS WHERE MOST OF THEIR LIVing took place. Violet pulled a cold towel from the icebox and pressed it to her forehead. The radio played Bing Crosby, a welcome diversion from updates on the battles taking place in Europe. It was hard to keep the names and the places in order, but Jean had hung a giant map on the living room wall so they had something to refer to when they heard that British troops had landed at Reggio Calabria or that the Italian fleet had surrendered at Malta.

"These Chinese names are impossible to pronounce. *Jiang Zhongzheng?* My mouth wasn't designed for them," Jean said.

Violet laughed. "The Russian ones are worse. Five consonants strung together?"

"Either way, I'm glad the Russians are on our side."

"Me, too. I just wish the Japanese were."

Jean stood next to Violet, husking corn and humming along with the music. Her hips couldn't help but sway, and her lips mouthed the words to every song. When Violet had first seen Jean in the classroom next door, she wondered why a movie star had come to town, but Jean turned out to be the newest teacher at Honoka'a High. Fresh off the boat from Seattle, where it had been *too damp and too cold.* Jean had been living with Violet and Ella for over a year. Ever since Herman disappeared and Violet's life had begun to unravel.

Campus housing was scarce and Violet had been happy for the company. Their cottage was the largest on campus, with three bedrooms and a living room big enough for a sofa, two chairs and a *pune'e.* Set back from the others, the cottage bordered a dense tangle of woods behind the school. Violet and Jean had painted the walls white and filled it with ferns and crawling plants and enough books to help them forget the outside world. The exterior of the house was another story. Sunflower yellow. For Ella.

One of the disadvantages to having the largest cottage was the abundance of windows. Windows that needed to be boarded up and blacked out at night. Houses in Hawaii were designed for the steady trade winds, with more screened windows than walls. When the school was built, no one had planned on a war. Soon after Pearl Harbor, and martial law, the shop teacher fashioned thin wooden slats that easily slipped into place. But the sliding screen doors that led from the living room onto the porch made blacking out that section of the house nearly impossible. So at night, Violet, Jean and Ella stuck to the kitchen, reading Dr. Seuss and listening to the radio. And once Ella went to sleep, Violet and Jean would discuss the war. And Jean's flame, Bud. He was one of the marines who showed up last December straight from the battle at Tarawa. The people in Hawaii had taken them in and made them their own. Jean fell in love with Bud, but now he'd been shipped out.

They also talked about Herman. And what might have happened to him.

"Ella asked me today if she could go to Japanese school," Violet said in a hushed tone so Ella, who was drawing in the living room, wouldn't hear.

Jean turned off the faucet and faced her, eyes big. "Our Ella?"

"I wasn't sure I heard correctly at first."

That morning, when Ella had asked, Violet fought to keep her face in order. "Japanese school is for Japanese. And you, my dear, are not Japanese," she'd said, brushing a lock of Ella's hair back.

"Why does it matter?" Ella had said.

"It's just how it is right now. With the war."

"Umi says all they do is make origami animals and sing." Ella was still too young to know the meaning of skin color, and how it mattered more than it should. "Please?"

It took Violet a few seconds to realize that Ella had made up her mind. "No promises, but I can ask."

These were the moments in childrearing that she longed to have Herman around. He was good at handling difficult matters. Violet tended to let emotions cloud her thinking. Anyway, it was the first time in the past year that Ella had shown interest in doing anything apart from Violet. She would spend a whole afternoon drawing pictures of dragonflies or petting the cats on the porch rather than venturing out on her own. Aside from when she was at school, which she hated, Ella could always be found within a thirty-foot radius of her mother.

Jean wiped her hands on a dish towel. "What did you say to her?"

"I pointed out the obvious. But now I'm wondering. Japanese learn English. Why couldn't she learn Japanese?"

Jean shook her head. "I know you hate to say no, but this might not be the best time. People are on eggshells about whether or not the school should even be open."

"If they were going to shut it down, they would have already."

"Nothing's for certain."

Before she could respond, Ella appeared in the doorway, bare feet white against the green linoleum. "Mama, there's a tall man at the front door."

She and Jean exchanged glances. There were few tall strangers in the area. Jean smoothed her skirt and they walked out to the living room together. Ella hung back. It was September and the remaining light sent streaks of gold through the *hau* trees. A figure in a green uniform stood in front of the screen door, backlit. Another stood on the steps below, looking out toward the ocean.

As she approached the door, Jean squealed. "Zach? Is that you?" She flung open the door and flew outside, wrapping herself around one of the men before he could get a word out. "What are you doing here? Oh, Lordy Lord, I can't believe this!" She turned to Violet. "This is my little brother, Zach."

When he managed to detach himself from Jean, he shook Violet's hand, nearly pulling her arm out of its socket. "Pleased to meet you, ma'am."

Zach motioned to the other man. "This is Sergeant Parker Stone, Fifth Division."

Parker squeezed her hand. His eyes were either deep-sea blue or silver, and she tried not to stare. Must have been the lighting.

"Please, come in," Jean said.

Parker remained planted. "I'll wait out here if you don't mind. I can't seem to get enough of this sweet air," he said, looking more interested in the whitecaps and cane fields than in either of them.

Jean pulled Zach in and dragged him into the light of the kitchen. Ella sat at the table, looking into her glass of milk. Violet could tell she was curious because she kept sneaking glances.

"Ella, honey, this is my brother, Zach. Can you say hi?" Jean said.

Ella's chestnut eyes were stubborn. She didn't look up, but in a small voice said, "Hello."

Zach towered over her. "Well, aren't you a sight for sore eyes. Pleased to make your acquaintance, Ella."

He looked down at the picture on the table. Ella ignored him.

"That's a fancy-looking creature. Do those actually live around here?" he said.

The drawing was of a butterfly with lacy wings and a cat's face. Ella nodded, ever so slightly.

"I wasn't aware that Hawaii had flying buttercats. But this is good information to know," he said, winking at Violet.

It didn't take Zach long to make himself comfortable at the table, and for Violet to decide she liked him.

Jean beamed. "Tell me everything, young man. Why didn't you contact me?"

Without his hat, he looked younger. Jean was twenty-five, so Violet guessed Zach to be about twenty-two. "They wouldn't let us. You know how that goes. If anyone so much as mentioned *pineapple* or *island* in our letters home, they were crossed out or returned."

"So you must have been in the convoy that passed through town this weekend. And you're just coming here now?" Jean asked.

"I searched for your face when we drove through. Trust me, I came as soon as I could."

"Your group looks different from the fellas that left us last month," Violet said.

"Camp Pendleton is a far cry from Betio Atoll. God bless those boys." Zach's face clouded over.

"What can you tell us? How long are you here for?" Jean asked.

Zach shared the same smile as his sister, toothy and nearly wider than his face. "That, I can't say. And when you contact Mom and Dad, don't say I'm here. The last thing we need is the Japanese to know what we've got going on. Though Lord knows they have their spies."

Violet's stomach lurched. "Not in this town." She was fed up to her teeth with outsiders assuming all Japanese were spies.

"You can't be too sure," Zach said.

"I can vouch for a good number of them."

"We're just here to protect our country."

"Just beware of blanket assumptions based on skin color," Violet said.

Zach backed off. "I've got to run, since we're supposed to be on official business. It's six o'clock and I don't want to get shot, but I'll come down when on liberty if that's all right?" he said. "And next time we'll bring Roscoe."

"Who's Roscoe?" Jean asked.

"Just you wait. You're going to love him." He glanced at Ella. "You, too, Ella."

At the sound of her name, Ella perked up, but still regarded her drawing instead of Zach.

"Please do! Oh, Zach, I'm so happy to see you. You look well," Jean said.

He placed his hat back on and bent his grasshopper legs

to bring him level with Ella. "And maybe I'll get to see that buttercat for real next time."

Ella looked at the floor.

Later in the evening, Violet peered through the window at Setsuko's house down the hill. Lights were out, which wasn't surprising, since lights were always out. She debated walking down to see if anyone was still awake. There was no excuse for being out past ten unless on official business, and she didn't want to get shot by the guards set up at the school entrance. Curfew was taken seriously. Even still, their houses were on campus, and she would be only a thin shadow against the backs of houses.

"I'm going to walk down to Setsuko's. Can you keep an eye on Ella?" she asked Jean.

"Now?"

If there was one thing in the world she wanted, it was for Ella to come alive again. "I need to ask." After all, why not Japanese school? It couldn't hurt to have Ella learning Japanese customs and language, especially living in a blended town like theirs.

Jean gave her one of her teacher looks, and planted her hands on her hips. "Wait until tomorrow."

"Don't worry. I'll be back soon."

She sneaked around back and padded down the pathway, following a thin trail of moonlight. Voices floated in and out from darkened windows along the way, and radios sent their noise into the black air. Everything seemed so desperately regular, except for the fact that she had to sneak to her friend's house in the cover of night. There would be no sleeping until she talked to Takeo.

From the road up to the school, the hum of an engine grew louder. Why hadn't she accounted for headlights in planning her route? A beam of brilliant light shot across her path as a truck came over the hill. She pressed herself behind a tree, cursing her hips for not being slimmer. But the truck continued on toward the gym. A few minutes passed without another truck.

Outside the house, she hesitated. A knock at the door might cause alarm, but it was too late now. A radio played in the kitchen, and she tapped on the door, while at the same time whispering through the screen. "Setsuko, it's Violet."

The radio turned down and feet shuffled. Silence filled the house.

"It's Violet," she said again, this time louder.

The door opened and she was pulled into the dark living room by strong hands. "What are you doing here?" Setsuko asked. She wore a rice-bag kimono. Her hair, which usually coiled on her shoulders in permed waves, was now pinned up. Violet smelled seaweed on her breath.

Takeo stood behind Setsuko and nodded to the kitchen. A hint of light seeped out from under the door.

She had to work up the nerve for her request. "Did you sell a lot of sweet potato in Waimea?"

Takeo squinted his already narrow eyes. He knew her too well. "Is that what you came here for, Violet? To ask me that?"

Not much taller than she was, he was strong enough to carry a whole bushel of cane on his back. As a *Nisei*, he had both feet planted firmly in Hawaii. What Violet loved about him was that he spent more time listening than talking.

"I have a favor to ask of you," she said.

"Go."

"Ella wants to come to Japanese school."

For a moment, everything in the room seemed to be listening. The crickets outside quieted and the wind hushed. Setsuko coughed.

"I don't understand," he said, throwing a hard glance at his wife.

"My daughter wants to attend your school. As a student."

His eyebrows lifted and he stood there barefoot and unsmiling.

"Please, Takeo. I need this favor." An uneasy feeling welled up in her stomach. She worried he would say no. Ella rarely asked for much, and Violet wanted to give her this.

"Bring her by day after tomorrow."

In the morning, Violet sat at the bureau, readying for school and applying cover-up to her lower lids. The blue of her once-bright eyes had rubbed off sometime in the past year. She only hoped her pink lipstick made up for the lost color. Worse than that, the waves in her latest permanent were falling out and her honey-colored hair now stood stiff like straw.

Last night after talking with Setsuko, she had tried counting convoy trucks to help her fall asleep. That hadn't worked. Jean said maybe it was the grape juice cans rolled in her hair that caused the insomnia, but Violet suspected it was more likely from thinking about things over and over. And over. There were so many layers to her grief. While Ella had a perpetual stomachache, Violet was prone to a perpetual heartache.

Jean was already in the kitchen banging pots around when Violet walked in. "Bad sleep?" she asked.

Violet nodded. Jean always looked fresh from the beauty parlor, not one hair out of place and as though someone had smoothed coconut oil over each strand. Even first thing in the morning. When they had first moved in together, Violet was unsure how two strong-willed women would get along under the same roof. It hadn't taken long for her to realize that having Jean around was like having her very own wife.

On some mornings, coffee was already made, banana pancakes already piled high on a plate, still steaming. And Jean knew how to scour a kitchen clean.

When Ella joined them at the table, dark smudges under her eyes were visible. Though she never complained about being tired, surely the nightmares had taken their toll. "Where's Snowflake?" she asked.

"She must be outside hunting for mice," Violet said.

Ella left her bowl of cornflakes and walked to the front door.

"Pumpkin, you need to eat before Hiro and Umi come for you."

Ella's voice cut through the morning stillness. "Snowflake!"

Snowflake didn't show up, but two other striped cats arrived on the porch and rubbed up against Ella's legs. She sat to pet them, leaving her breakfast unattended. Cats were more important than food and water, and Violet prayed that Snowflake really was out hunting for mice.

"Your cereal is getting soggy. Come on up and eat." Violet looked at the clock. The Hamasu kids were never late and she wondered what was keeping them. The twins were Ella's only friends these days, and the more she was around them, the better.

Ella remained in a fur huddle and acted like she didn't hear. Violet stuffed an extra ball of rice into Ella's lunch tin, then pulled her daughter along. "Come on. You'll have to eat when you get there."

Honoka'a School was the largest high school on the island, with almost one thousand students coming from as far as Paauilo to the east and Waimea to the west. The way the buildings stood on the hillside over town looking out on the Pacific reminded Violet of an exclusive manor. When the skies were clear, she sometimes imagined being able to see all the way to Alaska. On the way to her classroom, she poked her head into Setsuko's room and waved.

"We missed Umi and Hiro this morning," Violet said.

Setsuko met her at the door. "They're with their father, harvesting sweet potato. His worker fell ill."

Nowadays, when people weren't where they were supposed to be, Violet's whole body filled with unease. Only natural after what she'd been through, but there was always something to worry about, between Ella and the war. There was also the matter of all her Japanese friends and their livelihoods. Everyone said it would only be a matter of time before they closed the Japanese school. When your country was at war with Japan, but the Japanese made up almost half of your population, life turned complicated.

Toward the end of fifth period, the bell hadn't even rung when Mr. Nakata showed up outside her classroom. He stood to the side and nodded, but didn't enter. The look on his face was familiar, one part pity and one part annoyance at having to trudge over here. Even though it had been more than a year since he took over for Herman, in her mind Nakata would always be the *new* principal. No one could replace her husband.

When she acknowledged him back, all her students turned their heads in unison toward the door. "Keep practicing your lines, class. I'll be right outside. And I expect that you will have no errors."

The typewriters clicked away.

"I don't want to alarm you, but there's been a small incident with Ella," Nakata said.

Her throat tightened. "Well, I am alarmed. Is she all right?"

He moved in closer and dropped his voice. Wafts of pomade rose from his slick hair. "She's fine, but she wet her pants during the air-raid drill and Mr. Hodges sent her to the infirmary. I'll watch your class until the bell."

The school nurse should have a change of clothes for Ella, but it never got easier. Violet turned and ran.

"Violet, don't you want to put some shoes on?" She ran back in, switched out her Japanese slippers for her flats and sped across the field to the infirmary. The campus was calm-before-the-storm kind of empty, minutes before school got out. She reached the infirmary, a converted old classroom, in one minute flat.

"Hello, Mrs. Baker. Where's Ella?"

Mrs. Baker wore her whites crisp and clean, even though she had outgrown them several years ago. Nevertheless, her overabundant body made for good comforting to sick children. Or scared children, which had become more common these days with air-raid drills and gas-mask practice.

"She's in the back. I got her changed but she refused to go back to class," Mrs. Baker said.

Ella didn't look up when Violet walked into the room. In the oversize PE uniform, her arms looked like small wires sticking out from the sleeves. Red spots patterned her arm, one trickling blood, which meant she was picking at herself again. If Ella noticed her arrival, she didn't let on. She was drawing. Violet sat down on the worn-out carpet next to her.

"That's a lovely cat, honey." Nothing but silence. "Want to tell me what happened?"

Ella shook her head and filled in the wings of a giant bird hovering overhead. The bird appeared to be ready to snatch the cat away in its claws. "You worried about Snowflake? She'll be there when we get home. She always is." It better be the case. "Come on. We can bring that."

Ella remained rooted. "Where are Umi and Hiro?"

"They had to help their father today, selling sweet potato."

The distance between them narrowed when Ella's focus shifted from the drawing up to Violet. Her brown eyes were still too big for her face. "I don't like it here without them."

Violet fought to keep her expression in order. Watching Ella suffer was the worst part of this whole war. "They'll be back tomorrow. Plus, you know how close my room is."

Luther Hodges, the shop teacher and Herman's friend, popped his head in. "Everything okay here?"

"Just having a rough day. We're fine."

Ella began picking the scab on her arm vigorously. She wouldn't look up.

"The sirens seem to set her off. I'll keep an extra eye on her," he said.

Ella seemed much more comfortable around the women teachers and women in general, but any help would be welcome. "Thank you."

To Ella she said, "Did you hear that? You can always seek out Mr. Hodges if you are feeling scared."

Ella began quivering and Violet pulled her in for a hug. "What is it, honey?"

"The air-raid drills scare me."

"They're just practice. Nothing is going to happen to us, especially with half the marines in America just up the street."

There was some measure of comfort having so many armed men around. Soldiers with enough heavy artillery to sink the island and fancy new amphibious landing boats. A small piece of her wondered, though, if that also made the Big Island more of a target.

Chapter Three

ELLA

I WAS ALREADY AWAKE AND STILL WRAPPED IN my horse blankets when Mama came in this morning wearing slippers. Being from Minnesota, Mama doesn't understand walking barefoot. Even in the house. She wears socks when it's cold and Japanese slippers when it's hot, the kind with velvet straps and woven straw where your foot goes. I'm her little native, she says, because I hate wearing shoes. A lot of the Japanese kids from the plantation don't even get to choose because they're so poor. For them, an umbrella is more important. It's one or the other. Rain comes down in buckets here, so the umbrella wins out.

I pretended I was still sleeping because I worried there might be another air-raid drill at school. The noise sets something off inside me. We always have them on Tuesdays. So even if there was a surprise one yesterday, it could happen again. Half the time, I wet my pants. I guess I forgot to mention that earlier. Talk about embarrassing. It smells up the room and everyone turns to me. Sally Botello and Gina Chang pinch up their noses and fan their faces like they're dying. Even Mrs. Hicks looks at me with such pity I want to ask her to please leave the classroom and head over to detention. Teachers should know better. At least the Japanese kids ignore it.

From halfway across the floor, Mama smelled like cinnamon and morning sun. When she shook me, I acted groggy, but she was wearing a huge smile as she sat on the edge of my bed. Snowflake, who showed up last night wet but alive, turned on her purr even louder. It's almost like someone put a little motor inside her throat. I call it a purr-box.

Mama smoothed down my hair. "Good morning, sun blossom."

She calls me weird names. Jean started it. And in case you're wondering, I call Jean *Jean*, not Aunt Jean or Miss Quinlan. She said if we're going to live together, I might as well save my breath. Which was smart, because I have less breath than other people. But I do also call her Honey Jean, mainly because *honey* is her favorite word. I called her it once and the name stuck.

"I have good news," Mama said.

"School is canceled?"

She laughed. "Something even better."

Nothing would have been better. My eyes stung with the coming of tears. I cry a lot for no reason. But the doctor says this is normal behavior for someone who has been through a difficult situation. Which I have.

"What?"

"Takeo said you could start Japanese school today! You'll be the first non-Japanese in the school."

Now, this was news. If I could have picked one thing to do in life, it was go to Japanese school, especially now that it was just fun stuff. Before Pearl Harbor, they taught them to write and talk Japanese. Not anymore. No one wants the kids to be spies.

Somehow, being white made me feel like an outsider, like the only piece of corn in a barrel of rice. Mama said we're corn people, being from Minnesota. But I consider myself Hawaiian, or even partly Japanese. If you spend even five minutes around them, you will know that Japanese people are smarter, neater and more interesting than us. They also don't talk as much, and are probably good at keeping secrets. Sometimes I wonder if I should tell Umi what I know. About my dad.

"For real?" I asked.

Mama pulled out a small wooden box and handed it to me. "You'll need this, to write with."

I sat up and opened the box. Thin bamboo brushes and bottles of ink were neatly packed in on top of white see-through-looking paper. I held it up to my nose and sniffed. It smelled of tree bark mixed with some kind of chemical.

A thin smile crept onto my face. The first one in a while. After the incident with Papa disappearing, it took about a hundred years before I smiled again. At least it seemed that way. Mama, too. Neither of us had anything to smile about, and I think we were both afraid to let ourselves have any kind of happiness. Then, about seven months later, I heard laughing in the kitchen. When I cracked open the door, I heard Jean telling jokes. I don't know where she gets them, but she always has new ones.

"What's the difference between an orange and a matter baby?" she asked.

Mama sat at the table with Betty Crocker opened in front of her. "What's a matter baby?"

"Nothing, honey," Jean said, in a sweet syrupy voice.

A laugh came out of Mama, and from then on, I knew laughing was allowed. We were moving on. But that was a lot easier said than done.

Chapter Four

VIOLET

IN THE MONTHS AFTER HERMAN'S DISAPPEAR-ance, Violet had dragged Ella to one form of specialist after another. They began with the plantation doctor, who prescribed small pink pills that caused Ella to walk around in a fugue state, bumping into walls and drooling. After a week, Violet flushed the pills down the toilet.

The psychiatrist turned out to be even worse. On the day they made the three-hour drive to Hilo, an angry rain forced its way in through the window cracks and drenched them before they had even arrived. Then they dashed through ankle-deep puddles only to find that the doctor would have to reschedule; he had gone to Kona. On their next visit, Dr. Stern spent a full hour interrogating Ella behind a closed red door. Violet knocked several times throughout and poked her head in. Ella never raised her gaze.

After the session, he invited Violet in. Looking over his wire spectacles, past a razorback nose, he said, "Mrs. Iverson, I'm afraid that shock therapy is the only thing that might bring your daughter around."

No expert in medicine, she knew enough to take Ella by the hand and walk out the door.

When it came to Reverend Dunn, his answer was much the same, only in this case it wasn't shock but prayer that would be her only salvation.

In desperation, Violet decided to enlist the help of a Hawaiian named Henry Aulani. He lived in a modest house at the bottom of the road down to Haina. More prison guard in appearance than healer, his mellifluous voice and coffee-colored eyes told a different story. Kids played in the yard and dogs wandered in and out the open back door. He brought them into the high-ceilinged kitchen, where dried plants hung from the rafters, filling the room with sharp and sweet scents of mint and forest.

"Please, sit." He motioned to the table.

Violet felt her throat constricting at the thought of explaining Ella's condition to yet another person. But he didn't ask her anything about Ella.

"Tell me about your home," he said.

"What do you want to know about my home?"

"Whatever you want to tell me," he said.

Violet thought it a strange question. Weren't they here about Ella? "Well, to start with, it's bright yellow..."

She continued on. Ella remained mute until a few minutes later, when a black cat with yellow eyes jumped onto the bench and climbed into her lap. "What's his name?" she asked Henry.

"*Her* name is Pele. And you must be special, because this cat doesn't do that with most people," he said.

"She purrs real loud," Ella said.

On more than one occasion, Ella had asked Violet why

humans don't purr and if there was any way possible to learn how. *"We purr. You just can't hear it,"* Violet had said.

If at all possible, the air in the kitchen now seemed easier to breathe. Whether it was the cat or Henry pulling Violet out of her own mind full of hidden fears, she couldn't be sure.

Henry took both Violet's hands. The warmth in his palms made her own tingle. "Now, tell me what happened."

The date was forever etched in her mind. Friday, September 10, 1943. Violet had been with the sewing circle in the small blue-and-white church below town, assembling cardboard slippers for the wounded men still in the hospital at Tripler, in Honolulu. The group met every week. The horrors of Pearl Harbor were fresh in everyone's mind, even though it had been over a year ago. As usual, Ella stayed next door with Mrs. Cody, who had most of the neighborhood playing in her yard.

When Violet returned to the Codys' cottage, Ella was nowhere to be found.

"What do you mean, she's not here?"

"Maybe she doesn't know that hide-and-seek is over," Mrs. Cody said.

A brief search found Ella two houses up at the Hamasus'. Violet had to steady herself when she saw her daughter. Ella lay on the living room *pune'e* with blankets piled up around her and a warm cloth on her forehead.

Setsuko sat with her. "She wandered in only ten minutes ago. Something's not right."

Ella's skin was the color of cooked rice and her eyes were shut tightly. Right at that exact moment, a feeling of cold ran through Violet, turning her blood to stone.

"You should have told me you weren't feeling well, honey," she said.

Ella didn't answer. It was only the beginning.

★ ★ ★

Back at the house, darkness set in and Herman still had not returned. She assumed he was on a patrol, though he hadn't mentioned he would be out that night. Soon after the bombing, Herman and half the plantation workers formed a group they called the Hawaii Rifles. The members would ride around on horseback, keeping an eye on anything out of order. None of the men had any experience, but that didn't stop them. People wanted to feel like they were doing something.

With the onset of the war, predictability had become a thing of the past, but his absence seemed wrong in a way she couldn't explain. Call it a hunch. She fixed a pot of sweet potato soup up for Ella, who refused even one spoonful. Her forehead felt clammy and her little body shook in small fits.

"That settles it. I'm taking you to the doctor in the morning," Violet said.

A few minutes after midnight, Sheriff Souza knocked on the door. Standing on the porch, he was a mere shadow with a hat, and Violet invited him into the kitchen, where she turned on the light. Instinctively, she hugged herself. His hands were plastered in his pockets. "Mrs. Iverson, I don't want to alarm you, but do you have any knowledge of your husband's whereabouts? His car is down at the lookout below Kukuihaile."

The old Ford. Why on earth would he be down there at this hour? Her mind raced to imagine the possibilities. Submarine spotting. Airplane spotting. Aside from those, there was no reasonable explanation. Not for Herman.

"I don't, Sheriff. Maybe he was on watch duty?"

Souza's expression looked wooden and unreadable. "I yelled around. Did he mention he would be going anywhere?"

She shook her head. "I was at the sewing circle and he usually works at school until dark."

"I'll be honest with you—this seems fishy. With curfew and all."

More than fishy. Herman was the kind of man who never missed an appointment, showed up on the dot. He was reliable to a fault. If he'd had duty tonight, he would have told her.

"Maybe he said something to Luther?" she said.

Souza seemed relieved to have somewhere else to go. "I'll have a word with him. You stay here in case Herman shows up."

As she waited, minutes expanded to hours and Violet was no longer sure if she was awake or dreaming. She closed her eyes and willed herself to wake up, only to understand that she already was. Rain began to bucket down, pelting the windows with tadpole-size drops.

Before long, Souza returned. "Ma'am, Luther didn't know a thing. But he was pretty liquored up. I'll talk to him more tomorrow."

"If anyone, he would know."

"Try to get some rest. I'll put a call out, see if anyone knows anything. And send a car out first thing in the morning. Meantime, stay here. I'm sure there's an explanation."

They were the most feeble words she'd ever heard him speak.

In the kitchen, where Violet waited, the rickety icebox kick-started into high gear every once in a while, startling her with its hum. The wetness of the air caused her hair to stand on end. She felt torn in half.

Sheriff Souza called at eight o'clock with no real news. Mr. Fujimoto had been sweeping the sidewalk in front of his store when he thought he had seen Herman driving north toward Waipio, but that was all. Friday afternoons in town were usually crawling with people, now that the evenings were off-limits. No one would have been paying attention.

"I'm going to head back to the car right now with a few of my men, search the area for any signs. I'll get back to you just as soon as I can," he said.

She hated to think of what that implied. As of now, she was suffering from a trembling in her gut that would not stop. Scenarios played out in her head. Herman meeting up with Japanese soldiers who had crept ashore and scaled the cliffs. Or slipping and falling from those same cliffs. It was simply impossible that her husband would not be found alive and in one piece with a perfectly rational explanation.

Ella slept uneasily through most of the morning, thrashing about in her bed and tangling herself in the blankets. Violet felt her forehead, which had cooled but was still clammy against the back of her hand. Low clouds blocked the sun, allowing only gray light in through the windows. In despair, she called Setsuko, careful not to say much on the line.

Within minutes, her friend stood in the living room with her arms wrapped around Violet. "It will be all right, Violet, I promise you."

"Did you see him after school?" Violet asked.

"No, I went straight to Japanese school. I didn't get back until five, just before Ella showed up on my porch."

Footsteps announced a visitor, and Luther appeared at the door. A veteran of the Great War, he'd arrived in Honoka'a eight years earlier to take over the position as shop teacher and unofficial handyman. Deaf in one ear, and the size of a bear, he and Herman became fast friends. Luther had lost a nephew at Pearl Harbor and had been drowning his sorrows in the bottle, which worried Violet since he had no wife and no other family around.

Overnight, Luther's face had turned ashen and his clothes crumpled. "Any news?" he asked.

She repeated the sheriff's update and added, "Herman drove out there without telling anyone, which concerns me. He didn't mention anything to you?"

"Nope. I've been up most of the night thinking on it. Would it be possible he was meeting someone to fetch a new batch of *okolehao*?"

"He would have mentioned it. Plus, he still has a few bottles left," she said.

"Yes, but you know how much it's worth these days, now that everything's being rationed. We both know he's a shrewd businessman."

True. *Okolehao* was a Hawaiian ti-root moonshine, but some of the locals also used pineapple, taro, sugarcane or rice. Just up the road, Waipio Valley had become a hotbed of illegal *okolehao* production during Prohibition. Violet hated the stuff.

"I feel like he would have told me. But I suppose it's possible."

She wanted to believe him, and wondered if Herman had gone down into the valley to meet someone. There was a Hawaiian man down there he had mentioned once or twice. And maybe the river had overflowed and he was stuck down there. It made sense and was about the only thing that could possibly, remotely, hopefully have been true. But truth, she was finding, didn't always want to be known.

"I'm heading over now to talk to the sheriff," he said.

Violet dropped down on the cracked red paint of the front step. She watched him walk away. Unable to do anything else, she lay back and let the tears come. Setsuko sat next to her and held her hand while she went numb from the inside out.

★★★

Just before lunchtime that day, Ella called out, "Mama?"

Violet rushed to the *pune'e*. "Good morning, love. How you feelin'?"

There was a new vacancy in Ella's eyes, like someone had taken an eraser and removed all the brightness, leaving a dull brown. Ella didn't answer, just closed her eyes and rolled to face the wall.

Setsuko had slipped on an apron and said from the kitchen, "Ella, I have your favorite. Rice cakes."

Violet began to wonder if Ella's condition might not be a sickness at all. The timing was peculiar. *Disease is in the mind*, her father used to say, never allowing anyone to skip chores because of a sniffle or miss school due to a burning throat. As though you could think yourself well. Was it possible that we could also think ourselves sick? Violet reminded herself that Ella had been playing at the Codys', so what could she possibly know?

"Did you happen to see Daddy yesterday afternoon? Before he drove off." Ella shook her head. "Did he say anything to you at all yesterday about going someplace in the afternoon?"

In the silence between them, her fear began to spread.

"Honey, I need you to talk to me."

"My tummy hurts," Ella whispered.

"Setsuko, would you mind fixing some poi?"

A voice inside was telling Violet that the two incidents were connected. Her tough little girl suddenly seemed so fragile. "Where were you when the other kids were looking for you?"

"I had a good hiding place. I told you that," Ella said.

Violet watched the rise and fall of her ribs. Tenderness rushed through her.

"Sometimes, when you hold things inside, it can make you feel sick. Is that what's happening?"

Ella shook her head again, limply.

Violet let out a big sigh. "We can keep it just between you and me, but I need you to tell me anything that seemed out of the ordinary. Even if you don't think it matters."

"There's nothing to tell."

She prodded Ella for more information, but Ella refused to answer. Frustration was building up inside, causing every cell in her body to hurt. She wanted to scream.

When Sheriff Souza returned, his face had *bad news* written all over it. He didn't waver as he asked her to accompany him into the kitchen and swung the door shut. Her heart dropped.

He chewed on his lower lip for a moment before speaking. "Now, I can't say that we found anything conclusive, and there was plenty of rain last night, but we combed the area around his car and there appear to be some broken bushes. And blood. Just a small amount, but it was near the edge of the overlook."

The word *blood* was all she heard. "Did you look below? Could he have been hurt and fallen?"

She pictured the cliffs. Lofty, vertical slabs that plunged straight into the roiling blue. In some areas, small outcroppings of land jutted out.

"Anyone falls, they end up in the water. Or on the rocks. We didn't see a body on the rocks."

A *body.* She felt herself unraveling at the seams and had to check to make sure her upper half was still connected to her lower half. Strangely, she felt as though she were listening to a radio detective show. Herman dead was impossible. Husbands were not allowed to die. Especially young ones. Especially hers.

The words came out in a whisper. "Luther thinks Herman went into Waipio with someone for *okolehao*. That blood could have been from anything, couldn't it? A pig, a goat."

"Could have been. I sent Boy Rapozo down to check. No one coughs down there without him knowing about it. Gonna have the blood tested. Do you know his type?"

"O."

The ringing in her ears ramped up and Violet focused on Souza's bristly mustache and the way his lips jutted out underneath. How his gaze moved around the kitchen, trying to find an anchor.

"Thank you, Sheriff."

"We'll get to the bottom of this. People don't just disappear in Honoka'a. Not on my watch."

As it turned out, they did. The only lead that turned up was from a chicken farmer up the way who claimed he heard two gunshots that afternoon. But even he couldn't be sure from which direction they had come. Speculation in town was rampant. *Herman worked for the Japanese. A moonshine deal had soured. He was gambling on cockfights. Working for the FBI.*

That people thought someone as upstanding and well liked as Herman could be a spy boiled her insides. But she had to admit most things Japanese did have a special place in his heart. His secretary was Japanese, he boasted that some of his best teachers were Japanese, and many of his friends were Japanese. He liked Japanese food, drank Japanese wine, and grew Japanese sweet potatoes in his garden. But did that make him a spy?

Violet swayed back and forth between her own two theories. One was that he might have been on watch for the Hawaii Rifles, and been ambushed by the Japanese while out patrolling along the cliffs. But no one else had seen anything suspicious and no one else had up and vanished. The other idea was that he had upset someone in the spirit business, because he had on several occasions voiced an interest in making his own. She had argued against it.

"How will it look if the school principal is also a moonshine distributor?" she had said.

"Honey, it would just be for a few of us around here. And we could use the extra money to buy more land."

"Not a good idea," she'd insisted.

If only she could find his calendar, which he also used as a sort of journal. It was not on his desk where it usually was and had yet to turn up. Either he had it with him, or someone took it. This was the one piece of information that didn't fit. How could someone have taken it? Sheriff Souza had interrogated everyone in the school on this small fact, reasoning that if someone had taken the journal, someone had access to his office.

For an entire week, Ella wouldn't eat solid food and Violet took to feeding her spoonfuls of chicken broth and rice. She refused to go back to school, and so Violet had to bring her to class once she returned to work the following week. There was no way for Violet to hide the swollen redness of her eyes, so she didn't even bother. Sleep came sparingly. By mornings, her pillow was soaking and covered in clumps of hair. *Herman, where are you?* As best she could, Violet tried to stay in that slice of time just after waking, before she remembered. It never lasted more than three seconds.

Eventually, the blood results came back. Human. Type O.

Chapter Five

VIOLET

THE NEXT DAY AT SCHOOL PASSED WITHOUT INcident, and Violet met Ella at her class. They stopped at home for a quick snack of chocolate pudding, then continued across the worm-eaten bridge over the ravine and up the hill to the small building where Japanese school was held. They passed clumps of ginger, a thick stand of guava clouded with fruit flies and a dilapidated chicken coop with rusted wires, full of vines instead of chickens. Ella held her hand like she was trying to strangle it.

Before Pearl Harbor happened, students learned to speak the Japanese language, practiced calligraphy, and were schooled in common traditions like ikebana and *yukata*. Violet guarded her opinions, but she thought it a miracle the school had been allowed to keep on. The military had ordered Takeo to stick to arts and crafts. None of the kids minded.

Please, God, let this work out. Umi and Hiro already knew about Ella coming, but there was concern over how her presence would go over with the other students. Takeo had said, *"Do not worry."* But worry was everywhere, as plentiful as the stalks of sugarcane in the fields. The elongated one-room building contained two sections, and Ella would be with the six- to twelve-year-olds.

When they approached the school, Ella stopped. "Do you think they will like me?"

"You already know most of the kids."

"That's what I'm worried about."

The words tugged at Violet's heart. "The sensei is like your uncle, so no one will dare bother you."

Even before Herman's disappearance, Ella had been shy and considered *different* by the kids. Partly because of her skin color, but more than that, she was the kid in the group who chose green when everyone else chose blue. She picked animals over people, and once punched Robbie Iwase in the nose when he tried to torture the class rabbit. From then on, kids steered clear.

They stood there, staring at the whitewashed wooden house. Two mynah birds chattered on the road in front of them. Ella looked around, and Violet followed her gaze.

In front of the schoolhouse, a row of garden boxes overflowed with lettuce, kale, plump tomatoes and eggplant. Off to the side a large square patch of sweet potato crawled through the grass. The students had painted VICTORY in red, white and blue on the boxes, which might have helped their cause. Several fat hens scratched about, reminding Violet of home. Leaving her hens had been one of the hardest parts about leaving Minnesota. On the sagging plank porch, two girls played jacks, too engrossed to notice them.

Ella tugged at her hand, and together they crossed the yard and entered the building. There were no desks, no tables and chairs, only tatami mats spread out across the floors. The walls were lined with shelves and everything had a place. The sills were painted a deep red and several bonsai plants caught sun through the mottled glass. Violet felt a stab of envy. Her classroom had never looked so tidy.

The chatter of young voices filled the room, and Takeo stood near the front. In the other half of the house, Setsuko taught the teenagers. After the war broke out, the school lost many students, parents fearing to seem overly Japanese. Though how could you be anything other than Japanese, if you were Japanese? She had yet to determine exactly what constituted one's Japanese-ness, but being born in Japan was at the top of the list. Takeo and Setsuko had destroyed, or possibly hidden, all photos of their family back in Japan, some of whom had been members of the Imperial Navy. The predicament caused an ache in the middle of Violet's chest.

Little by little, voices quieted. Heads turned. Ella's fingers curled around her hand more tightly, and Violet squeezed back. Takeo spotted them and hurried over. "Violet and Ella, welcome."

"Thank you, Sensei," Violet said, feeling safe to address him here, but certainly no place else.

"Are you going to stay?" he asked her.

"Should I?"

They both looked down at Ella, who was staring at the back corner of the room. Giant origami butterflies and cranes, fish and frogs hung from the ceiling. "Sweet pea, would you like me to stay?"

At that very moment, Umi marched up and grabbed Ella's hand, leading her to the back of the room. She pointed at the folded paper creatures, while her two long braids twisted down her back like origami snakes. Violet had been looking for some kind of sign. To tell her that life was ready to flip-flop. Maybe this was it. She took a chance and slipped out the side door.

The house felt strange without Ella, almost soulless. Violet had grown used to her always being underfoot, filling the cracks with her presence. Strange how you noticed something more once it was not there. In the kitchen, Jean was listening to the radio and grading math worksheets. She looked up and her lashes fluttered when Violet walked in.

"Don't tell me she let you leave her there," Jean said.

Violet had spent the half mile home wondering if she should go back. "I sneaked away while she was distracted."

"Baby doll, that is wonderful!"

The throbbing in her feet from standing all day prompted her to sit. "Ella wishes she was Japanese, so it couldn't be more perfect."

Jean smiled. "I'm feeling hopeful. For Ella. For me. Even for you."

"What's that supposed to mean?"

"Just that Zach is here. More than anyone alive, he will take my mind off Bud. And things are now looking up for Ella, in which case you won't be able to help but be happy."

Jean and Bud met a month before the first batch of soldiers left town. He had ridden the school bus into Honoka'a with her students one morning and asked for directions to the theater as he climbed out. When the bell rang, she found him hovering outside her room. That was it for both of them. All his liberty time was spent holding tightly to Jean's hand. Aside from being a marine, Bud was a grass-chewing, rough-riding Texan. He also liked to spit. Violet had put up with him for Jean's sake.

If someone could stop Jean from ruminating about Bud, Violet would be eternally grateful. That kind of pining was not helpful. Sewing, movies, trips to the beach, nothing worked. She'd even involved Jean in their victory garden up the hill. And Jean had gotten her hands dirty for possibly the first time ever. But in the midst of harvesting, Jean said the cucumbers reminded her of Bud and alternated between sniffling and sobbing the whole time. Violet had her own thoughts about Bud but she kept them to herself. Mainly that he seemed interested in only one thing. She didn't quite trust the man.

Violet reached across the table and squeezed Jean's hand. "I hope you're right."

Happy was a word out of another lifetime. Sure, she no longer felt like she was living underwater with the whole ocean pressing down on her. Life had become tolerable.

"Even if I'm wrong, you still better love me forever," Jean said.

Thank goodness Jean's moods were catching. "You? Wrong?"

"Oh, by the way, Zach called and said he might come out this weekend. They'll be on liberty. That fine with you?"

"You don't need to ask. Just keep him away from Irene Ferreira or he's a goner."

Jean winked and stood up to check on the meat loaf in the oven. By now, the entire kitchen smelled like tangy sauce and sage. Wednesday was Jean's night to cook, and she commandeered the kitchen. With rations, they'd had to get creative. Packing sardines into sushi or fashioning Spam into casserole.

Jean poured Violet a tall glass of passion orange juice. "In high school, he was a goofball with the ladies. Sweet as can be, but his tongue tied up in knots."

"Just warn him," Violet said.

Chapter Six

ELLA

WHY DON'T THEY HAVE US MAKE ORIGAMI ANI-mals in regular school? Instead, Mrs. Hicks forces us to make cardboard slippers and painted egg crates for the wounded soldiers. Everything is about the soldiers. Sometimes I wish they would just go away, even though we need them for protection. I wish we could just erase the war and erase the fact that now Japanese people are bad. Maybe the ones in Japan are different, but I like most of the ones here.

At home, Umi always folds miniature origami animals, and she tries to teach me, but mine come out ugly and smooshed. I thought it was because my fingertips are too big, but Umi says I need proper lessons and lots of practice. Any paper Umi gets her hands on ends up a tiny perfect creature. Now was my chance.

These origami in the classroom were huge enough to breathe on their own or fly away. I couldn't wait to make Snowflake into a folded paper cat the first chance I got. Big fingertips wouldn't matter with these.

When I finally remembered where I was and looked for Mama, she was gone. I felt the usual pinch of fear, but instead of rising into a panic, I got drawn into the singing at the start of class. Sensei, as he told me to call him, hit a small gong that made my teeth ring. Everyone was singing with their full hearts. They all knew the words. I had no choice but to sit with Umi, feeling dumb since I didn't know the songs. Some of the other kids gave me weird looks and scooted away. But kids don't worry me too much, especially singing ones.

I knew I might be lost learning a new language, but Japanese words seem easy to me. I already know some. *Sensei*, *obake*, *satoimo* and *arigato* were just some. We have an *obake* living in our house. It might even be Papa. The words have trickled down to Umi and Hiro from their parents. Sometimes I feel jealous, because they have a whole family. At night, I imagine that Papa will be home in the morning, cooking coffee and waiting to pick me up and kiss the ribbons in my hair. Whenever he hugged me, I ended up smelling like Old Spice afterward. I still have his bottle, and when I really miss him, I put a dab on my wrist before I go to bed.

Singing took up a lot of the time that day. And just when I thought we were finally going to stop, we started another song or sometimes repeated the same one forty-seven times. *Itchi ni san shi.* I was sneaking glances around me. The boy to the left had a string of snot dripping from his nose, but he kept singing. June Higa, right in front of me, swung her silky hair back and forth as she bobbed her head in time. All Japanese girls have nice hair. It must be a God-given right. And straight parts. I don't even have a part.

After the singing, Mr. Hamasu, who no longer allows anyone to call him *sensei*, talked to us about plants, and how we were going to expand the victory garden to the other side of the building, which meant we would need to help clear the bushes away. Work clothes were required for next week. After that, we were going to grow our own bonsai plants! In honor of the soldiers, of course.

He told us, in his very even voice, "Bonsai plants are different than our garden plants because they're for the mind, not the body. Caring for your own bonsai will teach you patience, ingenuity and focused effort. Some of them won't survive, but that, too, is part of the process."

He passed around several bonsai trees, which seemed old and wise. Hiro says that one at their house is over a hundred years old. He sometimes makes stuff up, or at least stretches out the truth, but this time I believed him.

By the time class ended, I knew I wanted to come back. Even if I heard one girl whisper to her friend, "What is Ella Iverson doing here? She's *haole*."

As if that were some kind of great revelation. Of course I was *haole*. I had always been *haole*. I would always be *haole*. *"So, what's the big deal?"* I wanted to say.

It was easy to pretend they didn't exist. I'd had practice.

Chapter Seven

VIOLET

WHEN THE SHADOWS HAD LENGTHENED AND the thrushes broke into song, Setsuko and Umi showed up at the door with Ella. Violet had been checking the window every few minutes, watching for their arrival.

"Auntie Violet, your daughter is home!" they called.

She ran out to greet them. Ella walked straight to the coffee table and set down a folded red crane before coming back to hug her. The hug was double what she usually got.

"How did it go?" She eyed Setsuko, who smiled.

Waves of excitement were pouring off of Ella. "I'm going to make a bonsai, and help in the victory garden!"

Violet bent down, not wanting to tamper with her success by making too big a deal. "Well, that's wonderful news. I'm sure they can use you with all of your gardening expertise."

"They sing a lot, too. I don't mind singing, but today I didn't know the words."

Setsuko risked a laugh. "The words will come."

"Did you learn anything else?" Violet asked.

Ella thought about it for a while. "I learned that it's a whole lot more fun than regular school."

"Oh, honey, I'm happy you had a good time. You still have to go to regular school, but this will be something to look forward to."

With Ella on the mend, their lives could take on a whole new orbit. She envisioned Ella plumping up, waking to dry sheets in the morning, not being terrified senseless by air-raid drills and letting her skin heal over. The hurts of her daughter commingled with her own, but instead of seeming double, they more than quadrupled. Certainly Violet missed Herman as a husband and the man she counted on in life, but more so she missed him as a father to Ella, as a fellow parent. Every now and then she felt guilty for having those feelings. That she should have loved him more passionately. But that was the truth, and lying to herself would serve no purpose.

On Thursday and Friday, Violet held her breath while Ella was at Japanese school, at any moment expecting to have her show up at the door. But on both days Ella returned with new stories and an extra spot of color on her cheeks.

"Today Sensei told us a story about Tanuki, and I want to get one," Ella said, folding her hands on her chest like it had already been decided.

"A what?"

"Tah-noo-key." Ella rolled her eyes and drew the word out as though speaking to a four-year-old. "A Japanese raccoon dog. He says they're jolly and mischievous and some can even shape-shift into other animals."

If Ella had it her way, they'd be collecting animals like most people collected stamps or coins. "Ask Umi to help you make an origami one for now. That's about the best I can do."

Their meager food rations and low wages were just enough to feed their own mouths, let alone a zoo. Sugar had been the first to be rationed and then came milk, butter, oil, meat, coffee, and other canned and processed foods. Thank goodness for their garden and those of nearby folks, with whom they often traded. Gasoline was another story. It wasn't something you could grow. Most civilians got an A sticker, which entitled them to only three to four gallons a week, which couldn't get you very far. Everyone stayed close to home.

When Saturday dawned a honey-colored sky, they piled into the Ford and drove up to their garden plot above town, in a place called Ahualoa. The road was steep in some places, rolling in others. Thickets of koa and smaller clusters of ohia attracted bees, and even native honeycreepers. Ella kept her eyes glued to the window, waiting to spot the tiny red birds darting from tree to tree like forest sprites.

"Honey, I've got a feeling we aren't in Minnesota anymore," Jean said.

Ella giggled. Jean wished she was Judy Garland and was the first to admit it. Ella had joined her on the bandwagon.

"You've never even been to Minnesota," Violet said.

"California, then."

On a small patch of land at the two-thousand-foot elevation, Herman had planted potato, corn, peas, cucumber and watermelon. At first Violet had shied away from anything to do with farming, after the disintegration of her family farm in Minnesota and the unraveling of her father. But here in Hawaii, there was no dust or frozen winters and everything grew with a vengeance. Over and over, in a silent mantra, Violet had reminded herself that Herman was not her father.

Violet renewed the lease after Herman's disappearance.

Some weeks, there was enough overflow that she and Jean brought bushels into town to sell.

Not only that, but Violet swore that the minute Ella stuck her hands in the dirt, whatever gave life to those plants gave life to Ella. Just add water and a touch of sun.

They rode in silence for a while, which meant Jean was stewing over something. "I want to fix those boys something special tonight. Fatten them up and keep them coming back for more," Jean said.

Violet had to keep her eyes on the rutted road. "Even if you served Spam, they'd want to come back."

After Zach's call, Jean had flown around the house in a flurry, dusting cobwebs and wiping down lizard poop. Violet was more reserved about having a house full of soldiers, but maybe they would bring some cheer. It sure seemed that this group of marines was more prone to smile than the last. There had been piles of them spilling out of buses and into the bars in town. The military had made an arrangement to let them hitch rides on the school buses. Many of them looked no older than her own students, and when they stepped onto the street in their uniforms, some of them could have been playing dress-up. But these boys were about to step into the blood-seeped battlefield of the Pacific. Her heart stung for them, and their mothers back home, who no doubt had a love-hate relationship with the telephone and the mailman.

Jean slipped on her purple gardening gloves and busied herself singing "Mairzy Doats." When the song had first come out, Violet had wondered what kind of nonsense they were singing.

"What on earth is a Mairzy Doat?" she had asked Jean.

Jean quickly set her straight. "He's saying *mares eat oats.* Listen carefully."

Sure enough, Jean was right and the song soon became one of Ella's favorites. Now the two of them belted it out.

Jean rolled down the window, letting in a burst of lemony eucalyptus air. Even while watching the road, Violet could see Jean's foot tapping on the floor. Her hand fidgeted with an unraveling thread on the seat.

"What?" Violet asked.

"Say, I was just thinking. Maybe you should finish off the Limburger before the boys come. Or store it at Setsuko's for the night."

"It took me months to get that cheese. You know that."

The cheese had been a splurge, a comfort that reminded her of home. Jean once said it smelled like a dirty soldier's feet. Herman had tolerated it. Barely.

Jean sighed. "Do you think the boys might have heard anything about Bud's division? Or where they've sailed off to?"

"Probably, but you know what they say."

As if on cue, Ella answered, "Loose lips sink ships."

Jean turned around. "You don't miss a thing, do you?"

When they arrived at the plot, Violet parked under an enormous ohia tree with sun-kissed red blossoms. She let herself out and opened Ella's door, since the inside handle had broken off and there was no money to fix it.

The minute Ella climbed out, she pointed. "What is that?"

On the other side of the tree, a whole mess of rust-colored feathers was strewn on the ground. It reminded Violet of a feather blizzard.

Ella bolted.

"Honey, wait!"

The tree trunk blocked any view of whatever disaster had transpired. Ella's voice was shrill. "It's still alive. Hurry!"

Alive was a generous term, she saw when she reached the scene. Large chunks of feathers were missing, including all tail feathers, and half a wing hung limp. Violet hated for Ella to see the carnage, but as a girl growing up on a Minnesota farm, she herself had seen a whole lot worse than injured or headless chickens.

The hen squawked. "Mrs. Chicken, we're here to save you," Ella said.

Huddled on the bare ground, the hen cocked her head to the side and stared warily at them with one blinking eye. She ruffled what few feathers she had left and tried to settle into the dirt and leaves.

Jean stood back. "I hate to say this, but I'm not sure she can be saved."

Ella ignored her and ran to the car for a burlap sack. "Mama, can you help me?"

Violet hesitated, knowing that once they went down this chicken-saving road, there would be no turning back. Ella would fall in love and there would be another mouth in the house, another soul to worry about. *If it lived.* Yet she had lost the ability to say no to her daughter. Without waiting, Ella scooped the hen up and cradled it in her arms. The injured bird hardly put up a struggle and let out a few soft clucks.

That was how they ended up with a featherless chicken.

Chapter Eight

ELLA

AT THREE O'CLOCK, WHEN MAMA WAS POKING around in the closet for linens and Jean was swaying like she always did in the kitchen to Louis Jordan singing the "G.I. Jive," I decided to post up near the window to keep an eye out for our visitors. High swirly clouds floated in the sky and a group of mynah birds were in the grass, fighting over what was probably a bug carcass. From a built-in cushion area right next to the screen, you can see the whole lay of the land. Who's coming up the driveway, the other teacher cottages on our lane, and even the rusty tin roofs of houses below the school.

Our new chicken was still alive and wrapped in an old blanket next to me. The whole way home in the car, I rubbed just under her eye. Mr. Manabat, who lives out near our land and sells eggs, said that's how to hypnotize a chicken. I thought maybe it would cheer her up. Mama agreed that we could call her Brownie, which I came up with all on my own.

For some reason, I was curious about Zach. He was nice, even if he thought my butterfly was a buttercat. And I didn't want to disappoint him by telling him that no such thing existed. I decided to draw another butterfly that looked more like a real one, with orange-and-black lacy wings. I wanted him to see it. I got the crazy idea that if I got on the soldiers' good side, they could help me sort out my problems. Maybe we could teach God a thing or two. I had been asking God repeatedly to tell me what to do about this horrible knowledge inside of me, but for some reason He never answered. I was beginning to wonder if at some point in my short life I did something to upset Him, or if He was just too busy with the war going on and all the new prayers to answer.

The problem is, I don't know who to trust outside the house—besides the Hamasus and Irene Ferreira. Not talking to strangers is getting harder with so many strangers around. I am pretty sure I can trust Zach, though, since he is Jean's brother and he has honest eyes and one of those faces that smile from the inside out. I call them trust faces.

Did you know that about people? You can tell a lot about them by the way they look at you. Take Miss Irene Ferreira, our telephone operator. Her eyes are huge and chocolaty and clear. They're always so open that you would know right away if she was hiding something. She is simply unable to keep a secret by manner of those big eyes.

Old people also have interesting eyes. It seems like their eyes know so much that they hardly have to say anything. Mr. Hayashi is like that. He sits in the back of the store, carving things out of wood. I'm not sure he can even see, but that doesn't stop him. He still has all his teeth, which is rare for old people, and he shows them off when I sit down on the stool next to him. Mama takes her ration tickets there, and while she picks out flour and rice and things for the kitchen,

I sit with him. He used to carve Japanese characters onto small blocks of wood, but now he sticks to American letters, or stars or animals. Even though his eyes are milky, it seems like he can see right through me.

Sometimes that makes me nervous. I don't want anyone to see into my head. It's bad enough that I'm in danger and scared of my own shadow, but I don't want anyone else to know what I know. Then they could be, too.

Chapter Nine

VIOLET

"LATENESS IS RUDENESS," SO HER MOTHER ALways said, but Violet wanted to give Zach the benefit of the doubt. Jean paced on the porch, as her lips moved with the words playing on the radio. A picture of lovely, she wore a red pleated skirt and a white blouse. As always, the fire-engine-red lipstick set off the gold in her hair. Violet had stuck with a plain blue dress with red buttons. She had sewn them on herself one night while feeling patriotic.

"I'm sure he has a good reason. Once you're in the military, your time is not your own," Violet said.

"Zach never was good with time. I should have guessed he'd be late."

No sooner had she spoken the words than a military jeep rattled into the driveway. Three men hung halfway out the windows, waving. Singing must have run in the family, because Zach and a redhead were hollering like fools. By the time they arrived at the front door, it was obvious why they'd been late.

"Alma Jean Quinlan, are you ready to dance?" Zach called from the steps as they filed up.

Jean shot Violet a look before answering. "Where have you boys been?"

All three of them stood in varying degrees of leaning and swaying, and removed their hats. Her cheeks heated up. If late was rude, late and sauced was inexcusable.

Zach's smile must have been a mile wide. "Ladies, I believe you've met Parker, and this here is Tommy O'Brien, the fastest man this side of the Pacific Ocean. I apologize for our lateness, but we had to meet up with a few members of our company at the hotel."

Violet stood on the front porch, deciding whether to say anything. But since she had nothing nice to say, she kept quiet. Jean ushered them into the living room, where Ella still sat by the window, only now she was drawing rather than watching.

"Where's my talented little friend Ella?" Zach said.

"Ella, honey, please greet our guests. These are very important men, so we need to treat them with respect," she said, wondering if Ella would pick up on their drunkenness.

Ella waved at the men and said, "Hello, it's a pleasure to meet you." And immediately went back to her paper. The hen began clucking at the intrusion.

"What do you have here?" Zach said. In two strides, he was at Ella's side.

"Why don't you tell them how we got it," Violet said.

Everyone crowded around the chicken in the blanket, whose clucking had taken on a frantic tone.

Parker bent down for a closer look. "She's just about in tune with the radio. This little lady yours?"

Ella nodded.

"Looks like she got in a fight with a lawn mower. What happened?" he asked.

Ella pinched her lips together and without a word climbed down and started rubbing under Brownie's eye. Violet was impressed at the tenderness of her touch. How her small fingers were so precise, delivering just the right dose of love. Not more than a minute later, the hen stopped her ruckus. Ella beamed up at them. "She likes that."

"Where'd you learn that trick?" Parker asked.

"From Mr. Manabat. He knows everything."

That got a laugh from the men.

"Does he, now? Well, then maybe we should be talking to him about a few things," Zach said.

Tommy finally spoke up. "Like where on earth we're headed. All I care to know."

Ella traded a look with her mom. "I meant he knows everything about chickens. He wouldn't know about that stuff. But you could ask."

"Good advice. I just might do that," Tommy said.

Jean disappeared and came back with trays full of peanuts and Saloon Pilot crackers with chunks of salted codfish. She set them out on the card table. Violet realized that this was the first group of adults she had entertained since Herman's disappearance. Sure, the Hamasus came over often, but they were like family. These were men, and even though it was only Jean's little brother, she suddenly wished she had worn something prettier.

Zach's voice was several notches louder than the other night, and he scooped up almost the entire batch of peanuts in one hand. "Lord, it's nice to get out of that wind-blasted tent city for a change. You ladies been up to Camp Tarawa much?"

"Now and then. We go to sell vegetables if we have too

many," Violet said. "Waimea is not always like that. Just you wait. It's about the loveliest place on earth when the weather's right. With all those pastures, the sky always seems bigger up there."

Tommy laughed, revealing a missing tooth to one side. "You mean to tell me there's a sky up there? I haven't seen anything but that crazy sideways rain and heaps of clouds. It's enough to drive anyone mad."

"Once the weather turns, you won't want to leave," Violet said.

The words had already come out when she realized her error. As if they had any choice in the matter. Parker nodded as if considering the implications.

"Speaking of Camp Tarawa, guess what?" Jean said, clasping her hands together.

"What?" all three men said in unison.

"We're going to be setting up a pie stand outside the USO on Saturdays pretty soon, so that should cheer you up!"

The pie-selling plan had come about after driving into Waimea one day to sell greens and sweet potato with Takeo. Jean took one look at all the soldiers milling about and a light bulb flashed on.

"These boys need some home-baked love," she had said and then continued, "We'll make them pies and end up with change in our pockets and a whole new set of handsome friends. And we will be doing something important in the war effort."

"You're serious, aren't you?" Violet had questioned.

"Somehow having Zach here has made me feel more protective of these soldiers. Instead of a big horde of smelly men in uniforms, I see them like brothers, sons, husbands," Jean had said.

"I suppose it might not be a bad idea. But we'd need to work on boosting our gas rations."

Jean had stood with her hands on her hips. "Of course it will work. Boosting morale, fattening them up. In my eyes, comfort food is better than any pill."

"Well, I guess it's settled, then."

Zach now slapped his forehead and fell back. "Fellas, once you taste a Jean Quinlan apple pie, you may just want to up and marry her. Don't say I didn't warn you."

Jean's cheeks reddened, but she loved this kind of thing. "Oh please! No apple here, but we'll have Okinawan sweet potato or chocolate honeycomb."

Tommy's nostrils flared and he stiffened. "You ladies selling Jap pies to the soldiers?"

"The potatoes aren't Japanese," Violet said. "They come straight from our garden, and I get the starters from Mr. Otake, who has lived here for a hundred years or more."

"That may be the case, but you ought to rethink what you call your pies if you want to sell any," Tommy said.

"Mr. O'Brien, I see your point, but let's get one thing straight. Here in Hawaii, there are far more Japanese than *haole*. And as far as any of us are concerned, most of them are just as loyal to America as you or me. These are not the same people we are fighting," Violet said, feeling her cheeks burn.

His voice was taut. "Ma'am, I'm afraid we may have to agree to disagree."

Jean gave her a halting look, and then trained it on Tommy. "Let's talk about something else, please? Remember we have a young lady in our midst."

That was how they learned Tommy O'Brien was from a big family in New York, and he was a Yankee to the bone. Also, given the chance, he would talk himself to death. Halfway through his monologue, Violet left to check on the creamed corn and beef stew. Ella followed.

"Are you going to show Zach your new butterfly watercolor?" Violet said.

Ella shrugged and fiddled with one of the scabs on her arm.

"I could use your help filling up these glasses with water." It appeared they had consumed enough alcohol already, and she kept the beer in the icebox.

A few moments later, the volume on the radio shot up. It was Bing Crosby, only now he had company. "Swinging on a Star" also happened to be Ella's favorite song, and she knew every word. She pushed the kitchen door open just a sliver and peeked out.

"It's the dark-haired one," she whispered.

Violet came over for a look. Parker was leaning up against the radio and snapping his fingers. His moves were fluid, but there was nothing fluid about his voice. It was like sandpaper on a chalkboard. On the next verse, Tommy and Zach both joined in. How could this be happening? The house had become a concert hall for drunken soldiers, and yet she couldn't draw her eyes away. The way they were singing with every ounce of heart made her dense with longing.

When the song ended, Parker caught Ella's eye and winked. She jumped back. Then he nodded at Violet. She felt her cheeks flush, and she let the door close.

"They're funny," Ella volunteered.

"I think we're going to like them."

Before supper, they bowed their heads and Jean gave God an extrastrong thank-you for bringing her brother to town. Even after scarfing down the peanuts and dried fish, the men tore into the food as though this was their last chance to eat. The table was drowning under mounds of beef stew, creamed corn and white rice. Violet sat at the head of the table with Parker to her left and Ella to her right.

"So, Ella, have you ever been to a zoo?" Parker asked.

Ella glanced up at him as if deciding if he was worthy of an answer. She looked to Violet, who answered for her. "We don't have a zoo here, and Ella's never been to the mainland."

"I used to work in a zoo," he said, again to Ella. "We had lions and monkeys, crocodiles, even hippos. And I learned a thing or two about animals while I was there. I could look over your hen if you'd like, after dinner."

Ella brightened.

Violet wondered at their good fortune. "That would be nice. Thank you. How did you get involved in a zoo?"

It was easy to forget that the soldiers had lives back home before this whole war started up. That they had left education, careers and families to come here. Inside those uniforms you could find the same measure of love, fear and hope as in anyone else. Often more.

"I've wanted to be a vet as long as I can remember. Left the ranch up north for school in San Diego, and I was halfway through premed when the war broke out."

"Well, I'll be," Jean said.

Jean had been caught up in conversation with Zach and Tommy on the other end of the table, but now turned her eyes on Parker. It had only been a matter of time. Jean would flirt with the Pope given the opportunity. Violet felt a lump of jealousy form just below her ribs. *What on earth?*

Parker continued, still focusing on Ella and Violet. "I was the lucky one that got the buckets of slop ready for the animals. That's about all you want to hear, trust me."

Jean flashed her most irresistible smile, dimples and all. "Tell us more about home. Do you have a family waiting for you?"

"My folks and my little sis, Alice. And then there's Bella."

Jean wilted. "She your sweetheart?"

He wore no ring.

"My dog. Black as midnight and truer than the Bible," he said, grinning.

His smile was straight across, with only the sides turning up. He had olive skin that was too dark to be from the sun and smooth like a baby's bottom. Then there were the broad shoulders and tapered waist. All things considered, he had the kind of looks that could only lead to heartache. And no doubt he knew it.

"Surely you must have a woman back home?" Jean persisted. Lord, she could be pushy.

"When I first enlisted, I was with the Paramarines. It was a tough unit to get in with, but they had a rule you couldn't be married," he said.

Tommy laughed. "Sergeant Stone, married?" His mouth was full and he nearly choked on his bite.

Zach slapped his knee, which was almost level with the tabletop, and laughed out loud.

"Fellas, cut me some slack here," Parker said.

"He's on his best behavior here, but..."

Parker cut Zach off. "But nothing. Am I going to have to make you do an extra hundred push-ups tomorrow?"

Violet turned to Ella, who had finished eating and was watching the men's banter with her mouth hanging open. Surely there had been nothing like this in their house before. Herman had been a straitlaced family man. Once in a while, he and Luther would have a few beers on a Saturday, but there was never this kind of loose conversation and maleness.

Out of the blue, Ella spoke. "Do you think the Japanese are going to bomb your zoo?"

"The Japanese will never get close enough to bomb my zoo. Rest easy. We'll be taking care of them long before they ever get near California."

"What about here? Miss Ferreira says that you guys are here because the Japanese submarines are sneaking up on us. And we should move back to the mainland before it's too late," Ella said.

Where had Ella gotten this information? "Darling, you know not to believe everything Miss Ferreira says. She tends to exaggerate." Violet would have to have a word with Miss Ferreira, sooner rather than later.

Zach cleared his throat and Tommy stared at his corn, but Parker addressed her concern. "You bring up a good point. A lot of unexpected things happen during war. But I can promise you this—the animals are safe, and you're safe, so quit your fretting."

Over Ella's head, he winked at Violet.

"I wouldn't want to leave anyway," Ella said. "Without my papa."

Silence dropped onto the table. Jean had probably mentioned Herman to Zach, but Violet had no idea what the others knew. Everyone in town knew the story, so she never had to explain it.

"Nor should you have to," Parker said.

Jean mouthed the word "Sorry."

"Thank you for your confidence in our safety, Sergeant. You may or may not be aware that my husband disappeared a year ago," Violet said.

Ella folded her arms and looked into her lap. There was that word again. *Disappear.* Violet was conscious of the difference between *disappeared* and *died.* And how she always chose the former. The likelihood of Herman coming back was slim to none. That much she knew. But without a body, would she ever be able to draw the line? Would she grow old wondering with an ache in her soul? There was no easy way to talk about it, but people needed to know. These men especially, if they were to be sharing meals with them.

The truth was the truth, and the sooner everyone knew it, the better.

"Did it have anything to do with the war?" Tommy asked.

"Unfortunately, we don't know. There was a search and an investigation, but they turned up nothing." Violet told them her practiced version of the story while she rubbed Ella's shoulder, at the same time tasting bile in her throat. Talking about this had that effect. Maybe having the men over hadn't been such a good idea.

Parker didn't seem to have a problem talking about it. "Either way, I'm sure that you loved him and he loved you. And that will never go away. Not knowing's got to be hard."

She nodded. By now, the whole house smelled like baked coconut and Violet excused herself to check on the pie. "Ella, I could use your help."

Ella scooted in with her. The pie still had another minute or two before browning. She sat Ella down at the table and looked into her eyes. "Sweetie, we both want your father to still be alive. More than anything. But we've been over this before."

Ella bit her lip like she was holding back tears. "I know, but sometimes it helps me to pretend."

"Oh, Ella." Violet hugged her in tight as the burning in her gut intensified.

If only it could be that easy. She could pretend forever that Herman was out getting milk, that he was just around the corner. That she would wake up to him snoring next to her, filling the whole room with his sounds. She had to hold back a laugh at the thought of their first night together, and how she had woken in a panic, certain that a tornado was pulling off the roof. But it had only been his god-awful snoring. She caught herself. This was happening more lately—thinking about him without tears. *Where are you, Herman?*

Violet sliced up the pie with freshly polished silver, and she and Ella carried out double slices to the soldiers. Living on the farm, especially in her later years, her folks had been so poor, meals were about staying alive, not about pleasure. But since moving to Hawaii, and especially since living with Jean, all that changed. In Hawaii, crops grew year-round and in such abundance, you could pluck the fruit off a tree whenever you pleased. Fruit designed for baking outlandish desserts.

A late-afternoon shower drizzled down outside, adding steam to an already muggy day and chasing the mosquitoes away. Violet and Ella set plates down in front of each man and you could have heard a pin drop. Then forks began clinking on china.

After taking a whole minute to chew his first bite, Parker was the first to speak. "So, which one of you is responsible for this?"

"Why, that would be Violet," Jean said.

"Don't blame me. This is your recipe," Violet said, not wanting credit, or any marriage proposals.

Tommy put his fork down. "Zach was right. I think I'm going to have to marry you."

"Me, too," Zach said.

"Is there a reverse word for *polygamy*?" Jean asked.

"Polyandry," Zach said.

Jean looked confused that her brother would know such a thing. "And you know this, how?"

He shrugged. "No idea, but it sounded interesting."

All this talk of husbands made Violet nervous, but she knew they were teasing. Then Parker said, "The whole war would be worth it if I knew I was coming home to this." She felt her body go motionless and her heart pick up speed.

He put another piece in his mouth and chewed, all the while staring into her as though she were some kind of conundrum.

She wanted to be clear on one thing—she wasn't up for grabs. There were more important things to worry about. Not that Parker would ever be interested.

"Well, that is awfully kind of all of you. And, Sergeant Stone, I have no doubt that you will find what you're looking for. We have no shortage of lovely single women on this island." Her eyes couldn't help but flicker to Jean as she said it.

Even then, he didn't look away. Eventually Violet had to turn to look out the window, at the sun-laced trees and the town below.

"Please call me Parker, ma'am."

"How about this. I won't call you Sergeant if you don't call me 'ma'am'?" Violet said.

After dinner, Parker stayed true to his word and inspected Brownie's wounds. They brought her into the kitchen, and she squawked at first but settled down when he tucked her tightly under one arm. The arm in question had sharply defined biceps and a ropy forearm.

He pointed to where her right wing attached to her body. "This one here looks like it needs some care. You have any kind of healing salve?"

"I have drawing salve," Violet said.

"First I would use a honey ointment to prevent infection. You got any honey on hand?"

Jean climbed into the conversation and laughed. "Do we have honey?"

Violet explained. "We have more honey than we know

what to do with. Mr. Keko'olani keeps bees. He feels sorry for me, so he brings us honey once a week." The jars were piling up, but he kept coming. Kind of like Mr. Macadangdang with the coconuts. Anyway, Mr. K. kept thirty-eight hives at his place and had another zillion spread out in the woods and nearby farms. Honoka'a was a perfect place for beekeeping. The bees loved the honeydew from a certain grasshopper that fed on the sugarcane, and the forest was abundant with ohia-lehua blossoms.

"I have a few jars of salve back at camp. I can bring some next time, but it's easy to make, too," he said.

Herman would have probably just cut the chicken's head off and asked Violet to stuff it for supper, so this was a surprise. Tommy and Zach lost interest quickly and retreated to the porch.

Darkness was almost here. They needed to leave, but Parker seemed so genuinely concerned for the chicken that she let him continue.

"Olive oil, comfrey, marshmallow root, witch hazel bark and honey," he said. "You put that on Brownie, she'll be good to go in no time. Ella, maybe you can help your mother make the salve. It would be good for your cuts and scrapes, too. I use it all the time." He lifted his forearm to show a long pink scar. "I got in a scuffle with Roscoe. He didn't mean it, of course."

If Ella had any doubts about these soldiers, they would be blotted out by now. "Zach said we would meet Roscoe. Where is he?" Violet asked, unsure about meeting anyone who inflicted wounds like that.

"Roscoe is otherwise occupied, but you will. I promise."

Chapter Ten

VIOLET

BACK IN BADGER, MINNESOTA, VIOLET'S FAMILY had always gone to church, even in the bitter freeze of winter, when it was risky to breathe outside. They would bundle in worn-out blankets and extra layers of wool socks, and trudge to the church in the middle of town. *"Acceptance, deliverance, repentance,"* the minister had drilled into them. But understanding those words was another matter altogether. As a girl, Violet had thought acceptance meant standing on the stage and getting your award for having the biggest goat or the fattest pig, not making the best of a situation gone wrong. Later she learned it was not an easy thing to master.

Despite the new routine of Japanese school, which seemed to be going well, and the night with the soldiers, Ella still ate less than a squirrel and picked her freckles until they formed angry red mounds. Sometimes Violet wanted to tear her own hair out, unable to protect her daughter from invisible grief, but that pesky word *acceptance* kept rearing up in her head.

Maybe now was the time to revisit what acceptance really meant.

Maybe acceptance meant moving forward with what you had.

Violet first met Herman in a church. He was sitting in the front row, shoulders tight with shudders, trying to hold it together, which was hard to do when your sixteen-year-old brother was lying dead from pneumonia, a by-product of the dust storms, people said. Herman was the older one who had come back from Hawaii for the funeral. She wasn't even sure where Hawaii was, but she liked the sound of the word. It sounded sweet and warm and green.

Her mother insisted she come, knowing there would be men there. The sooner Violet found a man, the sooner she could get out of the house. Violet ended up in the kitchen helping clean up, when Herman walked in. Without a word, he rolled up his sleeves and picked up a towel. They stood side by side at the sink, she washing, he drying. After the tenth plate, she broke the silence.

"Is that where the pineapples come from?"

For the first time, she saw the hint of a smile. "Hawaii is a lot more than pineapples. But don't tell anyone."

"Like what?"

"Well, for one thing, it only snows on the very top of the mountains, which are tall. You could wear a dress all year there."

She thought she had misheard. "Be serious."

"Scout's honor. The place is paradise. They weren't lying."

"Who's they?"

"The education corps that brought me out there. I'm a teacher, but soon to be principal."

Herman didn't say it in a boastful way, but she was impressed nonetheless. He could be only four or five years older than she was, at the most. His manner was sparse, and she wasn't sure if it was his nature, or because he was sad about his brother. If she wasn't mistaken, his arm had gotten so close to hers that soon they would be touching. They talked until her mother came in to tell her their time was up.

It was the first funeral that Violet hadn't wanted to leave.

Herman took her to dinner the following night, and the night after. But he was returning to Hawaii the next week. What was the point? Still, Violet enjoyed his company, and the distraction he provided from going home in the evenings to her mother and Mr. Smudge and her stepbrothers, who fought constantly. Herman got her considering that there might be life outside Minnesota. They spent the week together, walking in the fields behind town, holding hands and stealing kisses. He told her stories of natives riding canoes down the face of waves and of the white-sand beaches with palm trees and fresh coconuts. It sounded magical.

Two weeks after his departure, an envelope arrived in the mail holding something stiff and colorful. Violet's heart tap-danced on her ribs. A ticket on the SS *Lurline*. To Honolulu.

Herman had written a note:

Dearest Violet,

Should you wish to see for yourself, I would be most honored.

Yours, Herman.

PS: Remember that winter is on its way and what I said about wearing dresses all year round.

She smiled at his reference. There were so many reasons not to go. Another two years of college. The town newspaper job, even if it only involved sitting in meetings, taking shorthand and not getting paid. Of greater concern would be leaving Lady, her faithful collie-dog, and her lovely hens.

Her mother was another matter. Every so often, Violet would see glimpses of the way she used to be. Bright-eyed and full of song. She sang to the cows, to the family of sparrows that flew in and out of the barn, to the wheat crops when harvest time arrived. That was before Violet's dad up and left them under the guise of finding work, before they moved in with Mr. Smudge, the town butcher, who had lost his own wife and had two sons of his own. For the first time, Violet had siblings—ones she didn't much like. Mr. Smudge smelled like blood and sweat, drank enough vodka to turn his face purple, and had a case of the shakes. But he provided for Violet and her mother and he taught her how to shoot a gun well enough to pop a can from across the field. He put food on the table. On one level, she knew her mother had chosen survival, but all joy had squeezed out of her and she'd never found it again.

Violet had been fourteen the day her father hopped on the train and headed for the city.

They stood at the station, her face in his hands and his ice-blue eyes searching into her. Sometimes at night, she could still feel the sandpaper of his skin and the sunken pit that came from saying *goodbye*. "Darling, I promise I will be back before you know it. Or else I'll send for you when I have enough money."

"Take me with you!" she cried.

"Your mama needs you."

Violet's lip quivered and she willed herself not to cry. But her face was wet for weeks after. Letters came, but no money. *"I have hope,"* her father would say.

I have another interview tomorrow to sell vacuum cleaners. The city is full of men looking for work. They say I need to have experience.

The letters came less often. The letters stopped coming.

She hadn't blamed him like her mother had, at least not at first. Between drought, grasshoppers, insufferable heat and orifice-filling dust storms, their farm had been doomed from the start. What happened to the land happened to him, turning him into a hard, cracked and hopeless man. Several years later, a letter came saying he was still out of work and to move on with their lives and he was sorry. So sorry.

Herman seemed like a far cry from her own father. Dependable, employed, ambitious. Anyway, there was no law that required her to stay in Hawaii if she didn't like it. She held the ticket up to her nose, and swore she smelled flowers and sea salt.

She went by boat train to San Francisco. At her first sight of the ship, she nearly fainted. It was massive, with smokestacks like small buildings and decks layered up to the sky. How could such an enormous object stay afloat? Flags were flying, and once they cast off the python-sized ropes, Violet joined the passengers in confetti-tossing and cheering. She was alone with nearly seven hundred people on a voyage to Honolulu. What in God's name was she doing?

For Violet, the ocean was a new and wondrous body of water, and its blue was unfathomable. Salt layered everything, and she was constantly tasting the breeze. On the first two days of the voyage, she gained her sea legs, for despite the size of the ship, the seas were rolling. Plates and glasses slid back and forth during dinner, and many people took to their bunks, ill from the motion. When she saw all the green faces, she felt lucky not to be seasick herself.

All Violet wanted to do was be on deck, where she caught

sight of whales and watched the albatrosses glide overhead. Much of her time was spent wondering and guessing. She had seen pictures of Hawaii, people riding waves, pineapple fields with migrant workers and women dancing in colorful dresses or grass skirts. Herman had also made it sound larger than life. But a part of her thought that there must be more to the story, more than coconuts and rainbows. In her short nineteen years of life, Violet had seen enough to know that not everything was as it seemed. People were starving and dying of cold, half the country was out of work, and her own father had abandoned them on account of losing his farm.

Many of the passengers were stopping in Hawaii, but many were also headed to Pago Pago, Suva and onward to Australia. After the second day, the ocean smoothed out and people began emerging from the depths. The deck chairs filled up and drinks began to flow. There were hula dancers and steel-guitar players, card games and even wooden horse races. Rumor also had it that there were movie stars in first class, and even Amelia Earhart. For a time, Violet imagined herself working on the ship, traveling the South Seas and seeing another side of the world.

When the SS *Lurline* pulled into Honolulu Harbor, the docks teemed with people. But Violet was more interested in the green of the mountains, which to her seemed impossible. There was also something strange going on with her sweat glands, which wouldn't seem to turn off. Herman was right where he said he would be. Standing in the front row off to the left, wearing a white suit. As she got closer, she could tell that she wasn't the only one sweating in the melting Hawaiian heat.

Herman waved at her and smiled. He wore his goodness like a badge. His giant hands held a yellow plumeria lei, which he placed around her neck. His neck smelled like sardines and sweet flowers. His touch was tentative, and even after a week together and weeks of almost daily letter writing, she realized they hardly knew each other.

After the initial hug, Herman pulled out a small box.

He knelt down.

The people around them disappeared and she could see only his mouth forming words.

"Violet, will you marry me?"

In her mind, she began to frantically recall the letters and if she had possibly missed one. In all of their correspondence, marriage had not been mentioned. But then why else would a man buy a woman a ticket halfway around the world?

"We have your mother's blessing."

His eyes were so open and expectant. Was there any other answer than *yes*?

A loud pounding rattled Violet from her daydream. "Hello?" a voice called.

It was Luther. "Thank you for coming."

"Anytime, you know that. What can I do for ya?" he said.

"Jean and I are going to sell pies in Waimea on Saturday mornings. Give the soldiers a feeling of home and make some pocket change," she said.

Luther had to bend his neck straight down when talking to her. "I'm afraid I'm not much good at pie making, so if you've invited me here for that, you're fresh out of luck."

The thought of Luther with an apron on, baking a pie, caused her to laugh. He only cooked meat. She knew this because they shared an occasional dinner together, along with Jean and a few other faculty members. Being around Luther was a link to Herman, and she was glad for his company, even if he seemed preoccupied these days and kept more to himself.

"Now there's a sight. But we do need a pie stand, something that we can fold up and is easy to assemble. I know you would be good at that," Violet said.

"Now you're in business. I can have something ready by the weekend if you'd like. How many pies you looking to sell?"

"I think we'll start with twenty and go from there. But I have a little extra time now that Ella's in Japanese school in the afternoons," she said.

His voice boomed. "That such a good idea?"

Violet was fed up with paranoia. "It was *her* idea. And why the hell not?"

Luther tucked his hands in under his belt, lowered his voice, looked around as though someone might be hiding between the walls and leaned close enough that she thought she smelled liquor on his breath. "Just between you and me, I've been hearing rumors that they might close the school."

Violet about fell over. "What? Where did you hear that?"

"Oh, in and about town. People talk. You know that."

Closing the school would ripple through their small community, ruining her friends' livelihood and cutting off her daughter's newfound independence. Somewhere between the September heat and a rising feeling of dread, her palms broke out in sweat.

"Is there anything you can do about it? Herman talked to someone not long after Pearl Harbor, when there was mention of closing it then. Do you know who?" She had to take a breath to steady herself.

He shrugged it off. "No idea."

"You must have connections. Please, Luther, we need this. Ella needs it," she said.

He held up his hands. "I'm not privy to the government's

agenda. There's a lot going on we don't know about. Hard to trust anyone these days."

She would have to warn Takeo.

October 2 turned out to be a good day for the Allies. According to the radio, they'd breached the Siegfried Line and would now be able to penetrate Germany along the northwestern border. The Germans had just crushed the Polish resistance in Warsaw and needed to be stopped. Maybe someone would finally do something about that mustached pig.

Violet was boiling coconut and listening to the news when Ella burst through the door, arms flailing. She was home far too early for Japanese school to be over.

"Mama, there are armed men at the school. You have to come!" Ella said.

Violet almost fell over. "What?"

Ella could barely get the words out between gasps. "They came while we were singing and stood outside. Sensei told us that school would be ending early today and to go home. The men didn't look nice."

"Honey, you stay here with Jean."

Jean had heard Ella and hovered nearby. Shaking, Violet slipped her shoes on and ran up to the school. Branches tore at her dress and the dense air pressed in on her lungs. By the time she arrived on the small porch, she had to fold over to catch a breath. Two army jeeps were parked in front. *Too late to warn Takeo.*

When she opened the door, the chirping of the birds halted and the entire room froze. Papers were strewn across the room and drawers piled haphazardly on the floor. Without the singing children, the place felt stingingly cold.

"What the devil is going on?" she cried.

Three men stood around the desk, and an older one with a

scar carved deep into his cheekbone stepped forward. "Ma'am, this is a government matter. I'm going to have to ask you to return to wherever you came from."

Violet couldn't restrain herself. "How dare you come in here when the kids are in class. Have you no common decency?"

The soldiers all began fidgeting. "We were prepared to wait but Mr. Hamasu requested for the children to leave," the scarred one said.

Takeo stood off to the side with a blank face and unreadable eyes. He nodded toward the door.

Still, she wasn't leaving. "I want to know what you're doing here. Takeo already went through this after Pearl Harbor. They're not even teaching Japanese, for heaven's sake."

The man spoke as though she was just a small annoyance. "That may be the case, but we're doing what we see fit to keep the country safe. This is a matter of national security. What concern do you have in the matter, anyway, Mrs....?"

"Mrs. Iverson, sir. My daughter is a student here."

The men exchanged glances and a look of confusion spread across their faces. "At Japanese school?" the spokesman said.

"Yes, and she loves it. She comes home with folded paper animals and is learning how to create a miniature tree. Terribly dangerous stuff."

It seemed odd that they would be coming now. The threat of direct attack had lessened and the Japanese were being forced back toward their homeland. Violet knew Takeo like a brother. He had stepped in after Herman disappeared and been a second father to Ella. If she was sure of one thing, it was that Takeo was no spy.

The spokesman leaned against the desk and folded his puffy arms. "As of now, the school is officially closed and we are taking over the building. Sorry for your daughter but she doesn't really belong here anyway." The look he gave her said he wasn't sorry at all.

Violet shivered from the understanding that these men had poisoned minds and were unable to think for themselves. The war had created some kind of mass hysteria. "My husband was the principal of Honoka'a School and the head of Hawaii Rifles. He vouched for Takeo. Shouldn't that count for something?"

"Leonard, please escort Mrs. Iverson home so we can wrap things up here and get a move on," the spokesman said to one of the younger men. And to her, "We are done here."

Violet stepped back toward the door. "I don't need escorting." Her eyes met with Takeo's, and behind his calm exterior, his eyes gave her the impression of a murky pond, one without answers. He failed miserably in his attempt at a smile.

Takeo spoke. "Violet. Thank you."

Her name sounded lonely without the *san* at the end.

Rather than returning to her house, she went straight for Setsuko, who she knew would be at home with the kids. She didn't bother knocking and let the screen door slam shut behind her. Glancing across the room, she saw Umi and Hiro on the floor listening to the radio. Setsuko stood by the window, her face drawn down and her eyes bloodshot.

They were about the same height, and when Violet hugged her, Setsuko trembled and wouldn't let go. "I'm scared. They said they were searching for something of vital importance," Setsuko said.

She had never seen Setsuko like this. "They probably always say that. If they close the school, we can do crafts with the kids here. And they have our little garden here and Ahualoa."

"That's not what I'm worried about. I think they're taking him."

Violet pulled away, still holding both her hands, and looked her in the eye. "Taking him?"

"To the relocation camp at Kilauea. The captain said something about the Ni'ihau incident," Setsuko whispered, then put her finger to her lips.

They were practically nose to nose and Violet could see the salt from the dried tears on Setsuko's cheeks. "That was years ago. And what would it have to do with Takeo?"

Everyone knew about the Ni'ihau incident. In 1941, a Japanese pilot had crashed on the small island after raiding Pearl Harbor. Initially, the Hawaiian people of the island didn't even know about the bombing, but when they got wind of the attack, they apprehended him. The pilot sought aid from three local Japanese, who assisted him in breaking loose, finding weapons and taking hostages. In the mind of the Americans, it proved that anyone of Japanese descent could not be trusted.

"Nothing at all, but they already have their minds made up," Setsuko said.

Violet gripped her wrists. "We won't let it happen."

Chapter Eleven

ELLA

ALL OF US KIDS WERE SCARED WHEN THE ARMED men showed up, but Sensei told us not to worry when he went outside to talk to them. I wondered if I was the cause of this. Maybe I wasn't supposed to be there and they had come for me. But that wasn't it. Over and over, I could hear Sensei saying, "I'm an American, you have to believe." It turned out the men wanted to search for something in our schoolhouse.

Sensei came back in and told us that school would be closed until further notice, and that we should head straight home. Sumiko and Ethyl in front of me started crying. On the way out, the men gave me funny looks. Everything went orderly, but I got a taste of despair coming off of Sensei, like he wanted to fold himself into an origami crane and fly away. A single tear ran down his cheek when I turned to wave at him. All I could do was give him my biggest smile, one that I rarely use.

I hated the thought of Mama alone in the near darkness. There were a lot of bad people around. Or good people, depending on who you asked. One time, just after the army moved into town, we were walking up to see Papa, who was working late at school. At that point we were used to being able to do whatever we wanted, and being the principal's family gave us what Mama called *clout*. It was just after sundown and I was telling Mama about the book *Lassie Come-Home* that Mrs. Hicks read us, and how they made it into a movie. Neither of us paid any attention to a man giving commands. Mama had her big blue eyes turned on me as though I was the only person alive—until we heard, *"Stop or I'll shoot!"* We both turned into statues and Mama yelled who we were. He said he didn't care and curfew was curfew. That was when we knew things had really changed.

It was dark by the time Mama came home. Her eyes were swollen and I ran up to hug her when she came into the kitchen.

She wiped her nose with a dish towel. "They took Takeo away."

"Oh heavens, no!" Jean said.

I could see Mama was on fire. "You know what gets me? This whole hysteria. I understand that we need to protect ourselves, but there's a line of human decency that has been crossed."

Jean set down her glass of milk. "That may be true, but a lot of these people from the mainland don't know our Japanese like we do. All they know is that we are at war and our lives are at stake."

Well, that got my mama going, and her nostrils flared like they did when she was fuming. "Alma Jean, are you siding with them?"

"I'm not siding with anyone. It's a complicated situation, and I can see both sides. You know I love the Hamasus."

One thing about Mama mad is that she takes action. "We

need to talk to everyone we know. I'm going to see if Irene can get me on the line with the governor tomorrow. Takeo is the most harmless man around."

Jean nodded and I hugged Mama harder. I didn't want her to get herself in a situation like my papa did. She looked down at me like she just noticed I was there. Her hands rubbed my scalp. "I'm sorry, Ella. That you had to be there for that."

"Where are they taking him?" I said.

"To a camp near the volcano."

If they called it a camp, it must not be so bad, and I wondered what all the fuss was about. "Will we get to go, too?"

Mama and Jean looked at each other like they knew something that I didn't.

"No, but maybe we can visit," Mama said.

When we sat down to eat, Jean asked God for an extra helping of love for Takeo and his family. To my surprise, she also asked for Brownie to grow a new set of shiny feathers. She had a special way with prayers, which made me wonder if I should ask her to pray for me.

Brownie had managed to live, but it would be a long time before she looked like a proper chicken. The top hen in the yard attacked her when we set her down outside one sunny morning, and I had to run screaming at them with a shovel to break it up. *Pecking order* is something real, not just a made-up phrase. So we still keep them apart and Brownie sleeps in a cage on our lanai.

I knew I should feel sorry for Takeo and his family, but I was caught up thinking about myself. And how I wouldn't be able to go back to his little schoolhouse. "Can we do Japanese school here?" I asked.

Mama and Jean had been talking about the war and they got quiet. "No, we can't. But that doesn't mean that Umi and Hiro can't come over and practice origami. And I'm sure Setsuko would be happy to help you keep your tree alive since she won't be helping out at the school anymore."

It wouldn't be the same as in the old wooden house. I liked how our voices bounced off of the floor and the walls, and I wanted to make an *oshie* out of old kimono material. I had only seen ones of people, but I planned on making a chicken. More than anything, I knew I was safe there.

Suddenly, it looked like a light went on in Mama's head and she said, "Say, I have an idea!"

Chapter Twelve

VIOLET

THE WEEK WAS SHAPING UP TO BE ONE OF THE worst in recent memory. Sleeps were fretful, Ella wet her pants in class for no apparent reason and the trade winds had taken a vacation. By the end of each school day, Violet's dress was stuck to her back and her hair looked more like feathers. Setsuko had no option but to keep teaching, and spent her lunch breaks crying, as though she'd spent her whole life saving up the tears, and now they wouldn't turn off.

On Friday morning, none of Violet's students wanted to follow instructions. All anyone could talk about were the marines that were coming at noon to display their tanks and latest artillery. The boys wanted to see the weapons and the girls wanted to see the soldiers. The only good that would come out of it was that Zach and the boys would be joining them afterward for supper. The house could use a happiness boost.

Even before the bell rang, her students lined up at the door, spilling into the hallway. You could hear the thrum of engines down near the field.

"Johnny, keep your toes on this side of the threshold," Violet said.

Johnny Martinez was the kind of young man who tested her at every turn. Constantly in motion, he had an affinity for breaking things. "But, Miss, I want to get picked to ride in the tank." She had long given up trying to change the fact that all teachers here were called Miss, regardless of their marital status.

"When the bell rings, we'll go. No sooner."

She had to stand in the doorway to keep them in. Finally the bell rang and everyone beelined to the field. Johnny Martinez tore off on his own. Even so, she had a hard time being upset with him. When it suited him, he could be sweeter than fresh sugarcane, and she had learned that her most difficult students were often the most lovable.

Several olive-colored tanks were positioned across the field, along with artillery carriers and an amphibious vessel that looked like a big metal dinghy with wheels. Johnny ran straight for the tank, which didn't have as many people around it as she'd have expected. Under the midday sun, she could already feel her dress melting onto her back. Near the flagpole, a crowd had gathered. Violet raised herself up on her tiptoes to see what the draw was, but saw only a military jeep with a few soldiers standing around it. The elementary kids were already there and she looked around for Ella without any luck.

At this point, she gave up trying to control her class and nudged her way to the front of the crowd. When she saw what the fuss was about, her knees almost buckled. A lion lounged on the hood of the jeep as though it were the most natural thing in the world. She blinked several times to make sure her eyes were not making this up. A handful of kids crouched on the front of the jeep, petting the lion. One of those kids was Ella.

Violet's first instinct was to holler out, but Ella looked spellbound, and beamed at the lion with her whole heart. All of her features were scrunched together in an enormous grin. This was ridiculous. Whose idea was this—bringing a lion and letting it loose with the kids?

For the first time, she noticed the men in charge. Zach and Parker. If one of them was responsible for putting Ella up there on the hood, she would be having a word with them. Ella might be happy, but the lion had paws the size of baseball mitts, even though it was clearly still just half grown. Kids sat on the hood, smashed into the seats and balanced on the wheels. Everyone wanted in. The men ushered new kids in to get their chance, but Ella remained firmly planted. Parker turned to Ella and said something, and she shook her head. *"Sorry, I'm not leaving,"* Violet imagined her saying. Ella had always contained an extra helping of headstrong.

So this must be Roscoe. She had to laugh. Everyone had been expecting to meet a dangerous man. The scratch on Parker's arm, of course. Aside from a light panting, and the occasional twitch of his tail, Roscoe looked as though he might fall asleep.

With her feet planted in the grass, Violet resigned herself to watching. Ella would cling harder if made to leave. Several of Violet's students now gathered around her. The girls had taken to giggling and she realized their attention was on Parker, not the lion. Zach spotted her and waved her over.

She smoothed out her hair and stepped forward. "This is about the darnedest thing I've ever seen. You boys have any other surprises up your sleeves?"

Zach grinned like a proud father. "Isn't he grand? Good ol' Roscoe."

As far as lions went, he was a grand specimen. Not that she had much to compare him to.

"I have to admit, a lion was about the last thing I expected. When you mentioned Roscoe, I pictured a scrappy man."

Parker turned and smiled. In the sunlight, his pale eyes stood out against his almond skin. "Hello, Violet."

"Hello yourself. So, which one of you is the lion tamer?" she asked.

Zach pointed to Parker. "This fella. A handful of us are in charge of Roscoe, but Parker here is the one who got him."

How one ended up with an African lion in a small town in Hawaii, she couldn't wait to hear. "Where on earth did you find him?"

"Long story," Parker said, just as Ella caught sight of her.

"Mama! This is Roscoe!"

"Sweetie, I see. He seems to like you, but be careful," she said.

Her own mother had always told her to *"watch out for snakes, don't talk to strangers, keep away from beehives."* And then she collapsed after her husband left. Too much fear and not enough living. Violet swore she would be different as a mother, and yet she found herself wanting to shield Ella from all of life's perils, large and small. Was it so unreasonable to be wary of a lion?

The next thing she knew, Ella reached down and wrapped both of her arms around Roscoe's neck, burying her face in his sand-colored fur.

Violet grabbed the nearest arm, which happened to be Parker's, and squeezed. "Ella, get off him!"

"Roscoe is about the most gentle-natured animal you'll ever meet. He was raised with humans," Parker said.

"He's a wild animal. And wild animals are unpredictable," she said.

"Last time I checked, life was unpredictable. People. Animals. We all are." The faintest smile brushed his lips. "When was the last time you had any fun?"

How could he possibly know that the last time she'd had fun was…well, quite frankly, she couldn't remember. A line of heat shot up her neck, and she felt like smacking him.

"This isn't about me, Sergeant. I just don't want my daughter's face bitten off by the lion that never hurt anyone." Her words made her sound like she was angry at the world. Maybe she was.

Parker remained in place and fingered his dog tag. "I promise, she's going to be fine."

Whether he was talking about Ella and Roscoe or Ella in general, she couldn't be sure. Against better judgment, she swallowed her doubt.

After school, Violet walked with Ella into town for an ice-cream float. It was their end-of-the-week tradition. Mamane Street bustled with soldiers on their way to the People's Theater to see *Casablanca*, or to shoot pool in the saloon down the way. Swarms also spilled in and out of the Honoka'a Club Hotel, loud voices filling the air. Someone had plastered the town with banners advertising the upcoming rodeo. All in all, the war had infused their little town with a new vitality.

As much as Violet hated to admit it, Parker's question had spread through her like a dust storm. She searched her memory for any occasion of real fun since Herman's disappearance, and was not surprised to find it empty. Even more troubling was that before that, she was hard-pressed to come up with anything. Life had always been about the school, and then about the war. There had been a few weekend excursions to see the snow on Mauna Kea or to visit the volcano. Defensiveness of her way of life rose up. What did Parker know, anyway?

On the way, they stopped off to say hello to Irene Ferreira, who was dressed in a pink-and-orange-checkered dress with white pointy heels. Nowadays, she dressed for work as if her life depended on it. You never know who you might run into, she always said. When people like Bob Crosby, Bing's brother, and Joe DiMaggio were rolling through town, you'd best be prepared.

Irene worked the switchboard frantically.

Violet called from the front door, "Just saying hello. We can stop by another time."

Irene waved them in. After a few moments of plugging and unplugging wires, she turned to them and said, "It sounds like the island-hopping toward Japan is progressing. Our forces are dropping something called napalm that burns away all the foliage. Wait—hang on." Irene made a few more connections before taking off her headphone. "Don't say I told you this." Irene ran her hand across her mouth like a zipper.

"I know how to keep secrets," Ella said in a way that caused Violet to wonder all over again what kind of knowledge was wound up inside her. Every so often she made a remark like this.

"So tell me something I don't know," Irene said to Ella.

"We had a lion at school today."

Irene looked to be reconciling this. "You don't say."

"It's true. I saw it with my own eyes," Violet said. "The soldiers brought him along with the tanks and Ducks and artillery. He's their mascot."

Ella raised herself up on her tippy toes, like she used to when she got excited, and the words flew out of her mouth. "And guess what? His name is Roscoe and he's coming for dinner."

Irene never passed up an invitation, even though technically she hadn't been invited. "The soldier or the lion?"

"The lion. But the soldiers are coming, too. You would like them. They sing and dance and have stories," Ella said.

Of course Irene would like them. Every last one of them. And before the night was over, would probably issue a few marriage proposals herself. But Violet was still hung up on the part about a lion at dinner.

"Wait a second, Ella. They didn't say anything about bringing Roscoe. We can't have a lion in our house."

Ella shrank back. "Why not? I asked Parker."

"Well, Parker doesn't own the house, does he? We have chickens and cats, and Lord knows what he might do to the place."

All the pink drained from Ella's face. "Mama, please?"

The word *no* was impossible to say.

Chapter Thirteen

VIOLET

WHILE WAITING FOR THE MEN, VIOLET FOUND that she half wanted to see the lion again. Her earlier panic had transformed into a prickly feeling of anticipation. An engine sputtered outside. She peeked out the kitchen window and there was Roscoe, leading Parker, Zach and Tommy O'Brien up the steps on a long chain. Before he reached the top step, he had already spotted the chicken coop. For a young lion, one whole chicken might go down like a handful of peanuts.

She had taken more care in dressing this time, and wore a red-and-white-flowered dress with a wide waistband. After a few failed attempts, she managed to pin her hair in a loose bun on top of her head and used a drop of oil to smooth the flyaways. Jean had demanded she borrow a red lipstick that matched her dress perfectly.

"You look delicious, my dear," Jean said, as she stood back and fanned herself.

The thought of those men seeing her like this caused a palpitation in her chest.

Ella left her perch by the window to greet the soldiers on the lanai. Between Zach's goofy smile and the delight in Parker's eyes at seeing Ella, Violet felt any reservations softening around the edges. Maybe Roscoe would be okay tied up to the post out here. Or if worse came to worst, in the jeep.

"Good evening, ladies. We come bearing wild animals," Parker said, mainly to Ella, who now pressed herself into Violet's hip.

"Hello again. A little warning about Roscoe would have been nice. I suppose he's welcome to stay, just not in the house," she said, her voice sharper than intended.

"Sometimes warnings get in the way," Parker said.

He seemed determined to rattle her.

Zach cut in. "Roscoe is nothing more than an oversize kitten. I'll wager he could win over Adolf Hitler or General Yamamoto in a heartbeat."

Parker leaned closer and Violet smelled the sharp smell of sweat mixed with engine grease. He lowered his voice. "Don't tell anyone, but he's our secret weapon."

He winked at Ella, whose eyes about fell out.

A crack of sun lit up the wooden slats on the lanai. Everyone sat. Setsuko and the twins showed up a few minutes later, at the same time as Irene Ferreira. Since their earlier visit, she had piled up the front part of her hair into a large dome on her head, making her look taller than she already was. On the other hand, Setsuko had gone from slim to scant. She felt anxious having Setsuko with the marines, and Setsuko hadn't wanted to come, but Violet won her over in the end.

"You have to stand your ground. This is your town and you're no different than Jean or me. They need to see that," Violet had pressed.

There seemed a blurred line between those who were rational and those who had blanket opinions about the Japanese. And the reverse might have been true. Some marines could make the distinction between an honest and dishonest Japanese American. Others couldn't. Violet was determined to show them that Setsuko was part of the family.

The twins had seen Roscoe at school earlier from a safe distance, and now they both moved in a little closer to where he sat in the shade of the table. Jean handed out drinks and Violet decided a cold beer sounded refreshing. Something to calm her nerves. Roscoe's tongue hung out and he looked thirsty, too.

"Might Roscoe need water?" she asked.

"Please," Parker said.

He followed her into the kitchen. The only thing around large enough for his head to fit into was the mixing bowl she used for her pies. She wondered about African diseases, but rinsed it out anyway and turned on the faucet. The kitchen was sweltering, and had she been alone, she would have rubbed ice on the back of her neck.

"Your daughter is smitten," he said.

"Plain as day."

He came around and stood next to her at the sink, the space between them smaller than she would have liked. "Animals are good for the soul. Seems like Ella has already figured that out," he said.

He was right, of course. "She chooses animals over people every day. Why do you think that is?" Violet concentrated on the water.

"How I see it is that animals don't have all those annoying thoughts that humans do. They don't name things. They don't fret about the future. They're busy just *living*," he said.

Violet glanced up at him. "Sounds like you've thought this through."

She was keenly aware of a tickle of sweat running between her breasts and the buzz of the mosquitoes outside the screen. *"Animals are good for the soul"* echoed in her mind, and the way he said it with such conviction.

Parker wore a mix of amusement and seriousness on his face. "Like I said, I worked at a zoo. Animals are my business. Ever notice that feeling of peace you get when you're petting one of your cats?"

She thought about Snowflake, whose purring could make the whole room feel still.

"I think I have."

"So you know what I mean. And I got to noticing the look on those kids' faces when they connected with one of our animals." He paused as if dredging up some old memory and then chuckled. "A few ended up leaving in tears, though. Trust me, you don't want to upset a gorilla."

"Suppose I did?"

"I'd say you were in for it. True story. There was a real obnoxious young fella. He kept making faces at the gorillas and grunting sounds. Thought he was real funny. Bobo was never happy about being on display and he let people know it, pounding his chest and making faces and showing his rear end. On this particular day, he decided to go to the bathroom in front of everyone. A big pile of it. Of course, the boy thought this was about the best thing he'd ever seen. Until Bobo picked up his pile and threw it smack-dab in the boy's face."

"No!"

When he laughed, a new dimple showed up on one side of his cheek. "I swear on a stack of Bibles."

"Ella would love that story," she said.

Half a voice behind her said, "What story?"

She turned, and there was Ella, standing at the swinging door. "A zoo story. I'll let Parker tell you later. Want to help bring this for Roscoe?" Ella took the bowl.

On the porch, Roscoe stretched across the dusty planks with his spotted stomach exposed. His chest rose and fell and his whiskers twitched in the contented rhythm of dreamland. Everyone had arranged themselves around him, watching him sleep. Ella placed the water bowl quietly next to him.

"So much for water," Violet said.

"Busy day, with the kids and all," Zach said.

Irene had strategically positioned herself next to Zach and flashed her teeth. "Where on earth did you get him? I want the whole story," she said.

Zach turned to Parker, who sat on the top step, rubbing Roscoe's spots. "You tell 'em."

All eyes focused on Parker, who didn't seem to mind. "When I was stationed at Pendleton, our division elected me to find us a mascot. Now, I don't know if you are familiar with military mascots, but the marines have always had bulldogs. The first one, Private Biggs, even rose in the ranks to be a sergeant major. On my way to look at some bulldog pups, I decided to swing into the zoo for a hello. There was a new litter of lion cubs, wee little things. When the zookeeper told me they only had room for one, I got to thinking."

Zach chuckled. "You want to watch out when Parker gets thinking. He's got what you call an overactive imagination. Grandiose ideas."

Parker just shook his head. "Why get a bulldog when you can have a lion? Or a mule. Army uses mules. Anyway, he sold me the lion cub for twenty-five dollars, said I got a deal because he was the runt. It took a little work convincing Lieutenant Colonel Boyd, but in the end, he let us have him."

"I'm surprised they let you bring him on the ship," Violet said.

The boys all laughed. "They didn't. When our orders came to ship out, Tommy here had the bright idea of putting him in a crate and covering it up in canvas. By some miracle, we got him to Oahu without being caught. But when we arrived, there was no way of getting him past the inspection. They made us put him in quarantine, which is why he only recently got here," Parker said.

Violet tried to imagine hiding a lion on a ship crammed with soldiers, and was having a hard time. "How did you feed him?"

"Well, it got a little tricky, and each of us lost weight on that trip over. Sharing our meals with Roscoe. It took us about six days to Oahu. When we first left Point Loma, we had no idea where we were going. Some people were saying San Francisco, or Tokyo. Scuttlebutt was rampant and Billy Worthington kept telling us there were girls on board. It wasn't until the second day at sea our unit commanders said Hawaii," Parker said.

Ella crawled forward from her place on the *lauhala* mat and buried her hand in Roscoe's fur. "I'm glad it was Hawaii."

Parker fixed his eyes on Ella and patted her hand. "Me, too."

Violet felt a bump in her chest. She looked over at Jean, who was shaking her head in a way that reminded Violet of her own mother, when she knew something Violet had yet to figure out.

Back in the kitchen for napkins, she saw Mrs. Cody peering out at them from her window. Violet waved and Mrs. Cody ducked behind the curtain. Poor woman was always nosing into their business, probably now concerned about all the single men and women under the same roof and what kind of inappropriate things might be going on. Meanwhile, her own husband was probably hitting the bars about now. Violet could hardly blame him.

Just then, she heard boots pounding up the steps. Only one person made that kind of noise. Luther. She hadn't invited him and now felt sorry. She rushed out. Jean was already making introductions.

He had puffed himself up an extra inch, if that was possible. "Pleasure to meet you boys. I served in the Great War. You need any words of advice, don't hesitate to call on me. But you're up against an entirely different breed," he said.

Violet hated when people talked like that in front of Setsuko, but Setsuko didn't flinch. She hoped it wasn't taken personally. Which was an empty hope, of course. Luther had never been one for sensitivity and said whatever came to his mind.

"You're welcome to join us," she said.

"Thank you kindly, but I have a roast in the oven. I just have a couple of questions on your pie stand," he said.

Luther gave Roscoe a wide berth. "Mr. Nakata sees that thing here, he's likely to flip."

"Official business, sir," Parker said, grinning.

"Well, my business is with the lady, so I'll steal her off for a moment if you don't mind. Violet?" Luther said, nodding to the living room.

As she followed him in, she caught a whiff of booze. It seemed like every time she saw him lately, he'd been drinking.

Luther bumped into the coffee table and dropped onto the couch. "What color do you want it?"

"Whatever color you have on hand. You sure are fast. I appreciate it," she said.

Paint was hard to come by these days, which was partly why they'd painted the house yellow.

Luther leaned in a little too close. "It may cost you a few ration tickets, since you don't use the liquor ones, that is."

"I am happy to pay you with pies or vegetables," she said, stepping back and letting the implication speak for itself.

Luther crossed his arms over his massive chest. "Fine."

She suddenly felt like crying. What was wrong with her?

"How's Ella doing, by the way?" he asked.

Violet hugged herself and blinked away tears. "She was devastated that the Japanese school closed down. But as you can see, Roscoe here is the greatest thing to ever hit this island."

When she looked out, she noticed Parker had backed up to the screen door. Close enough to hear the conversation.

Luther lowered his voice, but it still carried. "These boys all seem nice enough, but you'll want to keep your distance. Marines have a reputation."

Violet placed her hands on her hips and looked at him. "Oh? And what kind of reputation is that?"

"Bad boys, hell-raisers, you name it. I'm afraid they don't have a lot of respect for women. Which means that having them over with all you young gals might lead to trouble. Nor does it appear proper," he said.

A voice right next to her caused her to jump. "You know, we'd be happy to help with your pie stand, too, Violet. Marines aren't all bad. Oh, and I meant to give you this." Parker said it with a straight face and an even tone, but a vein pulsed in his temple. He held out a small jar full of something yellow.

"What's this?"

When he placed the jar in her hand, his fingers brushed over hers and squeezed in for the tiniest of moments.

"Chicken salve. How's she doing?"

"Hanging in there. I'll let Ella show you later. Thank you for this. Fellas, let's go back onto the porch, shall we?"

Jean had outdone herself with a Spanish casserole and roasted fall vegetables—carrots, squash, potato and sun-colored beets.

Everyone took their seats but Ella, who had been parked next to Roscoe since his arrival.

"Honey, come on up to the table," Violet said.

Roscoe sat up now and had his eyes trained on a lizard climbing the post. The tip of his tail twitched. Ella ran her hand along his back, her fingers disappearing beneath his sand-colored coat. Either she hadn't heard, or was lost in that dark place she retreated to. Sometimes Violet wasn't sure.

"Ella, we're eating now. Please join us."

Zach waved his fork in the air. "You know what happens to kids who don't eat dinner, don't you?"

That got her attention and she looked at him. "No?"

He continued. "Well, I'm not sure about here in Honey Cow, but in Waimea town, you might be in danger of blowing away in that wind. You need to keep a little weight on you to stay anchored."

Irene snorted in laughter. But Ella kept her eyes on the lion.

"Honey Cow?" Violet had to ask.

"No one can remember how to say Honoka'a," Parker said, butchering the word in the process, "so the boys refer to it as Honey Cow."

Hono-kah-ah. Irene Ferreira had drilled it into her head soon after her arrival. "Never heard the term, but it doesn't surprise me. No one can say any of these Hawaiian names properly," Violet said.

"Honey Cow is a weird name for a town," Ella said.

"Weird is good, isn't it?" Parker said.

Ella shrugged.

"Well, we don't have the same wind down here, but, Ella, if you want to come to Waimea to sell pies with us, you'd better come to the table. Now!" Violet said.

The last thing she wanted was a standoff and she could feel her tolerance stripping away. She held Ella's gaze and silently counted to five. Ella finally detached herself and came to sit between Violet and Setsuko, folding her hands in her lap. Roscoe watched Ella leave, and stood up, too. He was still tied with a long rope, but sauntered over and stopped behind Ella, rubbing the side of his face against her chair.

"What does he eat?" Setsuko asked.

It was only the second thing Setsuko had said tonight, and the first directed at the soldiers.

"The fellas at Parker Ranch have been good about giving us meat for him. So he's well fed. No need to worry about your kids," Parker said.

Ella made a face, as though trying to decide if Parker was for real. "Do you think he could eat a grown-up?"

Almost as a father defending his young, Parker launched into a speech. "Let me set things straight here once and for all. Roscoe is about as dangerous as Snowflake. We've had him since he was a tiny cub, and he's been raised with people. Trust me on this one." Parker looked over at Roscoe with tenderness. "He knows that we're talking about him, don't you, boy?"

The lion moved behind Parker, who reached out and rubbed Roscoe's ears, jostling him around. Up close, Violet could see that his whiskers were as sturdy as wires. His yawn exposed a set of canines three inches long. Regardless of what Parker believed, he could bite you in half if he had a mind to.

"A playful swat could be deadly," Violet said.

"He's gentle. You'll see," Parker said.

Irene Ferreira set her beer bottle down a little too hard, shaking the whole table. "Where's his mane?" she asked.

"The manes don't usually fill in until they're two. And Roscoe is only about six months," Parker said.

Roscoe moved back toward the post and suddenly sprang up, batting his paws in the same way that Snowflake did. The translucent lizard shot up the post toward the ceiling, narrowly escaping. Roscoe kept his eyes glued.

Ella squealed. "He's so cute! Can we get a lion, Mama?"

Cute was not the issue here. Violet could already see the problems that would arise once the soldiers shipped off and took their lion off to war with them. Ella's heart would crack to pieces. Again.

Instead of settling down in front of the radio after dinner, Violet put Ella to bed and returned to find Setsuko waiting on the front step to say goodbye. In the last residue of dusk, the outline of her face reminded Violet of her own, after Herman. Strange how vacuous a person could look. But there was more hope for Takeo than Herman. At this point.

She whispered into Setsuko's hair, "The truth will come out."

Setsuko squeezed a little harder and took Umi's and Hiro's hands. Watching them walk into the shadows, Violet wished she could do more. A chill ran through her.

Back in the living room, Tommy sat with an ukulele in hand and Parker, an old guitar. Jean had lit one small candle, which moths were now dive-bombing.

"I think we should move into the kitchen," Violet said.

Everyone looked at her as though she had come specifically to spoil the fun, but Parker spoke up. "She's right. We don't want to get them arrested."

In the full light of the kitchen, they all crammed together. Violet was thankful it was a cool night, or they would be roasted alive within minutes. When both men started playing, she would have sworn fingers couldn't move so fast. The song was a flurry of notes. She recognized it as Spanish, from listening to the *paniolo* play. Parker might not be able to sing, but he sure could play. Tommy's heel thumped on the floor in time, adding to the beat. He was the first *haole* she'd seen on the ukulele.

Zach clapped wildly when they finished, and Violet could tell Irene was itching to dance. Boy, could she swing those hips. Any images Violet had seen of hula girls in grass skirts and coconut tops had been surpassed by the performances she'd seen once arriving in the islands. Women wore colorful skirts and long flowered muumuus and moved in the most elegant ways. Even the men danced their own kind of hula. "You fellas should form a band!" Irene said.

"Tommy, how'd you learn to play the ukulele so quickly?" Violet wanted to know.

Zach answered for him. "Tommy O'Brien, the Irish Hawaiian."

Tommy just shrugged and kept his fingers moving up the four-stringed neck.

The next song was even bouncier, and Zach decided he wouldn't be left out this time. He stood and began stomping his foot and waving his arms around like a mad elephant. Parker called out a few words in Spanish and Irene clapped in time. Zach plucked Irene from her chair and twirled her around. His hands got stuck in her hair and he nearly brought her down. Between the bunch of them, Violet couldn't help but laugh. Zach was all elbows and knees, but once Irene took over the dance, they smoothed out.

The feeling of despair that often came around at this time of night was no place to be seen. Maybe that was the way of life, to fold moments of color back into your everyday living, little by little so you barely knew it was happening. Violet closed her eyes.

At that same moment, a roar like nothing she'd ever heard before filled up the entire house, most likely bouncing off the moon, it was so loud. The vibrations caused a fullness through her whole body. Both men stopped playing midsong.

"You think they heard that out on the ships?" Parker asked.

Tommy fanned his face with his free hand. "Imagine being out in the jungle on some faraway island at night and hearing that. I'd swim back here to Hawaii before facing such an animal," he said.

Parker had slipped out and returned with Roscoe, who looked at each of them with lazy eyes. *Try to top that*, Violet could almost hear him thinking.

After another round of songs, Parker gave Zach his guitar. Zach was passable, but he couldn't pick. Parker held out his hand. Violet turned around to see whom he was reaching for. But Jean and Irene were planted in their chairs. Her pulse drowned out the music.

With no choice but to join him, she stood. The music slowed and Parker placed his other hand on her waist. All she wanted to do was fade into the night. He pulled her in, then spun her out, and her hand hit the icebox.

"Sorry," he mouthed.

Her dance moves were limited to a simple waltz or foxtrot, and whatever he was trying to get her to do didn't seem to be working. She stepped on his feet and bumped into him on more than one occasion. The next time he pulled her in close, he whispered, "Relax, and follow me."

That only turned her anger on. "I'm trying, Sergeant."

Parker let her out again and pulled her in even tighter on the next go-around. "I like how you call me Sergeant when you're upset."

"I'm not upset!"

She saw a hint of a smile in the corner of his eyes. Tonight they looked more lake blue than silver. His hand on her waist sent heat through her skin, roasting up her entire midsection. Or was that her imagination?

Nothing she did made any difference, but Parker did not give up. By the end, Violet had to admit that he made an excellent dance partner, one with an extra helping of patience. She was, in all probability, the worst partner he'd ever had.

They sat. "I'm better off watching," she said, dabbing her brow with a towel.

Once again, he was sitting too close. "Give it time. No one ever got any better by just watching."

She crossed her arms. "Fine." He had an answer for everything.

Roscoe, who sat below Parker's chair, rumbled again, and Parker reached down and stroked him. "He likes to be included."

Next, Jean and Irene performed a hula to a song that only Tommy could play. Irene was more practiced, but Jean's red fingernails stood out, adding flair to her wavy hand motions. Violet decided they made a nice team, chocolate and vanilla.

Above the music, from somewhere down the road, came a slurred holler. "Quiet down! Any Japanese submarine passing by is going to hear that racket. You're going to get us all killed."

Mr. Cody. It could only be. They all looked at each other and tried to suppress their laughter. Zach responded, "Roger that!"

It was getting late, and she wondered if Ella was sleeping through this. "It's probably time to turn in," she said.

The truth of the matter was, Violet was having a wonderful time. Despite Parker. The men led Roscoe out and said their goodbyes, and when Parker leaned in to kiss her cheek, he whispered, "I bet you'll change your mind."

She opened her mouth to say something, but he had already turned to go. *Change my mind about what?*

Chapter Fourteen

ELLA

I HAVE DECIDED THAT I CAN TRUST ZACH AND his gang. Anyone who keeps a lion for a pet can't be half-bad. I can't say for sure that I like all of the soldiers, though, especially the mean and unreasonable ones that took Takeo away. It seems like you should have a good reason for taking someone to camp, but they couldn't answer any of Takeo's questions. Which makes me wonder how bright they were, or fair. But Jean says they are here to protect us, so who knows.

I thought I would be scared to touch Roscoe at school when I first saw him, but anyone could see that he was no different from one of us. Just an oversize cat who wanted to be noticed and loved. When Zach lifted me up onto the hood of the jeep and Roscoe looked at me, I swear he looked right into me. His eyes were bronze-colored and the way his mouth curved up made it seem like he was smiling.

The first thing I did was reach out and feel him. I couldn't help it, even though he might have bitten my arm off. Lions are not soft like cats. His fur felt bristly and slightly oiled. The men didn't seem concerned; in fact, they encouraged us to pet him. Roscoe tilted his head and nudged my hand.

"Does he have a purr box?" I asked.

Zach gave me a funny look. "Lions don't purr. But, boy, can this one roar."

I knew at that very moment that a lion was what I needed most in my life. For many reasons. I could picture him sleeping with me in bed with his polka-dot belly. I would wake up and all those internal things that troubled me would be erased. I could also bring him to school and people would be nice and want to be my friend. Or in the forest he could protect me while I search for caterpillars. I used to spend a lot of time in the forest. Takeo called it forest-bathing. *Shinrin-yoku.* It's supposed to be healthy. Now I'm too scared.

Most important, a lion might be able to take care of my problem, once and for all. Then life could go on like before.

Meeting Roscoe at school made me happy. But it also made me sad. It made me miss my papa and wish he could have been there to see a real live lion. In the past, whenever we had any kind of assembly or field day, you would see him a head above most of the other people, like the tallest tree in the forest. The funny thing was, just before I would notice him, a tickle ran across my skin. I would turn around, and there was Papa, looking right into me. He'd smile and wink and I would feel like the luckiest person in the world. He had nut-brown eyes with dark eyebrows that pinched together in the middle and made him look a little mad. A lot of the kids at school were scared of him. Kind of like Roscoe—he seemed scary, but he wasn't. In fact, he took care of everyone and treated all the kids like his own.

Here's a good example. This was one of those days that stick in your head, and when you look back on it, you remember every tiny detail. Papa and I sat at the table sorting *lilikoi* for the butter we were going to make later in the day when the phone rang. Mama picked up and handed it over, mouthing, "It's the sheriff."

In about two seconds, Papa's face went baby-powder white. He groaned and nodded and ran his fingers through his hair and shook his head. He looked sick. Mama and I shared worried glances.

He hung up and jumped to his feet. "Japanese planes are bombing Pearl Harbor and Oahu. We need to get to someplace safe."

That was the beginning.

But before we ran off, he knelt in front of the radio and fiddled with the controls for some time before a staticky voice came through from KGU… "We have witnessed this morning the severe bombing of Pearl Harbor by enemy planes, the Japanese. The city of Honolulu has also been attacked and severe damage has been done. It is no joke. It is a real war. The public of Honolulu has been advised to keep in their homes…" A telephone operator interrupted to make an emergency call.

Papa stood up completely straight and turned around to look at us. His face had turned from white to gray, and you could see the fear wrapping around him.

"I'm going to make sure nothing happens to us," he said.

But I wondered.

We rounded up cans of sardines and Saloon Pilot crackers, filled jars with water and ran across the field to the mouth of the closest bomb shelter, a lava tube in the gulch next to our school. Papa herded us inside, and then went to find the other people on campus. We were left alone with an old lantern that barely lit up the damp walls pressing in around us. I squeezed Mama's hand.

"Are there rats in here?" I asked, not really wanting an answer.

"Sweetie, don't worry about rats. It's safer in here than it is out there for the time being."

Rats were not to be taken lightly, almost as much as bombs, since they had been spreading the plague to plantation workers in our area. Only last year, Dickie Ramos woke with a fever on a Saturday and was dead by Tuesday.

Mama was pretending to be calm, but her voice had a waver to it. I heard her tell Mrs. Hicks when she came in, "How could this have happened with no warning whatsoever? It's no secret that the Territory of Hawaii is a strategic location, but an unannounced military strike?"

"Lord have mercy on us all."

I felt the dampness leaking onto my shirt and spreading through my whole body. At some point, I started crying and tears and snot plastered to my face.

Papa came back with another group, including Setsuko and her family. He led them over to the last remaining spot near Mama and me. Everyone sat on wooden planks or burlap bags thrown over the rock floor. I could hear other kids crying and felt better that I wasn't the only one. Papa kissed the top of my head, sat down next to me and held my hand. The smell of sweat and mildew and Coca-Cola floated off him. We sat there for a while, and I felt some of the fear leaking out. He had that effect.

After several hours of sitting in the dark and listening to each other breathe, us kids began to get restless. Someone had thought to bring cards, and games of War and Go Fish sprang up. You could hardly see and no one's heart was in it, but we played anyway.

Papa left us again and was gone for at least a few hours. When he came back, he said that people could return to their homes, although nothing was for certain. When we got back, we turned on the radio right off the bat. "Plane down off of Diamond Head! Bomb dropped in Manoa, civilians hit! Dog-fight over Waikiki!" Web, the man in the radio, also told us to fill bathtubs and containers with water in case the water supply was cut off, or worse—poisoned.

He said that invasion now seemed not only possible but likely, and if the Japanese had attacked Oahu, which was well armed, what would stop them from hitting the other islands?

"Honey, should we let Ella hear this?" Mama whispered to Papa.

"No point in hiding anything."

"But it's just going to scare her."

"She'll be more scared if we keep her in the dark."

Papa was always my ally. A word I hear a lot nowadays.

Later in the afternoon, the sheriff called again. He said that the bombing had stopped but no one could predict what might happen next. There was worry about another raid, coastlines being shelled by submarines, and Japanese paratroopers landing. A total blackout was being ordered, and a curfew would be enforced. I had no idea what a curfew was then, but I didn't like the sound of it. It turned out it just meant that no one was to be out after dark. Papa got busy organizing the men to watch for parachutes and setting up volunteers to enforce the blackout.

I was proud to be his daughter.

Mama and I hung blankets over the windows and made forts out of mattresses to sleep under. As though that might somehow protect us from a bomb slicing through the house. When we finally went to bed that night, under the mattresses, I laid my head on Papa's chest and heard the thumping of his heart with one ear and the retelling of the day's events on the radio with the other. You could almost smell the black smoke from the three burning ships.

"The navy had made no statement as of yet, but the army ordered everyone off of the streets. Lives had been lost, planes were shot down and antiaircraft gunnery was heavy. Bombs were dropped in front of the governor's house and in front of the *Honolulu Advertiser*, nearly hitting their mark. It was difficult to believe that these were Japanese planes, until the red meatball insignia was seen on the wing. Three hundred and fifty men killed at Hickam!"

On one hand I wanted to keep listening, but I didn't want to hear what I was hearing. I don't know who had been right: Mama about me not listening or Papa about letting me in on it.

Either way, the war kept on happening.

When the soldiers showed up at our house with Roscoe, I was pretty sure I had died and gone to heaven. Parker also brought me my own special chicken ointment for Brownie. She has a new tuft of feathers growing in, but the other hens still peck at her. Then she goes tearing around the yard like an old lady who's lost her bloomers. My one concern with Roscoe is that he might want to eat our chickens for dinner. But you never know. Animals can get used to each other. Even ones that aren't supposed to get along. People should be the same.

Mr. Macadangdang has a big blue dog—at least, he says it's blue, but it looks gray—that nursed a baby mongoose. I swear on a stack of grenades. The mongoose was orphaned and one morning he said he woke to find its tiny mouth attached to her udder with the other four puppies. He still has the mongoose, which he calls Dog, and it rides around on his neck when he brings over the coconuts.

Anyway, last night was one of the best nights we've had lately. No one knew, but I sneaked out of my room and watched them dancing last night. My poor mama. She was the worst of the bunch, but she still looked pretty. Even though she thinks Jean is so glamorous with her blond hair and nice figure, Mama is the one that people stare at. Her eyes are shiny, with yellow speckles in the middle of a splash of dark blue. And no one I know has skin like her. When she smiles at you, watch out. It's like she knows the secret to life, and if you're lucky, she might share it with you. So what if her hair is prone to static electricity? All the pieces of her come together so nicely, they overrule the hair.

All I can think about is when I'm going to see Roscoe again. I know we'll be going to Waimea town next Saturday for our first day at pie selling. Mama asked Setsuko if she wanted to be a part of our operation, since Takeo is gone and they are short on money. It was a big deal to include someone else because we need the extra income, but friends come before money, Mama said, and I'd best remember it.

Chapter Fifteen

VIOLET

NOVEMBER 1 ROLLED AROUND, AND JUST LIKE she did on the first of every month, Violet visited the sheriff's office. It was one of those occasions she dreaded, yet who else was going to remind Souza that Herman was still considered a missing person? *Presumed dead* was not good enough.

The tiny office was one block off of Mamane Street, the main drag of Honoka'a. Not much of a police station, it was sandwiched between a barber and the music shop in a red-painted building. After spending so much time there, Violet came to understand that the secretary, a Miss Iris Watanabe, ran the whole affair. The office was in such order that no pen or particle of dust was out of place. Souza called her Admiral Watanabe, or just Admiral, but with such affection that on more than one occasion she wondered at the nature of their relationship.

Violet pushed the door open. "Hello, Iris."

Without turning her back from the filing cabinet, Iris said, "Have a seat, Violet. The sheriff will be back in two minutes."

Exactly two minutes and ten seconds later, Souza strode in. He took off his cowboy hat and threw it on the coat hanger. "Violet, always a pleasure."

"Sheriff, how are things in town?"

"Run-of-the-mill. Missing goats, drunken soldiers."

Even after this long, they still continued with niceties. For months after the disappearance, once the investigation dried up, Violet went door-to-door in town and out of town, asking people if they had seen or heard anything. She made her rounds at the plantation, at the dairy, and even in the neighboring camps. No one could give her any answers that led very far. And as much as Violet hated to put Ella under pressure, she'd had Souza ask her about that afternoon and what had upset her so badly. Or had she been merely sick? Ella held firm. She stayed mute as a stone on the matter.

One man at the plantation seemed sure that Bernard Lalamilo, the old man in Waipio Valley who made the Hawaiian moonshine, had something to do with it because he had a reputation as a trigger-happy drunk who hated *haole* people. And Herman had been down there on more than one occasion. Violet thought the two had been on good terms. But what if Herman had mentioned his dumb idea about making his own? She pressed the sheriff to investigate him fully, but after questioning the old man, Souza said you can't arrest a man based on hearsay.

Souza had handled her taking matters into her own hands graciously, even going with her when crime was slow.

"Anything turn up on Herman?"

"Now, you know I would be at your house in a heartbeat if I had anything," he said, leaning forward in his chair and glancing at Iris, who had stopped filing.

Before the last few visits, Jean had suggested that maybe it was time to stop. The look on Souza's face said the same thing. Violet clung to her seat, feeling faint and prickly.

Iris rolled over in her chair. "The case is cold. Everyone has done what they could. Time to move on."

The words were a shock to her system, as though someone just hit her in the gut with a sledgehammer. No one had ever been this blunt. She stammered, "Why…why… I'm trying."

"There are times in life when you just have to let go," Iris continued.

Souza looked at the wall. The phone rang and rang, but no one moved to answer it.

"In order to move on, let go, whatever, I need to know what happened," Violet said, ordering herself not to cry.

Iris stared through her, to that wounded place in the center of her chest. "You may never know what happened."

Without another word, Violet stood up and walked out. The words reverberated through her skull. *"You may never know."* Could she survive the rest of her life wondering? At some point, maybe a choice would need to be made. To wait without living, or to live without knowing.

Throughout the next week, the radio was abuzz with news on the ongoing battle at Saipan. The Allied forces had destroyed three Japanese aircraft carriers and hundreds of planes in the battle of the Philippine Sea, which meant that there was little hope for the Japanese garrison defending Saipan. Without reinforcement, they were toast. But in typical Japanese nature, all would continue fighting to the last man.

Violet and Jean listened with horror as the radio announcer described Hell's Pocket or Purple Heart Ridge. The Japanese were being wiped out by the thousands, but it sounded like American casualties were also mounting.

Jean looked ready to weep. "I hate to think of Bud in the middle of that. He's just the type to get himself blown up."

"Hush! That's an awful thing to say."

"Well, it's true, isn't it? He was always the one breaking things and wounding body parts. You saw how he was," Jean said.

It was the truth. In a few short months, Violet had learned that Bud was more bull than cowboy. Why, he'd even broken the handle right off of the icebox. Right now, any kind of consolation seemed phony. "Instead of dreaming up worst-case scenarios, let's see if Zach and the boys can find out anything," Violet said.

Violet had called a meeting that afternoon with Jean and Setsuko to prepare for their pie-selling debut on Saturday, only two days away. As promised, the stand was gleaming white and perfect. Fashioned with two-by-fours and shipping pallets, it came apart in several pieces. The stand would be easy to transport in the school flatbed, which Mr. Nakata had generously lent them.

As soon as Setsuko arrived, Umi and Hiro joined Ella in the living room. Ella was supposed to be practicing her letters, but Violet would return only to find drawings of lions and chickens strewn across the floor. Together, with the chicken perched on some part of the lion. Top of the head, shoulders, nose.

"Ella, we made something for Brownie!" Umi said, holding up an empty rice sack.

Ella looked up.

"Close your eyes," Umi said.

"Violet, can you fetch Brownie?" Setsuko asked.

A minute later, she set Brownie on the wooden bench on the lanai. Umi led Ella out to meet them, while Setsuko pulled out a small knitted item from her bag. On first glance, Violet thought it was a bright yellow sock. But the bottom belled out.

"Hold her for me, will you?"

Violet held Brownie firmly while Setsuko slipped the knitted piece over Brownie's head. There were two holes on each side for her wings. Brownie gave them a nervous look, then promptly started squawking. Luckily, Setsuko was sure-handed and swift.

"Open your eyes," Umi said.

Ella's eyes shot open. When she saw the sun-colored chicken sweater, her whole face lit up. Brownie ruffled her remaining feathers under the sweater and clucked a few more times before dropping down to a low crouch.

"Do you think she likes it?" Ella asked.

Violet was pretty sure Brownie hated it, but animals were adaptable and seemed to be able to keep right on living, even with missing feathers or limbs. "It fits her perfectly. I have no doubt she will love it."

"It'll keep her warm at night," Setsuko said.

Umi glowed with pride. "We took her measurements before we made it."

"Now there's a business idea for you," Jean said from the doorway, shaking her head.

Enterprising folks from around the Big Island had taken up peddling their goods to the soldiers. Just beyond the barbed-wire borders of Camp Tarawa, the marines could find hamburger stands, newspaper kiosks, *manapua*, chop suey, you name it. The Magnolia and The Chuckwagon had become permanent vendors. Anything was better than the slop served in the camp mess hall.

It had taken Violet some finagling with the ration board

to get a coveted B sticker for their gas rations, but she won out in the end. It hadn't hurt that Herman used to play cards with one of the board members. That allowed them an extra four gallons a week, which they would need to get to Waimea and back.

The women congregated in the kitchen and Violet began. "Let's revisit the name, Honoka'a Pies. Do we want something more interesting?"

"It's simple and straightforward," Setsuko said.

"Jean says it's too boring. So does Ella," Violet said.

Anyone knew that three women in one kitchen were too many, but here they were, elbow to elbow. Jean rolled up her sleeves and wiped the sheen from her forehead. Herman always said the houses were built out of paper and that's why the sun heated them up like furnaces. She didn't doubt it.

"We need something catchier," Jean said.

"What about Mama's Pies?" Violet said.

Jean rolled her eyes. "Please, something that will lure the soldiers in like bees on honey."

"You try, then, if I'm so terrible at it," Violet said.

She was stacking ingredients into a mountain on the table. Their plan was to make two varieties of pies each week, depending on available ingredients. Again, they'd traded alcohol ration tickets for some items. Coffee beans, cream, flour, cocoa, to name a few. Violet found she was happiest in the kitchen. The outside world fell away and the war turned off. Nothing else mattered.

"How about Sweetie Pies?" Jean said, sneaking a chunk of coconut.

"Too sugary-sounding," Violet said. "Setsuko, what do you think?"

Setsuko had been staying out of it. "I like all of your choices so far. Keep it simple. Honoka'a is as good as any."

"But no one can pronounce it," Jean protested.

Oh, how she sometimes wanted to wring Jean's neck. "Instead of Honoka'a, why don't we use their name? Honey Cow Pies."

For a moment, silence. Then all three erupted in laughter—the kind that folds you in half and makes your insides burn. Every time Violet looked at Jean, her laughter started back up again. When the peals finally tapered off, Jean managed to speak. "Now if that isn't a play on words, I don't know what is. But it's perfect!"

"We wouldn't dare," Violet said.

"Oh, we would, and we will. The boys are going to love us!"

The following afternoon, Violet couldn't wait for the bell to ring so she could get home and finish off the pies. Crusts were formed and dusted with egg whites, and the sweet potato and coconut all chopped and prepared. In well-orchestrated time, the moment her foot hit the bottom step of the house, the first raindrop landed on her cheek. For days now, the air had been as still as the surrounding mountains. You could almost taste the storm hovering just beyond sight, but the black curtain of sky to the east now looked to be moving toward them. *Please, let tomorrow be dry and clear in Waimea.*

They were going to need all the eggs they could round up. "Ella, darling, can you please grab me some hen-fruit for the pies? And take the umbrella."

Ella had a knack for picking up war slang, and *hen-fruit* was her new favorite way of saying *eggs*.

With her apron fastened tight, Violet set out the mixing bowls and dragged the radio closer to the kitchen, leaving the door open so she could hear the music. Cooking before dark with doors and windows open was the only way to go;

otherwise everything steamed up and they'd be standing in puddles of sweat.

Jean and Setsuko both showed up within a quarter of an hour. Jean disappeared and walked into the kitchen wearing her red-and-white-checkered apron and only her underwear, a beige ruffly affair. "I'm ready."

Setsuko's eyebrows lifted, but Violet wasn't surprised. Jean opted for fewer clothes when at all possible. "Put some clothes on, for heaven's sake. We have kids nearby," Violet said.

"My apron covers anything of interest. And I can't take any more of this heat. It's causing me to break out in hives all over."

Violet crossed her arms. "The rain should temper it, but suit yourself. I'll go ask the children to stay out of the kitchen if they don't want a big scare."

Jean stuck her tongue out, then turned to Setsuko. "I hope I'm not offending you?"

"Underwear in the kitchen is nothing." Her words were flat. Violet knew how she felt. When you've lost a big chunk of your heart, the top layer of life stops mattering. Only those big things—love, survival, hope—have any effect on you.

When Violet returned from speaking with the kids, Jean stood at the wall chalkboard, writing Chocolate Honeycomb & Coconut Sweet Potato Pies. "These names all right for tomorrow? I brought home a small chalkboard from school to lean up in front of our stand."

"Perfect," Violet said.

Earlier in the week, Jean had insisted on the chocolate honeycomb pie. "This one will land us husbands for sure," she had said.

Violet immediately looked over at the picture wall, where Herman smiled out at them from a silver frame. "None for me, thank you."

"Oh, V. At least keep an open mind."

No one understands. On more than one occasion, Violet had stated clearly that she would not be with another man until she knew whether Herman was dead for certain. The unknowing burned through her in the wee hours of the night. But as time moved on, him being found alive grew less and less likely. Still, a place inside her heart couldn't close the door.

"Think of it as more for you," Violet said.

Anyway, wasn't Jean losing sleep over Bud? One minute she cried over him, and the next, she exposed her dimples to any handsome man who so much as looked her way. On the account that they needed to use up the honeycombs from Mr. Keko'olani, Violet agreed on the chocolate honeycomb pie.

The ladies promptly got to mixing and pouring and layering. Honeycomb in chocolate, coconut on the purple sweet potato. These pies seemed far more exotic than anything Violet's mother would have made in Minnesota. Apple, cherry, pumpkin, thank you very much.

"Any word from Takeo this week?" Violet asked.

"Wednesday a short postcard came. Most of the prisoners have been sent to Oahu, so there is plenty of space and enough food, but he said that the guards follow them everywhere, with their bayonets fixed. He promised he's fine, but I know he's worried sick they're going to send him to the mainland. If he goes to the mainland, we go, too."

"I never got in touch with the governor," Violet said. "I guess he doesn't accept calls from schoolteachers in Honoka'a. He has more important things to tend to. But there has to be a way to get Takeo out."

Setsuko's once-round cheeks had flattened. Her jawline stood out as she spoke. "No one has yet told him what the new information was that caused his arrest. Maybe if we find that out."

"The sad thing is, no one needs a reason," Jean said.

Setsuko said, "Being Japanese is reason enough."

The words hung thick between them.

"Not everyone is so dumb, but unfortunately, a few people in charge think that way," Violet said. She had asked Irene Ferreira first thing, but Irene hadn't heard a peep. "Jean and I can ask around, because it sounds like in Takeo's case, they suspect something."

"I'm only thirty, and look, I have gray hair now." Setsuko held her head down. Sure enough, a few strands of silver had sprouted almost overnight.

"You and me both," Violet said.

Setsuko attempted a smile.

They decided on baking sixteen pies for the first day of selling. Better not enough than too many, in case no one was buying. But with twenty-three thousand homesick marines, the odds were in their favor.

Jean scooped out the last of the chocolate. "Call the kids in to lick the bowl. Oh, by the way, I ran into Irene Ferreira on my way back from town. She asked if she could stop in and I couldn't say no."

"She has her sights on Zach. That's plain as day," Violet said.

"That woman can't keep her mouth shut, but she usually has a lot of valuable information. I'll ask her to keep her ears open for Takeo," Setsuko suggested, having to shout over the rain, which was spilling down and now blowing sideways.

"I already asked."

The leading edge of the storm had arrived, and with it much cooler air.

"Lord Almighty, that rain is about my best friend right now," Jean said.

With the rain, which sounded like marbles being poured onto the tin roof, came a pounding on the door. "Come on in, Irene. We're in the kitchen."

Ella poked her head in, her face pale. "It's not Irene."

Violet walked out. Two uniformed men stood on the other side of the screen, faces deadpan. The tall one wore two bars on his shoulder. "Jean Quinlan or Violet Iverson?"

"I'm Violet." She turned around to see strips of Jean's and Setsuko's faces peering out from the kitchen. "Can I help you?"

The short one held the door open. "Mind if we come in out of the rain?"

They were on a tight schedule and Jean was in her underwear, but she swung the door open. "Please, come in, but we're quite busy, so if you'd get to the point of your visit."

The kids stopped their card game and stared. "Ella, please take Umi and Hiro into the bedroom to finish your game."

All the life had drained from her daughter's face and she made no move to leave. Umi grabbed Ella by the hand and dragged her down the hallway.

"Mrs. Iverson, I'm Officer Beckworth and this is First Lieutenant Decker. We're here on official business. Please ask your friends in the kitchen to join us."

"I'll need to get something from the bedroom first," she said.

A dress for Jean, to start.

Lieutenant Decker cleared his throat, but there was nothing in it to clear. "I'm sorry, but I'm going to have to ask you to stay where we can see you." He hollered toward the kitchen. "Ladies, please come out here."

She didn't like the threat in his tone. "Are we in some kind of trouble?"

The aroma of baking chocolate seeped into the room,

mixed with salt carried in with the rain. It was a smell to win hearts and steal alliances. Most regular folk would have commented on the sweetness of it. Not these men.

"We've reason to believe that messages are being sent from this house, possibly to the Japanese. I'm afraid you ladies are going to have to come with us."

Violet laughed. "I assure you, you have the wrong house."

Both men remained stone-faced. "No question, ma'am."

Setsuko appeared next to her, a study in solemn.

"We're schoolteachers at Honoka'a School, and my husband used to be principal. Look at us. Do we look like spies to you?" Violet said.

She fought to keep her heartbeat down, while time seemed to turn to cotton. Her mind flipped through questions. Was Herman somehow involved with the Japanese after all? But they had lived in a different house. *Jean? No way.*

Jean marched out of the kitchen in her apron and underwear, waving a chocolate-covered spoon. "Fellas, in case you haven't noticed, we have pies in the oven. Pies that we are baking for the soldiers, no less. Leaving right now is out of the question." Jean sneaked a wink in when the two men glanced at each other.

Officer Beckworth kept his gaze on the rug. "Ladies, I suggest you get yourselves together, turn off the oven and put some clothes on. It's cold where we're going." When he spoke, his upper lip folded under, exposing a set of rat teeth. All he needed was a set of whiskers.

More than a few seconds passed and no one moved. That was precisely when Irene Ferreira walked in, wearing a long pink skirt and a white blouse dotted with rain. "I hope I haven't missed the party!"

The cheer vanished from her face as soon as she saw the men.

"And you are?" Lieutenant Decker asked.

"Irene Ferreira. A friend. What's this all about?"

"Well, Irene, if you're not busy tonight, maybe you'd like to stay here and mind the children. Your friends will be coming with us to headquarters," he said.

"What about the pies?" Jean said.

With an ugly sneer, Decker looked Setsuko up and down. "You sure you're not putting poison in those pies?"

If Violet had had the guts, she would have slapped him hard across the cheek. Instead, she glared. He was the sort of miserable man who overinflated when given power. "Please, this is all a big mistake. You have to tell us more."

"Back at camp. Go get your dress on," he said to Jean, then turned to Violet and Setsuko. "You two stay here."

As best she could, Jean swung that peachy bottom of hers slowly into the hallway, giving them a little wiggle before she disappeared. If Violet hadn't been shaking in anger, she might have laughed. But it was wartime. People had been carted off, shot at, locked up. Times were different.

A small voice called out. "Mama?"

All three kids stood at the edge of the hallway. "Irene is going to stay with you guys. We're going to Waimea to straighten up a misunderstanding. Nothing to worry about."

Ella didn't look convinced, and Umi was crying. Violet feared especially for Setsuko, whom she'd persuaded to join them and now was being carted off to who knew where. Even a seed of suspicion would be enough to cause real trouble for her friend.

"Officers, our children have lost their fathers. Can you see what this is doing to them?" Violet pleaded. She was struck by how much these children had to endure.

The men softened. "Say your goodbyes, and if all is as you say, you'll be back in no time."

When Jean returned, Irene had her arms around the children. All faces were wet. "Thank you, Irene, and please put the next round of pies in for an hour. The timer should ring soon."

"You got it."

The last thing Violet heard as she hoisted herself into the jeep was the splitting sound of Ella wailing.

Chapter Sixteen

VIOLET

THEY DROVE THROUGH FOG AND FIERCE RAIN. In the front seat, every time Violet opened her mouth to speak, Beckworth, who drove, said, "Wait." She felt soaked, inside and out. At the very edge of Camp Tarawa, they crossed a line in the sky. The downpour stopped and a tangle of stars was visible all the way to the horizon. He hadn't been kidding, either. Waimea was a good ten degrees colder than Honoka'a.

Unable to contain her shivers, Violet tucked her legs up underneath her skirt. The jeep bounced down the dirt road, past the tent barracks to a small wooden building. Whatever these men had in mind for them, she didn't care. Her thoughts were on Ella.

The men marched them into an office with an older man sitting behind a desk. Even in the dim light, the first thing she noticed were the bushy eyebrows, and how they shadowed his eyes so you could barely see them. "Well, well. What do we have here?"

"The suspects from Honoka'a, sir," Lieutenant Decker said.

At the word *suspects* Violet felt ready to explode.

Swirls of smoke rose up from the man's nose. "Ladies, have a seat. I'm Captain Riggs, chief intelligence officer."

"Captain, I demand to know why you've brought us here," Violet said.

He nodded slowly. "Fair enough. Last week, one of our ships noticed flashing lights coming from the area in which you live. The code guys on board believed it to be a signal being sent to Japanese submarines that we know are still out there."

Jean piped up. "And you think it's us? Horsefeathers! Someone isn't doing their job."

Riggs stared at Jean, whose glossy red lips were about the only thing of color in the room. "We sent a plane out and determined the exact location. Which, I hate to tell you, is the house you three were found in tonight. You two are the only adults presently living in the house. Correct?"

"Correct," Violet said, wondering where the dickens he was going with this.

"But you live near Mrs. Hamasu." He nodded toward Setsuko. "And she frequently visits with you?"

"She does, with her kids. We make paper animals, knit dresses for chickens and bake pies for soldiers. It's a dangerous operation, sir," Violet said.

The two officers standing behind split up laughing, but Riggs remained stiff as a plank. "You understand we have to investigate anything suspicious. And this is, especially knowing that Mrs. Hamasu's husband is believed to have ties with the Japanese."

Setsuko stood still as a mountain, scarcely breathing.

"Captain, please. My brother is a marine at this camp, Zachary Quinlan. Call on him to vouch for us," Jean pleaded.

Violet thought of Parker. "And Sergeant Stone. They've been with us for dinner."

Riggs scratched his chin, then picked up his radio. "Jed, ask Sergeant Stone to come to my office." He hung up and turned his attention back on his detainees. "In the meantime, we're going to interview you all separately."

Decker and Beckworth escorted Jean and Setsuko down the hall, where they disappeared behind closed doors. Alone with Riggs, Violet wrapped her wool scarf tighter around her neck. He stretched out his legs and plunked his thready boots on the table, even offered her a cigarette.

"No, thank you."

"So, you're a widow?"

"My husband is missing."

Widow was about her least favorite word in the world. The first time someone had used it on her, it was like a full-body slap.

"Must get lonely," he said.

"Loneliness is a convenience I don't have time for. Can we keep on the subject of my alleged espionage?"

Riggs stared up at the ceiling and blew smoke rings, one after another, into the already stale air. "So your husband disappeared. Rumor has it he was sympathetic to the Japanese. Care to elaborate?"

The dead could not defend themselves, so the work had been left to her. She hated that Herman's honor be questioned as it had been along the way.

"My husband was sympathetic to the human race. To friends. In case you haven't noticed, we live in a town full of Japanese. When you live and work side by side, you befriend them. Simple. But he was loyal to America. Head of the Hawaii Rifles here in Honoka'a, for goodness' sake."

Outside, a row of tanks rumbled past, drowning out her

final words. Riggs paused. She tried to imagine what it would be like across the ocean, trapped in a place where the threat of being blown up loomed constant. Hawaii was bad enough, hiding behind blackened windows from Japanese Zeros and mortar shells.

When the quiet reassembled, Riggs continued. "What about Takeo Hamasu? Your husband helped keep him out of camp right after Pearl Harbor. And then your husband vanishes. How do we know you're not in on it?"

"My husband was helping an innocent friend keep a little school running."

"Pearl Harbor changed things. People became spies overnight," Riggs said.

"Sir, no offense to my husband, but he wasn't inventive enough to be any kind of spy. He operated strictly by the books, and all he cared about was running his school and keeping order in our small world. He had a garden, sold vegetables. That's it. I would have known he was up to something else."

Violet had given herself headaches over this—wondering how well indeed she knew her own husband. She felt confident in her statement to Riggs about Herman, but there was always a side to people never known to anyone else. Even a spouse. His words rang through her. *"People became spies overnight."*

"Maybe you're the ringleader, not your husband."

Her lungs burned and she was losing patience. "Ringleader of a secret pie operation."

"Who knows? Maybe you're putting some kind of poison or moonshine in your pies?" He lifted an eyebrow.

A laugh escaped. "Sir, you have this all wrong. Describe the signals from our house. There must be another explanation."

"I'll ask the questions."

"You're wasting your breath."

Violet worried for herself, but even more so for Setsuko. Who knew to what lengths Riggs and his men would go to force some kind of confession out of her? Even if she had nothing to confess to.

A few seconds later, the door opened. Parker walked in with a cool gust of wind. He saluted. "Captain Riggs."

"Stone, this woman says she knows you."

Parker looked at her and his face softened. She suddenly felt stupid for involving him. What did he really know of her, anyway? Aside from the fact that she made a swell pie and was a terrible dancer.

"Why is she here?" he said to Riggs.

Violet burst out. "Not just me. Setsuko and Jean are in the other rooms."

Riggs lit another cigarette. "Your gal friends have been sending signals out of their house."

A wind gust tore through the camp, shaking the thin walls and groaning as it moved through the cracks. She felt her chair vibrate.

"Was anyone able to decode the signals?" Parker asked.

At least maybe Riggs would listen to him.

"Not in front of the woman, Sergeant." Riggs nodded in Violet's direction.

"And you are sure of the location?" Parker asked.

She watched the way the sides of his mouth curved up when he spoke. How his hands joined in the conversation, waving around with a life of their own. When he caught her looking, he gave a subtle thumbs-up. Instantly it was like someone smoothed a layer of healing salve across her worried parts.

"One hundred percent," Riggs said.

Even in the cold air, sweat formed on the back of her neck,

and her palms heated up. Was Jean or Setsuko—or maybe both—involved in something sinister that had also gotten Herman killed? Was she the naive one in all this? Violet combed her mind for anything out of place. Her friends acting strangely or other subtle clues. She came up with nothing.

"You know what makes me mad?" she said, glaring at Riggs.

His bushy eyebrow arched. "Tell me."

"That all your allegations made me question my friends for a few seconds there. But you're wrong, sir. None of us are spies. I know this one hundred percent."

Stone cut in. "Captain, I was at the house last Friday with some of my boys. The women were with us the whole time, and in the kitchen. Even Roscoe was there."

"And in the kitchen." His words tickled at her unconscious. Was someone in the kitchen flashing lights? Maybe Ella had been playing and somehow the plane had mistaken whatever she was doing for signals.

"The boys know what they saw. Stone, watch this one. I'm going to go check on the others."

Riggs disappeared down the hallway. A door opened. Then another.

Out of the corner of her eye, she felt Parker looking at her. "What?"

He smirked. "Spies, huh?"

"What kind of fool arrests three schoolteachers on espionage?" she said.

"Captain Riggs might be gruff, but he's a fair man."

"I don't like him."

His face clouded over. "What did he do?"

"I just don't like his kind."

Their eyes locked and Parker offered a smile. Nothing

big. But enough to put a dent in her annoyance and weaken her knees.

He leaned back on the desk. "I know you don't want to hear this, but is there any way Setsuko might be working both sides?"

Violet wanted to tear her hair out every time an allegation was made toward her friend. "She's not working anything."

"I hope you're right."

"I am right."

He stood up and walked over to the window, stooping to look out. "Your friend being Japanese doesn't help matters."

"Tell me something I don't know."

"Violet, I'm here to help. But you're up against a war and people who have done terrible things to our country."

"What ever happened to innocent until proven guilty?"

"Rules change in wartime."

She closed her eyes and concentrated on the pattering of rain against the flimsy tin roof. On not breaking down, though her heart felt pinched and pressed and ready to burst. Fairness was a thing of the past. Reason skewed.

Riggs returned a few minutes later and looked at Parker as he spoke. "We'll be keeping them here. Until further notice."

The room froze around her. "Sir, you can't do this. Our kids are at home."

He looked down at a paper on his desk, avoiding her gaze. "With an adult, are they not?"

"That's beside the point."

"I'll allow a phone call. How about that?"

Parker broke in, "What if you release them to me? I'll take them home, sleep in the jeep and be accountable."

Riggs had developed a shiny film on his forehead. "That's

not how it works here. They aren't going anywhere until we get to the bottom of this."

Violet felt herself turn to stone. Immobilized. Petrified.

The jailhouse was really a jail tent. Gusts of wind pumped the canvas roof and rainwater dripped in the corners, leaving small pools on the wood floor. Anyone with a mind to get out would have only had to slit a hole in the wall and climb through, and Violet half wished she had a knife.

Jean stomped her feet back and forth for warmth. "We would have all been better off using the gas mask sitting on the shelf in there."

Violet shuddered. "Be serious, Jean. We're in a heap of trouble here."

"I am being serious, and by the way, I'd like to get ahold of the knucklehead who reported this," she said.

Setsuko had a deep crease in her forehead and Violet felt the fear coming off of her in waves. This was no longer about *those people*, intangible others, but scraping across their very own skin.

"This feels like one of those awful nightmares that you want to wake up from, but can't. Where you're screaming but no sound comes out," Jean said, slipping onto one of the cots against the back wall.

Setsuko stood just inside the doorway, not bothering to move. "We wouldn't be here if it weren't for me being who I am."

"But you haven't done anything wrong," Jean said.

Violet grabbed a scratchy army blanket and tossed it to Setsuko. "Come. Sit."

Setsuko was right, of course, but the fact was that all three of them were here. Until they sorted this mess out.

"The bottom line is this—we know we are innocent. We

just have to prove it," Violet said, pulling her cot closer to Jean's and Setsuko's.

"I will never be innocent. As long as this war is going on. Look at all the *innocent* people living in relocation centers on the mainland."

"The difference here is that only people who are considered a threat are being taken away. So if we can prove we aren't a threat, you'll be in the clear," Jean said.

"She's right."

Silent tears wet Setsuko's cheeks. "There's no decency to these men. Umi and Hiro are probably sick with fear."

"Aww, honey, it'll be okay," Jean said.

No, it won't. Not for a long, long time, Violet thought.

The phone call home had not gone over well, but Violet had minimized their situation as best she could, telling the kids it was too late for them to be driven home in this kind of weather. Ella would start up on bed-wetting again and likely open a whole new row of scabs on her arms. Umi and Hiro would probably be developing stomach ailments if they hadn't already. And who knew what would happen to the pies.

"I don't know how much more of this I can take. Maybe it would be easier for all of us to be in a relocation center. At least we'd be together," Setsuko said.

"We are getting out of here. Tomorrow. So, stop talking like that," Jean said.

Violet unfolded the scratchy blanket that smelled like horse and kerosene, and lay back on the cot. A cloud of dust formed around her head. "It's going to be a long night. Let's try to get some rest," she said.

Jean sighed and Setsuko sniffled. Between the thumping of the tent and the echo of men's voices, morning seemed years away. The sound of breathing filled the room.

Just when Violet's eyelids were growing heavy, Jean piped

up. "What do you think they would do to us if we really were spies?"

"We aren't really spies," Violet said.

"But say we were."

She nudged Jean in the ribs.

"I'm just curious."

"I suppose we would go on trial and they'd have to show evidence. Like the Doll Woman."

A small laugh escaped Jean's mouth. "I had forgotten about her. Velvalee Dickinson. What kind of name is Velvalee, anyway?"

They had read about the Doll Woman earlier that year, sending coded messages about the US Navy to a woman in Argentina who also worked for the Japanese. The letters mentioned dolls and doll repairs, but were really talking about ships. Velvalee had gone on trial and was eventually convicted. Ten years and ten thousand dollars.

"Worst case is that we get charged, but they wouldn't have any evidence against us," Violet said.

"How awful would that be? To be imprisoned and have our names and honor dragged through the mud?" Jean asked.

"It won't happen," Violet said.

Setsuko then voiced what Violet had been wondering all along. "I'd like to know what the signals coming from your house said."

"You and me both."

No one spoke for a while and Violet could almost hear her friend's thoughts, fervently sorting through possibilities. And then the bagpipes started up, sorrowful notes jabbing at the night sky.

"Am I dreaming?" Jean whispered.

"I wish you were."

"Not only is it ice-cold, but that music is fit for a funeral and this blanket is liable to give me a rash," Jean said.

"My teeth won't stop chattering, either," Setsuko said. "Let's combine blankets and use body warmth."

They rearranged themselves, cot to cot and under three blankets hardly big enough for one man. Being sandwiched between two of her closest friends in the world added a small measure of warmth and comfort, and despite the pit of worry in her stomach, Violet felt herself drifting off. Her last thoughts were of signals flashing from her house to a Japanese submarine lurking off the cliffs, beneath the wind-battered surface of the ocean. She wondered what the message said.

How did I end up here? was a question that Violet pondered as minutes dragged past as sleep came intermittently. On an island in the middle of the Pacific, no husband, a fragile daughter, surrounded by American soldiers, bolstered up by friends, terrified of Japanese attack, and now being accused of working for the very people who had turned her world upside down—everyone's world, for that matter. Life sure had a knack for surprises, and she was growing tired of it.

The three of them were just stirring when someone opened the flap that served as a door. The early-morning light flooded the room for a second and in walked a young man in uniform with a jug of water and a plate of biscuits. He set them down on an empty cot.

"Morning, ladies. Eat up," he said, then turned and left.

"I need coffee, not food, to face this day," Jean said to the door behind him.

Violet immediately pictured their kitchen at home thick with the smells of dark-roasted coffee and morning rain. Pies would be stacked in the icebox, waiting for the journey into Waimea that now wouldn't happen. Irene was probably frantically trying to calm the kids and find out what on earth to do with them. Maybe making porridge. Surely she couldn't keep the three kids indefinitely.

The kitchen had always been the hub of the home, even more so now that it was the only room with blackout windows. Sitting in the kitchen, listening to the radio and helping Jean cook was a balm for her soul. She imagined Ella coming and going through the swinging door to show her drawings, grab a cup of milk or tell her about a new red-beaked bird in the yard. Wait.

Violet bolted upright.

"I know what it was!"

Jean, who was already sitting cross-legged with her hair piled in a bun, jumped. "What was?"

Setsuko sat up, too.

"Riggs was right about it being from our house, but there was no signal being sent. What they thought was a signal was our swinging door opening and closing. And that was the night the soldiers were there when we did a lot of coming and going," Violet said.

Jean focused hard on her face, then leaned over and hugged her. "Violet, you are a genius! We need to tell them, right away so we can get out of this god-awful tent. It smells like putrid socks."

Setsuko wore a look of hesitant optimism.

"Is the tent door open?" Violet asked.

Jean scooted over and tried to pull the flap open. It must have been secured from the other side. "They don't trust us." She called out as she wiggled the handle. "Hello?"

Their jail tent was three tents down from Riggs's office, and who knew if any of the other tents had inhabitants. This tent had no windows, just cracks in the floorboards that let the cool air in.

"Hello!" Jean called out again.

"I imagine they can't just leave us here all day."

"Actually, they could," Setsuko said.

Jean put her lips to the fold in the canvas and belted out. "Somebody let us out of here. Right now!"

"Calm down. We aren't out of the woods yet," Violet said.

The interior of the tent was dim and stuffy, and she wanted out just as badly. Wanted to get home to Ella. A few minutes later, the canvas parted and Riggs himself entered. He tied the flap to one side. "What's all the ruckus here?"

A few seconds later, Sergeant Stone poked his head in. Violet's hand immediately went to her hair and smoothed down her flyaways. He smiled.

Jean's cheeks were pink, and her words came out stacked on top of themselves. "Violet figured it out, Captain! The swinging door in our kitchen is responsible for the flashing lights coming from our house."

"Sir, we are not spies," Setsuko said.

Riggs squinted at each one of them, huddled together on the cots. "Explain."

Violet continued. "Especially when we have company over, we go in and out of the kitchen a lot. The swinging door lets a brief burst of light out with each pass. It would look like a blinking light from afar."

It made perfect sense. Riggs scratched his chin.

Parker eased in closer, but still hung back. "We ate outside on account of the heat, so there was a lot of coming and going through that door. Look, Captain, these women are solid characters. There is not one bad intention in that house. I would swear on a stack of Spam cans."

Riggs began pacing, the stale scent of smoke in his wake. Violet couldn't wait for fresh air and to be clear of this ridiculous charge.

"You don't think our men would know the difference between a swinging door and a signal?" Riggs said.

"Mistakes happen, sir. And this would be an honest one," Parker said.

She remembered every detail of the night the soldiers had visited. Bursts of light from the kitchen, music filling the night, Parker's hand on her waist.

Riggs growled. "I will need to see this for myself. Investigate."

"You know where we live, and we have nothing to hide," Jean said, flattening her skirt.

To Violet, it seemed as though Riggs wanted them to be guilty, whether they were or not. She suspected it had something to do with skin color. "Come over tonight and we can demonstrate," she offered.

"Let me drive these ladies home. They've been held long enough and they have kids at home," Parker said.

It took some persuading, even a little posturing, but Parker won out in the end.

As soon as Violet stepped outside, she was reminded of the bitter cold in Waimea. Perhaps the air was thinner, or maybe it funneled down from the high summits after skimming the snow. Whatever the cause, she felt the cold sticking behind her knees, on the back of her neck. The three of them huddled on the small porch, waiting for their ride, as the wind tried to strip them of clothing.

"I was worried I may never see the light of day again," Setsuko said.

Jean squeezed her shoulder. "Let's just be thankful we sorted it out."

"I don't know about sorting it out, but at least we bought ourselves some time," Violet said.

"He'll change his tune once he sees," Jean said.

Violet only wished she had the same faith. "If they treat a couple of schoolteachers like this, I'd hate to see how they treat the men they're hauling off."

As soon as the words came out, she realized her error. Setsuko's arms hung at her sides, and she stared off into some unreachable place. No sobbing, no overt show of anger, just the look of pure pain in her eyes.

"Sorry, that was dumb of me to say," Violet said.

Setsuko blinked rapid-fire. "It's nothing I don't think about twenty-six hours a day, so don't worry."

Violet tightened her arm around Setsuko. She, of all people, knew the weight of losing a love, and the way it pressed in on you from all sides, draining away your own life. Even worse was watching what it did to your kid. Why couldn't there be a Band-Aid for patching up shattered hearts?

A jeep swung around the corner, kicking up a cloud of dust. Parker jumped out and ran around to open the passenger door. "Hop in, ladies. I grabbed a few blankets for the ride."

Jean and Setsuko climbed into the back, leaving Violet up front. She draped the scratchy blanket around herself. It smelled of mothballs, but she wasn't complaining. Once they hit the edge of town, the sun emerged from behind a row of eucalyptus trees. Last night's downpour had left the air smelling somewhere between tree bark and melted cow pies. If they hadn't just been terrified to pieces, Violet would have wanted to pull over and soak it all in.

Parker had to yell above the engine. "You know, one of the reasons everyone is so touchy is someone claims to have spotted another Japanese sub off Hilo."

"Recently?"

"Don't say I told you. It's probably just a rumor. But no one wants to be caught off guard again, so all threats are taken seriously."

Put in those terms, Violet could hardly blame the captain. But that didn't excuse his insinuations. What scared her the most was the fact that they could no longer count on anything to be normal. Black was green. Orange was blue. The element of living on the edge of her seat wore away at her seams. In a sense, this episode had been a drill. What if the Japanese landed? What if they were taken in by the enemy?

Smoke in our faces would be the least of our worries.

Moments later, a speckled brown owl swooped low across their path. Setsuko called out from the back, her words nearly stolen by the wind. *"Pueo!"*

When a pueo flew across your path, you counted yourself lucky. She had learned at least that much in her years in Hawaii. Not big on superstition, but any luck that came her way was more than welcome.

As they bounced along, Violet swore she could feel Parker sneaking glances her way. She held firm and kept her eyes on the rutted road ahead. "The morning glow suits you," Parker said in a voice so low, she thought maybe she'd misheard.

But when she looked over, the grin on his face confirmed it.

"Everyone looks better in low light, Sergeant."

He laughed. "There you go, calling me Sergeant again. Not good with compliments, are you?"

He was looking at her again. She could feel the burn of his stare. "Keep your eyes on the road. This stretch is dangerous," she said.

"You want to know dangerous?"

"I don't think I do."

Why did everything he say cause her skin to heat up, like someone had taken a warm stone and pressed it across her cheeks? He reminded her of Johnny Martinez, at whom it was impossible to stay mad. That same earnestness worn on his sleeve. Only in this case, she was dealing with a bona fide man.

"Can I ask you a favor, Sergeant?"

"Fire away."

"We are supposed to be selling pies near the USO. Ella is dying to see Roscoe. He's all she can talk about. Would you bring him by?"

"You ladies are going to turn around and come back?"

"We need to."

"Well then, we'll be there."

Violet looked back to check on her friends, who had fallen quiet. Jean's head was down and bobbing, while Setsuko stared out the window. Violet leaned her head back and watched the outline of trees beneath the sky. Each branch formed its own pattern against the gold-tinged sky. She wanted to think about Herman, but her mind kept yanking her back to the soldier sitting next to her.

"Why are you doing this?" she eventually blurted out.

"Driving you ladies home?"

"That, and more. Coming over, talking to Ella, bringing salves for Brownie."

"Does a person need a reason for everything? How about because I like to."

Violet knew she was being nitpicky, but for some reason couldn't stop herself. "For the record, we aren't a charity case."

Parker slowed the jeep. He blew out a big breath and shook his head. "You have no idea, do you, Violet? This might be the last stop any of us have. Being with you all has given us some semblance of home. Of family."

His words squeezed her heart. "I just don't want to give you the wrong impression."

"Noted."

What kind of selfish person was she? Lord, she had spent so

much time focused on her own problems that she had completely ignored the bigger picture. As they descended toward Honoka'a, blankets were no longer needed. Before folding hers up, Violet wiped a stream of tears from her cheeks. She tried not to sniffle.

"I reckon the captain will want to see for himself your swinging door. Aside from that, I believe you're in the clear. You would make a good spy, though," Parker said, the lightness returned to his voice.

"Why is that?"

"Your eyes are hard to read. All that blue? It distracts."

Even though she had sworn not to look, she turned.

Their eyes met. "Yep. Pure distraction," he said.

Chapter Seventeen

ELLA

WHAT A SCARE. I STARTED BREATHING REALLY fast when they took Mama and her friends away. So much so that Irene had me lie down so she could hold a cold towel on my forehead. My whole body started shaking in fits and there was nothing I could do to stop it. I felt like a human earthquake.

"Ella, your mama will be back before you know it."

I had already lost my papa. Would God do that to a child? Take both parents? Umi picked up my hand and started singing one of our Japanese songs really loud in my ear. But her face was wet and she was dripping tears on my shoulder. Hiro's face was unreadable. He probably got that from his dad.

All I could think was that, somehow, those men had found out about me. But I hadn't even opened my mouth to a soul, not even the animals, so why were they taking her? And Jean and Setsuko. Maybe because they knew I loved them both, too. This was the dreaded moment I had been trying so hard to prevent, and now I'd gone and gotten them all hauled off to who knew where. We'd never see them again. Then Irene mentioned something about a misunderstanding, that Mama and Jean were sending smoke signals out to the Japanese ships. We all knew they weren't. That reassured me a little.

I will tell you this. It wasn't until Hiro came over with my chicken in his hands that I calmed down. Brownie has this soft cackle that I love. She does it whenever she's real content. Her very own way of saying that life is good. As soon as she nestled down into my side, her cackle leaked out. It filled me up with a warm sensation.

I thought about poor Mama and how much she'd been through. Losing Papa, living through war, having a daughter with big problems, and now this. I promised myself that when she came back, I would do my best to be a regular person again. I wasn't sure I could manage, but I would try.

At some point, Irene asked us if something was burning. Her eyes got huge and she tore into the kitchen screaming. In all of the turmoil, no one heard the timer.

Poor woman was almost in tears. "They're ruined! Oh, kids, I'll never be invited back."

I don't know much about cooking, but I do know that chocolate is supposed to be brown, not black. *Scorched* is what Mama would have called the pies. All eight of them.

"Miss Ferreira, they won't be mad," Umi said, waving an apron over their tops to help cool them down.

But I knew different. Setsuko might not be, because she was the most levelheaded woman alive, but Jean and my mama would be furious. Mama would hide it, but not Jean. I felt bad for Irene, so I nodded in agreement.

"Let's just make sure we don't burn these ones," Hiro said.

The other half of the pies were waiting patiently to be put in the oven. Originally they were meant to go into Setsuko's oven, but that was before the men came. While the next batch cooked, we stayed in the kitchen and Irene checked the pies every minute of the hour. I was getting tired watching her, so I started drawing.

"So, what do you kids know of Jean's brother, Zach?" Irene asked us.

I had no idea what she was getting at. "I know he likes lions. And he's nice."

She laughed. "I mean if he has a family back home. A wife. What's his story?"

We all looked at each other and shrugged. Taking history of adults is not what kids do, but Irene must not have known that. She always acts like we are miniature grown-ups.

"No idea. Why? Do you like him?" I said.

Tiny spots of pink showed up on her cheeks and she suddenly got bashful, looking everywhere but at us. "I just think he's nice, is all. Don't say I asked, okay?"

Another secret to keep. But this one was easy.

Chapter Eighteen

VIOLET

THERE WAS ENOUGH BLUE IN THE SKY TO LAST a lifetime. As if the night before had been one of those dreams you wake from, shake your head and think, *That sure seemed real.* None of them really wanted to turn around and head back to Waimea, but at Violet's insistence they decided it would boost morale for the kids. And wasting the pies would be a punishable crime.

Bleary-eyed, Violet sat pinched between Setsuko, who drove the truck, and Jean. It had taken some persuading to get Setsuko to come.

"Take Umi and Hiro," she'd said.

"Look, you belong on this island. You were born here. And you're not the only Japanese in Waimea. The Hayashis, Tsugi Kaiama and the whole Kimura family are out there selling away."

"But their husbands haven't been taken away," Setsuko said.

"True, but we need to prove to the marines you have nothing to hide."

She thought about it for a minute, but that got her.

Each of them held a box of pies in their lap. A measly start for so many soldiers, but it was all they had. In the back, the three kids all stood against the cab. Now and then, laughter fell in through the window.

With the sun still low, long shadows fell across the rolling pastures. They passed a single ohia tree whose knotted form was void of leaves or flowers. The tree looked lonely, and got Violet to thinking about loneliness and how it wasn't something you could outrun. Sitting here with Jean on one side and Setsuko on the other was about the best way to stamp it out.

Setsuko held in her lap the one chocolate honeycomb pie that survived. Initially, Violet hid it in the icebox to keep for themselves, but in the end they all agreed it would be better off taken to town, sliced up and sold by the piece.

"We don't want to deprive the soldiers of this treasure of a pie," Jean had said.

Once in town, Setsuko backed the truck up in the tall grass of an empty lot right across from the USO, a red-and-white plantation-style house with an extrawide porch. Nearby, a newspaper kiosk advertised war stories and a Portuguese family on the other side advertised coffee and the world's best *malasada*. This looked like the only spot left.

Thanks to Luther, their stand practically set itself up and looked sharp and professional. With help from the kids, Jean had stenciled in Honey Cow Pies in bright blue, with red stars around the words. Being Saturday, groups of marines milled about. To Violet, it seemed as though they were looking for anything that might take their minds off what they were really here for.

"Do you think it's too early for pie?" Ella asked.

Jean stopped what she was doing. "It is never too early for pie, pumpkin. Maybe you could help us lure them in?"

Ella shrank back.

"All you have to do is sit here next to us, cute as a button, and wave if anyone catches your eye."

Violet said, "You're the one that should be waving."

Jean sighed. "I have been. My charms must be waning. Even last night, none of those men so much as looked at me."

Setsuko waved a giant horsefly away from the pies. "The men that arrested us?"

"What other men were there?" Jean asked.

"You need to learn to differentiate. It would do you a world of good," Setsuko said, shaking her head.

Jean turned up her nose. "What's that supposed to mean?"

"Just that not all men are created equal. Especially ones like Decker and Beckworth. You want to choose the man, not the other way around."

Violet could tell from the frown on Jean's face that the conversation was deteriorating. "Hey, these guys look hungry. How about we offer a sample?"

A group of young men in khakis ambled over. "You selling real cow pies?" a squat, jovial one said. "Boys, maybe we should get one for Captain Turner. I'd like to see the look on his face."

Jean smiled and held out a plate with slivers of honeycomb and chocolate. "Try this. But I'll warn you..." She looked around as if making sure no one could hear. "One bite and you're in for it."

The man cocked his head. "That right?"

"You boys will be lined up here next week waiting on our arrival. Don't say I didn't warn you." She picked up a piece and gently eased it into her mouth, chewing with her eyes closed. "Mmm."

You could pretty much count on Jean to turn any situation up a notch. The men all stood there, hanging on every word as if their lives depended on it. A skinny one with freckles stepped forward and picked up a piece. The rest followed.

Pretty soon, heads bobbed up and down. "How many of those you got?" the spokesman said.

"Just one."

"One? You come here with one pie to sell? Now there's good business sense."

Setsuko stepped in. "We have seven sweet potato pies. Which are even better."

They sold half their merchandise before eleven o'clock.

Before long, Umi and Hiro grew bored and went up the road to the park to play with a group of other kids in the field, but Ella stayed back. There was no way she would miss seeing Roscoe, and she kept her eyes trained on the hard-packed dirt road that came from Camp Tarawa. Business sped up around lunchtime, and they sold slices to go with hamburgers or a plate lunch.

Word must have spread quickly, because everyone asked about the deadly chocolate honeycomb pie. Speaking of deadly, Jean got the bright idea on the ride home last night to create a special just for Captain Riggs, should he stop in.

Violet spotted him first. "Here he comes. Flip the sign."

Ella reached around and turned the chalkboard from front to back. She noticed for the first time that Captain Riggs walked with a slight limp. When he saw who was behind the stand, he saluted. "Look who it is."

"Captain."

As he read the words on the board, his caterpillar eyebrows pinched together. "Moonshine Pie." What might have been a smile showed in the creases around his eyes. "I don't know whether to arrest you again or buy a piece."

"Try it. We baked this one especially for you," Jean said.

Riggs grumbled, "Women. I've never been able to understand you."

"What's to understand?" Violet said.

"With men, you know what to expect. With you folk, everything comes out of left field."

Violet ran the knife through a chunk of honeycomb. "Living in a camp with twenty-three thousand of them, I imagine you'd start to forget how the other half thinks."

"It's not by choice," he said.

"The way I see it, Camp Tarawa is nothing but an oversize boys' club. A necessary one, but still, it could use some female influence."

Jean scooted next to her. "You ask me, the military would be a lot better off run by women."

For the first time, Riggs laughed. "Just give me a piece of that moonshine pie. If it works, maybe we'll have to bring a container full and serve up the Japanese. The Hawaiian stuff is deadly."

"In that case, you'd never know, would you?" Violet said in her sweetest voice.

"I guess I'll have to take my chances." He walked away with chocolate smeared across his chin and seeming half as intimidating as he had last night.

Moonshine pie would do that to a person.

By closing time, they had only half a pie left. Ella leaned against the stand, hugging her folded legs. Disappointment tugged at the corners of her mouth. Violet knew the feeling, for as much as Ella waited for Roscoe, she had been hoping to see the boys.

Jean leaned down and patted Ella's knee. "They must be training, sugarplum."

What had she really expected? While the regular folk went about their daily lives, these guys were out marching halfway across the island, carrying fifty-pound packs under the pounding sun.

"Look," Setsuko said, pointing toward the main intersection.

A beanpole of a man walked toward them with what could only be a lion at the end of his rope.

Jean waved madly. "Zach!"

Ella tore off toward them.

"Careful, honey. Don't scare Roscoe. He may not remember you," Violet called after her.

Ella stopped far enough away to let the giant cat get used to her again. Zach said something to Ella and handed her the rope.

"I wonder who's walking who," Violet said.

"My money is on the lion," Jean said.

Violet continued to glance toward camp for Parker, but it appeared Zach had come alone. She felt caught in that place of not wanting to admit her feelings. The lie was that she had been waiting for all the boys, when in fact Parker was the one.

Zach tied Roscoe to the post and hugged everyone in turn. "Glad you're all still here. But it looks like you've sold out?"

"We saved a half a pie for you. And Tommy and Parker..." Violet said.

Jean interrupted. "Little brother, I need you to do something for me. I'm worried about my friend Bud that left for Saipan with the Second Division. We keep hearing god-awful accounts of the battle." She pressed her hand to her chest. "Of beaches full of bodies. Can you ask around and see if anyone knows whether he made it?"

"Friend"? Everyone knew he was more than that, but Violet kept her mouth shut. She sincerely hoped he would find out news to settle Jean.

Jean continued. "It terrifies me to know that you boys are shipping off to war, too. I'm losing sleep over it. Any news on when you're to leave or where you're headed?"

"Tight lips. But the scuttlebutt is before the end of the year," Zach said.

Less than two months away. Far too soon.

"I'm already a wreck," Jean said.

Zach's face brightened. "Hey, we're having a steak fry tomorrow down at the beach in Kawaihae. Why don't you join us, bring the kids?"

"Oooh! That sounds like fun!" Jean said.

Violet nodded, though she wasn't sure. "Say, where are Parker and Tommy today?"

"Out in the field. One of our amphibian Ducks got hung up on the far end of the beach, collapsed into an underground hole or something like that. But he asked me to get Roscoe here."

"We would have had a very sad girl on our hands," she said, glancing around for Ella.

Behind the stand, Roscoe had stretched out under a nearby jacaranda tree. Umi, Hiro and Ella sat around him. Ella wiggled a long stick with purple flowers at the end, and he swatted at it, trying to grab on. The natural way they all sat there, Roscoe could have been just another family pet, not so different from a cat or a dog. But if Violet wasn't mistaken, he already looked bigger than that first day at the school.

Zach ran his hand over his crew cut and looked directly at Violet. "If Parker makes a promise, he'll move hell and high water to see it through."

Chapter Nineteen

VIOLET

EVERY TIME THEY WOUND THEIR WAY DOWN from Waimea toward the rocky coast of south Kohala, Violet felt a swelling in her chest. The unending blue reminded her of the choice she'd made to leave everything behind in Minnesota. Though *everything* mainly consisted of a mother with no zest for anything and a dog named Lassie. Looking back, she sometimes wondered if it had been the magnetic pull of the ocean, and not just Herman, that brought her here.

During summers, Herman would pack up the school truck with cots and coolers and fishing poles, and bring them down for a week. They would collect shells and driftwood. He'd made friends with a family who owned a lava rock house at Puako, where the water was so clear that Violet contemplated drinking it on more than one occasion. Having grown up in a place where people froze to death on a regular basis, the beach seemed too good to be true. As it turned out, it was. They ended up sleeping with their cot legs in bowls of water to keep the scorpions from crawling into their beds. She couldn't help imagining the sound of insect feet scurrying up the walls and that had kept her up half the night. After that first trip, Violet pulled the cots onto the sand and slept outside.

Kawaihae was a few coves north of Puako. Only now, the beaches were lined with barbed wire. It hadn't taken long to persuade Ella to come, since she loved the water, and Jean was always in. Irene Ferreira rode in the back, gushing thanks every three minutes at being included. Violet had been the one who resisted coming. She couldn't even say why, but suspected it had to do with Parker.

"Do lions swim?" Ella asked as they approached the turnoff to the beach.

"Cats sink, honey," Jean said.

Ella frowned. "How can they take Roscoe on the boat when they leave, then?"

"The boats they go on are as big as floating towns. I wouldn't worry. Plus, cats can swim if they have to," Violet said, but she wondered. Would they take him or leave him?

"Maybe we can keep him with us?" Ella said.

"He belongs to the soldiers. Not to mention that people don't keep lions as pets."

Ella inspected one of her scabs. "Are you sure Roscoe is going to be there today?"

Jean laughed. "Sweetie, you sure have a one-track mind, don't you?"

"One-track minds seem to be the theme around here," Violet said to Jean, who had been talking Bud for breakfast, lunch and dinner these days. *"Say, remember that time Bud serenaded me?" "This beach reminds me of Bud." "I stayed up all night worrying about Bud." "Bud hasn't written lately. Do you think he's okay?"*

Anyway, she didn't care if Ella was obsessed with the lion.

Whatever it took to settle her emotions, especially after their night in the brig had left her so anxious that there were new open scabs on her arms, and chunks of hair on the pillow in the morning. Each time Ella seemed to be improving, something happened to yank her back.

"Roscoe will be there and you can love him all you want."

The car bumped and rattled down the road. Dust blew into the windows, and Violet had to roll them up. Instantly the car turned into a furnace. By the time they pulled up, all of their faces were bright red. Even this late in the fall, the heat moved in waves, shimmering above the black lava rocks.

A volleyball net had been set up and the soldiers were midgame. A cluster of young women frolicked on the one portion of the beach without coils of wire. Violet suddenly had the sense that coming here had been a bad idea. Large groups made her uneasy, at best. And the last thing she wanted was to appear to be *after* any of these men.

Right away, she picked out Zach and Parker on the sandy court. Both men waved.

"I feel weird," she said.

"As in sick?" Jean asked.

"No, as in out of place."

Jean draped her arm around Violet's shoulders. "Turn that mind of yours off. Zach invited us. We're here for a Sunday picnic. End of story."

Here she was, fraternizing with a bunch of men, some young enough to be her students. She'd already had a career, a husband, a daughter. A life.

They set up camp at the far edge of the beach, under the sprawling branches of a huge kiawe tree and apart from the others. Violet scanned the sand for three-inch thorns before throwing the blanket out. Bees hummed overhead, lured in by the nutty, sweet blossoms. Ella grabbed the black inner tube and ran straight to the water, apparently having forgotten about Roscoe for half a second.

"Don't go too far out," Violet called.

Irene sat down on the floral beach blanket and peeled a banana. She wore a serious look. "I didn't want to mention it in front of Ella, but I heard something peculiar on the phone lines yesterday."

That got Violet's attention. "Oh?"

"The call was between Captain Riggs and a man by the name of Lieutenant Swift. Swift said he believed the letters in the school were bogus. That the Japanese colonel they were addressed to doesn't exist."

"Letters in which school?" Violet said.

"He didn't say, and Riggs suggested they meet in person."

Her pulse quickened. "Did he say what the letters were about?"

"Nope, and you know I could get in trouble for telling, so keep it between us."

Had someone tried to frame Takeo for being a spy? Violet looked out to the horizon, trying to call up a reason why someone would want him locked up. But she knew well enough that reasons did not always present themselves. Irene swallowed the last bite of her banana and jumped up. Violet turned and saw Parker and Zach trotting over. Parker was now shirtless, revealing muscles twisting up his torso that she hadn't even known existed. It took all her wits not to stare.

He seemed genuinely happy to see them. "Glad you made it. You know you ladies are the talk of the barracks?"

"On account of our arrest?" Jean said.

"More on account of those pies, which I was awful sorry to miss out on," Parker said. There was nothing to do but stand and greet them, though Violet was overly aware of her swimsuit pinching her thighs. She had to tippy toe up to kiss the both of them, especially Zach. But it was Parker's hand that lingered on her hip. Backing away, she stepped on the lunch basket and lost her balance, and she grabbed his arm to save herself.

"Sorry," she mumbled.

Parker steadied her, even though his arm was slippery with sweat. "Easy there. I know I'm irresistible."

"What you are is smelly. You need a swim." She stepped out of his reach.

"Come with me?" Without waiting for an answer, Parker sprinted to the water and dived in. Zach, Irene and Jean were already halfway there and Ella floated just off shore in her tube. Violet didn't move. She saw his dark form swimming underwater toward Ella. Next to her, he erupted out of the water. Ella squealed, but Violet suspected she'd seen him coming. He pointed to the pavilion, where Roscoe watched from the shade.

Joining the group, Violet waded in up to her waist. The water was bathtub-warm, almost to the point of not being refreshing. The small group of women who had been down the way now migrated over with Tommy and a couple of other soldiers.

A pretty young Hawaiian swam right up to Parker. "Sergeant Stone, I want you for my partner in chicken fights." She had polished almond skin and hair that went on for weeks. Violet instantly disliked her.

Two girls clung to Tommy's arm, threatening to pull him apart. Violet wondered if he was going to try to fit both girls on his shoulders. "Buddy, you're going down," he said to Parker.

Parker hesitated, glancing Violet's way. Before he could object, if in fact he was going to do so, the girl climbed up his back. Tommy ducked underwater and let one of his girls on. The men were up to their chests in the water. Parker had the height advantage, but Tommy's speed was immediately evident. Above, the women cajoled and flapped their arms around. Eventually, Parker toppled. They came up choking. And laughing. His partner still had her arms around his neck and hung on like a baby monkey. Violet's stomach twisted. She had to look away.

Someone splashed behind her. "Can I try?" Ella said.

This time, Parker didn't hesitate. Parker swam up under Ella and scooped her onto his shoulders.

"Any takers?" he said.

Ella gripped his head with one hand and held tight to his other hand. She broke into a gaping smile.

"Us!" Irene grabbed hold of Zach and pushed him under.

Violet worried that the weight of Irene on Zach's shoulders might break him in half. Not so much overweight as she was big-boned. Irene stood at least six inches taller than Violet, and was thick any way you sliced her. And with that thickness came strength. From all her hula dancing, Irene's legs were strong as tree trunks. Ella wouldn't stand a chance. Zach came up swaying under her weight, but Violet gave him credit for even standing. The boys danced around each other like boxers, a featherweight and a heavyweight.

"Come any closer and you're down," Parker said.

She worried that Ella might be choking Parker, but his face hadn't turned blue yet. With arms the size of Irene's finger, Ella somehow managed to catch her off balance, giving a hard shove. A huge splash later and Irene disappeared beneath the cool water. Ella stood up, wobbling, and raised her arms before diving from Parker's shoulders.

She popped up two feet away. "Did you see, Mama? I won the chicken fight!"

Violet wished she could bottle the look on Ella's face and serve it up to her on a daily basis.

"You were like a crab up there. We better make sure Sergeant Stone still has his ears."

When Parker swam over, she thought he was coming for Ella, but he tapped her on the shoulder. "Your turn."

"No way."

Irene chimed in. "Get up there, Violet. Don't be such a sissy."

Well, that did it. So much for keeping her hair dry. Parker lowered himself. His shoulders felt slippery beneath the backs of her thighs.

"Lock your ankles behind my back," he said.

Zach and Irene came at them with a new kind of fury. Poor Zach, he would have been better off as the top part of the team, as tall and gangly as he was. One thing was always true about chicken fighting, though. It made you laugh. There was no way around it. By the time Irene tipped them backward to the point of no recovery, Violet was squawking like one of the hens awaiting breakfast.

Underwater, she worked to untangle herself. But every time she pulled a body part away, Parker pulled it back. When she finally surfaced for a breath she felt drunk from salt water.

"Are you trying to drown me?" she asked.

He was close enough for her to see drops of water on his lashes.

"They say that salt water cures anything. Just helping you out."

Her heart squeezed a little bit. "Is that how you see me?"

"We all need to be cured of something."

There was no denying the truth of those words. He must have been able to see her softening, because he smiled. Violet looked away first, into the water, as if she might find answers in the powdery sand below. *More important, what is the question?*

Roscoe lounged in the cool shade of the pavilion with both paws planted sphinxlike in front of him. A family of sparrows pecked at crumbs nearby and his tail twitched as he watched them. Zach pulled out a butcher knife and hacked up a thigh-sized slab of raw meat. He tossed a piece to Roscoe, who missed it with his mouth. The meat fell to the sandy floor, where he swatted at it before swallowing the chunk whole.

"It must cost a fortune to feed him," she said.

"The people at Parker Ranch give us the cuts they don't use, which is a big help."

"Is Parker Ranch named after Parker?" Ella asked.

He laughed. "No, the ranch is old enough to be his grandfather. From what I understand, it's been here for almost a hundred years, and is bigger than any ranches on the mainland."

Ella considered this, then promptly sat next to the lion and stroked him with her wet hands. This time, Roscoe seemed to recognize her and rolled to his side. When he yawned, a child could have stuck her whole head in his mouth. And he still had a lot of growing to do.

In the midst of this lazy day at the beach, Violet wanted to pretend that this was life. That Ella was recovering, and the soldiers and Roscoe would always be here. But beneath the dinners, the pie selling and the outings, the ache of war still found a way in. You could see it behind the men's eyes, in how they immersed themselves in the seconds and the minutes. Looking for a quick brand of living. Everything here was a by-product of war. And war was messy.

On the far end of the long beach, Violet noticed a Duck parked along the rocks. These amphibious military vehicles were supposed to be the latest, best thing for beach invasions. It didn't look like much—a hulking olive metal-hulled boat on wheels. Apparently the men trained on these things until their feet bled.

"They let you bring that here for fun?" she asked Parker.

He was leaning against one of the rock posts that held up the pavilion roof, peeling an orange. "That depends on your definition of *let.* Want to go for a ride?"

"Can we?" Ella said.

"I'll stay with Roscoe," Violet said.

Irene and Jean were already heading down there with Zach and a few others.

Parker turned to Ella. "You can be the captain. Come on."

At the water's edge, Zach slipped an orange life vest over her head. It turned out there was only room for Ella and the ladies, so Parker volunteered to stay ashore. Ella didn't want to leave Violet behind. That much was obvious. Torn between mother and boat, she looked back and forth between them.

"You've got Jean and Irene and Zach to watch you. Go. Have fun," Violet said.

Only a month ago, Ella wouldn't have considered it. This time, the boat won out.

As they watched the boat disappear around the rocky point, the space between Violet and Parker thickened. All of a sudden, she wished she had gone. The way she lacked anything to say around him bothered her.

"You want to see something around the point? It's pretty neat," he said.

She risked a look at him. "I think I'll wait in the shade of the pavilion."

"Get your slippers on."

"You don't listen, do you?"

Who knew how long the boat would be gone, so she relented. There were plenty of extra pairs lying around, and he poached one for her. At the far end of the beach, a path of foot-worn rocks led across a black field of lava. The rubber-soled *zoris* were good protection from the jagged rocks, but every now and then her foot slipped off. Parker was like a goat.

"You're good at this," she said.

"I've had practice. We do this ten hours on some days. And after that, we drag our sorry butts the eleven miles back to camp. The heat is brutal and men collapse, but it's a day at the beach compared to where we're going."

After a lengthy pause, in which she tried to think of something useful to say, all she came up with was "All this training will pay off. And Jean says the best prayers in town. We'll put her on your case."

He half turned. "We're going to need 'em."

Walking might have gone more smoothly if her eyes hadn't been glued to his back. The first time she tripped, she had been contemplating the trickle of sweat running down his spine. She felt like she was walking into trouble but couldn't stop herself. Had she ever looked at Herman like this? Or anyone, for that matter? Herman had come along at a time in her life when she needed a savior. She knew that. A solid man and a good friend. The love had come on slowly and over time, his goodness catching. Never, ever, had she felt this kind of bursting-at-the-seams longing.

The coconut trees announced freshwater springs up ahead. But they stopped just before the trees. At a small outcropping, they looked straight down into a perfectly round pond with high walls. A school of yellow tang drifted in the middle.

It struck her then how the world would just keep on being beautiful, whether you wanted it to or not.

A pair of wooden swim goggles materialized in Parker's hand. "You ever used a pair of these?" he asked.

She'd seen some of the Japanese and Hawaiian women out on the reefs wearing them, coming in with nets full of octopus. Setsuko even had a pair. But Violet enjoyed the water perfectly fine from above. "Never."

"You're in for a treat, then."

She was wondering how they would get down to the hole, when Parker stepped from the ledge. Seconds passed before he hit the water. When he came up, he shook his head like a wet dog and hooted.

Violet peered down, unsure of her free-falling ability.

"Oh, I think I'll stay up here."

"Come on. You'll love it."

It was the look of expectation on his face, almost like a young boy. She stepped to the edge.

"On the count of three. One, two..." He was nice enough to hold on to *three*, to give her a few more seconds. On the way down, she pinched her nose and hoped there would be a graceful way out. She instinctively pulled her legs in when she hit to avoid kicking the rocks below. The water was crisp and refreshing.

"Try them on." Parker handed her the goggles.

Even in this small aquarium of a pond, she saw red pencil *wana*, blooms of purple coral and several fat sea cucumbers. She floated in circles, taking it all in. The goggles were loose and kept filling with water, but she couldn't pull herself away.

"Come over here. Let me tighten them," Parker said.

He sat on a seaweed-smoothed rock. She checked for sea urchins, which the local folks called *wana*, and then climbed out next to him. There was just enough room for both of them without touching. As he fiddled with the straps, she watched him. In concentration, his brow wrinkled in single-minded focus.

She pictured him looking through a rifle, or fiddling with

a grenade. That same determination would be valuable in a war situation.

"You don't seem afraid of anything," she said.

He stopped. His Adam's apple moved up and down. "Oh, I'm afraid all right. I'd have to be crazy not to be. You want to know what scares me the worst?"

"What?" She wasn't sure she really wanted to know.

"The fact that you can never be truly prepared. Sure, we're fit and we know how to shoot and all that. But I have no idea how I'm going to react when I come face-to-face with the enemy. Or worse, when my men's lives are on the line and people are getting shot up around you."

Her eyes scanned his face.

"Will I have what it takes?" he said.

"That's not just true in war. It's true about life. You do what you have to," she said.

He was quiet. With his free hand, he reached over and tucked a piece of unruly hair behind her ear. It crossed her mind that he might kiss her, but instead he slipped the goggles over her head, adjusting and tightening. For all the racket her heart was making, it might have been the first time she'd ever been touched by a man.

As he shifted to face her, his leg pressed against hers. "I make you nervous, don't I?"

He made her lots of things, and nervous was among them. But nervous was not what caused this strange hum that dropped down from her chest, swarming below her navel. Rather than answer, Violet returned to the safety of the water. Once she was about as far away as she could get, she said, "Not at all."

Parker plunged in and came up only inches from her face. He must have sucked in most of the air around them, leaving it empty. "I want to go on record as saying you're beautiful."

In a moment of complete distraction, Violet shoved her foot down to stand. A sharp burning shot into her heel. She screamed.

Parker wasted no time in grabbing her leg. "Lean back."

As he examined the damage, a slow burn ran up her leg. Reflexively, she yanked it away. "How bad?" she asked.

"I'm not going to lie. There's a load of spines in there. Unfortunately, they break off when you try to pull them out."

Fighting back tears, she looked. Blue-black spikes stuck out from her pale skin like stubble. Over the years, she'd seen kids carried from the water screaming. Because of that, she watched herself near the coral when she had a mind to. Today had been another matter.

"You know the best way to dissolve it, right?" Parker said.

"Unfortunately, yes."

Nothing dissolved *wana* spines better than a healthy dose of urine.

"First, let's get the spines down. I'm going to pull what I can out. Hang in there," he said.

Violet drifted while he performed the delicate task of plucking fragments of urchin from her foot. Many deep breaths later, he hoisted her out of the water and onto a ledge.

"Shall I do the honors?"

"I don't have much choice, do I?"

"Just so you know, urinating on women is not my usual thing."

She laughed, despite herself. Then strangely, the laughing turned to tears.

"That bad, huh?" Parker said. "I shouldn't be making jokes when you're in such pain. But if you promise to close your eyes, I can go on your foot and make it better. Something about the ammonia."

She nodded, still sniffling. The tears were not only from

the pain in her foot, she realized. They were for Parker. For the way his hand felt on her skin, and the dimpled smile he so generously gave. And for how in another time, something might have happened between them. She'd already thought the whole thing through and come up with so many reasons not to fall for him. A missing husband. A promise to find him. A troubled daughter. And Parker sailing off to war in less than two months' time. Her heart couldn't take another loss.

He stopped a tear in its tracks with his finger. "I promise, you're going to live."

If only she could say the same.

After urinating on her foot—while Violet turned her head and closed her eyes for good measure—Parker helped her scale the rocks, pulling her up with one arm, while clinging to the cracks with the other. Walking on her toes, she was able to hobble along for a ways. But the going was so slow that she finally agreed to let him piggyback her to the beach. His back was hot with sun.

"Good training," he said.

She didn't want to think about why he would have to be carrying another person on his back. If only she could erase those images she'd seen in the newspapers. Black-and-white anguish. How different the pictures would be if they were of those you knew. With the whole world as witness.

"Glad I could be of service," she said.

"You ladies are a lifeline. Like I said before, it feels like we have a home away from home at your place. It matters."

She swore he pulled her in closer when he said it.

At the beach, the Duck was back. Everyone rushed over and demanded to know what happened when they saw Parker carrying her on his back across the sand like a stalk of bananas. He lowered her onto the cool concrete of the pavilion and the pressure burned.

"You're a verifiable pincushion," Jean said.

"Lie down over here," Irene said, bringing a blanket to the sand next to the pavilion.

"I'm fine. Let me be."

Even with the foot, she was content to sit and fill up on afternoon breeze and the smell of kiawe pods. Her shoulders were pink and her cheeks warm, as were Ella's. Everyone seemed to be having such a fine time, she hated to burden them. Irene brought her half a coconut.

Another volleyball game started up, and Parker and Zach joined in. For such a gangly person, Zach was awfully quick. Just when there was no chance of saving the ball, he shot an arm up and sent it right back over. After watching for a while, she also noticed that Parker knew exactly where the ball would end up, always crouched in waiting.

Tommy sat at the picnic table, strumming his ukulele with two fishermen with buckets full of bait fish. One of the men threw a hand-sized fish to Roscoe, who swallowed it whole. Half an hour later, Violet's foot started throbbing and her skin grew hot and prickly. The leathery Hawaiian man who had been collecting opihi out on the rocks came around to have a look. "Girl, go soak 'em in vinegar. You don't wanna wait too long."

She was relieved to hear of another cure. Jean and Irene rounded up their gear. Ella was still in the water, probably wrinkled and half-cured in salt by now. Violet called her out. Ella ran up the beach, her bathing-suit bottoms hanging with a load of sand and too loose on her legs. There was something so fresh and honest about that face of hers, so impossible to not love.

The volleyball game had ended, and Violet was thinking

she didn't want to leave, when the chicken-fight girl intercepted Parker across the sand. Her flat stomach and narrow hips were hard to ignore. Whatever she said caused him to throw back his head and laugh.

When Violet looked away, she saw Jean was watching her intently. "What?"

Jean leaned in close. "Looks like you want to scratch someone's eyes out."

She didn't bother to answer.

Chapter Twenty

VIOLET

BY MIDWEEK, VIOLET WAS ABLE TO WALK WITHout trouble. The vinegar worked wonders, as did the salve that Parker had left for Brownie. Her skin was still streaked blue, but the pain diminished. On top of the blue in her foot, she and the rest of the household had been lobster red since Sunday. That was now fading, too.

The only thing not fading was her memory of riding on Parker's back through the lava. What concerned her the most was that in all her years with Herman, she had never come close to that kind of stinging jealousy she had felt down at Kawaihae last Sunday. Parker was some kind of stubborn affliction. The more she tried not to think about him, the more she did.

On Thursday afternoon, she and Jean had their hands white with flour, making piecrust, when Zach called.

She picked up with a dish towel. "Hi, Violet. It's Zach. Would it be okay if I stopped by tonight?"

"Tonight? What about curfew?"

"You didn't hear? They've moved it back to ten. Which means you may be seeing more of us, by the way."

"Good news. Must mean that they're feeling more confident in the war's outcome?"

Even with the good news, Zach sounded somber. "I need to speak with my sister about a matter."

Jean had no problem interrupting. "Who are you talking to?"

"Of course you can come over, and save some room for dinner."

Violet hung up. "Your brother. He's coming by and they've pushed curfew back to ten."

Jean's expression clouded over. "Did he say why he's coming?"

"I didn't ask."

"Tell me what he said," Jean demanded.

"Just that he wants to speak with you."

Jean backed up against the wall and slid to the floor, knees to her chest. "It's Bud. I know it."

"Honey, don't jump to conclusions. Maybe Zach just wants to see you, get away from camp." Though she had a bad feeling, too.

Jean's fingers wound around themselves like she was trying to tie her hands into knots. "Something terrible has happened. You know when you know?"

Unfortunately, Violet did know, but she wanted to remain hopeful. "Before you get all worked up, let's hear what he has to say."

Jean let out a sigh that spilled through the house.

Even with her reservations about Bud and his intentions, Violet wished him no harm. And if her friend loved him, then so be it. No one could take that away from Jean. People fell in love with the wrong people all the time. Love wasn't just blind. It was dumb. Violet sat down beside Jean and picked up her hand. Jean swallowed hard. They waited.

Outside, the wind groaned as it passed through the floorboards on the lanai. Ella always kept her eye on the chickens in high winds, worried they might blow away. Today they'd brought Brownie in—the other hens now tolerated her—and she hunkered down in a box in the living room. Violet's father had always believed that the wind brought in the ten thousand evils, stirring up towering dust storms and sickness in their Minnesota town.

Here, the wind was mild in comparison, but Violet's hairs bristled nonetheless.

Zach drove up at seven o'clock sharp, alone. He wore his civvies with a tan jacket buttoned up to his chin. Jean stood with her face pressed against the screen door, oblivious to the dust. Next to her, Violet held her arm around Jean's waist. She had a feeling that this was one of those times that friends held each other up.

The look on Zach's face gave away most of what was coming. His eyes focused on the steps as he trudged up to the house. Jean opened the door and rushed into him, smothering herself in his broad chest. "Tell me!" Her words were muffled and tear-soaked.

"Oh, sis. I wish I didn't have to be the one coming here to tell you this. But it's not what you think."

Jean lifted her face. "What do you mean? You're here about Bud, aren't you?"

He glanced across the driveway at the neighbor's house. "Let's go into the kitchen."

Ella sat on a rice bag pillow next to the radio, which they'd turned down low, listening to Bulldog Drummond and his latest detective story, but her eyes were on Jean and Zach. "Ella, why don't you run off to bed. I'll be in soon," Violet said.

"But I have to hear the end," Ella whined.

Violet walked over and turned up the volume. "Fine, but stay in here. This is adult talk."

In the kitchen, Zach sat his sister down on a chair. "I'll start by telling you that Bud is alive." He swallowed hard. "On the final days of Saipan, there was what they're calling a banzai charge, where what was left of the Japanese attacked our front lines. Three thousand armed troops, plus wounded and bandaged, barely armed men, engaged our guys. It was a bloodbath, and Bud was shot in the leg. But he made it out and, from what I hear, is going to make it."

This *was* news. If Bud was alive, why was Zach so grim?

Jean looked like she had ten thousand questions, but couldn't quite get any of them out. Instead, she held her hand over her mouth and started bawling. "Dear Lord above, thank You. My baby is coming home with breath in his lungs. Did you hear that, Violet? He's alive!"

"I heard. It's wonderful!"

Zach glanced up and cleared his throat. He still had something to tell, that much was obvious. But no man wanted to make a woman cry. Especially his crazy-in-love sister. He let the good news sink in for a while, until Jean had worn herself out from crying.

"When I asked around about Bud, I found out something else," he said, fidgeting with his cuffs.

The room felt hot all of a sudden, dense and uncomfortable. "What?"

"Shucks, I hate to have to tell you this, but he has a wife back home. And a kid."

Jean's mouth opened and closed without spilling any words

out. "Impossible." She looked at Violet with a deep question in her eyes.

Zach's head wobbled on his long neck. "I confirmed with at least three reliable sources."

Outside, the wind picked up speed and rattled the blackout boards all around the house. He reached out for her hand, but she shook it off. As understanding colored her face, she jumped up, grabbed the fattest tomato from a basket on the counter and whipped it at the icebox. A red explosion splattered across the whole kitchen, which up until this point had been a shiny white.

"That bastard. He's going to wish he had died over there!"

Another tomato, *splat.* At least her aim was good.

There was no point in putting a stop to Jean. Sometimes it was better to let a fit run its course than to intervene. And, boy, did Jean have a right to be north of upset. Bud had charmed the skirt off of her and all but proposed during his stay here. He never showed up without a flower—ginger, plumeria, even lehua, which were known to bring on rain when picked. And he had a penchant for saying things like, *"You're my once in a lifetime,"* or, *"I get goose bumps when I hear your name."* He also liked to spend a lot of time in the bedroom. A right miracle Jean hadn't gotten pregnant.

"You are one hundred percent sure about this, Zach?" Violet asked.

"As sure as Jean is my sister. If he's unlucky enough to show his face on this island again, I'll make him wish he'd stayed in the trenches."

Jean changed course, flopping back down on the floor with her skirt spread out around her. She broke into tears. "This can't be happening. He told me he loved me."

Zach handed her his handkerchief.

"Some men have a funny way of being able to love more than one woman," Violet said.

"Then it's not love," Jean said.

"To him, it may have felt like it, is all I'm saying."

Jean looked defeated, with streaks of black staining her cheeks. "It's not fair."

"Mean is what it is. And hurtful and dishonest," Zach said.

Violet grabbed Jean's hand again and squeezed. "What burns me up is that we took him in, cooked for him, prayed for him. He betrayed all of us."

She had heard stories about people like this, but when you grew up in a small town of fewer than two hundred people, it was hard to get away with so much as taking an extra breath. With the military in town, people came and went all the time. Men sailing off to meet their fate might invent stories, too. It was harder to judge them when she thought of it like that. But heavens, this was hard to swallow.

Jean's face was now as red as the tomatoes on the wall. "Men are nothing but trouble. A pack of liars and scoundrels."

"Come on now. What am I?" Zach asked.

"Brothers don't count."

Violet's stomach twisted. "There are good ones. I know from experience."

One look at Violet and Jean burst out crying again. "Oh, I know. Herman was as good as they come. I didn't mean him. He was a real man. Maybe the problem is I've been dealing with boys."

When Violet had first seen Jean around Herman, she noticed right away that Jean didn't bat her eyes around him like she did with most men. He treated her like the respected schoolteacher that she was, and she responded in kind. He had a way of keeping people level—one of his gifts.

"There you go. Set your sights higher. Like Bud, most of these guys here wouldn't deserve you," Zach agreed.

What about Parker? How does he measure up?

"Keep on living your life, and someone designed just for you will show up. You have to kiss the toads to get to the prince," Violet said.

"No more toads."

"Only princes."

All of a sudden, Jean's eyes narrowed into one of her knowing looks. "Will you help me get back at him?"

Here was the Honey Jean she knew and loved. "Anything you want."

Chapter Twenty-One

ELLA

AS SOON AS MAMA CLOSED THE KITCHEN DOOR, I turned the volume back down and went to listen. They had other things on their mind and I knew no one would notice. Bud had been over here a lot, but he was nothing like the new batch of soldiers. Whenever he came over, he would mess up my hair and say, *"Hey, kid."* Besides that, he mostly ignored me. Being around Bud was like being invisible and I even tested it out a few times, making faces he didn't notice or even talking to myself. I was fine with that because he didn't have a trust face.

He stayed over on more than one occasion, and I don't think Mama approved. One night, he gave me a good scare. I remember waking up to someone dying. At least it sounded that way. Mama was snoring next to me, so I knew it wasn't her. Which meant it had to be Jean. I broke into a sweat as I lay there in the pitch black, terrified about Jean, but more panicked that whoever it was would come for us next. This was the moment I had been dreading. The cane knife was under my bed.

I shook Mama awake. "Mama, I think Jean's being murdered. We have to hide!" I whispered.

Someone was banging against the wall, over and over, like they were hanging a picture. And you could hear Jean whimpering, all strangled-sounding. Mama listened for a moment and then shot out of bed. "Stay here, Ella. Jean is fine."

In the hallway, Mama pounded on Jean's door. "Keep it down in there if you want a roof over your head come morning," she yelled.

The noises stopped instantly, and I could hear the crickets again. When Mama came back, I asked what had happened, and she told me it was something adults sometimes did when they were in love.

"Are they mating? We learned about that in science class," I said.

She gave me a funny look. "Something like that."

Her tone said to stop asking questions. And I was just happy Jean was alive.

I never heard them again, but they did an awful lot of hand-holding and kissing. The kissing made me embarrassed, so I usually went outside to draw or play with the chickens. Whenever Bud was around, Jean's voice changed, too. Words came out sweeter, like she was talking to a baby or an animal. It was a different kind of love than my mama and papa had. They were more like good team members, not all lovey-dovey.

When Bud left town, you'd have thought Jean was at a funeral every day for a month. I knew she was really bad off when she stopped wearing lipstick. Up until then, her lips were always cherry. Now they were ginger, like the kind you get at Hayashi store with your *musubi.* Things got better slowly, but she still talked about him constantly. So when

Zach said he was here about Bud, I wanted to hear for myself. One good thing about a swinging door is that it's easy to push open just a tiny crack, enough for one eye to see through. I had to tell my heart to stop beating so loudly or they would see me. From what I knew about grown-ups, they were able to love only one person at a time. This new information went against my current set of beliefs. If Bud was married, then what was he doing with Jean?

If a husband or a wife dies, only then are you allowed to marry someone else. Like Mama. Eventually she might take a new husband, once she is able to stop being sad about my papa. I know I should tell her the truth because it might help matters, since she doesn't really know he's dead yet.

Only I do.

Chapter Twenty-Two

VIOLET

PEOPLE ALWAYS SAY THERE ARE NO SEASONS IN Hawaii. That isn't true. In the blurred lines between fall and winter, Violet had come to recognize the subtle shift in the light and a less ambitious sun, ohia blossoms that wouldn't stop, and the need for an extra blanket at night. Plovers and sanderlings returned and the waves marched toward the island in towering lines, crashing against the cliffs in explosions of white.

She could almost say the same for herself, a changing of seasons. But hers was more a winter to spring thawing, when ice cracks and begins to melt and shoots poke through the earth. Not Jean, though. Jean was in the midst of a bitter-cold winter ever since the Bud news. Moping, brooding, staring off into space.

On Saturday morning, a new layer of dew covered the car windshield. Violet hadn't seen dew since spring. When they pulled up to Waimea town, a pack of men and a lion milled around in the grassy field where they were to set up their pie stand.

"What's going on?" Violet asked.

"*We* are going on," Jean said. "Those boys are waiting for us."

"We ought to have matching aprons," Setsuko said.

"Agreed," Violet said, thrilled that Setsuko was sticking it out amid the tension and getting more involved.

"If I'm Honey Jean, you two need new names," Jean said, pausing to contemplate the idea. "Guava Bee and…"

"I'll be Coco Mama," Violet offered.

"Guava Bee? We're not even making guava pies," Setsuko said.

"We could be," Jean said.

Setsuko shrugged. Right now, any of them would walk to Hilo and back barefoot to turn Jean's mood around.

Parker guided Violet as she backed the massive truck into place. In the mirror, she could see the sunlight catch his dimple. Ella had already jumped out and had her arms around Roscoe.

"Sweetie, what did I say about hugging him?"

"He likes to be hugged. Especially by Ella," he said.

For some reason, she was irritated by the sight of Parker, decked out in his utilities. While she had gone home to an empty bed and a bowl of vinegar last Sunday, in her mind he and the light-handed Hawaiian had danced under the stars and swum bare-skinned in the lagoon. "Is that what you came here to tell me?"

He looked as if she'd slapped him. "Actually, it's not. I came because I wanted to be the first person in line this morning for your honeycomb pie. And I dragged these fellas along with me. Told them it was part of morning training."

What had gotten into her? "I'm sorry. That was rude of me.

My fuse is a little short right now with Zach's news the other night." She nodded toward Jean, who was also bent over Roscoe and vigorously rubbing the loose skin around his neck.

"Tough situation," he said.

As a rule, marines kept their mouths shut about other marines. No one kissed and told. It was a brotherhood. She knew that. They were just lucky Zach had a higher obligation to his sister; otherwise Jean might have never known the truth.

The boys erected the stand in eight seconds flat, and before Violet knew it, Honey Cow Pies was in business again. The only problem was that Roscoe decided he wanted to lie in the middle of the stand, under the shade of the tin roof.

Violet tapped his flank with her foot. "Excuse me." He didn't budge.

One ear moved forward, one back. He looked at her as if to say, *"Good luck."* The mother in her felt sorry for him, having to be dragged around all day by the soldiers. Parker clearly hadn't been thinking about the lion's well-being when he bought him. But he was a man, and worrying was a woman's job.

"Fellas, your lion is in the way, and he's likely to scare away all our customers," she said.

Ella found another stick and wiggled it in front of him. He batted at it before grabbing the leafy end with both paws and kicking at it with his hind legs. The maneuver was bad enough when Snowflake performed it, but with Roscoe, one risked being shredded like the chicken *hekka* Mr. Tavares sold a few stands down.

Roscoe stayed in the stand but sat upright instead, with his face just high enough to look out over the counter. Violet couldn't resist the urge to scratch behind his ears. With all his weight, he leaned in for more.

"You like that, don't you," she said.

When she looked up, she caught Zach and Parker exchanging glances. "Only a matter of time," Zach said.

"Before what?"

"Before you're hugging him, too."

"Nonsense."

After serving up slices—about half chocolate honeycomb and sweet potato coconut—Violet pulled Parker aside. "I have another favor to ask of you." The favors seemed to be stacking up, but she didn't know who else to ask.

He held his fork in hand, waiting to take the first bite. "Not making any promises, but shoot."

"Of course you're not."

Her stomach rolled. One side of her knew that her anger was misdirected, even ridiculous. Parker was not her father, not Herman, but he was leaving. Of that she was sure.

"Jeez, you wake up on the wrong side of the bed?"

The wind had picked up speed and her hair blew in every direction. She had to hold her skirt down with one hand. "We heard that the evidence they have against Takeo is bogus. I was wondering if you could talk to Riggs, since he's involved in the case. If the military doesn't have any reason to keep Takeo, it's only fair they release him."

Parker formed a quiet whistle. "Where'd you hear that?"

Unable to implicate Irene Ferreira, she said, "I overheard two men at the bar the other day."

"You were at a bar?"

Did it seem so far-fetched that she might be out? "I was. I had to trade some of our ration tickets."

"Captain Riggs is what you might call hard-boiled, but I'll inquire. And I hate to tell you this, but if you're of Japanese ancestry, fair went out the window after Pearl Harbor," he said.

"Asking never hurt anyone."

"Well, that may not be technically true," he said, smiling.

Her heart thudded and she wondered if he could hear it. "Gravity is sometimes a by-product of circumstances, Sergeant. I wasn't always this way." She turned to escape this line of talk, which was likely to end in tears.

"Just trying to make a joke, ma'am." He saluted.

It was impossible to be upset with him when he had two pieces of pie on his plate and now tried to maneuver both into his mouth at once. The way he chewed, slowly and with his eyelids half-closed, reminded Violet how much these men appreciated the smallest specks of life.

He patted his stomach. "Trying to gain some weight for Island X," he said with a piece of crust stuck to his chin.

"Island X?"

"What we're training for. It'll be our first combat experience as a group." When Parker spoke, his eyes flickered. He shifted positions the way a cornered dog will.

"When will they tell you where it is?"

He grinned, returning to his usual cocksure self. "Not until we're coming in hot."

She had seen enough war propaganda to know that secrecy came before all else. "Keep mum—she's not so dumb," or "Don't kill her daddy with careless talk." Everything was kept strictly need-to-know. All this talk now struck her in the kneecaps, causing a near buckle.

As it turned out, Violet got the chance to speak with Captain Riggs personally when he showed up for a piece of moonshine pie. A cigarette dangled between his gray lips. "I survived the last piece. Figure I must be immune. Age does that to you."

She wasn't especially glad to see him, but forced a smile.

"Instead of paying, how about you answer a few questions for me."

Setsuko found a reason to walk away at that very moment, and disappeared behind the truck. Violet had told her about Irene's overheard phone conversation.

He coughed. "I'm not in the habit of answering questions."

Violet plunged ahead anyway. "I overheard some men talking in town the other day. One of them mentioned something about bogus evidence at the school. Would that be Takeo and the Japanese school?"

"We don't talk about ongoing investigations to civilians, ma'am, even if they do make a fine pie," he said.

She knew this was her big chance, and something about the shift in his gaze told her she'd struck truth. "What worries me is the fact that someone would fabricate documents. That there's such a dangerous individual among us. Maybe you should look into that instead of hauling off innocent family men."

Riggs worked to take a deep breath. "We have eyes on the ground, everywhere. And I don't take my job lightly. If you knew half of what went on, you might change your tune."

"But if the evidence is bogus, you need to release Takeo, sir."

He was one of those men who had no trouble blowing smoke in a woman's face. "*We* don't need to do anything, ma'am."

By two o'clock, Honey Cow Pies had sold out. Before heading back, they took some of their change and splurged on hamburgers up the street from Tsugi Kaiama, who almost always sold out before they did. She claimed it was because the whole cow went through her gas grinder. Violet thought it was from the bread crumbs and celery.

As they bounced along the rutted road home with stomachs and pockets full, she caught herself smiling out the window at nothing in particular. Bees swarmed in the tops of the eucalyptus, and a low bank of clouds cast the fields in a blue light.

Pretty soon, a picture of Parker emerged in her mind. Standing an inch away in the pond. She imagined feeling the drumbeat of his heart through salt water, her whole body wrapped around him. Up close, she could see how his lashes lightened at the tips and salt caked onto his lids. He tasted like sardines and beer, and his tongue was bold.

Bam. She flew up, banging her head on the lightly padded roof. Everyone else went with her. "Horsefeathers! Where were you?" Jean cried.

She checked the rearview mirror to see that all kids were still in, and spotted a pothole the size of a drinking trough. Hiding a blush, she focused on the road. "Sorry. It's just so lovely out, I was admiring the scenery."

"Admiring the scenery in your mind, more likely." She could feel Jean filling up on questions. "What really went on when you disappeared with Sergeant Stone last weekend? You couldn't wait to get left behind," Jean said.

"That's not true!"

Any talk of men right now might have been enough to send Jean smack over the bridge. Thus, Violet had kept her conflicted feelings about Parker unvoiced. Jean was no dummy, though.

"You have a pulse," Jean said.

"We swam. I stepped on *wana*."

Jean shook her head, unconvinced. "Damned if you do, damned if you don't."

"What's that supposed to mean?"

"Either way, you end up crushed. But he *is* the cat's meow. Not a crumb like Bud."

"Nothing happened, nor will anything. End of discussion."

Jean gave her a knowing look. "You remind me of myself not that long ago. Only I wasn't afraid to admit it."

Chapter Twenty-Three

ELLA

IF THE AMOUNT OF CHOCOLATE HONEYCOMB pie I ate today is any indication, things might be looking up for my stomach. I've wanted to eat more lately, in general, and I wasn't sure if lions liked pie, but I got my answer after Roscoe wolfed down his piece. There was cream all around his mouth, which gave me away. Mama wiped it off with a napkin and said, "Ella, no more pie for Roscoe." But I could tell she didn't really mind too much.

The day had been such a good one up until then, I was afraid to count my chickens. Good thing I didn't. We were headed home around four o'clock in the afternoon. Mama had already hit a huge hole in the road and I was starting to wonder if she was driving blindfolded. We were barreling around a bend when she jammed on the brakes. We skidded to a narrow shoulder with our front wheels in the tall grass. Us kids rolled into the cab like bowling pins and I had to disentangle myself from Umi's braids.

We all stood up to see. Just ahead, a jalopy had been cut down, blocking passage. How Mama explained it was that these cars had been hoisted up along the roads all over the island, ready to be dropped to slow advancing Japanese troops. I always wondered who would be there to drop them, since most of the time, there were no soldiers anywhere to be found. And if there were Japanese on our roads, wouldn't it be too late?

No one spoke for a moment. We were far enough in the boondocks that air-raid sirens would not be heard. Suddenly I felt cold. If we were being attacked, where would we go? As much as I loved my Japanese friends, I had heard enough about the Japanese soldiers to worry. The fact that we were women and kids might not even matter. I concentrated on keeping my bladder under control.

Us kids jumped out and ran to the cab. "Are the Japanese here?" I asked.

"More likely it was a prank, or the cables broke," Mama said, opening the door.

My first thought went to animals. "What if they burn our houses and the chickens can't get out of their coops?" My lips were quivering now and I had a funny feeling that my knees were loosened.

Mama smoothed out my hair, which didn't help this time. "I'm sure the Japanese aren't here, but we need to be tough in any event. Remember what the doctor said—deep breaths."

Still, I wondered. What if we had been lured into believing Hawaii was safe again, that the war had now moved closer to Japan? There was no question that the Japanese military people were sneaky, and smarter than most Americans. Ambushes were their specialty, after all. Jean started mumbling a prayer.

"Would you not do that? You're scaring the kids," Mama told her.

"A prayer never hurt anyone."

While Jean stood talking to God, the rest of us scouted out the jalopy to see if there was a way around. Hiro scrambled underneath and to the other side. One thing that's happened since his father was taken away is that he acts more like the man of the family. Jean says he has stepped up to bat. His eyes are always on Setsuko—I guess kind of like me and Mama. Where before Setsuko had to ask, he now does stuff on his own. Lately I've been thinking he would make someone a good husband one day—when he's older. "See anything?" Setsuko called.

"Looks like it was cut, but no telling by who or what," he said.

In the distance, I thought I heard a low rumble. Hopefully just someone driving up from Honoka'a. But from the raspy sound, it might have been a tank or a heavy truck. We all looked at each other with big eyes.

On the far side of the road we saw a small hill with a thick stand of ohia bushes.

Jean was the first to speak. "Run! Hiro, hurry!"

I froze in place. "Ella, come on!" Mama said.

My legs somehow kicked in and we wasted no time scrambling up and leaving the truck where it was. Mama's fingers strangled my hand and I gulped for air. My heart was beating about two hundred beats per minute and thudded against my ribs like it wanted out. We crouched down low. Between branches, we could see down to the jalopy, which was upside down.

"Stay calm," Setsuko whispered.

Staying calm was about as unlikely as me turning Japanese. My kneecaps were pressed into sharp pieces of cinder, and mud streaked across my overalls. Everyone held their breath. Time moved like dripping honey. I noticed a red bird twittering away on a bare branch. Clouds swam past. *Please, God, let me be a bird in my next lifetime*, I asked.

Have you ever tasted fear? It tastes like you're sucking on pennies and then you swallow them and they pile up in your stomach. I sank onto the ground, wanting to scream and cry and disappear all at the same time.

"Ella's shaking," Jean whispered.

Mama turned and looked me hard in the eye. "I need you to be strong right now."

It's one thing to *be* strong. Another to act strong. I stood back up. It was all I could do.

Setsuko risked talking out loud to all of us. "If it's anything other than an American truck, we run down that hill and follow the stream as far back as we can."

We all knew what she meant.

Several clouds later, a tank emerged from the stand of eucalyptus. From this distance, it was hard to make out what kind. As it approached the roadblock, it slowed, making a loud *chunk-a-lunk* sound. That was when we saw.

One big star.

Jean leaped up, sniffling. "I thought I was going to lose my lunch for a moment there." I was worried about losing more than my lunch. I was so relieved, I stood there mute. All the air-raid drills in the world won't teach you how to behave when faced with the real McCoy. A saying I picked up from the soldiers. I burst into tears and hugged Mama's waist.

"It's an American tank, honey. Probably training. We're safe."

I tore my face away and looked down at the tank. A man stood atop, next to the gun turret. Jean jumped up and down, waving, and he waved back. Probably wondering what a bunch of women and kids were doing in the bushes. The hatch opened and four more soldiers spilled out.

One of the men climbed over to our side of the road. He took off his helmet and smiled. "Sorry to inconvenience you ladies," he yelled. "We were on a drill to block the road. We'll have it moved out in no time."

"Inconvenience us all you want. We're just glad to see you," Mama said.

When I settled into bed that night, I practiced my thank-yous. Uncle Henry, the kahuna healer man, told me this was an ancient Hawaiian remedy. Instead of wasting thoughts on what bad things happened, or might happen, I am supposed to concentrate on what I am lucky for. Depending on my mood, I come up with a short list or a long list. Tonight, I noticed my list was growing longer. Soldiers protecting us, chicken sweaters, butterflies, sugarcane lemonade, Hiro, Umi, Roscoe, Coca-Cola, an endless supply of coconuts and honey, Mama still alive, Spam, American tanks.

One thing led to another, and before I knew it, I was lulled to sleep with the unspooling of good thoughts.

Chapter Twenty-Four

VIOLET

FALL CONTINUED TO DEEPEN AROUND THEM, with its thin air and windless nights. When she passed the soldiers marching roadside, their faces were no longer flaming red. For Violet, it meant getting through the school day without her dress plastered to her back.

"Mama, what's an intern?" Ella asked as they washed rice one afternoon.

"Well, that depends. Why do you want to know?"

"Because Umi says her dad is being transferred to an intern camp in California."

Explaining war things to children took a special kind of measuring. She always wavered between telling too much or not enough. Maybe it was a woman thing, wanting to shelter them from all the fear. But one thing she had figured out early on was that the kids usually found out on their own. "In the case you're thinking of, to intern means to lock someone up. To make them a prisoner."

"But I don't understand. Takeo never did anything," Ella said.

Violet sat her daughter down, leaving the rice to soak. "You and I know that without a doubt. But there are people that want proof. And until they find that proof, he will stay in the camp."

"If they go, I won't have any friends. Except for the soldiers."

They're leaving, too, Violet thought, but didn't have the heart to say it out loud. Funny how the soldiers were both a blessing and a curse. But when you broke it down into individual beings, there were the good and the not so good, just like in any situation.

Since the night of the downed jalopy, Ella had taken a few steps backward in progress. For several days afterward, she refused to eat, her scabs looked raw and picked, and her mood turned sulky. Violet had been trying to sleep in her own bed more often lately, but gave in. She always gave in.

"You know what?" Violet said. "When I was your age, I had fewer friends than you do. Our farm was out in the sticks and there was no time to play. When I wasn't in school, I had to help Daddy plant seeds, cut corn and can anything that grew. Wilma Newman was the only girl close to our house, and I always secretly thought she was a boy."

Ella asked, "Was she?"

"No, it was just that they had three boys and not enough money to buy new clothes for their only daughter. It wasn't until high school that I actually had real friends. But looking back, having all that time to myself was a good thing. You know why?"

Ella thought hard, her face pinched in concentration. "Why?"

"Because I got to be friends with myself. I played chase with the wild turkeys, I discovered an old Indian campsite full of arrow tips, and I taught myself to read *Winnie-the-Pooh* and *The Velveteen Rabbit*. Those books were two of my sweetest friends, and after I mastered those, I read whatever I could get my hands on. By the time I was ten, I got through *Mrs Dalloway*, even though I had no idea what it was about."

"Who's Mrs. Dalloway?"

"Never mind. The point is, we have to learn to make do with what we have, sweetie, even if it's different from everyone else. If we learn to love our own lives, a magic doorway opens and our dreams become real."

Ella was frowning. "How come you never told me about this?"

She had to think an answer. "Of course, it's not an actual physical doorway. It's more like a door in your mind, or your heart, that when you're paying attention, leads you to places you want to go in life. But you have to tune in."

"How do you tune in?" Ella hung on every word and this new development involving magic.

"That's where it gets tricky. When you're happy where you are, not wishing you were somewhere else or someone else, the door begins to crack. Like when you're drawing, or with Brownie or Roscoe. In a way, you have to stop thinking."

Slanted sunlight fell in on the table between them and it dawned on Violet that she should listen to her own advice. In truth, the ideas had been from her grandmother, and as they tumbled from her mouth, she almost heard her grandmother's voice, scratchy but always ripe with an inner smile.

"How do you stop thinking?"

She squeezed Ella's bony hand. "Little Miss Curiosity wants to know everything, doesn't she? If I knew exactly how to stop thinking, I'd be one of those Shinto priests. But from what I gather, the best way is to become friends with this moment, and to live it with all your might."

Snowflake entered the kitchen then, arching up her back and making figure eights between their legs. Her purr sounded like a small motor, and it revved each time Ella bent down to pet her.

"I'm going to practice," Ella said.

"It's not always easy."

But the practice of emptying your mind of all thought was what mattered most.

One thing that nagged at Violet was that she and Jean had neglected the neighbors in favor of the soldiers. They'd spent their evenings gathering and preparing pie ingredients, and their weekends selling pies and socializing. To remedy that, they decided to invite the Codys, Luther Hodges, Ethyl Grimm, Bella Matthison and the Hamasus over for chili and rice one evening. As the sun dropped below the treetops, everyone stood around the radio munching on salted peanuts and listening to the account of the first B-29 Superfortress flying a raid over Tokyo.

"Brigadier General Emmett O'Donnell, in Dauntless Dotty, leads one hundred and eleven B-29 bombers from the tiny island of Tinian fifteen hundred miles away to Tokyo, where they unleashed their loads over the Musashima Engine Factory thirty thousand feet below. Folks, we have arrived in Tokyo! I repeat, Tokyo has been bombed by American forces!"

There was a small measure of comfort in knowing that all the marines who'd lost their lives on Tinian had done so for a cause. Violet had learned that Tinian was critical in the island-hopping tactic, allowing American forces to set up bases for their massive bombers so much closer to Japan.

Jean stood next to her, stone-faced. Any mention of Tinian, and Bud was immediately on her mind, even though she claimed he was a knucklehead. On tough days, she still set up bottles in the backyard as target practice using rotten tomatoes. "Our Second Division did well, didn't they?" Jean said.

The room filled up with hopeful feelings of victory—so strong, you could have scooped out helpings and served them up on a plate.

Luther showed up late, and when he walked through the front door, he carried with him the scent of liquor and tobacco. He'd been drunk last time he came over, too. Maybe the war was getting to him. He wouldn't be the only one.

His voice boomed. "What's all the hoopla?"

"Did you hear about Tokyo?" she asked.

"What about it?"

"That our bombers made it there," she said.

He walked over to the radio and bent down, holding his ear up to the speaker, even though it was plenty loud. He smeared his hands over his beard and said, "'Bout time. Teach those Japs a lesson." When he spoke, spit came out of his mouth.

Regardless that America was at war with the Japanese, she still grew rigid when people used the word *Jap.* At least when some people referred to her as *haole*, they didn't mean it in a bad way. Not the case here. She glanced at Setsuko, who had been quiet from her morning visit to Kilauea Camp and seeing Takeo.

"He's suffering from a bad case of hopelessness," she had said upon returning. "He's putting up a good front but his eyes are empty and he's lost a lot of weight."

She could have said the same for Setsuko, who looked downright miserable.

"Is there a date?" Violet had asked.

They had been told that as soon as the military could spare room on a boat, he and the other prisoners would be shipped off to a tent city in California. Setsuko would pack up the kids and follow him if it came to that. "No date. It could be tomorrow, for all we know."

Now Violet nodded toward Setsuko. "Please have some respect in our household, Luther."

He motioned as though he was zipping his lips, with no apologies. Perspiration matted his thin hair to his temples. This was a new Luther, not the jovial shop teacher whom all the kids loved and her reliable handyman. She decided that this would be the last time she invited him over. Manners mattered, even in war.

Over dinner, all Luther wanted to talk about was how the damn kamikazes blasted up the USS *Lexington* and how to handle them. "We need to just sink their whole island. And from what I hear, it's in the works."

"How can we sink a whole island?" Jean said, looking bothered by his ranting.

"Ever hear of an atomic bomb?" he asked.

No one had.

"My goons tell me the government has a top secret project in New Mexico, building bombs as we speak. Not the kind that destroys a building—the kind that will flatten a whole city, even sink an island like Japan."

Jean crossed her arms. "Japan is more than one island."

"Well, all the islands, then," Luther said.

Violet glanced over at the kids, who were eating at the card table off to the side. All of them stared at Luther with their forks down, mouths hanging open. "Please, Luther, the kids don't need to hear this."

A bomb like that sounded like bad news.

"Just giving you the dope."

Luther seemed to be so full of hatred. He scared her a little. And that made her not trust him. She couldn't say why, just that nagging feeling in the back of your mind saying, *Watch out.*

Chapter Twenty-Five

VIOLET

FOR WEEKS NOW, ALL ANYONE COULD TALK about was the upcoming rodeo. Local *paniolo* from Parker Ranch and leathernecks from places like Iowa and Wyoming would be putting on a show—bronco riding, steer roping, bulldogging. According to the posters hung around town, they'd even be holding a greased pig contest.

People placed bets on who would come out ahead, but Violet kept her ideas to herself. Most of the cocksure mainlanders had no idea what they were up against. She'd seen the *paniolo* in action. And having grown up on a farm, she knew her way around horses.

The first time Herman drove her through Waimea town, she had marveled at the high-stepping horses and the Hawaiians who rode them. These cowboys were three generations deep. Herman explained that it all began when George Vancouver presented King Kamehameha with five cows. Cows had a way of multiplying, and in the 1830s, when the wild cattle ranged out of control, the king sent a high chief to California to find cowboys who could teach the Hawaiians. He returned with three Mexicans, who taught them how to break horses and round up the cattle. The Hawaiians didn't have the letter *S* in their alphabet, and no one could pronounce *espaniola*, so they made do with *paniolo*. It was the start of the Hawaii cattle industry, long before any of the Western territories had ranching traditions.

Ella had never been to a rodeo and pestered Violet every two minutes about wanting her very own cowboy hat. "We'll have to see about that. A cowboy hat is something you have to earn."

The morning of the rodeo, they rose early. When Jean traipsed out of the bedroom in a long denim skirt and a checkered ruffly affair on top, Violet couldn't hold back a whistle. Jean's hair was braided to one side and her lips looked to be on fire.

"No woman in their right mind would want to be standing next to you today," Violet said.

Jean smiled. "I want to do some bulldogging of my own. But not with a steer."

"Oh, stop. Haven't you learned yet?"

"No, ma'am. Tie me to a tree and whip me—I'm still a sucker for a man in uniform."

"I guess sometimes you need a couple of doses of medicine before it works. So my father would have said."

Jean held the back of her hand to her forehead and moaned. "Give me another dose, please, Doctor."

Only Irene Ferreira could pronounce the name of the corral, Pu'uhihale. And Ella, who sounded like a native in her own right. Irene had them all practicing on the way to town.

"Come on—how long have you girls lived in Hawaii? You need to be able to say it right. Think Winnie-the-Pooh. *Pooh-ooh-hee-hollay.*"

Jean slumped back after several unsatisfactory attempts. "My tongue will always rebel against these vowel-happy words."

Violet kept trying.

As they approached the vicinity of the stone corral, which was just across the main road from Camp Tarawa, cars lined up in all directions. Violet looked over at Ella, who rested her chin on the car door. If only Umi and Hiro had come, but Setsuko insisted on taking them to church. From the looks of it, they might be the only people on the island in church today. Setsuko believed the more face-to-face time with God these days, the better. Who could blame her?

The edges of the corral were thick with people, who spilled over the rock walls and into the dusty field.

"Zach said to sit where we have a view of the chutes, over here. Look, there he is!" Jean said.

At the mention of Zach's name, Irene's hands immediately went to her hair and she fussed with stray strands blown from the wind. She stood up straighter and sucked in her stomach. Violet knew the signs.

He must have come early, because he had secured prime seating, even if it was just on the wall. Tommy and a few boys Violet recognized sat around him, lower lips full of tobacco.

Zach made room for their group. "Glad you guys made it in time for the pig scramble. Apparently, it's a crowd favorite." He grinned like a fool. "Guess who they put in charge of greasing the pig?"

"Let me guess. Sergeant Stone?" Jean said, winking at Violet, who had been wondering where Parker was and feeling guilty about it.

"None other. Want to go back and watch?"

"I'll keep your spots," Tommy offered.

They wound through the jeeps and trucks that formed the outer boundary of the arena to a smaller holding pen out back. The sun was out in full force, magnifying the scent of manure and wet morning grass.

Zach reached down for Ella's hand, and she skipped along next to him in her overalls. "Did you bring Roscoe?" she asked.

"Nope. He stayed back on account of some trouble he caused last night. Got loose and chased a herd of puppies through camp. Some hunters in Hawaii got the bright idea that our men would be suckers for an unwanted litter, and, boy, were they on the nose."

Ella looked worried, and Zach quickly continued.

"I know Roscoe just wanted to play. He wants friends. Imagine being the only lion in town. But not everyone saw it that way. With all the livestock here today, we thought it best to leave him."

Violet knew that as Roscoe matured, things might grow more troublesome, but she held her tongue.

At the back corral, Parker leaned against a kiawe-wood fence post talking with a *paniolo* whose copper face was crossed with fault lines. Like all the marines, Parker wore khakis, a cotton button-up and a piss-cutter hat. If you were judging on attire, the leathernecks had already lost. Every Hawaiian she'd seen was decked out in colorful plaid or *palaka* shirts, bandannas and hats ringed with flower or feather lei. Even some of their horses wore lei around their necks.

When he spotted Violet, he waved them over. There was that funny feeling in between her ribs again. Like a flopping fish, whacking her insides with its tail. Parker was causing feelings she'd never quite felt before. She hoped it was just a light-headed infatuation, but worried there might be more to it.

"Morning, ladies. Meet Sonny Huehue, legendary in these parts."

Sonny removed his hat and kissed each of their hands, lingering at Ella. Normally, she flinched in situations like this, but her eyes remained fixed on the old man's. "How old are you?"

"Ten."

"I have a granddaughter your age. Her roping skills are going to surpass mine pretty soon. Maybe she can teach you one of these days. Would you like that?"

"I've only been on a horse a couple of times," Ella said.

Why not add another animal to the list?

"You come down here on a Saturday or Sunday. I'm not here, tell 'em Sonny sent you."

Ella glanced up at Violet, who gave her a thumbs-up.

Parker seemed antsy. "What's the holdup on the pig?" he said to Sonny.

"You'll see."

A couple of horses grazed nearby, a sleek black gelding and a painted mare. The sound of ripping and crunching grass reminded her of Minnesota and little-girl days. The only difference was that there was no grass left back on the farm, only dust. Here, the moss-green grass grew knee-high. All the animals were fat from it, their coats shiny.

Sonny grabbed Ella's hand and led her over. His hand ran along the mare's rump. "That one is Pontiac, and this beauty is Waipio. Want to ride her?" Without waiting for an answer, he hoisted Ella up and sat her on Waipio's bare back. From the look on Ella's face, she was alive in heaven.

A man like that could be trusted to know his horses.

While everyone watched Ella ride in circles, Parker said, "I got an audience with Riggs last night, by the way."

"That was fast. How'd you manage?"

"On Saturdays, he's been known to sneak that god-awful Hawaiian hooch into his office, and indulges. You might say I caught him with a little extra give."

Just then, a rickety truck careened up the dirt road, skidding to a stop and kicking up dust on the far side of the holding pen. The men who poured out howled with laughter. Some kind of loud banging rocked the truck.

"I didn't get a lot out of him." Parker glanced at the truck, then squeezed her hand. "We'll talk later. I've got to deal with this."

Sonny scooped Ella off the horse, set her down and ran around to the back of the truck, where all the men had crowded. A gut-shaking roar erupted from their midst. Anywhere but Hawaii, and Violet would have thought it a bear. In a flash, one of the men released the truck bed, while the others, each with a rope in hand, dragged a cage out and dropped it into the pen. No one moved to open it.

"All yours," one of the men said to Parker, patting him on the back.

"Take a gander!" Jean said.

"These guys are nuts. As if anyone is going to be able to grease that thing," Irene said.

The wild boar was about three Roscoes molded into one black, wire-haired monster. The minute one of the men opened the cage, it beelined to the bronco standing in the middle. With ears flattened, the horse blew hurricanes out his nostrils. The situation was not liable to end well, but none of them could look away. The boar charged, while at the same time the bronco spun and connected a back left hoof to its snout. With a screech, the boar fell back.

"Get that boar away from my horse!" Sonny yelled.

All the *paniolo* had ropes in hand, even Parker. But the boar was in such a craze, no one could lasso the thing.

Jean jumped up and down, clapping. "Forget the bull wrestling. Anyone that snags that boar is the real winner today."

"My money is on Stone," Zach said, with a shadow of concern on his face.

With a few more well-landed kicks from the bronco, the boar turned its fury on the cage. Within minutes the entire cage was reduced to a twisted metal ball. Parker stood out in his military-issued clothing, but his roping ability looked authentic. In the end, it was Sonny who landed the boar. It took every last man to drag it to the pen opening.

"They better not let it loose out here," Violet said, looking around for the nearest escape.

Once the boar sensed freedom, he bolted toward the hills, dragging the men behind him. Eventually they loosened the rope and let go.

Parker returned, caked in dust and sweat. "Mean son of a bitch. Good thing they had the forethought to clip his tusks before bringing him in."

"I'm half-suspicious that boar was Japanese, with all that fanatical resistance," Zach said.

If that's what the Japanese soldiers were like, the American boys were in trouble. Violet only wished people could handle their differences with words rather than weapons.

Back at the main corral, they watched a far less thrilling version of roping. This time on calves. Next up was the bulldogging, and then the bronco riding. The weather couldn't make up its mind, with a light sideways rain one minute and bright sun the next. Once again, Violet found she was blindsided with joy. Thundering hooves, the cheer in the crowd, and watching Ella stuff a foot-long hot dog into her tiny mouth. All of it.

Her prediction proved true. The *paniolo* rode circles around most of the leathernecks. But not all. A handful of real cowboys from the Southwest were close to equal in roping and riding. Flair was another matter. The Hawaiians sat on their horses with an extra helping of swagger. Most had probably started on horseback before they could walk.

When it came time for the bronco riding, the crowd tightened in. Herds of men gathered around the newly constructed chutes. Parker and Zach were somewhere over there, but Violet couldn't make them out.

"Look, that bronco has giant horns," Ella said, her voice barely audible over the escalating roar.

When Violet focused in closer, she saw that Ella was right.

"If that's a bronco, I'm Franklin D. Roosevelt," Jean said.

A horn blew and the bull twisted and kicked out of the gate, ridden by a stocky *paniolo.* The man lasted all of three seconds, but when the bull tossed him, the rider contorted his body midair, so he landed standing. The crowd erupted.

"Looks like the ranch hands thought bull riding would be more fun than broncos. I just hope no one gets killed," Violet said.

After a few more *paniolo*, a gawky leatherneck rode out on the meanest bull yet. All four of its feet left the ground, if that was possible, as it twisted to the side with an arched back. The ring fell silent and Violet whispered an abbreviated prayer. But the man moved like water, and it seemed his upper half was not connected to his lower half.

Jean's red nails dug into her arm. "Mother of God, it's Zach!"

She was right. His bull appeared to be an expert in spinning, but by some miracle, Zach held on for another four seconds, barely making it to eight. Jean exhaled enough breath for all of them when it was over and Zach stood safely outside the ring. His turned out to be the longest ride so far.

"How do they know who wins?" Ella asked.

"At this rodeo? Who knows? They seem to have their own rules, but usually the rider has to stay on for at least eight seconds to even qualify," Violet said. "Then it depends on how well he controls the bull and how difficult the bull is. Uncle Zach should do well because his bull was so crazy and he made the time."

What she didn't say was that every last one of these men in the bull riding had a death wish. Either that or they were exercising their right to pack in as much living as humanly possible. A different set of rules applied to these men.

Parker rode last.

Whoever picked the bull must have wanted to see every bone in his body broken. It was twice the size of the others. With braided rope in hand, Parker lurched as the animal bucked and reared and kicked around the corral. His free arm waved around like it belonged to someone else, but he stayed on. Violet held her fingers over her eyes and peeked out between them. The ground thundered.

"Five one thousand, six one thousand, seven one thousand. Oh, no!" Ella cried.

The bull now stood violently still. Twice he pawed the red dirt before hanging his horns and charging the rock wall. Everyone began yelling their two cents. *Jump! Don't jump! Hang on to your hat!* Violet saw the look on Parker's face at the same time the breath froze in her lungs. There was no way this would end well.

At the side of the corral, spectators fled in all directions. The open grassy patch would have been perfect for landing, if not for the gnarled ohia tree in the middle. A scream rose up in her throat, but nothing came out. Violet forced herself to watch as Parker leaned forward. Time turned sluggish. Somehow, she had enough time to think that maybe she needed to make a decision. Or maybe it was too late. Parker unstirruped his boots and swung a leg over. With both hands, he pushed up on the saddle and shoved himself backward and into the dirt. She had never seen a body sail through the air like that, as though he had come straight from a howitzer M1.

Violet felt his fall between her shoulders, a searing pain. When the bull slammed on his brakes, Parker still lay on the ground unmoving. Men poured into the ring from all directions, and two *paniolo*, Zach and Tommy hauled him away. Even from a distance, she could see he was limp.

"Is he dead?" Ella asked.

She had no answer.

There was much buzzing around the huddle of dusty men. In the few minutes that it took them to make their way around, a bank of low clouds arrived, spinning the air white and oddly metallic. She could still hear the thud his body made as it hit the ground like a sack of wood.

Her resolve was unraveling. "No," she said to no one in particular.

No, he won't be broken. No, I will not feel this way.

Violet tried to make Ella stay back with Irene, but both ignored her. Loud voices floated out and she heard fragments. "Alive...broken...lucky."

The temptation to run overwhelmed her. She wanted to see for herself. Without care for manners, she nudged her way to the front of the crowd, with Ella, Jean and Irene hanging on to her dress. The only recognizable part of Parker was the eyes. Other than that, he might have been dipped in red dirt, clothes and all. He sat holding a cloth to his head, very much alive. Zach perched on a rock next to him.

When Parker spotted Violet, he reached his arm out and then winced. "There you are. Had a little trouble there at the end, but what'd you think?"

Zach shook his head and chuckled.

Violet regarded his swollen cheek and pinched eye. "What I think is that you are lucky your friends dragged you out in time, and you weren't skewered on the tips of those horns."

When she looked closer, she realized there was a glaze over his good eye. Something was wrong.

"That wasn't luck. That was finely honed skill. Luck is when you finally kiss the one girl in the whole wide world who refuses to look your way," he said with a light slur. A lopsided grin spread halfway across his face. Then his head wavered and he fell back into the soft grass.

"In the whole wide world"? Some nerve.

Aside from being more worried than she ought to be about Parker, Violet was confounded, disconcerted and alternately flattered. Those feelings followed her around all day Monday and into Tuesday. Why did he have to go ahead and speak his mind, in front of everyone, no less?

"He wasn't talking about me, silly," she said to Jean on the way home from the rodeo.

"If you believe that, you're dumber than I thought."

On Tuesday afternoon, when Ella was outside reading stories to the hens and Violet had her arms elbow-deep in the wash bin, the phone rang. She was expecting a call from Macadangdang on the next coconut delivery so had a towel lying on the counter nearby.

"Violet?"

"Yes, this is she."

A pause. "It's Parker. I'm told I owe you an apology."

She barely managed to choke out, "Oh?"

"I don't remember much after hitting the ground, but Zach filled me in. I imagine it must have come across as pretty arrogant, and if I made you uncomfortable, I'm awfully sorry."

The thing with arrogance was that it carried a certain appeal. If measured out right. Violet had encountered men with too much and men with not enough. She was still trying to determine where Parker fit in on that scale.

"With the sense knocked out of you like that, who can blame you? Plus, you could have meant anyone," she said.

"You believe that?"

She kept quiet.

"Anyway, you're stuck with us until we ship out. But that's not the only reason I called. We never finished our conversation Sunday." He cleared his throat.

Riggs. Japanese school. No way he would risk talking about it on the line, would he?

"Yes, I've been wondering," she said.

"They are going to hold off shipping the *cattle* to the mainland. While they look into what might be causing their disease. So that might ease everyone's worry, for the moment."

"Good to know. I'll tell our neighbors."

Finally, a small crumb of good news. She couldn't wait to tell Setsuko.

"It's not much..."

She cut him off. "It's something. And by the way, everyone around here wants to know how your head is."

"On the mend. The swelling's gone down and I can see out of both eyes now. Doc said I have a concussion, and my company kept me awake all Sunday night. Now, there's a good form of torture. Every time I nodded off, someone clapped in my face."

She laughed. "Dreadful, but they need you alive, Sergeant. They care about you."

We all do.

Parker sounded like he was in a busy room, with radio static and voices barking orders around him. The line went silent for a moment and she thought she'd lost him, but his voice came through a second later. "That rodeo was something else, wasn't it? Seeing all the boys cut loose like that. Earned me a new level of respect for your *paniolo*, too. Even if they are hell-raisers." The smile in his voice slipped through the wire.

"Men will be men."

Again a pause, as though he was debating what to say next. "Speaking of men being men, there's a dance next weekend at the USO, and I'm supposed to drum up women," he said.

Violet immediately pictured Parker with the girls down at the beach. "They put you in charge, huh? Why doesn't that surprise me?"

"I only know four women on the island. I swear," he said.

"Sure you do."

Setsuko and the twins were in the habit of eating dinner with Violet, Jean and Ella several nights of the week now. Strength in togetherness was something you could feel deep in your bones. They all knew it, as well as knowing there was an unfillable space in her heart.

"The kids need normalcy," Setsuko had said, and Violet wondered how different she would be without the kids to be strong for.

In the past month, Hiro had mastered the fine art of coconut husking, and now he and Ella and Umi sat on the porch in an assembly line. *Hack, husk, crack.* Sun filtered through the trees, covering them all in gold. Brownie supervised, dressed up in her sweater.

The kids were buried in their work, so Violet pulled Setsuko into the kitchen and sat her down. "I have news. Parker called, and he couldn't tell me directly over the phone, but it sounds like Takeo is staying put for the time being," she said.

Setsuko's hands flew to her cheeks and tears pooled in her black eyes. "How does he know?"

"He was talking about cattle, but I knew what he meant. He said they weren't shipping the cattle to the mainland while they investigated what was causing their disease. I'm guessing while they look into the planted letters."

A look of sheer relief fell over Setsuko. "Oh, Violet. You have no idea how much this means."

"I have an idea, being that I see you almost every day. It's hard for me to watch you living only half a life."

"I could say the same for you. But you seem better lately."

Without another word, Setsuko stood and wrapped her arms in a tight squeeze around Violet. Her hair smelled like sugarcane and coconut. They were still hugging when Jean walked in.

"Please tell me this is a happy hug. I'm about done with bad news."

Violet told Jean about Parker's call. She almost left out the part about the upcoming dance. It might be simpler. There was no way Setsuko would go, and equally no way that Jean would *not* go. Her own feelings were somewhere in the middle. Hordes of very young soldiers, girls of every shape and size, and roaring music. But she'd yet to attend one, and December had already arrived. This might be the last one.

Jean turned the radio up, grating and chopping to the music. "Better start moving those hips, Coco Mama. When was the last time you danced?"

"No idea."

"We'll have a practice night, then, before this weekend. Get you primed."

Violet contemplated saying no outright, but settled on maybe. "I haven't said I'm going yet."

"Oh, you're going all right."

Saying no to Jean rarely worked. Maybe it would be enjoyable. If Ella didn't mind staying with Setsuko for a few hours.

With the music off, crickets filled in with their own night songs. Coldness drifted down from the mountain, and Violet wrapped a shawl over her shoulders. The Hamasus had gone and Ella was in bed. Her sleep had been improving lately. Whether from time or the influx of new friends and activity, Violet couldn't be sure.

Jean left the kitchen and returned with a box of floral stationery. "Time to send Mr. Bud Walker a letter. What do you say?"

"You sure about this?" Violet said.

"His actions can't go unattended."

In her book, liars were the lowest sort of person. People came up with excuses and reasons for lying, but it all boiled down to one thing. Lack of guts. People who told big lies were missing courage to tell the truth. Either that or they had an empty conscience. But a small part of Violet felt for Bud. Poor man believed he was going to die in the war and Hawaii was his last bus stop in life. He had voiced it on more than one occasion.

"What's the game plan?" Violet asked.

Jean rubbed her stomach. "Hmm. I think I've come down with a bad case of pregnancy. Maybe that, and I am on my way to Texas with all my belongings?"

"What about his wife?"

"She's probably suffered enough. I'm just going to address the letter to Bud and seal it."

They used scratch paper first. Violet threw out ideas and

Jean scribbled them down. Jean laughed and then she cried, leaving blotches of tears on the paper. She whispered, "I thought I loved him."

"Listen, Honey Jean. Love happens, and once it turns on, you can't just turn it off. The way he wooed you, you didn't stand a chance," Violet said.

"Tell me, did you ever suspect he was married?"

"Lord, no. Not a once. But that's the thing. Us trusting folk just have to go on trusting."

Jean wiped her nose and kept on writing, transferring the draft onto a starched sheet of stationery. She finished with a large swoop of the pen.

"Read it to me," Violet said.

Dearest Bud,

I hope this letter finds you in good health. After the battle of Saipan, I got word from the current marines at Camp Tarawa that you had survived. This was of such great relief to me that I fainted and had to be lifted from the ground and given smelling salts. They say that mail delivery has been halted, so I'm sure your letters are somewhere at the bottom of a ship's hold. But enough of that. I have the most swell news this side of ocean. I'm pregnant! You and I are having a baby. I've decided to leave Hawaii and move to Texas, since I think the baby should grow up with his Daddy. And I miss you. Oh, how I miss you. For a whole month after you left, I cried buckets and didn't catch one wink of sleep. I'm better now that I have a part of you inside of me.

I have purchased a ticket on the *Lurline* and should be arriving sometime around Christmas. In addition, I would prefer not to have this baby out of wedlock, so

I'm bringing my grandmother's ring. Soon we will be together again, my most handsome love!

Yours,

Alma Jean Quinlan

In many ways, the letter was just short of real. And Jean would have been more than eager to row her own boat to Texas if Bud had so much as hinted. Why did females seem prone to doing just about anything for a man?

"Well, if that doesn't scare the living daylights out of him, nothing will. Worse than any Japanese soldier."

Jean didn't look convinced.

Violet softened her voice. "Even if he was married, he didn't fake his feelings for you."

Jean sighed and bent forward, laying one cheek on the table. She looked up at Violet with one blue eye. "I don't know what to believe. You really think I should send it?"

"Do what feels right."

The house creaked, even in the stillness. Violet could almost hear the sound of Jean and Bud laughing at their own inside jokes.

"It feels mean," Jean said.

There was something heartless about the whole thing. "Sleep on it, then. Main thing is you got the words out."

Chapter Twenty-Six

ELLA

THE DAY STARTED OUT YELLOW AND PROGRESSED from there. Yellow light on the walls, yellow eggs, yellow flowers on my nightgown. When I first wake in the mornings, I can usually tell what kind of day it's going to be by the first color I see. Some I like better than others, but yellow is my favorite because then I know happy things are going to happen. I'm not sure why this is the case, but it always has been.

Last year, it seemed like I might never see yellow again. Papa added a burst of sun to my life. I knew that some of the kids called him Herman the German because he could be strict, but he was the school principal. That was his job. He also had a small mustache, like Mr. Hitler. At home, he let his soft side out as best he could. More with me than with anyone, even Mama. He wasn't the kind of man who hugged a lot or said mushy things, but he liked to kiss the top of my head and hold my hand. He did stuff with me, too. Like take me bamboo pole fishing down at Kawaihae for yellow tang or show me how to stick seeds in the ground, whenever he had the chance. He was busy, but I felt important around him. Like I was his *number one*.

On some days since he's been gone, the night follows me into the day. Everything is black like one long night. Usually it takes a butterfly or a flower to make me see color again. The butterflies in our yard like the purple and orange lantana, and Mama says they are pollinating.

One more thing about yellow. I hear a lot of mention that Japanese people are yellow. I've been caught staring in school a few times, especially in gym class, trying to figure out why. So far, none of the ones around here look yellow. If anything, they are brown. I don't want to offend Umi and Hiro, or Setsuko, because they're a little touchy about that kind of thing, so I keep my mouth shut. To tell the truth, though, I'd rather be yellow than black or white. It's a nicer color.

Mama let me help her get ready for the USO dance in Waimea. She spent all her time worrying about me and I spent all my time worrying about her, so her going was probably a good break. Jean always pestered her that socializing with adults was important. Mama was still young, after all. I knew Zach and Parker wouldn't let anything happen to her, so I felt unusually relaxed about the whole thing.

Jean already knew what she was going to wear. A red skintight affair that dipped low between her bosoms, which were almost nonexistent. She said it was seasonal, with Christmas coming up and all. The front part of her hair was piled on her head like ropes of silk, pinned up with every bobby pin in the house. She looked like a pinup girl from the war posters. Minus the bust. The ones that sing for the soldiers in Europe.

Mama had three dresses laid out on the bed. "None of these are any good," she said to Jean in a whiny tone.

"If you weren't so well-endowed, I could lend you one of mine. And don't try to get out of it."

I was starting to understand that Mama was nervous about the dance. "You look like a movie star in the yellow one," I told her.

She tried on the yellow one again. When Jean zipped it up, Mama had to hold her breath. "I look like a hussy."

"You look nothing of the sort. If you've got it, flaunt it," Jean said.

Mama rolled her eyes. The dress really lit up the gold in her hair, which she had set earlier with big rollers and Aqua Net. She had curled mine, too, and now I looked like Shirley Temple minus the cheeks. I couldn't wait for Umi and Hiro to see my new look. Strangely, the thought of Hiro seeing me like this caused a flurry in my stomach. Not the kind I usually have. A good flurry.

Irene showed up ten minutes later. She wore a ruffly pink number and a crown of flowers in her hair. Her sparkly shoes, which she left at the front door, were the fanciest things I'd ever laid eyes on. "Cute as a button, Ella," she said as she bent to kiss me.

I blushed. No one ever told me I was cute. They usually told me to eat more.

By the time Jean dragged Mama out of the house, I was ready for them to leave. So much fretting over how they looked. I'd never seen Mama act this way.

It had to do with the soldiers, Parker especially.

Chapter Twenty-Seven

VIOLET

FROM THE MOMENT THEY WALKED UP, VIOLET wished she hadn't come. People were dressed to the nines, and spilled in all directions from the red-and-white schoolhouse. Right in front of them, a couple was necking against a post, oblivious to all passersby. The music could be heard from across town, and her teeth chattered from the cold. Waimea could get downright chilly, being at a higher elevation than Honoka'a.

At the top of the steps, she spun around. "I have to go back to the car and get my sweater."

Jean gripped her shoulder and delivered a menacing look. "Don't think you're going to hide out in the car all night, miss 'I'm too old for this.'"

"Back in a jiffy." Violet tore herself away.

Too bad hiding in the car was out of the question. There was also a side of her that looked forward to dancing. All that practice bopping around the living room with Jean would not go to waste. With sweater in hand, she returned. Jean and Irene were nowhere to be found.

You can do this. She stepped tentatively inside the room. Women lined one side, and men, the other. In the middle, couples danced away. The all-military band was playing Bing Crosby. In the dim light, Violet felt less self-conscious. She scanned the crowd. Across the room, one head stood out above the others. She navigated through bodies to reach him.

"Zach!"

Then she saw Irene and Jean and Tommy. But no Parker. Which probably meant one thing. He was dancing. With a woman.

Tommy wasted no time in pulling all three of them out on the dance floor. Violet felt stiff-hipped at first, but the crowd was dense enough that no one would notice. Pretty soon, Zach joined in. "Watch out—he's a shin cracker," Jean said, her voice nearly lost in the music. Irene didn't seem to mind, and before long, the two were on their own. Tommy had taken to twirling and dipping Jean, letting her hair fall back to the floor.

Nothing worse than feeling like a fifth wheel.

By the time Violet concluded that signing on as a chaperone would have been a better idea, she spied Parker. He was dancing with two women, one of them hula-hand girl from the beach, the other a tall blonde in a strappy red dress. Violet abruptly turned her back to them. Of course, he would be dancing with girls. All the same, her stomach flipped and flopped. Her mouth went dry.

"I'm going to get some fresh air," she yelled into Jean's ear.

Elbowing her way through the crowd, she finally arrived outside. Sweat froze on her arms. With any luck, there would be a beach blanket in the trunk of the car. A hand gripped her arm just as she reached the bottom step. She thought it was Jean, come to drag her back.

"Let me go!" she said.

The hand released.

It was Parker. "Are you all right?" he said.

She swallowed hard. "Oh, I thought you were Jean. Yes, perfectly fine."

"Where are you going?"

Trying to get away from you. She opted for a sliver of truth. "I enjoy being outside at night. Plus, that room was feeling stuffy with all those bodies crammed together."

"Agreed." He looked past her at the jeep parked alongside the road. "I have an idea."

"No, thanks."

The sooner she got to the car, the better.

"Please?"

It crossed her mind that Parker might be arrogant, but he was also human. Maybe he just wanted what everyone wanted. A healthy slice of love and companionship. Hard to fault someone for that.

She crossed her arms over her chest. "Tell me, first."

"You wouldn't do very well in the military." He pressed his hand to her lower back. "I'm going to need you to trust me."

She looked up, as if an answer might appear in the sky. The moonless night was spattered in stars, so much so that you could see trails of dust from one horizon to the other. *Why not?* "Fine."

Parker seemed caught off guard that she agreed and escorted her to the jeep. Along the way, he looked around nervously. Everyone was too huddled in groups, smoking cigarettes and caught up in their own worlds. Was he that embarrassed to be seen with her? What if he didn't want hula hands to see them leaving together?

They roared down the road, her hair standing up in all twelve directions. At least it was dark. Less than a minute later, he turned the jeep up a steep hill and pulled over at the top.

Parker gestured to the barely visible outline of a grassy cinder cone known affectionately as Buster Brown. "Seems like half my life has been spent running up and down this damn *pu'u*. But I've sort of formed a love-hate relationship with it."

A faint breeze moved in the window. "Going up that thing with a heavy pack would kill me," she said.

"You're telling me. A *paniolo* by the name of Teixeira told me that the Hawaiians called it Hoku'ula, which means 'red star.' That got me thinking and I sneaked up here one night. Just me and the stars as far as the eye could see. Now I can't stay away." He opened the door. "Come on."

"Up there?"

The alarm in her voice must have registered, because he laughed. "Don't worry. There's a clear spot right over here."

Parker grabbed her hand and led her into the pasture and away from a stand of juniper trees, whose tangy scent soaked the air. Unable to concentrate on anything but the sound of his breath and the warmth of his hand, Violet followed along blindly. The possibility of being kissed simultaneously plagued and thrilled her.

When he stopped abruptly, her chin hit his shoulder. "Ouch!"

In the dark, he felt for her face and rubbed lightly, his fingers rough against her skin. Violet had the desire to bolt. But instead, she shifted position so she was farther away from Parker. The entire western sky spread out before them, falling into the straight line of the sea.

"You ever notice how trustworthy stars are?" he asked.

"How do you mean?"

"Just that you can count on them being up there wherever you go. I could be sitting on the old log back at a campfire in California, or at the top of a mountain on Island X, and there they are."

She gave his thought space to settle, and wondered about this mysterious island the marines always spoke about. A stepping-stone in the Pacific. One probably full of gun-wielding men who had a single-minded hatred of the Americans. If nothing else, at least she knew these marines were training their *okole*s off.

"Do you know which star is the red star?" she asked.

"No, but I want to find out before we leave." His voice dropped off. "Which is going to be sooner than I thought."

"What do you mean?"

"December 25."

"Christmas? You're leaving on Christmas?" The words came out fractured.

Parker nodded. "Orders came down this morning that from Christmas on, we need to be ready at a moment's notice."

"But that's less than three weeks away." Violet could feel the blood rushing to her ears. She twisted her hair in her fingers. What kind of lunatic decided to ship out on Christmas?

"We need to keep pushing forward," he said. "They haven't said where we're going, but I have my ideas. It's not going to be pretty. You saw the first round of marines after Tarawa. I have a feeling this is going to be worse."

Send someone else, not our men, she pleaded silently. "Don't say that."

"Pretend I never mentioned it. We should get the jeep back before anyone notices it's missing. But I wanted to introduce you to my spot." He cleared his throat. "I also have a favor to ask of you."

"Wait—that's not your jeep?"

He draped his arm around her shoulders, steering her back toward the vehicle. "Technically, it belongs to the military. But Captain Riggs drove it tonight."

"Jeez, you fellas are too much."

Only last weekend, Zach had been raving on about how he and Parker had been on liberty in Hilo, stupid on beer, and needed a ride back to camp. They came upon an army command car and decided they would *borrow* it. They roared up the saddle road, only to run into a guard shack just out of town. Zach slammed on the Reverse madly, while the sentry was yelling, *"Halt!"* They made it back down the mountain with a few rounds shot over their heads, and parked the car a block from where they'd found it.

"What are they going to do to me?"

He had a point.

"So, what's the favor?" she asked.

"I need an accomplice tomorrow for a covert mission."

Violet laughed. "Come on. You can't be serious."

"I am."

"You have plenty of men to choose from, then."

"None of them can know. Plus, I want you, Violet."

Air-raid sirens went off in her head. She held on to the air in her lungs while thinking of an answer. Alone with Parker was a dangerous place to be. Where would they go? What would Jean say?

She thought about Herman.

"This isn't a date, is it?"

While a date was off-limits, a mission was perfectly acceptable.

"No, ma'am."

Chapter Twenty-Eight

ELLA

PARKER EXCHANGED ZACH AND ROSCOE FOR Mama this morning. There was no way I was going to tell her this, but I was thrilled. It was a pretty even exchange. All I could think about was wiggling a stick for him and running through the tall grass behind our house. I wanted to take him into town and show him off. Roscoe walked straight over and rubbed against my hip and sniffed my kneecaps. He was getting bigger by the hour, and stronger. If you've ever seen a movie in slow motion, that was kind of how he moved. Unless he was pouncing. You could also see that his leopard spots were disappearing, making him look more lionish. Parker said when he got to be full grown, his mane would fill in.

Even though milk was scarce, most of it going to the soldiers at camp who need it more than we do, Jean let me fill a small bowl for Roscoe. There was still cream on top, and when Roscoe was done, his muzzle stayed white.

When Jean and Zach get together, they talk a lot. Both

of them were sitting in the living room, listening to Christmas songs on the radio, babbling away. I entertained Roscoe as best I could, but he finally stretched out on the floor and yawned. Jean said we could let him in.

"Can we take him into town?" I asked.

"Sweetie, Zach and I are taking a walk down memory lane. We only have another two weeks until they leave and I want to soak him in. How about we go after lunch?"

Mama hadn't mentioned this and I wondered why. Probably because she didn't want me to worry. *"It's not your job to worry, Ella. It's mine."* "Two weeks?"

"They're on standby to leave."

"What about Roscoe?"

There I went again, more concerned about the animals than anything else. It was what the nurse Mrs. Baker calls a weakness. She says we all have them.

"Roscoe is staying," Zach said.

A ship was obviously no place for a lion. And neither was a battlefield. "Good, because the Japanese might end up eating him if they caught him."

Zach's face turned sour and I think he knew what I meant. "We wouldn't want that."

The kids at school liked to talk. And since I know how to listen without being noticed, I've heard a lot of stories. These are not the kind of stories that Mrs. Hicks reads us in class. And I don't even know if I should be mentioning this. But the Japanese in Japan eat Americans. How scary is that? Some people say it's because they're hungry and just trying to stay alive, others because they're evil. None of the Japanese I know are evil, but who knows.

The other thing I hear is that they are spraying germs all over everyone. Germs that make you bleed from your nose and choke to death. It's called the plague, like the one we have here from the rats, and a few other names I can't pronounce. That's why they drill us so often. So we stay germ-free.

I try not to think about it.

I wanted to stay out of Jean and Zach's business, so I decided I would make lunch for all of us. That way, we could get to town sooner. Midway through spreading mayonnaise on the bread, I heard a clucking at the door and a loud feather flapping, then a *bang*. I almost jumped out of my skin, remembering that Brownie was out. If we don't put her in the cage, she always shows up on the lanai for lunch.

"Roscoe, no!" Zach was already at the door, which now had a big rip in the screen. Brownie looked down from the rafters, huddled and ca-cacking.

I was frantic. "Did he hurt her?"

"Good thing she can still fly, or we'd be eating barbecue chicken for dinner," Zach said.

My frown said it all.

"Zach, that's a terrible thing to say. Ella, Brownie just had a scare," Jean said.

"Sorry, and I'll fix that screen for you right away," he said.

I didn't blame Roscoe, though, since he was a lion and that's what cats do. Eat birds. If they can. And I started to wonder about how weird and sad the world is. Why do animals have to kill other animals? Why do people have to kill other people? Mama says people who kill are broken, and I believe that. At least the animals use each other for eating.

After we put Brownie away, I finished assembling lunch. Mama's apron was just asking to be worn, so I put that on, and stacked the bread high with sliced ham, cold pickles, tomato, lettuce and onion. Zach was so skinny, I pictured him turning into a skeleton out in the jungle. Maybe this would help.

I marched out with their plates and set them on the coffee table, like a real waitress at a diner.

"Ella, are you wearing lipstick?" Jean asked.

I could feel my face heating up. Smoothing down my apron, I backed away and then turned and ran into the kitchen. My cheeks ached like someone had put one of those fireplace puffers in my mouth and started squeezing. Why had I thought they might not notice? Why did I care?

"Come back out here, Ella. We don't bite," Jean said.

I wanted to but my feet stuck to the linoleum. A moment later Jean walked in. She bent down and looked me in the eyes. "I used to play dress-up, too. All girls do. It's nothing to be ashamed of. In fact, it's the most natural thing in the world."

I swallowed hard and nodded at her.

Something about the soldiers made me want to be older. To have them notice me like they noticed Mama and Jean. It was the first time in a long time I had wanted to be seen, and I got to thinking. Life was trying its hardest to return back to normal. Still, there was a fatherless pit deep inside my stomach. Maybe that was the point. So I wouldn't forget him. Ever.

Mainly, though, I wondered how I could live the rest of my life knowing what I know.

Chapter Twenty-Nine

VIOLET

LOOKING A THOUSAND FEET DOWN TO THE VALley floor, Violet felt dizzy. Someone was once crazy enough to carve a road into the impossible cliffs of Waipio, and this was her first ride down in a car. Riding mules posed problems, too. Namely, not being able to walk for days afterward. But at least she hadn't had to worry about the brakes going out.

"It might have been better to blindfold me," she said.

"And have you miss this view? No way."

Parker had been tight-lipped about his mission. Only that they would be driving into the valley. Which turned her insides to one big mass of jelly. She hated heights almost as much as she hated war. Parker climbed out to fiddle with the wheels. After changing the jeep into four-wheel drive, he jumped back in. "Get ready for the most beautiful ride of your life. If you can stomach it."

In fact, her stomach climbed into her throat as they descended. Parker glanced over at her.

"Keep your eyes on the road, for heaven's sake," she insisted.

"You planning on taking that door handle with you?" he said.

Violet realized she had it in a vise grip.

In the lowest of low gears, the jeep hacked and coughed down the hill. "The face can't lie," he yelled.

"I'm prepared to jump if I have to."

In the end, she almost forgot about her apprehension and found herself grinning madly. A black-sand beach spanned the entire mouth, meeting with a gray and forbidding sea. Skies of the same color cast everything in a silver glow. In the middle of it all, a wide river split the valley. Rather than turning toward the beach, he veered upstream.

"Are you planning on telling me what we're doing yet?"

He pulled the jeep alongside the riverbank and killed the engine. "We have two missions today. One is to fetch a load of that Hawaiian firewater for the boys. And don't ask me to pronounce the name."

"Okolehao."

He nodded. "Since news of our departure circulated, tensions are high. I figured a little speakeasy in the camp might boost morale."

Waimea was a dry town, which was why the soldiers all swarmed to Honoka'a, Hawi and Hilo on their off days.

"They'll let you do that?"

He looked away, toward the slow-moving water and a hunched gray heron on the far side. "I'm not asking."

Violet only knew of one man who sold *okolehao* in the valley. "Wait—don't tell me we're going to Bernard Lalamilo's place."

"That's the one."

A lump formed in her throat. "That may not be a good idea."

"Why not?"

"For one, I'm told he hates *haole* people. And second, his name came up in regards to Herman."

Parker looked concerned. "You mean as a suspect?"

She nodded. "A man I spoke to at the plantation said he always carries a gun and is happy to shoot at anyone who happens by. If you catch him on the wrong day, you could end up facedown in the river behind his house. For some reason, he thought Herman had been down there that day."

"But he was never arrested?"

"Souza talked to him, but there was no evidence and no real motive and no witnesses. And the man swore that he liked Herman. So it dead-ended."

"Well, I trust the guy who sent me down here. Says the old man is more bark than bite."

Violet didn't feel good about meeting this Lalamilo character and was about to suggest they turn around when Parker added, "My other reason for coming is purely selfish. I want to see that double waterfall in the back of the valley before we leave. Don't ask me how to say the name, either."

She tried not to think. But, of course, that only increased the speed of her thoughts. That slow way that he drew out his words. The shade of his burnished skin. Eyes the same gray as the sky. In the end, she decided to give him this day.

"You're not selfish. You're honest."

They skirted the bottom of the cliff on the merest outline of a road. As they continued back, they crossed several shallow streams. There were no bridges. Parker drove with conviction, seemingly sure of where he was going. Violet kept her mouth shut and enjoyed the scenery. Moisture clung to every available surface—mossy trunks of kukui nut trees, undersides of the ti leaves, and lava rock. A place that swallowed houses and cars. The only people they saw were hunched over in the taro fields, knee-deep in water. Everyone waved.

At the next junction, instead of crossing, Parker turned into the stream and continued driving.

"Say, generally we drive on roads, not streams," she said.

"This is really a road disguised as a stream," he said.

Now that he mentioned it, Herman had said something of the same sort after fetching a batch of *okolehao* years back. The lengths that men would go to for a little alcohol. Or, in this case, salvation.

When they pulled out of the stream road and onto a grassy patch, an old shack appeared off to the side. With a rusted tin roof and vines crawling through the cracked windows, it looked uninhabited. On closer inspection, Violet spotted boots at the front door, a stalk of bananas hanging from the eaves and a fat pig tied to a tree. Clouds of mosquitoes swarmed around her head as soon as they stepped out. A distinctly rotten smell filled the air.

"Hello?" Parker called.

Only the pig answered, with a grunt. They poked around and waited for Bernard to appear, but he didn't come.

"We can talk to Lalamilo after the falls. I guess we leave the jeep here and hope it's in once piece when we get back. You going to wear that?" Parker looked her up and down.

She had on a casual beach dress. "If someone had told me what we'd be doing, I might have dressed differently. I have my swimsuit underneath."

He smiled. "Tell you what. I brought an extra set of utilities, small ones, so you don't have to soil your dress."

She wouldn't be caught dead in marine utilities and would suffer mud and mosquitoes if she must. It was an old dress, anyway. "I'm fine."

"Suit yourself."

It turned out the going was easier barefoot, and they followed a leaf-padded pathway. Every so often they had to rock-hop across the stream. Picking the right boulder proved harder than it looked, and more than once, Parker had to hold her up. His arm span was as nearly as wide as the water.

About twenty minutes in, they reached a pool with steep walls on both sides. "We swim across this one," he said.

"And then what?"

"I guess we scale up the other side."

She dipped a toe in. The water sent a chill across her skin. Once wet, it would be hard to warm up. She looked toward the thin slice of sky, hoping for any sign of blue, but none showed. In the midst of a conference with herself on whether to say something, Parker began stripping down. His body was leaner than last time she'd seen him shirtless. With his backpack balanced on his head, he swam across. Violet followed, keeping her feet close to the surface in order to avoid the pinchers of prawns or crayfish or whatever else might be hiding in the murk.

"Have you heard the legend of these falls?" he asked, once on the other side.

For some reason, his question gave her the jitters. "No."

"They tell me it was named for a young woman who vowed to never be separated from her lover, so she turned herself into a waterfall, and he ended up becoming the boulder that sits at the bottom."

"I suppose it helps to be part God when you can't have what you want. Anyway, where did you hear this?" Violet said.

"We have a local boy in our camp, the guy who told me about the *okolehao*. He's a wealth of insider information," he said.

At the far side, he pulled her from the water and they continued on. The contours of his muscled back made for good scenery. Then from nowhere, tears sprang up. What kind of an impossible situation had she gotten herself into? Wedged somewhere between a promise to Herman and the impossible hope that he might still be alive, and her own yearning. If only she could turn Parker into a boulder for the time being, maybe life would solve itself.

The farther they went, the narrower the valley. Twittering birds, bamboo and the echo of their voices bounced from wall to wall. As they drew close to the waterfall, its roar drowned out all sound.

They both stood with necks craned.

Parker whistled. "Would you get a load of that?"

The immensity threatened to crack her wide open. "Makes you feel small."

One stray sunbeam lit up the face of the falling water for a moment, and then disappeared. The pond was at least a stone's throw across, turquoise in the middle and deep green closer to the sides. Mossy vertical cliffs closed in around them, blocking out most of the sky.

"Humbling, isn't it? If you ask me, man is a little too self-important for his own good. Look how the spray has carved the rock out behind the waterfall. Now, that takes patience," Parker said.

"I can see why they made a legend about it."

Even standing on the boulders at the far end, a fine spray misted them. Parker found a flat rock and laid out a moth-eaten towel. He looked almost ashamed. "Sorry, it was all I could find."

He offered her a canteen while he searched through his backpack for their lunch. He'd offered to bring slop from the mess hall, but she insisted on packing a picnic. On such short notice, she'd resorted to Spam sandwiches, leftover red potato salad and chocolate honeycomb pie. Parker had not come empty-handed, and pulled out boiled peanuts and a bag of broken Saloon Pilot crackers.

Just as Violet was about to take her first bite, a foot-long red centipede crawled up the rock and over her foot. She shot into the air, causing Parker to yell and fall back. It took all her might to cling to her sandwich. After her heartbeat returned to normal, they looked at each other and burst out laughing so hard her face hurt.

"I'd rather face the whole Japanese army than one of those," he said.

"You and me both."

Parker swallowed his first sandwich in the same time she'd finished one bite. Fortunately, she'd made him two. They ate in an easy silence. Maybe it was the waterfall and the smell of wet leaves, or the undeniable closeness of the sky. The valley was weaving a spell.

"Can I ask you something?" he finally said.

"Anything."

"If things had been different—your husband, the war—would I have stood a chance?" His voice and face looked a new kind of vulnerable.

"Oh, Parker, do you really need to ask?"

"I hadn't planned to, but all of a sudden, everything has a new urgency. And sitting with you in a place like heaven, it's taking every ounce of willpower not to reach over and kiss you."

Yes. The answer was there on her tongue's tip.

Rain began to fall at the same time the willpower he'd just spoken of ran dry. He leaned forward slowly. First he touched his nose to hers with eyes open. Then he kissed her. In spite of herself, she kissed back. His mouth was hot, his breath tangy. Right away, her lips burned. His hand touched her neck and ran down her back, leaving patches of heat on her skin. Eventually he pulled back.

"Damn," he said, wiping his mouth.

"Maybe this isn't a good idea." Not that she really wanted to stop, but a panicky flutter had started up in her chest.

By now, they were both half drenched in rain. Violet was drunk from the heady combination of water and clouds and Parker.

"You're right. That was the worst kiss of my life." A stupid grin spread over his face.

She laughed. "Is that so?"

Without answering, he moved in fast. While the first kiss had been tender, this was desire and need and hunger all wrapped up in one. He pressed into her hip and ran a finger along her jaw. So this was how it felt to want something so urgently that you knew you shouldn't have. Or couldn't have.

By now, the rain wheelbarrowed down. A layer of black stood out behind the white puffy clouds.

"We better get out of here," he said.

Violet had lived in Hawaii long enough to know about flash floods. He was right. They scooped the towel and food into the backpack. Everything weighed twice as much.

When they stood, he cupped her chin. "I apologize for my behavior. I'll try to keep a handle on myself from now on. Let's go!"

She had no time to answer.

Stones they crossed on earlier were now submerged and the stream picked up speed. At each bend, there were fewer and fewer rocks to cross. The first clap of thunder split the sky when they reached the swimming pond. Even with the waterline two feet higher, they had no choice but to plunge in.

Parker yelled through the downpour. "I think from here

on out we hang to the left and try to stay on higher ground. No more stream crossing."

She liked his thinking. "You lead."

They scaled a steep bank, pulling themselves up with ti stalks. There was no trail and the mud squished through her toes like pudding. Every so often a flash of lightning lit the dark underside of the forest. Violet counted the seconds until the thunder. Even with her hands over her ears, it deafened.

Unlike Herman, Parker seemed to have a good sense of direction. In fact, this situation was probably nothing to him, with all that time spent training in these very conditions. He turned every so often to offer a hand. Below, the stream roared.

Despite all of this, Violet could only think of one thing. *The kiss.*

Chapter Thirty

VIOLET

WHEN THEY FINALLY REACHED BERNARD Lalamilo's house, their real reason for being there in the first place, nothing looked the same. Their stream road was now a roiling mass of water and the yard had shrunk to half the size. A light shone in the window. The old man was home. Only when Parker tore off ahead did she notice the jeep stood up to the grille in water.

"Shithouse!" he yelled as he jumped in. He turned on the engine and pumped the gas pedal but it sputtered and died. Again and again.

Violet watched, feeling saturated. She was about to ask if she should go to the door when a shot rang out. Without thinking, she dived behind the nearest banana tree, biting her lip in the process.

"Who goes there?" a deep voice called out.

Daring to look out between two fat stalks, she saw a dark

old Hawaiian man standing next to the house with a shotgun leveled at the jeep.

Parker raised his hands. "Don't shoot! Gizmo Santos sent us. From Camp Tarawa."

After an interminable pause, the man spoke. "I usually shoot uninvited guests."

"He said he would warn you we were coming," Parker said, looking around and probably wondering where she was.

"Nope."

A chill blew across her skin and Violet climbed out from her hiding place. She had nothing to lose. She ducked under his roof. "Mr. Lalamilo, it's Violet Iverson. I believe you knew my husband, Herman."

The man stared right through her and for a moment she wondered if he was deciding to shoot her. Then something like recognition lit his watery eyes. "Herman Iverson. One of the only *haole* I ever liked." Violet frowned, causing him to chuckle. "Men, I mean. Women are different. Any kine is good for me."

Her heart was pounding in her teeth, but she tried to smile. He gave her a cockeyed look that might have been his own version of a smile. She wasn't sure.

The engine turned over again without success.

Bernard shook his head and yelled, "Boy! Your jeep isn't going anywhere. Even if it was, the river's too high to cross. Come inside."

Parker hung his head out the window. "But we're soaking."

Bernard disappeared inside and returned with a towel, holding it up for Violet. "Here."

It didn't matter who was offering. A dry towel was a welcome sight. She patted off as best she could and hoped by some miracle their spare clothes were dry. Her hair was wringing wet and full of grass, and mud streaked the towel, which she hung on the door handle for Parker. Why was it always something with him? *Wana*, angry bulls, stolen vehicles and now this.

Bernard motioned them in. Two lanterns hung from the ceiling, adding warmth to the drab walls. A *lauhala* mat covered the entire floor and the room contained exactly one *pune'e* against the back wall, one table and two chairs. Bernard had also amassed an impressive assortment of glass fishing floats, which were piled in the corner. Some looked too big to wrap her arms around. Violet did a double take. There, lying on a mess of blankets, was the pig.

"Oh, look who it is," Violet said in surprise.

Bernard nodded toward the pig. "Akala. She doesn't like the rain."

The animal rubbed her nose around on the old blanket, grunting at the sound of her name.

Violet laughed. "You've chosen the wrong place to live, then, haven't you?" she said to the pig.

Bernard grumbled, "Smart, that one. She knew a good thing when she saw it."

Parker tapped his knuckles on the door as he pushed it in. "Sergeant Parker Stone, Marine Fifth Division, sir." He held out his hand. "I apologize for the intrusion. I was under the impression you'd gotten word."

The old man paused as if deciding whether to shake. "Lalamilo," he finally said.

Violet sized up the two men, who were about as different as a cat and a dog. Parker paled next to Bernard, whose umber skin looked like tanned leather. The top of his head barely reached Parker's chin, and there was a gap where two of his teeth should have been. In her estimation, he was ten years past handsome, with thinning hair and loose skin.

"Any suggestions for getting the jeep out of here?" Parker asked.

"Tomorrow. By morning, no problem."

"Morning?" Violet said.

It was probably the moisture making it hard to breathe. But staying here overnight was out of the question. Ella needed her home and Violet felt heavy with the weight of her daughter's fear mingled with her own apprehension. The man might be a murderer. And he had a pig in his house, for heaven's sake. Surely they could find a way out.

Bernard waved toward the window. His palms were pink. "We got five waterfalls in this valley. They all empty into this river. So until the water drops, you stay."

On cue, the rain started up again, sounding like horses galloping across the tin roof. Violet could make out swirls of rain as they pounded the window.

"At least our clothes are still dry," Parker said, holding up the bag.

"You don't understand. I have to get home. Ella worries and has nightmares."

"Zach knows my plan, and at least we know she's in good hands."

Trapped was how she felt. Coming here had been a mistake. She knew that now. "Where are we going to stay?" They both looked at Bernard.

He shrugged. "I have a bed in my shop."

"So there's no chance the water will drop before dark?" she asked.

"Zero."

Parker groaned. "Let's just hope the jeep starts up tomorrow or I'm going to have some explaining to do."

After changing into dry clothes, Violet felt mildly improved. She had broken down and accepted Parker's extra utilities, even though they were loose where they should have been tight, and tight where they should have been loose. Thankfully, there was a small mirror in the bathroom that worked if she stood on her tippy toes. The bottom half had tarnished with age. Her hair was a mass of tangled weeds, which she brushed with her fingers. She dabbed a smudge of color on her lips, while at the same time wondering why she bothered.

In the living room, both men sat at the table facing each other. Parker had changed into dry pants and a T-shirt, but the sheen on his face remained. Bernard stood up and offered Violet a chair. She sat.

"I was hoping to bring back some of your *okolehao.* It would do a world of good for my boys," Parker said, butchering the word in the process.

"*Auwe*, boy. I have one rule. You need to be able to say the word before I sell you any."

Parker turned to Violet for help. She enunciated each syllable for him. *"Oh-koh-lay-how."* He imitated her several times, until the word flowed out smoothly. He sounded like a real local.

"Better," Bernard said.

"Not supposed to have it at camp, but hell, we're shipping out at Christmas."

The old man scratched the white stubble on his chin. "I got a batch of something wicked. Brewed from red ti roots. I can spare ten pints, but it won't be cheap."

One sip of his special spirit would probably render her a bumbling fool. But maybe that was the point. Erase your worries, if only for the time being.

"Can we sample some?" Parker asked.

Bernard led them to a shack out back—this one even more dilapidated than the house. Violet had to look twice to make sure a banana tree really was sprouting through the window. Inside, oak barrels and iron pots and bottles lined the walls in neat rows. It reminded her of a science laboratory.

Akala trailed behind them. "Damn pig loves this stuff," Bernard said.

"The liquor?"

He nodded. "Got to keep a close eye on her. Found her once belly up and snoring in the middle of the floor. Turned out she'd gotten into one of the pots."

Akala sniffed around the floor, eventually tickling Violet's feet. "Ella would love her."

"Be my guest," Bernard said.

He wasn't fooling anyone. Violet could tell by the way he looked at the pig that he was well attached.

"What does *okolehao* mean, anyhow?" Parker wanted to know.

Bernard coughed and looked at the floor. "'Iron bottom.' It came from how the pots look like a plump woman's backside."

He launched into a description of how you had to wait for the ti plant to mature so that the stalk was at least the size of a man's wrist. Then you knew the root would be big enough, sometimes weighing as much as a small dog. After that, you baked them in an *imu*—where the magic took place. Distilling came next.

"Don't ask me to tell you my secrets," he said.

"What is it about the ti?" Parker asked.

"Ti root turns to sugar easily. You ask me, anything else is crap."

"When can we try it?"

"Dinner."

Darkness came early, along with the mosquitoes. Violet was ravenous from the hiking and so much nervous energy expended. Between her and Parker, all they had left was an apple and a bag of soggy crackers. Fortunately, Bernard had speared a papio that morning and planned to cook up rice, taro and watercress. All from his compound.

Violet offered to help, but he motioned her away, grunting the same as his pig.

Instead, she sat wringing her fingers and thinking about Ella. Parker went out to check on the water level of the stream. It was then that a ringing noise came from the cupboard, startling her upright.

"What the dickens was that?" she asked.

Bernard opened the wooden doors, pulled out a shiny black telephone and set it on the countertop. "Lalamilo," he answered.

He cast a glance at Violet and she heard a man's excited voice on the other end.

"Right in front of me," Bernard said.

Why was it so unthinkable he would have a phone? After all, Waipio Valley was home to several churches and hundreds of people. No doubt they'd run a line down. But she hadn't seen one in his house and assumed a man like Bernard would not own one.

He handed her the phone. "For you."

"Violet? It's Zach. Are you folks all right? Everyone here's been flipping their wigs."

She had to hold the phone away from her ear. "I can hear you loud and clear, Zach. We're fine. Until this very moment, I had no idea there was a phone in this house. The river flooded and the jeep is stuck. Mr. Lalamilo here has been kind enough to offer food and shelter for the night."

When Parker walked in, his look of surprise caused her to smile.

"Zach," she mouthed. "How's Ella?"

"Well, I don't want to offend you, but with Roscoe here, it wasn't until almost dark that your name even came up. Since then, she's been anxious. But we tracked down Irene, who helped us get ahold of Lalamilo's number. Took a little work, but here you are."

Violet wanted to kiss him for being so dogged. "Can you put her on?"

"Hi, Mama."

"Sweetie, I'm sorry to put you through this."

"When are you coming back?"

"We have to spend the night because we can't cross the river. But I promise we'll be back as soon as possible tomorrow. Main thing is we're safe and there's nothing to worry about."

Ella's voice sounded strained. "Are there any bad people down there?"

"No bad people. Just Parker, Mr. Lalamilo and a pig named Akala that you would adore."

She looked over and saw that Akala had burrowed under the blanket and was now invisible.

"Can Uncle Zach and Roscoe sleep over?"

"Of course they can, as long as Zach doesn't have to be back, honey."

This seemed to mollify Ella and she started on about how she spent the whole day with Roscoe. How they walked him into town to the soda fountain. And how half the people were terrified and the other half were dying to pet him. "He loves vanilla ice cream, too," Ella said.

"I'm proud of you."

"Uncle Zach wants to talk to Parker. But one more thing," Ella said. "Can Roscoe sleep in my bed? Actually, your bed, since it's bigger."

Violet had to smile. "How about on the floor?"

"Why not the bed?"

"Ella, most kids would just be happy to even see a lion. You don't need one in your bed."

Ella sighed. "I love you."

"Love you, too, sweetie."

A lion in her bed—that would be a first. She handed the receiver to Parker and felt fifty pounds lighter.

Bernard shuffled around the kitchen mumbling to himself. Every now and then he barked a peculiar question at one of them. "Do you believe in ghosts?" "Ever been to Louisiana?" "What do you think of Lana Turner?" "What's it like to fly?" He refused all attempts at help. "I have a system," he said.

Violet couldn't quite determine if he appreciated their company or was annoyed at the intrusion. Every now and then, she caught Parker watching her. He made no move to hide it, either, which raised a flush on the back of her neck. But now that Ella knew they were safe, nothing else bothered her. She would eat frogs from the mud outside if she had to, and sleep with the moonshine-drinking pig.

When dinner was ready, Bernard dragged in a barrel from the back lanai and used that as an extra chair. The fish flaked apart on its own accord and he had pounded a strange brand of white taro sweeter than the purplish-gray root she was used to. By the time she tried the watercress, she was drooling.

"How did you make this?" she asked.

"Lightly steamed and sprinkled in sea salt," he said, matter-of-factly.

A murky bottle stood in the middle of the table. If she didn't know better, she'd have thought he was bottling river water. Bernard twisted off the cap and poured two jarfuls. When he began to pour a third, she held her hand out. "None for me, thanks."

The one and only time she'd drunk *okolehao*, Herman had to carry her home from the bar. The next morning, she felt like she'd split her head open on a rock.

He poured anyway and raised his jar. "May the worst never happen."

Parker winked when their eyes met. "I'm all for that," he said.

Not wanting to offend the old man—since who really knew what he was capable of?—she first held the jar to her nose. It reeked of earth and roots and fermented fruit, possibly banana. She took a sip. All at once, her mouth caught fire and her eyes teared up. Fearing her throat had been badly injured, she followed it with sweet potato.

Bernard emptied his jar and slammed it down. "Puts more hair on your chest, every bottle."

"Just what I need," Violet said.

Parker managed a big gulp, and he looked panic-stricken when he swallowed. "This'll do."

She hated to imagine what the old man's insides looked like.

"Speaking of ghosts, there are two that live in the house. Just so you know," Bernard said.

Have we been speaking of ghosts? She gave Parker a questioning glance.

"Oh? Are they friendly ghosts?" she said.

"Plenty friendly. But they like to move stuff around and cause mischief now and then. Knock things over, open doors, that kind of stuff."

Violet thought it sounded more like a forgetful mind and wind blowing through open windows, but she kept her mouth shut.

"They have names?" Parker asked.

Her blood stopped, suddenly terrified he might say one was named *Herman*.

"Thelma and Birtha."

Something nudged her hand and she jumped a foot off the chair. But it was only Akala. A huge breath of relief. The old man must have been serious about his pig liking the *okolehao*, because she went from person to person, sniffing out hands and legs.

"*Akala*, go!" Bernard yelled, his eyes ablaze.

The pig ignored him, instead lying at the foot of Violet's chair and breathing on her toes. Parker was trying his darnedest not to laugh. Bernard shoveled food in his mouth, and from the clicking that accompanied each chew, it sounded like several of his teeth might be coming out with the meal. In between bites, he wanted to hear about the war and where Parker was off to. About artillery and airplanes.

As dinner progressed, he grew harder to understand, running his words together like *youasmewegonnablowemtasmithereens*. He was on his third jar when he said, "You two together?"

His unfocused eyes passed over Violet. The tiny house fell silent.

Parker was the one who answered. "No beating around the bush here, is there?"

"Parker is a good friend," Violet said.

Bernard continued to stare at Parker. A vein bulged in his temple. "What kind of fool are you, boy?"

"It's complicated, sir. Maybe someday?"

Violet opened her mouth to say something, then closed it again. Even with just one sip of the *okolehao*, her thoughts had blurred.

Bernard blew like an angry horse. "Nonsense. There is no someday. You live like that, you die alone, wondering what you were waiting for."

It took an act of forced concentration to sift through his speech, and Parker glanced over at her with eyebrows raised. A heaviness draped everyone in the room. The old man seemed to be just beginning.

"I spent my whole life in this valley, watching women come and go. Always knowing another would show up. I always found reasons to let them go. One wanted me to pick up and move, one didn't approve of my drinking, one hated the rain. I should have done whatever I had to keep even one of them. Don't squander your chance to live. You hear me?" By the time he stopped, he was panting.

He had a point.

Violet tasted fear—layers of it. From the ache of her own father heading out on the train that day, and the empty letters, stirring up hope every time; to the void of Herman and the hollow place in her chest.

"My husband disappeared, Mr. Lalamilo, and my daughter is only now recovering. But she's changed. There are some things beyond our control."

"How long it been?"

"A year."

Bernard sat back in his chair and stared at her. She could see his mind mulling over some big idea. For a hermit, he sure had plenty of opinions about the world. In fact, he reminded her of a Hawaiian version of her own grandfather, who always wanted to stuff her full of good advice. *"Why do you think they tell you to smell the roses? Because they're going to wilt and die. That's why."* The way of old people, she supposed.

"Speaking of Herman, I got a hunch where you might find him," he said.

Every drop of blood ceased to flow. Violet felt herself turning the color of Minnesota snow.

Chapter Thirty-One

VIOLET

VIOLET SLAMMED HER EYES SHUT. WITH HANDS that seemed to have a mind of their own, she clutched the jar of moonshine hard enough to crack it into pieces. To be sure, Bernard Lalamilo had been a man of contradictions, but these were about the last words she'd expected to spill from his mouth. Her most recent trip to see Sheriff Souza and the admiral had turned up plenty of nothing, as usual.

"I don't understand," she finally said.

Bernard fixed his eyes on her. "You have to swear not to tell."

"How can I promise if I have no idea what you're about to say?"

"Because the location of this cave is sacred to me. It's underwater."

In the search after his disappearance, men from town had searched the coast and scoured beaches and ravines without any sign. No one mentioned a cave. She was torn between wanting to believe and the truth of what they might find.

She stared back at the old man. "Wouldn't someone have noticed by now?" Unable to stop herself, she envisioned a body, or more accurately, a pile of bones. Her heart pounded against her ribs like it wanted out.

"Only one way to know," he said. "It depends on the tides. The swim is only makeable a few times a year. Even then, it's a couple-minute breath hold. Last January, so happened the surf was up on the full moon. Stayed that way for a few weeks."

"Who knows about this cave?" Parker asked.

"Just me an' Kawika, my nephew. My father showed me. His father showed him. It was a rite of passage to be taken in. Boy to man. Plenty tigers in the area, so nobody but us crazy enough to dive there." *Translation: tiger sharks.*

The possibility that Herman's body had washed into this cave was far-fetched, to put it mildly. But what if Bernard was right? "It seems unlikely. And wouldn't a body that washed in be gone by now?" she asked.

"Way the current moves it's almost a whirlpool. Debris collects on a high beach ledge. We go in for opihi, but it's also a boneyard. Cattle fallen from the cliff, driftwood swept in by storms, shipping ropes."

Lord God, why hasn't he mentioned this sooner?

"Can you show us where the cave is?" she asked.

"Because I liked the man, I will. But not 'til January, second night of the full moon."

"Last I checked, the full moon was the full moon," Parker said.

Bernard looked out the window. "*Akua*, *hoku* and *mahealani*. Three nights, all full."

Violet knew this only because Mr. Keko'olani had schooled her in the Hawaiian lunar month while explaining how his honeybees often swarmed during a full moon. By the next time a full one rolled around, Parker would be halfway across the ocean.

Bernard soon reached a state where conversation was impossible. One eye drooped shut and his mouth twitched to the side. Every so often, his head fell forward. Without warning, he stood up, pointed to the top shelf and mumbled, "Blankets." Then he burped and stumbled out the back door.

Akala lifted her head and watched him go. There was comfort to the pig's steady breath and Violet was glad to see her stay.

Parker pulled down the stack of blankets. "I can sleep on the floor, if you don't mind parting with a pillow," he said.

The bed was only a double. Curling up next to Ella was one thing, but sharing a bed with Parker was another matter entirely. Why, she was having a hard time erasing the kiss from her mind. Everything—pillows, blankets, sheets—smelled like mildew. Dampness and a proliferation of green.

Violet offered a weak smile. "Take them both." The floor was cold and hard and housed a pig.

He must have read her mind. "I'm used to it. I sleep in far worse conditions than this, regularly."

One of the blankets was wide enough to double up, and he spread that out on the bottom. She watched him lay the moth-eaten one on top and felt a stab of guilt for hogging the bed. Akala wasted no time in trotting over and rooting it with her wrinkled snout. "Hey, get out of here!" Parker cried.

"She just wants to snuggle."

"I don't suppose you want to switch places?"

"No, sir," she said.

Parker shook his head. There was that moon-sliver smile again. The one that sent her stomach lurching and stopped her lungs in their tracks. It crossed her mind that sleeping with Parker in the same room might prove problematic. She also wondered how she could be thinking such inappropriate thoughts. Perhaps time had been working behind the scenes, whittling down her edges like everyone said would happen. Violet bolstered up her willpower. For Herman, but also for her own heart.

After he blew out both lanterns, leaving only a glass candle burning on the table, he lay down. It was like being at camp, only your bunkmate was the man who scrambled up your thoughts and turned you half-crazy with longing.

Another round of thunder exploded around them and the sky flashed brilliant. Not two seconds later, Akala burrowed deeper into the blanket near Parker's feet. There was nothing for him to do but surrender.

"I feel sorry for the poor thing," she said.

"Me or the pig?"

"Both of you, actually."

She might not have the same affinity for animals as Ella, but that didn't mean she was heartless. She'd seen many a horse or dog lose their minds with fear during a storm. Something about a change in the atmosphere to stir everything up.

Parker rested his head in his hands and stared up at the ceiling. "So, what do you make of his story?"

"I don't know what to think, but I have to see for myself now."

"You think he had anything to do with it?" he said.

"My gut says no. What about you?"

"Same. I only wish I could help."

It grew quiet.

"The not knowing eats away at you. Finding out if he's dead or alive means everything to me," she said.

"I know it does."

The tenderness in his voice was too much to bear, unleashing a wall of tears. Gushing, drenching, clear-away-the-grief kind of tears. The best she could, Violet wiped her face on her sleeve. Her nose had turned on and didn't want to stop.

"Hey, sorry if I said something wrong," he said.

She shook her head and buried her face in the musty pillow. Words would have to wait. And then he was sitting next to her on the bed. His hand smoothed her kinked hair and rubbed her back. She hated to cry in front of people. For a year after her father left them, Violet's mother had cried to anyone that would listen, to the point where all the town avoided her—except Mr. Smudge.

Parker didn't say anything, just let her cry.

When her sucking breaths had slowed, and she thought she might be able to speak, she said, "I'm a mess."

"Who could blame you?"

Violet turned her face away from the wall so one eye looked up at him. "This is partly your fault," she said.

"My fault?"

"Because you're leaving us and who knows when you're coming back." The words tumbled out, and what was the point in stopping them, anyway? She burned for him in a way she never had for Herman. That was the simple truth.

Parker squinted down at her with a look that said she was crazy. "I'm not leaving *you*. Not by choice, anyway."

"Either way, you're gone. What would you do in my shoes?"

The faint smell of liquor still hung on his breath. She wanted to look away, but couldn't. "You really want to know?" he said.

It was difficult to answer with his mouth pressed hard against hers, like he was trying to breathe her in. Through his thin shirt, she felt his heart beating against her ribs. Warmth and hardness all wrapped together. Her arm was stuck, but she didn't stop to notice. "Violet..."

Finally, she pulled away, dazed by the force of his kiss. She shook her head and whispered, "I can't, Parker. I just can't."

She watched him back away and look at the floor, and in those seconds missed him. If that was possible. Her mother always said that when it came to love and death, no one was immune. Was that what was going on here? All she knew was that she was in big, moon-shaking trouble.

Say something. Put your lips back. Don't listen to me.

But he did listen. He slipped onto the floor and tucked himself into his makeshift bed without a word. She felt blindingly awful, like she was split down the middle and being pulled apart by both arms. All this feeling, and she couldn't accept it, not now, anyway.

After a few minutes, he said, "Try to get some rest."

If only she had earmuffs to blot out the silence.

Sometime later, Violet woke with a start. The candle had blown out, but a single star shone through the window. She inched to the edge of the bed and looked down. It took all of her might not reach out her arm and run her finger along his face, or to climb down and slip under the blanket with him. She stayed like that for a while, watching him breathe.

The night sounds were of a different breed, particular to this valley floor—the continuous croaking of frogs, dripping rainwater and a creak in the floorboards. At some point, maybe she had drifted off again, Violet swore someone was standing behind them. Was Bernard in the room? She held her breath and debated whether to risk waking Parker. That was when his eyes shot open. His body stayed motionless. Then, without warning, he bolted upright and swung around.

By now, her eyes had adjusted to the dark. Standing in

the middle of the room was the form of a small animal with pointed ears. Either yellow or white. It made no move. Parker reached over slowly and lit the lantern. As soon as Violet saw it, she squealed. The animal in question was a scrappy yellow dog. One ear pointed to the ceiling, one to the floor. It stared at them but made no move to come any closer. After a short standoff with Parker, the dog loped over to the blankets with Akala and lay down. Akala grunted and they rubbed noses.

"Jesus H. Christ, how did that thing get in here?" Parker said.

"The door must be unlatched."

He let out an enormous sigh and leaned back against the bed. A little bit of sleep seemed to have loosened the air between them and he ruffled up her hair. "You're beautiful when you sleep, you know that?"

"And how would you know? You were gone before I was."

"So you thought," he said.

Oh, boy, had he known she was watching him? She wanted to tell him plainly that her heart simply could not take another crushing. That this whole thing was doomed to begin with. Instead, she mumbled, "Good night. Sleep tight."

She sank farther into the dip in the mattress. After all her rejections, it was a small miracle he still wanted to be around her. A line of shudders ran the length of her body. This time, she had pushed him away for good. Sleep would not come. She tried counting sheep, but instead saw lions and pigs and lop-eared dogs. Not to mention piles of bones.

"Violet?" His voice rattled the after-storm calm.

"Yes?"

"Do you think I was meant to come here? To find you?"

She thought about the war in Europe and the four billion other places on earth he could have been sent. "Right now, I don't know what to think."

"To me, it seems that way. With Ella and Roscoe and you. We're like that puzzle piece that fits into place when you least expect it."

Violet sent him a sideways glance. "If you were meant to be here, why are you being sent away right off the bat?"

"I think this time you're going to need to learn to trust whoever is pulling the strings up there."

No doubt about that. There was a time when she had been a great truster. As a young girl, she trusted the earth to sprout food, that her father would eat dinner with them every night, and her mother would bake pecan pie on Saturdays. She trusted that she would go to college, become a newspaper correspondent, marry, and probably grow old in Minnesota. The house groaned as she remembered when that notion abruptly ended. On the inside of her mouth, she tasted blood and realized she'd bitten her cheek to a pulp.

"Right now, all I know is that I'm terrified about every last drop of life. Ella, me, you, Zach, Setsuko and Takeo. Even Roscoe, that poor lion so out of his element. I feel like I've swallowed all the world's problems."

"There's a law that says for every minute spent worrying, you have to spend another one laughing."

Violet laughed despite the heaviness in the room. The next instant, she felt his hand flopping around on the bed. "Give me your hand," he said.

It was an order.

His palm was like a siphon, draining out small bits of hurt. They stayed that way until sleep came.

Chapter Thirty-Two

ELLA

IN THE FIRST FEW DAYS AFTER COMING BACK from the valley, Mama hardly said a word. Usually I was the one having nervous problems, so this was unusual. When she walked me home from school she spent a lot of time looking at the grass, and at home in the kitchen, she wore one of those stares like her mind had traveled to some faraway place. Even I couldn't reach her.

I resorted to practicing origami and leaving Mama to her daydreams. Our Japanese home-schooling had never taken off because we had more important things to do in our spare time. Making pies and tending our victory gardens and listening to the radio as if our lives depended on it. Still, sometimes Setsuko would come over and show us how to do a new animal, like a carp or a crab or a dragon. I had trouble. Mine looked like little kid versions of Umi's, and I was determined to make a good lion, but I had miles to go. Hiro made nothing but airplanes of all shapes and sizes. I got the idea to make some for the soldiers, thinking they might want a small model of Roscoe to take to war with them. Setsuko said it wasn't smart. Nothing Japanese should go with them.

One afternoon, when I was laying out my plans for Christmas presents, Mama sat me down at the kitchen table with a glass of milk and told me that Bernard Lalamilo had an idea where Papa might be.

My mouth puckered up. This was such a shock that I could feel my heart pounding in my nose, of all places. She looked confused by my reaction. I couldn't blame her.

"You know you're the spitting image of your daddy?" Mama said, smiling through me, like she was looking at someone else.

A full minute went by as I contemplated telling her everything I knew and why I really kept the cane knife between my mattress and my box spring. Because I knew that one of these days, I might be the next victim. Or her.

I could barely feel the back of her hand as she touched my forehead. Instead, I poured all my concentration on the pincher bug weaving its way through the banana stalk on the table. Another thing Uncle Henry had taught me.

"What is it, sweetie?" she asked.

When I finally managed to speak, the words came out all jumbled. "What did you say?"

"Leave it be, Mama."

She looked at me and blinked. Her face had gone milk white. Before I knew what was happening, she grabbed me by the arm and shoved her face an inch from mine. I could have counted her eyelashes we were so close.

"Ella, if you know something, you tell me this instant. We've been through this again and again. The way you act makes me think you're hiding something."

I burst into tears and told her, "I just don't want you to die. Please, Mama."

"What makes you think I'm going to die?"

At that moment, if I had had one wish, it would be to rewind the clock to the morning Papa went missing. I would have been able to prevent it, knowing what I know now. But time only moves in one direction, and it's not backward.

Between sobs, I managed to say, "I just do."

"Look at me, Ella." I looked. Her chin was quivering. "Are you telling me everything?"

Lying is bad and I don't want to be a convicted liar, so I ramped up my crying. It was the only thing I could do. When our eyes met, Mama looked like her heart had split down the middle.

I hugged her with all my might.

Chapter Thirty-Three

VIOLET

THE FLOORBOARDS CREAKED AS VIOLET STEPPED into the police station and shut the door behind her. The smell of wood polish and hair spray almost knocked her back. This was one of those places that would forever be associated with the worst kind of anguish. The early days of loss. Iris sat at her desk, pounding away at the typewriter, and didn't look up.

"Good morning. I need to speak with the sheriff."

His door was closed.

Only then did Iris acknowledge her. "Mrs. Iverson, is this about your husband?"

"It is."

A moment later, Violet was sitting on a peeled vinyl seat across from Souza and a big mug of coffee. His eyes passed over her, disinterested. Violet felt her hair rise.

"How can I help you?" he said.

"I have news."

He put down the newspaper he'd been reading and leaned forward. "News about what?"

What else?

"Bernard Lalamilo says he knows where my husband might be."

Souza sighed for so long it sounded like someone letting the air out of a tire. "Violet, the man is a drunk. We've been through this. You can't put stock in anything he has to say."

She smoothed out her dress and sat rod straight, giving him her sharpest look. "Sheriff, I'm telling you that there may be a lead on my husband's disappearance and this is your reaction? Shame on you."

"Easy, ma'am. I just don't want you to get your hopes up."

A vein pulsed in her temple at being *ma'am*ed. "Hopes or no hopes, we need to follow every lead."

"I've already talked to him and got a load of gibberish. Nor do I think he had anything to do with this."

"He might know where to find Herman. Does that mean anything to you?" Her throat seemed to be narrowing and she had to push the words out.

"Not a day goes by that I don't think about this case."

It pained her that Herman, the man who had loved her with all his might, had been reduced to a *case.*

"Thinking about it and solving it are different matters," she said.

Souza took a gulp of coffee and huffed. "What did Lalamilo say?"

She left out the part about staying at his house with Parker, but told him about the cave. "He agreed to take us."

"That's some story."

Violet jumped to her feet. She'd had enough. "Do what you want. You can sit here and read your paper and drink your coffee, or get out there and help me find my husband. I'm going with or without you."

That got his attention.

"You sure Lalamilo will agree to me coming?"

"He's going to make you swear on a thirty-year-old bottle of *okolehao*."

Souza grinned. He was in.

According to Zach, Operation Detachment was in full swing. Preparing to mobilize twenty-something-thousand marines overseas was no small feat, and the soldiers were growing antsy. Tempers shortened. All nonessentials were packed and stored. Combat gear was checked and readied.

On possibly the last pie-selling day before departure, the line outside Honey Cow Pies was full of men with straight faces. All the easy banter and light moods seemed to have evaporated. Jean had suggested a special Christmas pie, made from ohelo berries, a ruby-colored berry found only on the upper slopes of the volcanoes. Mr. Hayashi sometimes carried bags of them in his store when the cowboys would come down from the mountain with sacks full.

"Everyone deserves to taste an ohelo berry pie at least once in their life," Jean had said.

Violet felt a stab. "Let's hope these boys get a lifetime to have their pies."

Jean was right, though. Nothing could compare. Tart and tangy and dazzling, the berries were a pie maker's dream. And by the changed look on the men's faces, it was clear they felt the same way. Just before they were to pack it up for the day, Luther stopped in. He wore his hair greased and pulled over the bald spot on his head. Violet had been avoiding him at school, not wanting to hear his rants on the Japanese and uneasy about his alcohol intake.

He gave them a hearty smile. “Been wanting to see the stand in action and I heard a rumor about some holiday pie that could knock your socks off.”

“You’re in luck. We only have a few pieces left. Why don’t you take them all?” Violet said, feeling a pinch of her old fondness for him.

He patted his paunch, which had grown in size. “Just one. Save the rest for the boys who really need it.”

Violet turned to Ella for a box. “Honey, can you…?”

But Ella was gone.

Jean handed her the box instead. “She may have gone off in search of Roscoe.”

“Where’s your Jap friend today?” he said.

Violet froze. That did it.

“Luther, please take your slice and leave. I won’t tolerate your insults any longer. Setsuko is a dear friend, and if you can’t see that, then I feel sorry for you. We aren’t at war with her.”

He shrugged. “Her. Her people. What’s the difference?”

“Guilt by skin color—is that how you see it?”

The broken capillaries in his cheeks flared red. “You have a lot to learn, Mrs. Iverson.” His eyes glazed over and he mumbled something about bombs and battleships as he stormed off.

Violet and Jean looked at each other.

“Good riddance,” Violet said.

Bitterness could eat a hole through anyone.

Violet hadn’t seen Parker since their overnighter, and she was growing despondent. He didn’t show at the pie stand that day, even though he’d said he would. Her mind was a flip-flopping mess. One minute, she figured he had lost interest. The next, she excused him because he was a busy sergeant getting ready for war. This was a different flavor of love than she was used to—*okolehao* instead of a smooth white wine.

She had about given up hearing from him when the phone rang one afternoon.

"Violet?"

"Yes."

There was a long pause. It was him. "I've been meaning to call, but it's been crazy tense here. Now we're restricted to only one small area of the camp, and everyone is running around like chickens without heads. The hooch from old Bernard has been a hot commodity." He dropped his voice. "Listen, I'm dying to see you before I go. We're getting liberty on the twentieth. Would it be too much to ask if we could stop in?"

By then, Violet felt like she would be on more solid ground again. "How about you and the boys come for a Christmas celebration? Just to be sure you have a proper holiday before you go."

"That would be nice, Violet. Real nice."

Closing her eyes, she saw Parker standing on the steps that first afternoon. A tall man in green. Only a few short months ago, but it felt like a lifetime.

"That's settled, then," she said.

There was a long pause. "Think Ella will mind if we bring Santa with us?"

"In Ella's mind Santa is only a notch below Roscoe."

"Done."

Preparations began almost as soon as she hung up the phone. That afternoon, they piled in the school truck and sneaked down a muddy lane on Parker Ranch property to a grove of Norfolk Island pine trees. Setsuko brought a rusted handsaw, the only one they could find, to cut down their own Christmas trees. Never mind that a Hawaiian Christmas, without freshly fallen snow, always felt like a poor imitation. But none of the kids knew any different, and Violet and Jean decided they would give the soldiers a December to remember.

"What do you want for Christmas this year?" Setsuko asked Violet, as she maneuvered around the ruts in the road.

Jean guffawed. "That's a loaded question."

Violet punched her in the knee. "It's an easy question. For the war to end today." She let the words sink in, then added, "Oh, and I wouldn't mind one of those fancy new electric mixers."

In so many ways, the war was stealing happiness. Taking away fathers and husbands, and returning them to the earth in wooden boxes. Or in many cases out in the Pacific, to the bottom of the sea.

"Santa Claus, I hope you're listening," Jean said, looking up. "And we all know what Setsuko wants. The sooner the better, please."

Setsuko produced a flat smile. "I'm with Violet. End the war. And give us our Japanese school back."

"Nothing else?"

"I could use some new yarn. In every color. All the Filipinos want chicken sweaters now, for their cocks," Setsuko said, straight-faced.

"What's not to love about a well-dressed cock?" Jean said.

Setsuko just shook her head, a thin smile appearing on her lips.

"One-track mind," Violet said.

"Just trying to add some cheer."

Speaking of Filipinos, why was it that in the islands, the Filipino, Japanese, Chinese, Portuguese, Hawaiian, *haole,* all managed to coexist? Neighbors became friends and families overlapped. Macadangdang was generous with his coconuts, Lalamilo provided much-needed moonshine, Hamasu shared his victory garden, Souza sold his meat and Pang produced rice. Of course, everyone had their squabbles, but nothing to go to war over.

"What about you, Honey Jean?" Violet said.

"Goodness, there's so much to want for. Mainly, I want our boys to come back safe. My little brother, Zach, if only I could steal him away and chain him to a tree in the back of Waipio Valley, I swear I would." She sniffled. "And that stupid, lying, cheating Bud Walker. I want to forgive him and tear up that letter."

The letter had been placed prominently on top of the icebox. Sealed with wax and dried tears.

"He's not worth all that goodness you have inside you," Setsuko said.

Well, that got Jean bawling, and pretty soon, all three of them were one big mess of tears. It was like someone opened up a dike and years' worth of pent-up feelings poured out, fish and all. At some point along the road, the crying turned into side-stitching laughter.

"Look at us. A cab full of hormones. Woe is the man who crosses our path," Violet said.

Jean caught her breath. "Right here in this very truck is the difference between men and women. And crying is heaven's way of washing away sorrows. It's God saying sorry."

One problem with a Norfolk pine in your living room was it could be as wide as it was tall. The branches hung their scaled needles like dark green skirts. It took all three of them plus Irene Ferreira to get the tree perfect. Even then, there was no way to manufacture smell. The tree gave off nothing. Fortunately, Jean had picked up a bucketful of pinecones from Mr. Suares, who had driven partway around Mauna Kea to pick them.

Ornaments were pulled out from their boxes in the hall closet and unwrapped. Soon after the war started, there had been a mass call to destroy German glass-blown and wooden ornaments. Violet had watched Herman burn some of her favorite carvings of tiny mice pulling sleds packed with miniature painted presents, and nutcracker men inside nutcracker men. But he had insisted. Now they hung origami made by the kids, glitter-dipped pinecones and stars fashioned from driftwood.

When they pulled out the ladder and finally finished stringing the lights, which had been absent since Pearl Harbor, Jean stood back and held her hands over her cheeks. "I'll wager that this is the finest Christmas tree I've ever seen," she said.

It was lopsided and sparsely decorated, but Violet had to agree that the tree had character.

They also decided to dig an *imu* behind the house, and keep it under wraps in case Mr. Nakata came sniffing around. He had heard about the lion, but anything soldier-related, he kept out of.

There was simply no better way to prepare a pig than slow-cooked in the earth with kiawe wood, hot rocks and banana leaves. Hiro and Setsuko supervised, and Violet enlisted a few of her football players to help. School had just ended for the break, and the boys were eager to earn a few extra dollars.

This would be the last weekend selling their Honey Cow Pies, and on Thursday afternoon, Jean found Violet sitting at the kitchen table chewing her nails down to the quick instead of peeling sweet potato like she was supposed to.

"Anybody know where Violet is?"

It took a moment for the question to register. "Check the icebox," Violet said.

"Ha! That must have been some night you spent in the valley."

Some night was putting it mildly. Since then, Violet had lost her toothbrush, forgotten to put her slip on before school and found her missing shampoo bottle in the icebox.

"I feel like I've been ambushed. Why can't I have more time to sort things out?"

"Nature has a way of piling up situations all at the same time. Some kind of universal rule," Jean said. Until now, she had been silent on Violet's bouts.

"Have you ever been so confused your mind went blank, just checked out completely?"

Jean laughed. "Have you forgotten who you're talking to? Listen, that heart of yours has a whole lot of protective layers, with good reason. But the signs were all there. You just turned up your nose at them."

"Signs?"

"Don't play dumb. You've fallen flat for him."

Violet dropped her face in her hands. "This was the exact thing I was trying to avoid."

"No one can avoid life, sweetie. And that's God's honest truth."

"I'm not trying to avoid life, just the agony part. I'm not ready and now Parker has complicated everything."

"Who is ever ready? All I know is that man has the patience of a saint," Jean said.

"I'm sure after Waipio he's washed his hands of me."

"Oh? And that's why he called today, isn't it." Jean stood there with her hands on her hips, reminding Violet of her own mother, about to dispense essential advice, whether she wanted it or not. "Being afraid of pain is like being afraid of the dark. You need to face it head-on, and if the pain comes at you swinging, swing back."

Violet stared at her. "But..."

"I'm not finished. If you arrange your life to sidestep it, that won't work, either. Each one of us has to be brave in our own way. Not one person in this whole world is immune." At some point Jean had picked up a wooden spoon and now waved it around. "So the moral of the story is you gotta take your chances, doll."

Chapter Thirty-Four

VIOLET

IN THE DAYS BEFORE THE CHRISTMAS PARTY, Violet, Jean and Ella all tried to bolster themselves up for the inevitable. Ella had taken to drawing pictures of lions with renewed vigor, and added in pigs after hearing the story of Akala. Every day, she asked how often they would drive to Waimea to see Roscoe once the soldiers left.

"We can sneak him in here on a weekend here or there," she told Ella.

With gasoline rations the way they were, *not often enough* was the real answer. Violet wondered if she could justify to the ration board the drive to Waimea if not to sell pies to the soldiers. Gas was one of the more closely monitored items.

"Mr. Nakata won't mind?"

A lion would be hard to hide, but let him say no to her daughter. "How about this. We won't tell him."

She looked at Ella, whose little face glowed at the news.

All the same, she suspected there was something else bothering her. Something to do with Herman.

Irene came over to help with the *imu* on the morning of the party. Cooking the meat was traditionally a man's job, but when short of men, they used the next best thing—a group of women and a ten-year-old boy. According to Parker, the soldiers had to stick around camp and wouldn't be arriving until afternoon.

"You'd make someone a great husband, Irene Ferreira," Jean said, as she stood to the side and fanned the coals with a piece of cardboard.

"Gee, thanks."

"In all honesty. A great wife, but also a great husband. You're the whole package," Jean said.

And then some, Violet thought.

"I hope your brother sees it the same way." Irene stood up and grinned, smearing ash through her hair.

After shoveling earth over the pig and the turkey, Jean looked up and asked the sky to please hold any rain until later.

Everyone reconvened in the kitchen and got to work on the potatoes and pies. Ella turned on the radio, which featured a daily Christmas program. It was playing "I'll Be Home for Christmas." As Bing Crosby crooned, Violet felt like someone had thrown sand in her eyes. Standing there up to her shoulders in mashed potatoes, she felt another round of crying coming on. Fortunately, the song ended, and "Jingle Bells" came on. Ella stood on her tippy toes, singing in her off-key voice. It was impossible not to smile instead.

When afternoon rolled around, she reached for her faithful red dress, the one that always made her feel like Christmas. Jean helped her pin up her hair, adding in glitter meant for the tree. Ella was awfully quiet. Eventually she showed up looking like an elf in a green velvet frock that pinched at the shoulders and fell above the knee. The dress had fit her when she was seven. Violet knew better than to say anything. Outgrown favorite dresses had always been a touchy subject with Ella. And this one Herman had brought back from Oahu in a fancy box.

"Mama, you look like a movie star."

"Now, that's an exaggeration if I've ever heard one, but thank you. Come on. The guests should be arriving."

On cue, men's voices rang out from the lanai. Violet felt her heartbeat ramp up. She peeked through the window before walking out. Roscoe stood alongside the men wearing a huge red bow on his withers and antlers on his head. He looked annoyed. Both Zach and Parker carried boxes with presents stuffed inside and Tommy held a six-pack under each arm. All three soldiers were dressed in their blues. Jean ran outside. "Say, don't you boys clean up nicely."

Violet went out a moment later, trying not to look at Parker. Which was a dumb notion. Of course her eyes went straight to his face. *Blink*, she reminded herself.

"Hi" was all she could think to say.

Irene hung a plumeria lei over each man's neck. "*Mele Kalikimaka.* It's what we say here in Hawaii."

The boys all laughed and smelled the yellow flowers. "Come again?" Zach said.

"You heard me," Irene said, swatting his shoulder.

Right then, Violet was grateful for Irene's ice-breaking skills.

Ella burst out of the house and beelined to Roscoe. And then she noticed the boxes. With paper in short supply, the presents were wrapped in brown sacks and the comic section of the newspaper. Instead of ribbon, they'd used cord.

"Come see our tree!" she said to the men, leading them all inside.

A band of fog had crept down from Mauna Kea, swallowing the house and everything around it. Not quite snow, but it would do. The Christmas lights spiraled up the tree, giving off bursts of color that shaped snowflake patterns on the walls.

"Doozy of a tree. Looks like something Paul Bunyan would have hauled in," Zach said.

It did take up half the room.

Parker pointed to the largest of boxes that he had placed under the Norfolk.

"This one's for you, Ella."

Tommy opened beers for everyone.

"Can I have one, Mama?" Ella asked.

Violet and Jean exchanged glances. "Ask me again in ten years, sweetie."

She went to the kitchen to check on the casserole and Parker trailed behind her. Even from across the room, she could sense him. Sitting through dinner, she realized, would be torture. He leaned against the counter and crossed his arms, watching as she opened the cupboard, turned down the stove and dabbed her face with a napkin.

"What?" she finally said.

"Nothing." His eyes had her pinned. "Just taking every last bit in."

The idea sent a nervous shudder down her spine and it was a relief to return to the safety of the group, where the air was easier to breathe.

Another jeep rattled up the driveway, and out piled Captain Riggs and two other marines Violet had met while selling pies and at the beach. Normally Riggs wouldn't be caught fraternizing with enlisted men, but this was Christmas. Rules could be bent. Anyway, she wanted to pry more information from him.

"So which one of you is going to be Santa?" Violet asked Parker, when Ella was out of earshot.

"We invited Gizmo Santos, our local marine. Said he had a Santa costume and would be more than happy to join us."

Irene announced that it was time to eat and wasted no time ordering the men around. "Dig here." "Stack the rocks there." "Don't drop the luau leaf!" By the time they'd unearthed the meal, the men looked like miners. But no one complained.

Using card tables to extend their own, they managed to squeeze every last person in. Violet wasn't sure how Setsuko would feel about Riggs in the house, but Setsuko remained stone-faced. Polite, but not all there. Having a Christmas celebration with one-third of her heart missing was no one's idea of a good time. But here was the thing: the other two-thirds was in the room. In recent weeks, Violet had come to wonder if hearts grew back. Maybe even bigger. As long as you had something to water them with.

Friendship, faith, love. Any of these worked.

Despite efforts to avoid war talk, the conversation inevitably folded back to it one way or another. The boys were fired up about recent news of the Ardennes Counteroffensive in Belgium, which the press referred to as the Battle of the Bulge.

Violet's insides had soured when she had first heard news of the surprise attack by the Germans. It reminded her of Pearl Harbor in the utter shock achieved.

Riggs, who was privy to the latest information, filled them in. "So get this, the Germans send a message to General McAuliffe of the 101st Airborne Division, who, along with the Tenth Armored Division, are defending the town. Actually, they send an ultimatum. Saying there is only one possibility to avoid complete annihilation of US troops. Our men are given two hours to surrender. When the general finishes reading the message, he crumples it up and throws it into the wastebasket, mumbling, *'Aw, nuts.'* Now the men in his command post are stuck trying to come up with a suitable response. Everyone in the room, including Colonel Kinnard, decides McAuliffe's initial response is as good as any. So they send the following official reply. This is word for word," he said, clearing his throat and taking a drag of his cigarette.

The room fell silent.

"'To the German Commander. NUTS! The American Commander.'" He nodded his head for emphasis. "And that is a capital *N-U-T-S*. When the German commander asks Colonel Harper, who hand-delivers the message, what that means, Harper says, *'In plain English, go to hell.'*"

All the men spoke at once. "Hot damn, that man has guts." "Or peanuts for brains." "I'd like to serve under McAuliffe."

Eventually Ella asked what Violet herself was thinking. "What happened next?"

Riggs showed a rare smile. "Good question. The artillery fire turned out to be an empty threat. The Germans bombed the town but we held 'em off until backup came."

"What does this mean for the Allies?" Zach wanted to know.

"I think we're at a turning point in the counteroffensive."

Parker looked grim. "Let's hope so. Too many lives lost over there."

Violet read the papers. So far, over sixty thousand too many.

Jean cast her a desperate look and she tapped her glass. "Let's talk about something more pleasant, shall we? I want to hear what each one of you has planned for after this war is over. Let's start with you, brother."

Violet admired the easy way between Zach and Jean. She'd often wished that Ella had a sibling, someone to split the weight of the world with. Someone to confide in. That way, maybe her hurt would have been manageable and not stung so badly. But what was her hurt?

When Zach spoke, Irene Ferreira watched him with such longing that anyone could see she was a hopeless cause. "Whether it's here or California, I want to start my own business, like Mom and Pop. But first, I'm coming back to this island for some well-earned R & R. Spend more time with all you ladies."

He glanced toward Irene, who had turned pink at his words.

It turned out Tommy wanted to be a race-car driver, which suited him perfectly. Riggs was a career military man and would never retire, he said. Regardless of whether the plans were big or little, every man at the table was banking on dodging bullets, staying afloat and, most important, not getting captured. They had lives to live and people to love.

Parker went last. "I had an offer from the ranch to come back and work, so that's my plan, maybe eventually finish up veterinary school. But it all depends." He raised his glass. "I guess he was impressed with my bull-riding skills."

Just before dinner wrapped up, bells and muffled singing emerged from the fog. The kids all moved to the edge of their seats as it drew nearer.

"Ho, ho, ho. Merry Christmas! Ho. Merry merry, quite contrary, how does your reindeer go?"

What on earth? Pretty soon, a red apparition half walked, half stumbled up the steps. A man in a baggy Santa suit dropped an empty-looking burlap sack on the porch and held out his arms toward Roscoe. "Rudolph, you beat me hea!" He spoke a heavy pidgin.

A low growl formed in Roscoe's chest.

"Easy, boy. It's only Santa," Zach said, standing up and holding on to Roscoe's harness.

"No more chimney, so was hard fo' find. Can Santa eat before he talk with da kine little ones?" Gizmo asked in a stilted pidgin. His long white beard was askew and he'd stuffed the pillow into the back of his suit, not the front. Which made him look more like the Hunchback of Notre Dame than Santa Claus. Each time he opened his mouth, a cloud of alcohol burst forth.

Zach walked over to Santa, escorted him to the table and sat him down. "Mind if I make him a plate?"

"Be my guest," Jean said, looking to the heavens and shaking her head.

Violet glared at Gizmo, then said to the kids, "Little ones, it seems that Santa isn't feeling like himself tonight. Maybe we'll wait until Christmas Eve to sit on his lap."

"I'm too old, anyway," Hiro said.

When everyone was up to their necks in smoked meat, mashed potato, cornbread stuffing casserole, pumpkin pie and frosted gingerbread men, Jean herded them into the living room. Homemade honeycomb candles had been placed on every available surface and the whole room looked like it was breathing.

Violet stopped in the doorway to take it all in.

"Don't move, woman," Parker said from behind her.

Without warning, he spun her around and planted a kiss on her surprised lips. Mouth closed, then open. When she'd about forgotten where she was, he pulled away and pointed up.

Mistletoe.

More flustered than she wanted to let on, Violet felt her face heating up. "And I thought you were just making a pass."

"This isn't my doing," he said.

"Well, whose is it?"

She turned to Jean and Irene, who were always looking for a good excuse to kiss someone. Jean pointed to Ella. "Blame this one."

Ella was grinning ear to ear.

Chapter Thirty-Five

ELLA

MAMA WAS TORN ABOUT PARKER. ANYONE could see that. After the kiss, she turned her big, shining eyes on me and smiled. I think at that very moment, she made up her mind. As Jean said, she was already in up to her teeth.

Last year, we didn't go caroling. It was our first Christmas without Papa and the island was still on blackout and curfew. Nobody bothered. Tonight, with Tommy and Parker strumming their guitars, our living room sounded like a lively concert hall. The soldiers sang themselves blue in the face and even Mama belted the songs out. After several rounds of "Silent Night" and "White Christmas," I asked for "Santa Claus Is Comin' to Town." Irene tried to teach them "Mele Kalikimaka," but it didn't go over so well. No one could get the words except drunk Santa, who burped loudly at the end of each stanza.

When that was over, Mama and Jean handed out presents. I didn't have any great expectations and Mama had said they'd gotten creative. I think for the soldiers, even a coconut or a rock would have seemed priceless. The only thing was, you couldn't send anyone away from the island with a lava rock. It was bad luck. When I looked around the room at the dressed-up tree and all the warm faces, I had the sudden urge to lock all the doors and never let anyone out. Nothing would be the same once the men shipped out.

Us kids unwrapped first. Zach gave me a deck of playing cards with a different animal on the back of each one. Even better than that was a leather cowboy hat from Parker. The edges were a little frayed and it blocked my vision, but still I didn't want to take it off.

"It's the real deal and you can grow into it," he said as he adjusted it back so I could see. "But promise me one thing."

"What?" I asked.

"You'll get your mama to take you to visit Sonny up at the ranch." He winked at Mama as he said it.

She scrunched up her forehead.

Zach and Parker also had gifts for Umi and Hiro. That was the kind of people they were. Thoughtful to a fault, as Jean would say. And over the last couple of months, they could see that kids were kids. No matter what color. A tablet of colored paper and a knapsack for Umi, and a fishing net and an airplane spotting guide for Hiro. On any given day, he could already identify seven out of ten planes that flew past.

Pretty soon, the floor was covered in paper and cord, all to be saved and reused next year. We had learned to waste nothing. Hard to imagine, but I saw a sliver of a smile on Setsuko's face. All this cheer must have rubbed off on her, and I decided then and there that Christmas didn't believe in war.

There was one present under the tree I was most excited about. I grabbed it and held it out to Parker. "Open this one next. It's for Roscoe, from all of us."

"You hear that, buddy?" Parker said to Roscoe, who sat crouched next to the tree. He had already batted more than one ornament off and was lying in wait for the next one to move. I went and sat with him and he bumped his head into my side. Lions really are nothing more than big cats, you know.

I felt my stomach doing flips as Parker unwrapped the box. I only hoped Roscoe liked his gift more than the antlers, which he tore up soon after arrival.

Parker held it up. "Is this what I think it is?" he said.

"A lion sweater! For when it gets cold. It will while you're gone, you know," I said.

"Did you make this?" Zach asked.

"We all did. Setsuko is the best, but we all helped. Everyone but Hiro, who says that real boys don't knit."

That got a laugh from everyone. I glanced at Hiro, who rolled his eyes at me. I smiled. Roscoe was the only one who seemed unsure of his new gift. When Parker tried to wrap it around him, he rolled onto his back and grabbed the sweater with his front paws, kicking at it with his rear ones and barely missing Parker's leg.

"No!" I yelled.

Eventually, Parker, Zach and I managed to hold Roscoe still and button the bottom together. He sniffed at the contraption, twitched his tail and settled back down. Other than one loop of pulled yarn, the sweater still held. Red suited him.

More unwrapping, and toward the end, the men insisted that Mama, Jean and Setsuko all open their presents together. On the count of three they each held up a yellow flowered apron.

"My word!" Jean cried out.

Embroidered across the front in brown were the words Honey Cow Pies.

"Our mother raised you right, didn't she?" Jean said to Zach, wrapping her whole body around him in a hug.

"We wanted to have them done up earlier, so you could wear them while you were still open, but Mrs. Kobatake had a long line of orders before ours," he said.

"I guess this means we'll just have to find a way to keep our business going," Mama said, looking at Jean.

Something must have passed between them because before I knew it, Jean was sobbing and going on about how she didn't want the men to leave. She started up her rant that mothers should be running the country and that war solved nothing. The mood in the room went south, along with Jean.

Do not cry, do not cry, do not cry, I ordered myself.

Chapter Thirty-Six

VIOLET

IN THE MIDDLE OF CLEANUP, RIGGS TAPPED VI-olet on the shoulder. "Can I borrow you for a moment?"

She led him onto the lanai, where he wasted no time in lighting another cigarette. When he blew the smoke out, it mingled with the fog, which now seemed to be holding up the house. Riggs hoisted his belt and sat on the top step, patting the wood next to him. He moved in the way of a man who wanted to postpone telling you something you might not want to hear. Sweat appeared in the creases of her palms even before he spoke. "Tell me, how well do you know Luther Hodges?" he said.

"Very well. He was one of Herman's close friends. Why?"

Riggs tapped his fingertips together. "I believe he was responsible for the letter in your friend's Japanese school."

Violet felt a stone forming in her throat. "You must have the wrong man."

"People do things."

"What makes you think it was Luther?" Her mind filtered through memories. Hadn't Luther been friends with Takeo and Setsuko? Gone with Herman and Takeo to the garden in Ahualoa and been to the beach with all of them? The man lived in Honoka'a, for heaven's sake.

"I can't give details, but he was one of our civilian watchdogs. Only now it looks like he took things a little too far. Fabricating stuff. Takeo wasn't the only one he's fed the military information on, either."

Violet stood so she was facing him. "Luther Hodges. Our shop teacher. We're talking about the same man?"

Riggs nodded and pushed out an exhalation. His neck and shoulder muscles bulged, probably from trying to get rid of all that tar in his lungs. "Same man."

"If this is true, what are you going to do about it?" she asked.

"*I* am not going to do anything, since we're shipping out any day. To tell the truth, this is low priority. Most of these guys would have been locked up anyway."

His words cut into her. "Not Takeo. He was minding his own business and teaching kids how to sing and grow food and be good humans. No one was being taken away anymore. You know that."

"He ran the Japanese school. He was a leader."

"Can't you at least talk to someone?"

"The Feds might pursue it, but I thought you should know about Luther, seeing as he's your friend. I would watch my back around that man."

"What did he have to say for himself?" she asked.

"He denied everything."

She pictured herself marching right over there and dragging him out of his house. Finding out the truth, one way or another. Telling Setsuko would be another story. "I'll make him talk."

Riggs frowned. "Don't say anything. Not yet."

"Why not?"

"Because he might be unstable."

"How do you mean?"

"The lying. You never can tell with some people. Just keep busy with your own life and let the Feds sort it out."

Easier said than done.

After Riggs and his boys headed out, Violet put Ella to sleep with her cowboy hat on, and said good-night to Setsuko and the twins. The news could wait until morning, when it would be just the two of them.

Back in the living room, Jean, Parker, Zach, Irene and Tommy huddled together on the *pune'e*, with their legs spread out in all directions and Roscoe at their feet. Tommy strummed the guitar softly, in tune with the occasional cricket.

Violet got the sensation that she wanted to slow down time.

"You ladies don't mind if we crash here, do you?" Zach asked a few songs later.

"I wouldn't have it any other way," Jean said.

Without making a sound, Violet lowered herself onto the rug next to Roscoe, who was by now sound asleep. His lip periodically lifted and small puffs of breath escaped. She wondered what he was dreaming. In that moment, she felt protective of him.

Conversation drifted well into the night, and one by one, people faded away. Jean roused herself to bring a stack of pillows and blankets from the closet, and Zach stretched out on the floor with his head under one of the tree branches. He spanned almost the whole width of the room. Jean fell asleep next to him with her head tucked under his armpit.

Parker sat up on the edge of the *pune'e* and grabbed a blanket from the chair. *Do something, Violet. Here's your chance, and it may be your last.*

"Want to go outside?" she said to him in nearly a whisper. Without waiting for an answer, she moved toward the lanai. He caught up with her at the door, holding it open. If anything, the fog had condensed into a wall of white, sending tendrils in through the windows and wrapping around the posts.

"An imitation white Christmas," she said.

"We take what we can get."

Violet bunched up her dress and sat on the top step, like she had with Riggs. Parker lowered himself next to her. Close enough so she could feel his heat, but not close enough to touch. He had to avoid a dollop of chicken poop on the third step. By now, the crickets were in full concert, their chirps magnified by the heavy air.

Words began to pour out of her. "Everyone thinks Hawaii is all paradise and rainbows and pretty girls in hula skirts. It took me a while to realize that it's so much more than just that. I don't think there's any place else on earth I'd rather be. And I have Herman to thank for that. He brought me here."

She didn't know why she was telling him this, but continued anyway. "If I hadn't met him that day at the funeral, I might still be in Minnesota, holed away in some office, raising four kids and married to the town plumber."

"Somehow I doubt that," Parker said.

"I hadn't expected a proposal so soon when I came, but he had it all planned out. I simply couldn't refuse. Sometimes I ask myself, 'Was I wrong for saying yes?'"

"It's neither good nor bad. It just *is*."

A moth fluttered in and landed on the underside of the eave. She contemplated the lacy pattern on its wings and envied such a simple life. "I grew to love him in a deep way—his stability and honesty. He was a simple but good man. Though to be sure, it wasn't my notion of how marriage would be. I had this expectation of passion and romance. That never happened."

"You had Ella," he said.

"Ella is the one thing I am sure of."

"Life doesn't come with directions, Violet. We do the best we can given the circumstances, which in some cases can be pretty bleak."

The words that she wanted to say were wedged in her throat, unable to come out. She picked up his hand and held on to it for dear life. He squeezed, offering her all the silence she needed.

Eventually she found her voice. "I think that being with you scares me in such an unfamiliar way that the only thing I've been able to do is shut down. Partly because I never felt this same kind of fire with my husband, and partly because you won't be here in a week. You were never meant to stay."

There you have it.

Parker lay back on the wood, tightening his grip on her fingers. She lay back, too, and he pulled her hand to his chest. "I would give anything to promise I'll be back. But it's not a promise I can own."

"I know."

A chill crept up her bare feet. Ella would be proud of her, not wearing slippers for once. She leaned her thigh against his. Wherever they touched, her skin burned.

"In case I forget or fall asleep, I left a small box for you in the tree," he said.

"But you already gave me something."

Parker laughed. "If you think I'd leave you here with an apron to remember me by, you're not as bright as I thought."

"Is that an insult?" She turned her head and met his eyes.

His look burned through her. "You know what I mean."

With her free hand, she reached over and traced her finger along his forehead, his nose, his clean-shaven jaw. Parker rolled onto his side and faced her, using his arm as a pillow. She did the same, moving three inches away, close enough to feel the heat of his breath.

"You won't believe how hard I'm going to try to stay alive," he whispered.

She blinked.

He exhaled.

She inhaled.

His breath.

She tried not to think about the war pictures. The twisted metal and sunken ships. Limp bodies half-buried in sand. Dead eyes. But images were one thing her brain couldn't seem to erase. Tears welled up in her eyes.

"Come on." He pulled her up and they blew out the last candles before repositioning themselves on the *pune'e* on the porch.

Heat collected between them, in the tender part of his arm where her head lay, under her palm. His uniform smelled like starch. His skin, salt. Strangely, she craved the ocean, even though it would lead him to more dangerous waters.

"What we're doing is important. I keep reminding myself," he said.

"It is."

"It has to be."

Violet leaned up on her arm to look down at him, though his face was now all shadow. "Listen, Sergeant, you fighting for our country matters more than anything. For all those boys killed in Pearl Harbor and those other islands. For us. And don't you forget it."

He stared at the ceiling. "I guess it's just that I've seen the other side of the Japanese while I've been here. Sure, there are the crazy bastards. But most of the population is probably not so different from Setsuko and her family, or Mrs. Kaiama and her love of feeding us with her hamburgers. It almost would have been easier not to know them."

"Maybe it will give you some compassion."

"Compassion's the last thing I'm gonna need."

"I beg to differ."

The stillness continued around them. While Violet memorized the sound of his breath, Parker rolled against her and buried his face in her hair. He made a sound like a hurt animal. Something inside gave way, and with two fingers, she felt for his lips, tugging on his bottom one until her own mouth reached his.

Parker lifted her chin and closed his mouth around hers. The kiss ran through her whole body, causing a flutter below her belly button. He brushed his hand lightly along her collarbone, and the next second pinned her to the bed. Her heart skipped. It was like a whole string of Christmas lights had coiled up inside her chest, blinking madly.

She ground her hip into his thigh.

His breath was hot.

Ribs. Abdomen.

Hardness.

In order to breathe, she eventually disentangled herself.

Parker wiped his mouth. "When I come back, I want to take you out properly to a fancy dinner with a big bottle of champagne," he said.

She felt a stab of panic. "Wait a minute. I'll see you again before you ship out, won't I?"

"Of course. Just getting ahead of myself," he said.

Here he was, not even gone and already planning his return. This was a man worth hurting for.

She missed him already.

Two mornings later, Violet dreamed that the school bell had broken and wouldn't stop ringing. All the students were gone for the day and she tried to type a letter but the ink wouldn't show up on her paper. She covered her ears, but that didn't help. A moment later, she woke with a start. *The telephone!* Wrapped in the blanket, she sprinted to the kitchen and picked up, breathless. "Hello?"

Dial tone. She called the operator with shaky fingers. When no one had picked up one hundred rings later, she slammed the phone down. The clock on the wall said four twenty. People didn't call at this hour unless it was important.

Jean showed up after a few minutes, bleary-eyed. "Who was that?"

"I don't know. I missed it."

"Did you try Irene?"

"No answer. I have a bad feeling." Her voice came out in a high squeak.

Jean walked over, picked up the phone and dialed. Again, no answer. "Either no one is in yet, or they're too busy fielding calls."

"The boys are leaving," Violet said, sureness settling in her chest.

"Don't jump to conclusions."

"I'm not jumping to anything. I got the distinct feeling that when Parker walked out the door yesterday morning, it would be for the last time." Before she knew it, she was gulping down air like a dying fish.

Jean grabbed her shoulders. "Get ahold of yourself. Even if they are leaving, he'll be back. So will Zach."

Jean fixed coffee while Violet tried the phone every two minutes, every time without luck.

"Enough," Jean finally said.

To distract herself, she ended up outside to let the hens out. High wispy clouds hung in the sky, each lit with a variation of orange. She noticed a lone plover on the roof, perched like a tiny weather vane. If you were going to sail off to war, this would be as fine a day as any.

Jean came onto the porch with a steaming mug. She turned an ear toward the mountain. "Hear that?"

In the distance, the ground thundered. It was a sound she had heard before, and she knew exactly what it meant. "Convoy!" she yelled.

They both tore into the house, and Violet shook Ella awake before throwing on a dress, brushing out her hair and dabbing a spot of coral on her lips. By the time the first trucks arrived, all three of them stood in wait on the edge of the slanted sidewalk. A few other townsfolk stepped out from storefronts, but other than that, the streets were empty.

The line of trucks extended past the last building. Soldiers smashed together in the backs, along with their duffel bags. Some stood and waved. Within minutes, more people filtered onto the streets, cheering and hollering, "Victory!" The marines were dressed in utilities, the air thick with anticipation. Long months of training now gave way to the real thing.

Irene appeared with her clothes looking like they were on backward. "I thought we'd get to say goodbye."

"We all did," Violet said.

Ella held on to her hand with all her might as they scanned the soldiers for any sign of Zach or Parker. Even Riggs. It wasn't until the second-to-last truck that she saw a couple of men hanging out from the side, waving their hats madly.

"Mama, it's them!" Ella squealed.

All four of them jumped up and down. As the truck drew near, Violet made out Parker's face. God, how she wanted one more day with him. When they were close enough, his eyes locked onto hers and never faltered. She stood forward and reached out her hand as he passed, and for a split second, their fingers met. "I tried to call," he shouted.

In her mind, she burned a photograph of the look on his face. One hundred ten percent honest-to-goodness love.

After the last truck passed, they stood there until the sound of chirping of birds took over. Violet's dress collar was damp with tears. In the distance, the whistle of the sugarcane train rose, shrill and sharp.

They held hands and prayed for a miracle.

Chapter Thirty-Seven

ELLA

CHRISTMAS IS SUPPOSED TO BE THE HAPPIEST day of the year. Not this time around, I promise you that. For the last two days all we've done is lie around in our pajamas and pretend to want to do things. Like get out of bed, or breathe. Mama has swollen eyes and Jean cries halfway through every song on the radio. For once, I'm not the most troubled person in the household.

Not only that, but the days are tinted red. I see everything through red cellophane and it has me concerned. I don't want to bother anyone by asking if they see it, too, so I keep my mouth shut. I don't like the color red. It reminds me of blood and blood brings up bad thoughts. Of Papa and now also of the soldiers and what's in store.

No one will tell us where our soldiers are going.

We know they took the sugarcane train—what is usually reserved for moving sugarcane from our area to Hilo—from Pauuilo to Hilo, then got on a really big boat called the

USS *Lubbock*. About now they're most likely turning green somewhere on their way to Japan. Every chance I get, I say a prayer that God spares them and brings them back whole and able to walk and see and eventually get married and raise families and have chicken fights and fun stuff like that. The newspaper shows pictures of facedown men on beaches, which gives me a funny feeling in my stomach. Their bodies are folded at strange angles and I can hardly believe they were once people.

All it takes is one or two bullets.

I felt heavy from lack of sleep and the feeling all over again that something was missing. Life was the same in some ways. We did chores, Mama and Jean cooked like maniacs, and of course we listened to the radio. It just seemed like all the brightness had been smeared away.

I wanted to see Roscoe right away, but Mama said we could visit him after Christmas. He would be living with the town veterinarian for as long as the soldiers were gone. He was growing bigger, and people had concern over how nice he'd be once he became an adult. Mama worried, too. I had convinced myself he wouldn't change—I prayed for it—but a part of me worried they were right.

Adults don't always think kids are paying attention and I heard Mama tell Jean that she felt like a tree that had just sprouted a new branch, only to have it unceremoniously hacked off. I knew what she meant. We avoided church on Christmas Eve, and on Christmas morning new gifts appeared under the tree from Santa, who is really a drunk Portuguese man. But that didn't stop my eyes from popping out when I saw the two big boxes. There was also a small box hiding high in the tree for Mama.

"Some of the kids at school say Santa isn't real," I told them.

Jean lay back on the *pune'e* and gave Mama a look that said,

You're on your own with this one. They were both visions of red in flannel pajamas and wool socks. Snowflake curled up next to them, purring like a lawn mower.

"Santa is real, sweetheart, if you want him to be," Mama said.

"I just don't see how he could get to everyone's houses in the whole world in one night. And we don't have even fireplaces."

After blowing out a big breath, she looked far into me. "Remember I told you that life has magic we can't always explain? This is one of those things. The key is believing."

Her words spun around in my head while I unwrapped her present, careful to salvage the ribbon and paper. "I want to learn how."

"We'll practice, all of us. How about that?" Mama said.

"Today?"

"Whenever you want."

Knitting needles and balls of mustard-yellow and green yarn. That was my present. Mama promised to teach me to knit so I could help Setsuko and Umi meet the needs of our chickens and those of everyone else in town. I started thinking of all the dogs and cats I knew that might need one, too.

"Can we also knit hats for the soldiers? So when they come back they won't be so cold all the time," I asked.

Jean leaned forward. "Right there is a good start in belief practice."

"What do you mean?"

She tapped me on the heart and smiled. "Because already, you see them coming home. You said *when* they come back, not *if.* That matters."

I nodded like I knew what she was talking about, but what I really wanted to know was what Parker got Mama. She plucked her box from the tree branch and set it in her lap, staring at it like a dog with a bone. The present was wrapped in a small piece of burlap and had a big red bow stuck to the top, made from real ribbon.

"Hurry the heck up," Jean said, after watching her try to untie the knot without tearing the ribbon.

Mama ignored Jean and took her sweet time. A bit of sun fell in the window, warming my skin. We almost seemed like a normal family, even though part of our hearts was missing, and I realized that with the three of us here, Christmas was salvageable.

Mama held up a metal beaded chain with a dog tag at the end of it. The silver shone in the light, and I suddenly worried how they would find Parker if Mama had his dog tags. Then I remembered what Jean said earlier and I tried to erase the thought.

"Is it a real one?" Jean asked.

Mama inspected the words and then smiled. She read it out loud in good Hawaiian. *"'Hoku'ula.'"*

"What the dickens does *Hoku'ula* mean?" Jean said.

Mama looked dreamy and her mouth bunched up like she might cry. "'Red star.' It's the proper name for Buster Brown hill. Where the men trained. We went there."

She handed me the tag. Someone had pounded in the letters in a very rough fashion, which made it seem like Parker had made it himself.

I think he loved her.

Chapter Thirty-Eight

VIOLET

AFTER BREAKFAST ON CHRISTMAS MORNING, the doorbell rang. It was Luther. He had called four times in the past couple of days. The first time, Violet said she had a roast in the stove and practically threw the phone away from her ear. From then on, she asked Jean to answer the phone. How could she face him and not say anything after what Riggs told her? Her gut had been telling her something was amiss with him all along.

"Merry Christmas. Anyone home?" Luther said as he pounded on the door.

Violet felt the pit in her stomach deepening. She shrugged at Jean as Ella disappeared into the bedroom.

"Come in," Jean said.

He wore a red hat, and with his white beard and paunch, he would have made a far better Santa than the drunk *paniolo.* Violet pretended to clean up paper and boxes around the tree. "Saw your friends shipped out," he said.

"They did."

"I have a gift for you ladies. Nothing big, but anyway." He fumbled around, clearing away a spot on the table to set down a jar of nuts. Were his hands shaking?

She commanded herself to act normal. *Aren't people innocent until proven guilty?* For that very reason, she hadn't told Setsuko yet. She wanted her ducks in a row. But Riggs had sounded convinced. After sweeping up imaginary dust and rearranging the tree lights, she fetched a coconut pie from the icebox.

"Merry Christmas. This is for you," she said to the wall behind his right ear.

When Luther took hold of the pie, his hands most definitely trembled. Alcohol or nerves? She felt a stirring of doubt. What if Riggs was wrong? Nevertheless, her main concern was how to get him out of the house.

During the next week, the mailbox became a central figure in their lives. Each day, checking the mail meant sweaty palms, a flurry of hope and, in the end, disappointment. Bursts of news slipped in through Irene Ferreira—the soldiers were laid over on Maui for one more bout of training; they had stopped at Pearl Harbor. Finally, they were gone from Hawaiian waters.

Violet and Jean both combed the papers for hints of where their men might be headed. Instead they heard about two drunk white US marines on Guam shooting and killing a black enlisted man. Hours later, another was shot to death.

"Horsefeathers! Black. White. Yellow. Why does any of it matter?" Jean asked.

Each night, Violet lay with Ella before bed. Since the men left, her sores had flared up and the nightmares resumed. She wet her pants twice in school, both times in shop class, which made her wonder. Was Luther going to work drunk? Was he scaring the kids?

"Who's going to protect us now?" Ella wanted to know.

She had also obsessed about having Roscoe come visit, to the point that Violet decided they would fetch him the next day, regardless of what Mr. Nakata might say. Chickens would be locked in the coop and they could keep him chained to the post on his long lead.

In the morning, Violet, Jean and Ella piled into the old Ford under a cloudless sky and set out toward Waimea. Their first visit since deployment. The main road looked about as lonely as they all felt. A few people rode along on horses, and a young boy pulled a red wagon full of helmets and dump treasures. Missing the soldiers intensified into a crushing pain between her shoulder blades.

When they arrived at the veterinarian's house, she saw Roscoe right away. He was lounging in a sunny spot on the porch, attached to a post with a long rope. At the sound of their car, he sat upright. Parker had reminded her that lions weren't like cattle or dogs. They climbed. So fencing didn't work.

Ella didn't even wait until Violet put on the brakes before flying out. "Roscoe!"

Roscoe bounded toward her as far as his rope would allow. Ella bent down and wrapped her arms around his neck. Violet watched the tenderness between them as he bumped his head into Ella's shoulder. Laughing, Ella fell back in the grass.

"Now, there's a good example of pure love. A kid and an animal," Jean said.

Violet thought then about her first reaction to Roscoe, and how silly she'd been. "Love is love, no matter the form."

Roscoe sat down next to Ella, yawning and exposing his ever-growing teeth. She beamed.

"You really love him, don't you?" Jean asked.

"Have you seen anything sweeter?"

"I'm not talking about Roscoe."

Love. An important word if there ever was one. "All I know is I want him to come home. Yesterday. It feels wrong, but most of the time I forget what I'm doing because my mind is on Parker. He's turned me half-crazy." Violet pressed her hand over her chest without realizing it. "If you call that love, I suppose I do love him."

Jean laughed. "Here you are, weepy-eyed and checking for letters like a schoolgirl, and you *suppose*. I knew it from the moment he set foot in our house, my dear."

Sometimes things were obvious to everyone but yourself. Violet had seen it in Jean. And now the favor was being returned.

Jean continued, "For heaven's sake, don't hold it in. That'll kill you. Say the words and say 'em often."

At that moment, she contemplated how much Jean had come to mean to her. "How about this. I love you."

"Please. That's not what I meant." Jean turned and flapped her lashes at Violet. "I love you, too, even if you are a bit khaki wacky."

"Speak for yourself."

Funny how love came in so many forms. Motherly love was steadfast and larger than life. Not up for debate. Friend love made you feel like you were never alone in the world. Love with men was different. With Herman it had been simmering coals and security. Parker a raging forest fire that would never go out. She was coming to realize that that was okay. Love was love, no matter its slant.

On the ride home, Ella chattered away in the back seat to Roscoe—now the size of a large German shepherd dog—who sat directly behind Violet. The best part of the ride was the lion breath heating up the back of her neck.

★★★

New Year approached, and each night, Violet watched the moon swell. Whether or not she would go into the cave with Bernard remained to be seen. The thought of swimming through a long, dark hole under the cliff caused a weakening of limbs. The water on this side of the island was not forgiving.

Ella begged to come. Violet said *no*, but the desperation in Ella's eyes cut through all resistance. There were no instructions on what to do in a case like this, and she went with her gut. "You can come. But not into the cave."

Throughout the days, Violet practiced holding her breath. Inhaling all the air she could muster and counting. The first time, she made it to thirty-four. The next, thirty.

"Let the men go in, for heaven's sake," Jean said, when she found Violet in the kitchen with her face turning blue.

"I have to do this."

"Not if you end up drowning in the process. Think about Ella."

"Why do you think I'm doing this?"

Jean squared off with her. "I know why, honey. And I'm praying for answers."

On the last night in December 1944, no one in the household felt like celebrating. Another year of war with no end in sight. But you couldn't tell that to the kids, so they invited over the Hamasus and Irene Ferreira, and got under way mixing hamburgers with bread crumbs and mayonnaise, slicing vine-ripened tomatoes and roasting marshmallows. They had enough food to feed a squadron, which turned out to be in Roscoe's favor. He was still with them, and aside from his love of lizards, he made a fine houseguest. Despite Ella's protests, he slept chained on the porch.

The kids all drifted off to sleep in front of the Christmas

tree. Ella always grew attached to the trees. In fact, last year they'd kept it up until March. Now, there was a fire hazard.

"Outside we go," Jean said just before the clock struck midnight.

Without argument, the four of them filed onto the porch. Jean toted a bottle in her left hand. Roscoe followed. When they had arranged themselves on the *pune'e*, Violet marveled at how they could be outside at midnight in January with nothing more than a thin blanket and body warmth keeping them alive. Still, there were no fireworks, no dancing, no men to kiss. The mistletoe still hung in the door frame, and every time Violet walked beneath it, she tasted Parker on her tongue.

The bottle of *okolehao* that Bernard sent her home with now made its way around. This time, she took more than a few sips.

"This stuff smells like the back end of a goat," she said.

"Or a soldier's rancid shoe," Jean said, burping.

"Excuse you."

Even Setsuko took a swig.

Irene must have been immune, the way she swigged from the bottle. "Nasty, but it does the job."

In the full moonlight, every tree in the yard cast its own shadow. Even the slits of the coconut leaves could be seen. The night softened. Violet felt giddy from alcohol and the closeness of her friends. She thought about how each was fashioned from her own unique pattern. All in this beautiful mess as one, lives sewn together with threads of love and loneliness.

"Anyone have a New Year's resolution?" Irene asked.

"Resolution, my *okole*," Jean said, taking another gulp.

"Nothing different than every day," Setsuko added.

Their faces were clear as day.

"Wait—you know what? I do have one," Jean said, sitting

up. "I'm going to tear up that letter that's been sitting on the icebox for the past two months, staring me in the face. In 1945, I vow to never think of Bud Walker again and to focus all my energy on Jean Quinlan, not some dumb liar."

Violet grabbed the bottle. "I'll drink to that." When she leaned forward to set it on the floor, she saw a flicker of movement beyond the chicken coop. She blinked, not sure if her vision could be trusted. A human-shaped blotch froze for a moment, as though aware of being spotted.

"Who goes there?" she called.

Roscoe immediately sat up, the fur along his spine raised.

The shadow bolted across the yard and merged with a grove of trees. Human for sure. All of the women were sitting up by now.

"Mr. Cody?" Setsuko whispered.

"He wouldn't even need to leave his house if he wanted to spy," Violet pointed out.

Jean stood and hollered into the yard, loud enough for the whole town to hear. "We have a lion here, so don't mess with us!"

A knot formed in Violet's gut. *Luther?*

Chapter Thirty-Nine

VIOLET

CRACKER AFTER CRACKER WAS THE ONLY WAY Violet could keep from throwing up her breakfast. Her eyes watered and her tongue felt like a thick slab of meat. Why had she gone and done this to herself? As they passed through the cane fields, she thought about Herman and how he used to bring home stalks of sugarcane to chew on. He and Ella loved the stuff. It seemed like anything Herman loved, Ella loved. A consummate daddy's girl.

Sheriff Souza drove a borrowed jeep that sounded like it might come apart at any moment. But there was no turning back now. Herman deserved this. Each bump on the steep road into the valley caused a churning in her stomach. Some start of the new year. Violet turned to check on Ella, whose head hung out the window like a dog. She seemed completely unaffected by the vertical drop a few feet from the wheels.

Souza wore a strained look. "You know, there's no need for you to go in there. I can handle this."

"I'm going."

Whatever the case.

Still, her heart rate had sped up to the point it was louder than the rattling jeep. *Calm down. Calm down. Calm down.* To make matters worse, driving into Waipio brought up images of Parker and the kiss at the waterfall. She blotted out those thoughts. Today was for Herman. Her hands trembled like an old man's.

The dirt road out toward the beach turned out to be far worse than the road to the back of the valley. Every ten yards or so, they had to slow for a mudhole the size of the jeep.

"Hang on," Souza said as he gunned it through the chalky brown water.

By the time they reached the beach they each looked like they'd taken a mud bath. Violet hardly cared.

On the near side of the river mouth, Bernard and his nephew waited with their four-man canoe pulled onto the black sand. There was a gray heaviness to the clouds, which stacked up on each other, but the ocean spread to the horizon, slick as oil. A lone fisherman with throw nets stood on the beach across the river. Other than that, two bony horses munching grass were the only signs of life.

Violet dragged herself out of the car, head throbbing.

"Hurry up! Low tide in an hour," Bernard said first thing, before adding, "My nephew, Kawika."

Kawika hardly nodded and Violet got the sense that he wanted them here even less than Bernard did. Ella, it seemed, had forgotten the purpose of their outing, because she ran down to the river and waded in, grinning like a wildcat. Violet let her go and turned her attention to the canoe, which was lashed together with frayed twine.

"This is going to hold all of us?" she asked.

Bernard scratched his chin. "We'll find out."

A terrible feeling washed over her.

They packed their gear under the seats, and Kawika handed Violet and Souza splintered paddles. "You ever paddle?"

Souza and Violet answered at the same time. "Yes." "No."

"Just follow uncle."

"Ella, come on!"

They slid the canoe into the water, and Bernard climbed in front and Kawika in back with a paddle blade the size of a car tire. Ella sat on the wooden outrigger facing Violet, and Souza sat in the seat behind them. As soon as they shoved off from shore, Violet knew she was in trouble. Sweat beads lined her forehead and the paddle felt like an anchor in her hands. She fought hard not to spit up, but within minutes, she found herself chest to the gunnel, releasing her stomach contents into the ocean.

The others stopped paddling. "Seasick?" Bernard asked.

"Okolehao," she said, splashing salt water over her face.

She wished they could turn around. Wished she could turn back the clock. By a matter of years.

The old man clucked. "Serves you right, then."

"You gave it to me."

"Not to drink in one night."

She waved them on, feeling slightly better.

"I'll paddle," Ella said.

"It's fine, sweetie."

"Girl wants to paddle, let her paddle," Bernard said.

For an old man, he sure could pull the canoe along. They switched places and Ella moved the blade through the water with far more finesse than Violet ever would. She'd learned how at Puako from the spear fishermen. Violet was now free to watch a gray wall of rain move in as they skirted the base of the towering cliff. With such a low tide, the exposed rocks displayed their abundance of opihi and scaly purple urchins.

Being so close in the normally rough seas would have been impossible.

One fat drop landed on her shoulder. Then another. The rain smelled pungent and sweet and stuck to her skin. No one made mention of the downpour as they paddled on down the coastline. Where the rain met the ocean, a thin fog of spray bounced up. With each stroke they took, her sense of unease rose. Ten minutes later, Bernard mumbled something to his nephew and pointed to an outcropping in the rock face. Twenty feet away, they dropped a rope with a rusty anchor.

"Current runs this way," Bernard said, pointing toward Hilo.

No wonder the boat seemed to be moving backward and tugging at the rope.

"Tide is good, uncle. Last time I saw the cave top was plenty years back," Kawika said in a lilted pidgin.

At the base of the cliff, a six-foot-wide hollow disappeared into the rock. Why anyone would want to swim in there, Violet would never know. But men could be counted on to do strange things.

Bernard pulled out two pairs of wooden swimming goggles and handed them to her and Souza. "Use these. Kawika no need."

Souza wiped his down with his wet shirt.

"What about you?" Violet asked.

"I stay with the girl."

"How will we see anything in there?" she asked, feeling the mountain of rock pressing down.

"Never mind," Bernard said, waving. "Go."

Already drenched from the rain, Violet pulled off her dress and handed it to Ella. "Use this for warmth if you need it."

Without warning, Ella burst into sobs. "Papa's in there. I

know he is!" She flung herself into Violet's arms. "I wanna come."

She held Ella, rubbing her back and rocking. "One way or the other, we'll know soon. You stay with Bernard. This is too dangerous for you."

"Wondering can be a curse," her mother once said. How many years had she spent wondering when her father would return? And then Herman. Every time a car pulled up, a phone rang, the dull hope that maybe, just maybe, it would be him.

A slice of sun pierced through the water all the way to the black rocks below. Kawika jumped in with a mesh bag slung over his shoulder. Souza hurled himself after him. Violet looked down, unable to move. Her body felt like it weighed three hundred pounds.

"You staying?" Bernard asked.

"No."

She forced herself in, surprised at the water's icy burn. Kawika led them to the opening, which allowed only a few inches of breathing space. She was taller than that. She glanced back at Ella, who clutched at the gunnels, her little wet body shivering. The look on her face was pure terror. Violet turned away. *You have to do this.*

Kawika let out a knotted rope. "Ten feet in, we go under. Hang on to this and don't let go."

She and Souza both grabbed on.

With heads tilted back, they proceeded. God only knew what kind of toothy creatures awaited, but not much she could do about it now. When the crack of air ended, Kawika took a deep breath and led them under. Gripping the rope with one hand, she kicked. *Relax,* she instructed herself. Through the goggles, she saw seaweed-lined boulders and a handful of fish. An eerie blue light came not only from behind, but someplace up ahead. *Thirty-nine, forty, forty-one, forty-two.* Just when her lungs pleaded for an inhalation, she burst through the surface.

Above, the cavern dripped water, but also muted light. Cracks in the ceiling.

From behind, Souza wheezed, unable to catch his breath. "Damn cigarettes," he said.

When Violet turned to check on him, she saw a dark shape moving toward him underwater. She braced for impact, unsure of whether to watch or turn away. But before she could warn him, another head popped up. Souza lurched away and yelled in surprise.

"Ella?" she cried.

"Don't be mad, Mama."

She should have known better than to leave Ella in the boat, but there was no time to argue. "Stay close," she told her.

Ella's fingers raked into Violet's arm. They swam to the rocks and clambered up. Her knee slammed into a rock but she ignored the pain. Once on dry land, they surveyed their surroundings. Driftwood and scattered bones lay piled high beyond the waterline on one side. Kawika pulled a flashlight from a jar and illuminated a cow skull and a tangled mass of shipping rope. "Graveyard," he said.

Enough light filtered through the rocks to make out shapes. A monk seal's flipper bone was easily distinguishable, as were fishing floats of varying sizes. Violet's eyes picked up another round object at the top of a pile.

"Over there. What's that?" She pointed.

Kawika swung the flashlight around. The beam stopped. *Dear God.* A skull. Violet's teeth chattered and the world around her spun. *Dear God.*

"Whoa, this is new," Kawika said.

"Looks human. When were you last in here?" Souza asked Kawika.

"Just over a year," Kawika said.

Their voices streamed past her. She stared up at the smooth white skeleton splayed over the mound of rocks. Remnants of tattered cloth lay in piles around it.

Souza moved first. "Bring that light up here," he said, climbing the little hill on all fours. He crouched down to inspect the scene and Violet gulped for air. A small crab scurried away.

"Looks intact," he said.

Violet forced her mind to remain on the simple task at hand, forming words. "Can you tell anything about it?" she asked.

"I'm going to say male. Based on rib-cage size and the pelvis. Give me that," he said, taking the light from Kawika, who then backed away and tripped over a rock. "More important than that, there's a hole dead center in the forehead. And maybe another in the sternum."

His voice bounced off the cave roof and struck her with a physical force. Violet crumpled to the ground. Ella clutched her hand, remaining upright and rigid and ice-cold. A moment later, the smell of urine hit her nostrils and she heard dripping on the rocks beneath Ella's feet.

"We're going to get you out of here, okay?" she said.

A low moan came from her daughter's throat and it was hard to tell if she was trying to say something or not.

"What, honey?"

The moan rose to a high-pitched whine. A frightened animal sound. Violet scooped Ella into her arms and squeezed. As sure as the ocean was deep, these remains belonged to Herman. Knowing rose in her body, along with the searing pain of loss. She wanted to swim out of here, to take the bones back to the top of the cliff and reassemble them, add on flesh and somehow breathe them back to life. *How can this be my husband?*

"I need to get Ella out of here," she said.

"Go if you must, but I need a few more minutes here," Souza said.

"We stick together," Kawika said.

Souza leaned down closer, his face almost to the skeleton. The light beam shone through the rib cage and onto whatever lay below. "Find me a stick," he commanded Kawika.

The way Ella's teeth chattered had Violet concerned, but there was nothing to do but wait. She felt a tide of panic swelling, and movies played in her mind about how Herman ended up here. Falling from the cliffs, bouncing like a doll and missing any trees that could have stopped him. Or was he pushed? Nothing made sense.

Souza poked around for some time at the decayed cloth. "Shirt looks like red *palaka*," he said, looking over at her.

On the day that Herman disappeared, he had left the house in a red long-sleeved *palaka* shirt. Her last image of him was standing in the kitchen with a piece of toast sticking out of his mouth. A glob of grape jelly stuck to his mustache. She swayed at the thought.

Souza continued his search. "Bingo!" he said, holding up a small shiny object.

A bullet.

Numbness came over her, same as the night he went missing. Then the numbness turned to rage at the unfairness of it all. Here Herman lay in a dark cave while she and Ella continued on with their lives. Someone out there was responsible. She wanted to scream. Or maybe she did scream.

Souza put an arm around her waist. "Violet. Someone is going to pay."

"Promise me."

Who could have done this?

Next, Souza held up a gold band he'd pulled from beneath the hand. Nothing fancy, just a small smooth ring.

"Recognize this?" he asked.

Violet took it from him. It was too dim to see the inscription, *H & V 1934*, but there was no mistaking the ring.

"Can I keep this?" she asked.

"For now, but I'll need it as evidence," he said.

"We need to go. I'm worried about my daughter," Violet said.

Ella was shaking violently. She pulled her closer and rubbed her hands along her back.

"Leave the body?" Souza said.

Body. Husband. Bones.

"I would like a proper burial," Violet said, "but I don't see how we will get him out of here. And it almost seems irreverent."

"You better get 'em now if you like. Or else the ocean will sooner or later," Kawika said.

A loud sucking noise filled the cave. Pretty soon the tide would make it impossible to get out. Bernard had been clear about that. She had the ring. It would have to be enough.

"We'll go without him. But give me a minute alone," she said.

After Souza took a few measurements and gathered clothing fragments and the bullets, he and Kawika clambered down the rocks to the water's edge and left her and Ella alone. Ella started panting.

Words spilled out. "Oh, Herman. We miss you more than you know." Violet wiped her cheek. "Someone really awful did this to you and I'm sorry."

She closed her eyes and hugged Ella into her soggy breast.

The wedding band burned the skin of her palm. Had she been without Ella she would have wanted to stay for days. She felt she owed him more.

"Tide's coming up," Kawika called.

Then a high-pitched cry came out of Ella that cut through the darkness and paused her heart. Ella's whole body rocked back and forth and she was choking on sobs. Without waiting any longer, Violet picked her up and carried her down to the water's edge, wondering how they were going to get out. She set Ella down and faced her.

"We have to swim out of here. Do you understand?"

Ella's eyes were glazed over. She seemed to be looking right through Violet. Souza and Kawika stood next to them. Neither said a word.

Violet tried again, at her wit's end. "If we stay much longer, we won't be able to get out. Do you think you can hold your breath again and swim?"

It was as though time had folded back on itself to the night of Herman's disappearance. The blank look, the trembling, the sobbing. The terrible feeling she'd had earlier now quadrupled in size. Now more than ever, she was sure Ella knew something.

Violet grabbed Ella by both shoulders. "Look at me."

Ella made eye contact.

"Can you do this?"

An imperceptible nod. It was enough.

"Goodbye, Herman" was the last thing Violet said before submerging her head beneath the water.

Chapter Forty

VIOLET

VIOLET AND JEAN SAT ON THE PORCH IN THE late-afternoon sun. Little by little, her limbs were thawing. Souza had dropped them off earlier. They'd both had blue lips and white fingers and toes. Worse than that cold was the cold that penetrated the chambers of her heart, a place where no mug of hot cocoa or warm bath could reach. All the same, she loved Jean for bringing them blankets.

Ella had remained mute and curled up in Violet's lap the whole way home. She now snored on the *pune'e* and Violet wondered how much more she could take. It was hard to be strong for Ella when she felt her own seams unraveling, her very soul emptying. No matter how many days had passed, dinners made, classes taught, pies sold, everything circled back to the day Herman went missing. Strange how one day could take up so much space in a life.

She leaned back in the chair and hugged her knees to her chest for warmth. Cool tendrils of wind rustled her matted hair. Tears started up again. Herman dead; Parker gone with a good chance of becoming dead; Ella catatonic, her spirit dead. She wanted to close her eyes and fall sleep and not wake up. But for Ella. Tomorrow, Violet would take her to see Henry Aulani since he had been the only one to help the last time around.

Jean kept talking and asking questions, and Violet heard only half of what she was saying.

"Why the dickens would someone want to kill Herman?" Jean said.

She was sick of that question. It haunted her day and night. "People have had their theories, but who knows?" Violet stared off at the gray horizon.

"But Souza got a bullet?" Jean asked.

She nodded. "American, he said. None of us felt like talking on the road home, but I could tell his mind was churning out theories. You think it's possible Herman was a spy?"

"No way."

"Then what? He didn't gamble. No enemies," Violet said.

"Maybe he was in the wrong place at the wrong time. Maybe he saw something."

Jean was only trying to be helpful, but Violet didn't want to think anymore. "Crazy people invent their own reasons for doing things," she said.

They contemplated theories for a while—disgruntled students, war stuff—but as always, ended up with an empty plate. When Jean went to prepare dinner, Violet lay down with Ella, food the furthest thing from her mind. She looked at the row of sea-urchin spines and shells along the windowsill, and at a piece of driftwood that Herman once brought her because it reminded him of a whale. Now driftwood would forever remind her of the cave where they'd found him. *Such a decent man.*

The hens came around, scratching and chattering, and Violet got up and went out to throw scraps for them. She sat on the steps and watched them for a while. What a simple life they led. Eat, sleep, poop. Maybe bringing Brownie in to Ella would help. After a few failed attempts, she caught the chicken, who now had a thin layer of fluff growing in. She carried her in and set her on the table next to the *pune'e*. Brownie hunkered down and clucked. Ella's eyes popped open.

"Someone wants to say hello," Violet said, smoothing down Ella's hair.

In the dim light, Ella watched Brownie from two feet away, but she made no move to pet her. If only there was a way to pry someone open and read their thoughts like a magazine, Violet would have given everything she owned and then some.

"Supper is ready," Jean called from the kitchen.

"I don't suppose you're hungry?" Violet said to Ella.

Ella scrunched up her face.

"We need to get some nourishment into you."

Ella closed her eyes. This couldn't go on.

Violet went to the table since Jean had bothered to cook for them, but she pushed her rice and carrots around the plate. As much as she tried, she was able to take in only a few bites. Food was the last thing on her mind.

"I know what you went through was god-awful today and you're still in shock, but at least you have certainty now," Jean said.

She nodded. That was the singular positive outcome. From here forward, she could focus on uncovering the how and the why and moving forward with her life instead of being mired in quicksand. "I'm going to lie with Ella. Thank you for being our nursemaid."

She reached over and held Jean's hand.

Under the auspices of the new year, Violet fell asleep on the *pune'e* swaddled in blankets and draped in black. Her dreams came in bursts and fragments, each a different version of finding the skeleton. In one, there were crabs living in the skull. In another it was somehow still alive. Ella tossed and turned, too, whimpering and drenched in sweat.

One of the worst nights in history.

Just before morning, Ella woke and sat up and shook Violet. Her bony arms looked milk-pale against the green blanket. She was sobbing in short bursts. "Mama," she stuttered.

"Honey, I'm here. What is it?"

Violet could barely make out her face, but she could see Ella's eyes on her, wide and glistening.

"Mama." This time louder.

The need to know flared up inside Violet. "Whatever you're holding inside, whatever you're afraid of is only going to get worse with time. Please, please talk to me."

The nature of secrets. They burn a hole through you, no matter how thick your skin.

"Mama. I was there."

Chapter Forty-One

ELLA

IT WAS DUMB OF ME TO THINK I COULD GO through life with a secret this big. But I was only doing the best I knew how. I spent lots of time making plans to tell Mama. Once or twice I almost whispered the news when she tucked me in at night or while we picked sweet potatoes in the garden, just the two of us. And then I thought of her going to tell the sheriff. So that usually ended that. Plus, after the soldiers left, she seemed so sad and lost.

I look back and see that half of me didn't believe we would find anything in that cave. The other half knew we would. The whole way into the valley and while we paddled, a terrible argument was going on inside me. *Tell. Don't tell. Tell. Don't tell.* When I saw the skull bone, and then the bullet hole and ring, it was like someone shut a curtain in front of my eyes and suddenly I was watching a movie called *How My Papa Died.* I don't even remember leaving the cave.

Now I had to tell. I was terror-stricken, but it was going

to come out sooner or later, and I had to warn Mama before she went digging around on her own.

On the day Papa died, us kids were playing hide-and-seek next door at the Codys'. The yard didn't have many hiding places, so I sneaked around Papa's car and climbed in, making sure to shut the door without a sound. I lay on the floor and pulled a blanket over me.

A few minutes later, someone opened the door. I held my breath. Then the car started up. Instead of saying hello to Papa, I stayed there and didn't make a peep. Who knows why? Maybe I was bored and wanted to see where he was going. Sometimes he met with the rifle people for planning against Japanese invasion. We drove and we drove and we drove. The floor heated up, but by now I was stuck. Even though I couldn't see him, I knew my papa was upset about something. Don't ask me how. I just knew. Maybe it was the way he zoomed around corners and slammed on the brakes.

After ten minutes or so of a very uncomfortable ride, he pulled onto a bumpy road. My head bounced like a bowling ball, and an "ouch" slipped out, but he didn't seem to notice. This was way more interesting than being stuck with the kids. From what I guessed, we were closer to Waipio Valley than to Honoka'a. The car headed downhill. I practiced my blind navigation skills, which would come in handy if the Japanese ever showed up.

When we finally stopped, salty air blew in the windows and Papa lit up a cigarette. Weird, because he hardly smoked. I remember thinking what a real adventure it felt like. And that I would surprise him and he would laugh and kiss the top of my head like he always did. Then he pounded the steering wheel and yelled, "Damn!"

Another engine approached. Louder and louder, until finally it turned off right next to us. A door slammed. I decided to stay put. Papa got out, too.

"Herman, what's this all about?"

"Tell me it's not true," Papa said in a husky tone I'd never heard him use.

A pause and then, "What do you mean?"

I would know that voice anywhere.

"That you're a goddamn informant for the military, which wouldn't be so bad if you weren't a liar on top of that," Papa said.

"Who told you that?"

"Cut the crap, Luther. And it doesn't matter who told me. You were the one who conveniently volunteered that the Shinto priests here were plotting something. That they were a threat to security. Which is a load of crap. They were nothing more than a group of old men who liked to pray," Papa said.

Earlier that year we watched armed men line up those old priests and march them into a big army truck. To their credit, not a one looked scared or even remotely concerned. Mama said they trained themselves to be like mountains and that way nothing bothered them.

"So what if I did? You're not my mother," Luther said.

Papa's laugh stuck in his throat. "How could you be so two-faced? And not even mention this to me. They also asked about Takeo and said you told them he's sending coded messages to the Jap submarines, which we both know is a lie. I had to vouch for him again so they didn't haul his ass away, too. What are you thinking?" he cried.

"Japs get what they deserve," Luther said in a really calm voice that caused all of my hairs to stand on end.

"We live in Honoka'a. Everyone here is Japanese. You want them to arrest the whole town?"

I heard the crunch of rock and grass and they moved away from the car. "Why not?"

"I know you lost Neil, and I'm sorry for that. But the people here are not responsible for that any more than I am," Papa said.

Luther hissed. "Are you saying you knew something? About Pearl Harbor?"

"No, I'm saying I know my friends."

"You're in with the Japs, aren't you?"

I didn't like the sound of Luther's voice.

"Get ahold of yourself."

Luther rambled on. "They're sneaky fuckers and none of 'em can be trusted. I always knew it. They killed my son..."

Their voices moved farther and farther away, and I heard Papa say something about a nephew and not a son, about not tolerating liars, that maybe Luther should leave town if he didn't like it here.

Luther was spitting out words and I strained to hear. "Some things I keep private...illegitimate."

But I was still stuck on the *son* part. According to Mama, he'd lost a nephew at Pearl Harbor. This poor nephew was locked in a ship at the bottom of the ocean. I had felt sad for Luther back then, and sad for the men who died. A son was a different story.

They yelled some more and I only caught every other word. "Insane..." "Fuck..." "Vigilante..." "My ass..." "Too much *okolehao*."

There was no way Papa could know I was listening to these dirty words. I prayed for them to hurry and finish the fight so I could get back to my game. Somebody might notice I was missing by now, or else think I had a really good hiding place. One day we forgot about Umi and she fell asleep in the laundry basket, so tired from working in the victory garden after school. Setsuko-san was frantic.

A gunshot jolted me into the bottom of the seat. And another.

My heart galloped but my body refused to move. I heard grunting and dragging and willed myself to sit up and look. Enough time had passed that Luther stood at the edge of the cliff dusting off his hands, alone. I ducked and knocked my head on my hand to see if I could wake myself up, but nothing changed. The sound of footsteps hurried toward the car. He jumped into the front seat and flung stuff around.

Please, God, don't let him look back here.

God must have been busy or not paying attention, because Luther did look. I will never know what drove him to pull the blanket off me. Maybe my uncontrollable shivering or the pounding of my heart against the floorboard. With one giant hand, he yanked me out of Papa's car and set me down in his.

"You idiot! What are you doing here?"

He was going to kill me. I closed my eyes, waiting for him to shoot. All this time in the war, they told us if we got captured by the Japanese, we'd be shot. Not in a million years had I thought I'd be shot by our own shop teacher. My body went numb. *Let it be quick.*

"Look at me!" he said. I looked. Foam built up on the corners of his mouth and one of his eyes twitched. "You saw and heard nothing. Got that, Ella?"

I nodded.

"Fucking mess," he yelled, pounding the dashboard with his giant hand. "This was all his fault. Your father was putting us all in danger. Lie down."

He shoved me sideways onto the bench seat, smashing my ear with his huge palm. If there was one thing I knew, it was that Papa would never put us in danger. Never ever. My cheek stuck to the seat with tears and strings of snot. I was trying to make sense of what just happened.

Luther was a madman. Papa was dead.

"If you say anything about this, your mother will die, too."

The whole time we were driving, I heard the two gunshots and felt them burning through my skin. What if Luther had missed? Even so, the ocean was miles below. Only birds knew those cliffs. No one would survive that fall.

Papa was dead.

"I have ears and eyes everywhere, Ella. If I end up in jail, others will come for Violet. I only did what I had to, to stop the spread of sickness. Promise me you won't talk."

Another car passed us, unaware of the terror going on inside. "I promise," I squeaked out.

Luther slammed his hand onto his forehead. "Ah hell, I should just kill you now." A battle seemed to be going on in his head. *Kill Ella. Don't kill Ella. Kill Ella.*

I wanted to say, "No, please don't," but I lost my voice.

Papa was dead!

"I don't want any more blood on my hands, but I will do it. I will. Keep your fucking mouth shut and you and your mother will live."

I nodded. I wanted my papa at that moment. More than anything I have ever wanted or probably will ever want.

But he was dead.

Chapter Forty-Two

VIOLET

BEFORE SUNRISE, ELLA FINISHED. VIOLET TREMbled. There was no air left in her lungs and her brain struggled to piece it all together. *Friend. Liar. Murderer.* Of equal concern was how Ella managed to exist without saying anything. Kids believed adults, plain and simple. And Ella would have done anything to keep her mother alive.

"Honey, I wish you had told me."

Ella looked up at her with those big brown eyes. "He swore he would kill you if I told. And if they got him, he had others to do the job."

"I know, but this was too much for you to handle on your own. Bad men lie."

"I didn't want you to die," Ella said, her voice cracking.

"Promise me something, okay? If anyone ever threatens you again, you tell me."

Ella nodded. "I was getting ready to, I swear. And then this happened."

Violet lay down and hugged her with every ounce of love she could muster. She knew that Ella would have told her if she'd been capable and not threatened into a state of terror. But Ella was her own little person. One with an iron will. Still, disbelief swarmed through her.

Luther taught her shop class, came by the house, did them favors. When in reality, the man was hiding a terrible secret. More than one, actually. In hindsight, Ella's sickness that first afternoon, the stomachaches and nervous picking, the fear of leaving Violet's side all made perfect sense. How had she not noticed the connection?

She hugged Ella tighter, wishing she could scrub away any memory of that day. Something this awful had never crossed her mind. Grief, sure. But not in this form.

Now would be a good time to march over and point a gun to Luther's head. To hell with the law. If a man killed your husband and threatened your daughter, he deserved an extra dose of his own poison.

Jean poked her head in the door. "Is everything all right?"

Violet sat up. "Everything is not all right. Call Setsuko and Irene."

For once, Jean didn't ask questions. She ran off to the kitchen.

Not five minutes later, Setsuko showed up. Violet told them everything.

"This is downright outrageous," said Jean, her cheeks wet with tears.

"I'll never be able to forgive myself."

Jean grabbed her arm. "Look at me, Violet. You are in no way responsible for any of this. Do you hear me? None of us suspected."

"But we knew something was wrong with Ella."

"Her father disappeared, for Pete's sake."

"I should have seen it," Violet said.

"Nonsense," Jean assured her.

They walked out to the living room and Jean smoothed down Ella's hair. "And you. To think you had such knowledge locked up inside you. I just want to hug you for the next thousand years."

Ella sat propped on a pillow, looking brave. Wisps of hair stuck out in all directions. Violet got the feeling that she felt relieved. No longer the lone keeper of the secret that had been gnawing away at her insides and festering in her tiny heart.

Setsuko stood and began to pace. "We need to call Souza."

"Oh, we will. Right now, in fact. But I also have a plan," Violet said.

Jean looked worried. "What kind of plan?"

"You'll see."

Irene arrived fifteen minutes later, wearing rubber boots and a look of surprise. She agreed to stay with the kids, and in the kitchen. Violet quietly instructed her to lock the doors and call Souza in twenty minutes. Leaving Ella was the last thing she wanted to do, but had to. She told her they were off to tell the sheriff.

A small lie.

They took Roscoe and went straight to Setsuko's house, where a gun lay hidden in a shoebox under the floorboard. Violet knew because the gun once belonged to Herman. She also knew how to shoot a fly from a hundred yards away. One of the perks of growing up in the boondocks of Minnesota. Setsuko pulled a chair to the closet and lifted down an old rifle.

"You never know," she said.

Jean paced behind them. "This is a bad idea. And don't point that thing anywhere near me."

"I need to see the fear of God in his eyes, before Souza shows up. Make him squirm." Violet fingered the cold, hard steel.

"I'm with you," Setsuko said.

"What if he's awake?" Jean asked.

"He won't be."

The moon had dropped behind the mountains, leaving only darkness and a thin announcement of sunrise. Violet held Roscoe close on the rope as they hurried toward Luther's cottage at the far end of campus. As they approached, the hair lifted on her neck.

The small one-room building used to be the shop, but a few years back Herman helped Luther transform it into living quarters. Concrete floors aided in their plan, which hinged on Luther being asleep. Violet held open the screen door, and Jean and Setsuko tiptoed in. The first thing that struck her was the stench. Bottles covered the table, and the rank smell of liquor overwhelmed.

No wonder he is drinking himself to death.

Maybe it was her imagination, but Roscoe seemed to sense an importance to their mission and remained glued to her thigh. They had to pick up bottles from the floor in order to avoid a clamor. She counted sixteen. She stopped at the bedroom door, with Setsuko pressed behind her and Jean in the rear with a baseball bat in hand.

They slipped in.

Funny how life could change direction overnight. When they'd gotten home from the cave yesterday, Violet had every intention of telling Luther about Herman. Even if he was suspected of spreading lies. Only there had been no answer when she called and she was too sapped to leave the house. The news could wait until morning. Now they were here with a different kind of news.

"Jean, stay over here," she whispered. And to Setsuko, "And you point the rifle at his chest. Give me ten seconds to get in place."

Setsuko nodded.

Once in the room, Violet's bare feet stuck to the gritty floor. Sweat and old socks stunk up the air. Enough light shone in the window to reveal Luther lying half under the sheets in a white undershirt. His mouth hung open. Two seconds later Jean flipped the switch and the whole room lit up. Violet raised the gun.

"Luther," she said.

He might have heard, because his mouth puckered up and he moaned, but he didn't wake. "Luther!" she said, louder this time.

His eyes popped open and he immediately shaded them from the light. "What's this all about?" he growled. When he removed his hand and saw Violet standing at the foot of his bed with a gun aimed at his face, he pulled the blanket up to his chin as if that might protect him. "Holy Christ, Violet!"

She held his gaze. His eyes were bloodshot and drool crusted in his beard.

"Why, Luther? Tell me why you killed him."

No answer would ever be enough.

His eyes narrowed. "Have you lost your mind?"

Violet studied his shortened breaths and the look of fear falling across his face. "We already know that you're a coward and a bully. But a murderer?"

"Don't forget liar," Setsuko said from the door.

For the first time, Luther looked away from Violet, catching sight of the rifle and the lion. Then his eyes went to his bedside table and he seemed to be measuring his chances of reaching something there.

"Take those guns off me," he said.

With both hands on the gun, Violet took one step closer. "And just so you know, I could hit a walnut from two hundred yards."

The blood ran out of his face.

Violet continued, not sure how she managed. "We know everything. We found Herman in the back of a cave yesterday. There were bullets. Ella broke down and filled us in on the rest. You son of a bitch, my daughter is going to have to live with this the rest of her life."

"She's lucky to be alive," Luther said.

The words shocked her into immobility, while she wondered what turned a human into a monster. Something in his tone caused a low hum in Roscoe. Luther took the opportunity to lunge across the bed, out of her line of fire. At the same time, Roscoe flew across the room and pinned him down with both paws, sitting over him like a dead bird. Violet had seen cats move at light speed to catch a lizard or a mouse, but she wouldn't have suspected Roscoe to be so quick.

Luther lay facedown, with Roscoe growling in his ear. "Oh, God, help me!"

All along, their plan had never been to kill Luther. Just pump him up with fear. The man who had killed her husband and instilled terror in her daughter, all the while coming over and acting helpful and concerned. She wanted to burn their pie stand that he had built for them. Let him think he was at the mercy of three crazy housewives and a lion. The plan seemed to be working. Soon, claw marks formed in the fleshy skin of his back. His whimpering gave her a small measure of satisfaction.

Jean came out of hiding and walked up to the bed. "You may not know this, but Roscoe has an affinity for fat old men."

Luther tried to wiggle free, but Roscoe bared his teeth and rumbled. Violet forced herself to sound calm. "So, what do you say? Want Roscoe to finish you off, or would you rather rot in prison for the rest of your life?"

With his face pressed into the mattress, Luther sobbed and mumbled to himself. "I didn't mean it. Going to hell. One last drink." Roscoe looked over and she raised her palm. In the month before Parker left, he had tried to teach him hand signals. Violet had laughed, saying that cats couldn't be trained. But Parker believed Roscoe knew exactly what they all meant. Whatever the case, it worked. He sat down on Luther and waited.

Outside, an engine roared up and tires screeched on gravel. Three doors slammed.

"We're in the bedroom," Violet called out the window.

When Souza got to the door, he about dropped. The way Luther lay like a dummy, it was hard to tell if he was still alive. Fear would do that to a person.

Two deputies trailed behind Souza, all armed. The men surrounded the bed from a distance and kept their guns pointed to the ceiling, away from Roscoe. "Luther Hodges, you are under arrest for the murder of Herman Iverson," Souza said.

Luther groaned.

"Want to call off your lion, ladies?" Souza said.

Violet patted her leg. "Roscoe, come."

He jumped off the bed and padded over, sitting at her feet and rubbing his scratchy head against her leg. She felt a swell of pride. Everyone in the room let out a sigh of relief. But she had known all along that Roscoe was not a man killer. All three policemen pointed their guns at the bed.

"You, get your slimy ass off the bed. You're coming with us," Souza said.

Violet turned and walked out. Luther had poured darkness over her family. How could she erase that?

Chapter Forty-Three

ELLA

MURDER IS BIG NEWS IN A SMALL TOWN. ESPEcially when the killer turns out to be the school shop teacher. That and the fact that everyone knows Luther and my papa were friends. Before the murder. Not that any murder is right, but somehow killing a friend seems more twisted. That's what Jean says.

It also came out that Luther made up a story about Takeo, and his being taken to camp was one big misunderstanding. Seems like a pretty big misunderstanding, but Sheriff Souza is working on getting him out. Most of the people in his camp have been sent to the mainland, where there are a whole lot more camps. There, you don't even need to have done anything bad. Just being Japanese is enough. I hope the sheriff has some pull.

Mama sat me down and explained that once in a while, a person goes bad, kind of like with coconuts. On the outside, everything looks fine, but you open it up and the meat is brown and smelly. I suppose you could say that Luther is a human version of rotten.

A few days after the arrest, early in the morning, someone came knocking on our door. I was already up heating cream for Roscoe. Mama was in the bathroom, so I peeked out to see who was there. Bernard Lalamilo stood with a newspaper in hand.

I walked out to greet him. "Hi, Mr. Lalamilo. Would you like to come in?"

He looked at me with sorry eyes and one less tooth than just the other day. "You doing all right, girl?"

"Yes, sir," I said.

I could tell that he wanted to make things better. He might drink a lot of moonshine, but he was a good man. I had seen that right off the bat. And I never told Mama this, but he helped me into the cave. He knew I had to see for myself.

Mama showed up behind me. "Bernard," she said.

"Ma'am, just wanted to give you this." He held out the rolled-up paper. "Glad you got the bastard. Luther came down plenty for *okolehao*. Something not right with that man."

"With all that guilt burning through him, he'd have needed it," Mama said.

She took the paper. Would you believe that even larger than the photographs of Papa and Luther was a photograph of Roscoe sitting on the front of a jeep, surrounded by all us schoolchildren. Someone must have taken it that first day the soldiers brought him, out in the school yard. Of all the kids in the picture, I was the only one petting him. In the picture, you could see my underwear, but I'm long past caring about that sort of thing.

We spread out the paper on the table and read.

LION NEW TOWN HERO

January 4, 1945.

Roscoe, the infamous lion of Camp Tarawa, helped catch a cold-blooded killer. On New Year's Day, new information as to the whereabouts of missing Honoka'a High principal Herman Iverson was uncovered. Sheriff Bobby Souza remained tight-lipped on details, but suggested that the remains of a body were found, with evidence of gunshot wounds and bullets still at the scene. Just before dawn the following morning, Souza and his deputies apprehended the suspected killer, none other than Luther Hodges, the shop teacher. Souza said that in the process of the arrest, Hodges lunged for his gun, but Roscoe the lion pinned him down, saving the officers from a scuffle, or worse.

No motive was available, nor information about how they found the body so long after the disappearance. Several unnamed sources revealed that Hodges had lost a son at Pearl Harbor and believed Herman to be somehow responsible. Iverson was a well-known supporter of local Japanese, and reports are that the two clashed and it turned deadly. Hodges had also turned to the bottle.

Violet Iverson, Herman's widow, has been helping to care for Roscoe while the marines are away. According to Souza, Roscoe is going to be deputized and honored in a ceremony. Police dogs are common, but this is the first known case of a police lion. Long live Roscoe!

I was so proud of Roscoe I cried. Big sobbing gulps. We all did. Mama said he was a hero in more than one way. Not only did he help them get Luther, but he helped nurse me back to health. Not that many people have a lion for a nursemaid. I guess that makes me lucky.

Planning a service for Papa with a real and proper goodbye, and a ceremony for Roscoe, kept us busy through all the next week. "Doing is the best medicine," Mama liked to say. And she was right. All that turmoil that had built up inside me was now slowly leaking out, little by little. I hardly had time to think about what I had been through.

We crawled through the forest, cutting ginger and ferns for the church ceremony. Mama even strung an extra long yellow plumeria lei for Roscoe. By Friday, we ended up with enough coconut pies for the whole island.

On the morning of the funeral, Mama told me to dress in color rather than black. She had insisted on Aloha attire as standard dress. Something about celebrating life, not death. Plus, we were in Hawaii. As usual, I picked a flowered yellow dress and Jean helped me pin a red hibiscus in my hair. When she bent over me, I smelled roses.

When we got to the church I felt choked up at how many people were packed into the tiny red building, overflowing across the yard and onto the cracked street. Not one person was going to miss this. Everyone loved my papa.

We stood on the curb. Mama looked down at me and smiled, and then we walked in.

Instead of organ music, three Hawaiian men strummed guitars and sang with uneven voices. When we got closer, I saw that one of them was actually Bernard Lalamilo. He winked when I caught his eye. A few old ladies in the audience sang along. The way their song circled around us and vibrated through the morning made me feel loved and cared for. We sat in the front row with Jean, Setsuko and the twins, and Irene Ferreira. True friends if there ever were. Mama sat ramrod straight.

I promised myself I wouldn't cry. Which is not something I recommend at a funeral. Once Minister Kaaua got going about Papa, and how he was a father to all the children in town, a guardian, a husband and an outsider turned *kama'aina*, I knew I was in trouble. He went on about what makes a man noble and honorable. A few other townsfolk stood up and added their own memories. Finally Setsuko walked to the podium and pulled out a folded piece of paper. Mama squeezed my hand. This was a surprise.

I was impressed by how loud her voice sounded and how she paused and looked us both in the eye after each line. The poem went like this:

I fall asleep in the full and certain hope
That my slumber shall not be broken;
And that though I be all-forgetting,
Yet shall I not be forgotten,
But continue that life in the thoughts and deeds
Of those I loved.

Poetry is not something I always understand, but I think I took in the meaning of those words and swore at that moment that Papa would always live in my deeds and my thoughts. I'm sure Mama felt the same. I had tears splashing onto my dress, but I hardly noticed.

All morning long, rain had been turning on and off. Now it stopped again, and a flood of sunlight shone through the windowpanes. You could see dust suspended in the air, and a couple of bees hummed around our flower arrangement. I wondered how I could feel so many things at once. The kind of sadness that tugs at the edges of your heart, pent-up anger that this happened to my papa, while at the same time relief at Luther's arrest. On top of that, I felt a big fat swelling of hope. The kind that would help me preserve my papa where it mattered most. Smack-dab in the center of my chest.

Chapter Forty-Four

VIOLET

IF THERE WAS ONE THING YOU COULD COUNT on, it was for the world to keep on spinning no matter what kind of heartbreak had transpired. Rain was predicted to fall indefinitely, which made for a wet first week back at school. Even in drowning downpours, Violet never missed a day of mail-checking. It had been over two weeks since the soldiers left.

On Friday afternoon, she opened the mailbox. *A letter.*

She dashed to the house through puddles and soggy grass, and despite her best efforts, the envelope wound up spotted with raindrops. Bleeding ink showed a post date of January 2. Violet flung the door open and stepped inside.

Jean sat on the *pune'e* painting her toenails red. "Horsefeathers, what's gotten into you?"

Violet held up the letter.

"Open the darn thing," Jean said.

"Give me a second. Where's Ella?"

"At Setsuko's with Umi."

This was good news. Ella out and about. She prayed school would no longer hold its place of terror. Air-raid drills might have been triggers, but more likely seeing Luther day in and day out was the main cause. Not to mention the continual fear that men might be coming for Violet.

Once the shock of finding Herman and catching Luther had died down, Violet had taken Ella to see Henry Aulani, the Hawaiian healer, again. If anyone, he would be able to siphon out some of the hurt and pent-up fear to help right the world for Ella. It turned out to be the best thing she could have done, not only for Ella but for herself.

While Ella played with the yellow-eyed cat, Pele, Violet filled him in on the details. Of course, the whole island already knew what transpired, but it felt good to sit face-to-face with the big man and tell him every last detail. He held one of her hands as she spoke. His palms were calloused and as big as baseball mitts, but his warmth settled her.

"The most troubling thing of all is the guilt I feel for Ella carrying around this time bomb inside her. I should have known. I should have done more," she said.

"Only natural. But you now know something you didn't know back then. Forget 'I should have.' You can't go backward. Show Ella the future and all the possibility it holds."

"But how? How can we not go back when there is so much unfairness, so much pain? If only..."

"No more 'If only.' It's the same as 'I should have.'"

A pressure built up in her chest. He was asking the impossible. "How?"

"Answers don't come when you're searching. They come when you're living. Kids know this more than we do. That's why they play."

He nodded to Ella, who rustled around a long mulberry

branch in the grass for Pele. The cat was frantically pawing at the stick. The look on Ella's face was pure innocence. Unadulterated joy.

He continued, "When you take your daughter home, do her the favor of honoring her choice. It was a noble one."

A sob erupted from deep inside and she broke down, her whole body shaking. *Ella's choice.* Henry picked up her other hand and began chanting in a very low voice. Hawaiian words she couldn't understand. But the meaning was beyond language. It felt like he was inflating her with eons' worth of love. That was the only way she could describe it.

She made a silent promise and had been reminding herself ever since.

"If you don't open it, I will," Jean said, knocking her out of her daydream.

"You'll do nothing of the sort."

The envelope felt like lead in her hands. She escaped to the kitchen to read it. Narrow block letters arranged themselves neatly, announcing Parker Stone as the sender. With trembling fingers, she opened the envelope. The words were jammed together, leaving almost no margins.

Dearest Violet,

To have held you one more time before leaving. A thought I have constantly. They woke us up before the roosters and gave us two hours to gather our things. I tried to call. Believe me when I say I already miss you.

After passing through Honoka'a, we transferred to the sugarcane locomotive. It wasn't a pretty sight, all of us boys shoved in the flat cars like anchovies. Those cars are not made for humans and everyone has spent the last few days removing splinters from their hands and other more sensitive parts. On the other hand, we got to ride across narrow bridges hundreds of feet high and saw lush valleys and waterfalls. None as lovely as ours. I will always think of Hi'ilawe that way—yes, I committed her name to memory. I can even pronounce it! Once in Hilo, we marched through town. Maybe you saw photographs? Our division ended up on the *Lubbock*, which is almost new but as cramped as the flat cars. I wish I could tell you more, but we are sworn to secrecy. Though we ourselves are mostly in the dark. I will say that we passed over the USS *Arizona* resting on the ocean floor like a massive tomb. It was a sobering moment for all of us.

I hope Ella is doing well and that you ladies get to visit Roscoe as often as possible. Seeing those two together was a heartwarming sight. My thoughts have also been with you, wondering if old man Lalamilo was right about that cave. I guess by now you would know. The unfairness of life sometimes astounds me. Who lives and who dies? Is there anything we can do to sway the odds in our favor? The best I can come up with is not always. But I'm open to suggestions. I have the highest regard for you and what you have endured. I will do my best not to put you through that again. Not that I in any way want to compare myself to your husband.

In some ways, it all feels like a dream. The exotic location and your luminous skin. Every moment we spent together is alive in my mind like a motion picture. All I have to do is close my eyes. Which I do more often than I care to admit.

Always,

Parker

PS: Give my regards to Ella, Jean, Irene and Roscoe.

PSS: He loves cream.

Violet held the letter to her nose and inhaled any traces of his scent. Maybe she imagined it, but the paper smelled like burned oil and sweat. She read it again. The ache between her ribs deepened.

Jean strolled in. "So, any news?"

For some reason, she felt protective of the letter and quickly closed it up. "He sent it from Honolulu, but you know they're mum about where they're heading."

"He must have said something."

Violet stared at the words that said a whole lot more than something. "He said to say hi."

Jean rolled her eyes and walked back out the door.

The students at school must have been in cahoots about being extra nice. Even Johnny Martinez. Most of the kids had Luther for shop and they begged her over and over to tell the story of Roscoe sitting on him. Violet had never let on that she was the one in the room that morning, but somehow word had gotten out. As much as she wanted to put the whole thing behind her, reliving Luther's fright brought a measure of satisfaction.

"What about the soldier that owns Roscoe? Is he your boyfriend?" Johnny asked one morning.

You could have heard a feather fall in the classroom. "And how is that any of your business?" Nosing into her personal life was a common ploy to avoid schoolwork. She knew that. Sometimes it worked, but not today.

"'Cause you're a good lady, Mrs. Iverson. And you're wearing a dog tag," he said.

His face was so earnest, and his words softened her. "Parker and Zach and Tommy are like family. We're all praying they come home safely. End of story."

He wasn't done. "Is it true the Japanese eat whales?"

"Johnny, you're digressing. Get back to work."

When everyone finally settled down and typewriters clacked, Violet pulled out the letter. She felt like a child sneaking ice cream in the middle of the night.

A second letter arrived two days after the first. And another three days after that. Jean heard from Zach. Irene heard from Zach. Which caused her already brown skin to turn several shades darker. The marines hadn't sailed into the thunderclap of battle yet. That was still to come.

There was nothing unusual about the following Sunday morning. Showers rode in on the trades, most of the townsfolk were at one form of church or another, and Violet, Jean and Setsuko stood around the kitchen flipping pancakes and listening to a sermon on the radio. Setsuko had taken the kids to an early service and it worked out, since Violet and Jean shared the opinion that church was best saved for weddings and funerals.

"If they took out this fire-and-brimstone nonsense, I might go more often," Jean said.

None of them noticed the sound of an approaching car. The kids were outside tending the chickens. They heard Hiro yell first. "Dad?"

Violet dropped the ladle. Jean placed the bowl of batter on the counter, her eyes huge. Setsuko ran to the window and looked out into the glare. Violet and Jean fell over each other trying to see out from behind her. All three kids stared at the car as a reed-thin Takeo unfolded himself from the back seat and stood with his back erect. A tattered suitcase hung from one hand. His shoulders were slightly stooped, but he might have been the tallest man she'd ever seen. Freedom had that effect on a person.

Setsuko flew out the door and into the driveway.

"How come she didn't say anything about this?" Jean asked.

"I don't think she knew."

Hiro and Umi wrapped around him, faces buried in his chest. Takeo held on to Setsuko for dear life. She had her face pressed into the crook of his neck and her shoulders shuddered, like she was setting free all that hurt and fear. He motioned for Ella. She gave him a quick hug before tearing toward the house.

"Mama! Jean! Look who's back," she cried.

They filed down to the driveway. Up close, Violet saw the color of imprisonment on his face, sallow and pale. But the look in his eyes told another story, one of being home. Somehow, all seven of them managed to cling to each other. When Takeo met Violet's eyes, she knew that he knew.

"Who would have guessed?" were his first words.

That night, they sat down to a feast of lemon-baked ahi that Jean ran down to the market for. They steamed potfuls of rice, freshly pounded poi and baked the first chocolate honeycomb pie since the soldiers' departure. Takeo ate until he had to lie down. More than once, Violet caught him gazing at Setsuko or the kids with the kind of tenderness usually reserved for newborns.

Takeo is home.

Chapter Forty-Five

ELLA

TIME HEALS. PEOPLE ALWAYS SAY THAT TO ME. While that might be true, animals are the real secret to surviving any upset. I promise. Without Snowflake, Brownie and Roscoe, I hate to think how I would have managed. The thing about animals is they love you 110 percent. They could care less if you're covered in scabs and don't feel like talking. Or afraid of the whole world. Something about their warm heartbeat and even breathing. You ask me, they're better than any kind of lemon-scented balm.

The soldiers helped, too. When the first letter came, Mama turned pink and stayed that way the whole night. She moved around the kitchen like she was floating in a way I never saw before. With a constant smile on her face. I guess love does that to people. Why else would she act like this?

Every night at dinner, Jean has us all hold hands, and we ask God to keep an extra eye out for our boys. I think of them as men, but hold my tongue. If where they're going is anything like the photographs in the newspaper, they need every last one of our prayers. To tell the truth, whenever I stop to think, I send a request out. I hope God is listening.

For Christmas, Jean gave me a notebook. I plan on writing this all down. About my papa and what a brave man he was. He stood up for his friends and Mama says that is worth more than anything. Also, everyone should know what it feels like to live through a war. I can't remember life any other way, which may not be a good thing. Blackouts and bunny suits. Shortages of sugar and air-raid drills. Collecting metal scraps. And how for each soldier out fighting, there are people suffering at home, hoping their loved ones are spared. On both sides.

But not everything is bad. We made pies, we made friends. We fell in love.

I just hope it ends well.

Chapter Forty-Six

VIOLET

DESPITE JEAN'S PEP TALKS, VIOLET WAS HAVING a hard time pretending that things would turn out okay. She had learned the hard way that all the wishing in the world couldn't make something happen. And how falling in love encompassed both bliss and despair and everything in between. You couldn't have one without the other. That's what makes us human.

On a particularly moody Thursday afternoon, she received another letter, or as the soldiers would say, a *behavior report.* How they came up with these terms for even the most reasonable word, Violet would never know. Drop a bomb, *lay an egg.* Nap, *blanket drill.* Chaplain, *GI Jesus.* Grenade, *pineapple.*

Each letter Parker sent had been slightly longer than the previous, and this was no exception. As though he was afraid he had to get it all out in case he didn't return. At least, that was how Violet saw it. The crinkled paper shook in her hands. Perspiration formed on the back of her neck.

Dear Violet,

The day has finally come. They fed us steak and eggs for breakfast, as if that might mask the fact that we were about to invade a foul-smelling volcanic rock called Iwo Jima. I guess they saw it as a final meal for some of us, and that it was. We lost a lot of boys today, Violet. The war has suddenly become crushingly real. You've probably already seen this all in the papers and I'm not even sure if our mail is getting out, but writing to you is a balm for me. Iwo Jima is colder than Hawaii and the sky looked unusually wide and blue this morning. It seemed like a good day to live. Or a good day to die. I am prepared for anything, though my goal is to make it back in one piece to see you. I am doing my best. Just before noon, word came. "Boats on the beach! Stay brave! Victory! *Semper fi!*" Our boat fell in line behind the lead and moved toward the beach. A new Stars and Stripes flapped in the wind, and it was quite a sight, a bold reminder of why we're here. To keep our freedom, because without freedom, what do we have? As we closed in on the island, smoke and dust hid the beach and everything but the hump of Mt. Suribachi. Right away I thought of its counterpart on the Big Island. Hoku'ula. Now I know why they had us march up and down that hill as if our lives depended on it. Because they do.

Aircraft fell from the skies around us and in the distance a landing boat was blown to pieces. Explosions went off every few seconds, near and far. Unnerving to say the least, but having Zach by my side kept me sane. Still, nothing could have prepared us for the sight on the beach. We ran past twisted tanks and shards of armored vehicles. The sand was deep and not like sand at all, more like ash. Bodies lay everywhere. Things burned that shouldn't be able to burn. But worse than anything was the stench. Rotting flesh and gunpowder. Numb and without options, we plunged on. Time moved like syrup and we found a shell hole already occupied with other marines. No room. The farther inland we went, the safer we would be. Or so we thought. The darnedest thing was, we couldn't figure out where the Japanese were firing from. How could any of them have survived the relentless bombardment of the past few days? Underground, as it turns out. The Japanese aren't on Iwo Jima, Violet. They're in it.

Maybe you don't want to hear all of this? The good news is by some miracle of God and Ella's extra helping of prayers, our whole unit survived our first day on the island. Other than a few scratches and bruises, I am uninjured. I wish I could say the same for everyone else. We are all in a somber mood and no one is talking much. I wish we could get a few homemade pies to boost morale or even just see your beautiful faces. This is only the beginning, I won't lie. By the time you get this, you may already know the outcome.

Please, keep your letters coming. Knowing that you have closure on Herman is comfort to me because I know what it means to you. You are a strong woman, Violet Iverson. And Roscoe! Some people said I was a fool for bringing a lion to Hawaii, but he's touched more lives than he ever would have holed up in some zoo. He was the cheer on those blustery cold days in Waimea. The best mascot a man could ask for in this war. I miss that chap. Take good care of yourself and Ella and try not to worry about me. Know that you are my reason. The other half of my heart.

Love Always,
Parker

Chapter Forty-Seven

VIOLET

THE LETTERS STOPPED COMING. AFTER A FEW weeks of no mail and radio silence, everyone knew something was up. Violet had trouble sleeping, so each morning she waited on the lanai for the paperboy, Shunji Izumi, who was as precise with his timing as he was his throw. The paper always landed on the seagrass doormat at 6:14 sharp. On this particular morning, the wind started early, whipping up the trees in the yard and stirring up dirt. *Thud.* Shunji was on time. Violet opened the roll.

The headlines read, US MARINES STORM ASHORE ON IWO ISLAND! A black-and-white photo showed six men crouched behind a mounted gun and a cloud of smoke from a freshly fired blast. Behind them were ammunition shells and rifles. One man scanned a large hill with binoculars. All around, scraps of unrecognizable debris littered the landscape.

So this was Island X.

Iwo Jima. The name meant nothing.

Days passed, and with each, a new story. Every time Violet opened the paper, she broke out in a sweat.

MEN AND GUNS AT IWO JIMA.

In every photo, she and Jean inspected the faces closely, looking for features of Parker or Zach or any of their friends. In uniform and from a distance, it was hard to be sure. But Parker she would know anywhere.

"That guy has Zach's height, but twice his girth," Jean said about one.

"How about him?" Violet said.

"No way. Too short."

OLD GLORY GOES UP OVER IWO. IWO PEAK CAPTURED.

A photo of marines throwing all their weight into raising the American flag swelled her chest with pride. There was something intimate about seeing those men at the top of the mountain, flat-out determination on their faces. In another shot of the same moment, a group of twenty-five or so men stood around the flag with their arms raised. Violet pulled out the magnifying glass.

"It looks like Zach," she said.

"Give me that!" Jean said. She peered through the glass. "I think it is. And Parker and Tommy over here. They're alive!" Jean straightened up and held open her arms, and Violet leaned into them as they closed around her. The battle to capture Iwo Jima dragged on. And on.

IWO CASUALTIES TOTAL 3,650.

Seeing the numbers pile up was a slow form of agony.

"Why do they have to torture us with this? I don't like this new up-close-and-personal form of reporting," Jean said.

They'd gotten in the habit of holding hands when reading the paper and Jean's palm felt sweaty. "Everything changes when you love someone out there, doesn't it?"

"How can capturing one small rock be worth all these lives?" Jean asked, sighing.

"Airfields. At least, that's what they say."

On a regular basis, whether or not their mail was being received, Violet, Jean and Ella wrote letters for their soldiers. Ella drew detailed pictures of Roscoe and they sent evidence of his recent growth spurt. The veterinarian in Waimea said Roscoe had gained twenty pounds since the marines left town. By the time they returned, he might be a full-grown lion. Violet included the newspaper clip with details of finding Herman, and how Roscoe was the new town hero.

On one of the rare mornings when Jean grabbed the paper first, she spread it out on the table for all to see. "You have to see this!"

The photograph showed two men in combat utilities. Dust caked their helmets. One sat on a piece of blasted concrete and held a plank of wood in place. The other was kneeling and finishing painting the words POST OFFICE. 4th Mar Div. Iwo Jima.

"Bless their hearts," Violet said.

"This means they're getting mail."

They continued writing with vigor.

MARINES SLICE IWO IN TWO AND CAPTURE MAIN AIRFIELD.

Though it looked like the Americans were making ground, the Japanese continually caught them off guard. Snipers, kamikaze and hidden heavy artillery took their toll. The Japanese soldiers also hid out in caves and tunnels, coming out only at night for ambushes. Violet was torn apart by the inability of the United States to end the battle once and for all. Too much killing.

Facial expressions on the living were enough to make you close your eyes and pray to a God you weren't sure existed. The faces of the dead were worse.

When Violet woke up a few weeks later, every bone in her body ached. *This is stupid*, she thought. Instead of going outside to wait for Shunji and the latest war news, she went to Ella's room and dropped into the chair next to her bed.

She watched the sun come up a fiery yellow, throwing light across the walls. A dove cooed outside. Jean always claimed that Violet worried too much, and maybe that was true. What was worry but a waste of time? Spending every morning entrenched on Iwo Jima would help no one.

In the kitchen, when Jean showed up, looking smooth-haired and rested, Violet made an announcement. "From this day forward, I'm on a newspaper diet."

"Newspaper doesn't taste very good, honey. You sure you want to do that?"

Violet folded her arms. "No more reading about that godforsaken island. I want to spend my time thinking about what's going on here."

"'No news is good news' now makes more sense, doesn't it?" Jean said.

The final straw had been a reprint yesterday of a Western Union telegram in the newspaper, received by a family on the day after Christmas. Unable to stop herself, she read the words on the small square of paper again and again. Two stars were stamped at the top of the telegram.

> THE NAVY DEPARTMENT DEEPLY REGRETS TO INFORM YOU THAT YOUR SON ######## FIRST MATE USN WAS KILLED IN ACTION IN THE PERFORMANCE OF HIS DUTY AND IN THE SERVICE OF HIS COUNTRY. THE DEPARTMENT EXTENDS TO YOU ITS SINCEREST SYMPATHY ON YOUR GREAT LOSS. ON ACCOUNT OF EXISTING CONDITIONS, THE BODY IF RECOVERED CANNOT BE RETURNED AT PRESENT. IF FUTURE DETAILS ARE RECEIVED YOU WILL BE INFORMED. TO PREVENT POSSIBLE AID TO OUR ENEMIES, PLEASE DO NOT DIVULGE THE NAME OF HIS SHIP OR STATION.—REAR ADMIRAL DICKENS THE CHIEF OF NAVAL PERSONNEL.

The irony of it caused her eyes to sting. She thought about closure and all those people who would have to live without. Always wondering. The idea wrapped her in heartache.

On March 16, Irene Ferreira called just before she and Ella left for school. "For heaven's sake, open up the paper," she said.

Violet threw down her coffee and ran out to the porch. She forced herself to read.

IWO SECURED BY AMERICANS!
6,800 DEAD. 20,000 WOUNDED.

Chapter Forty-Eight

VIOLET

VIOLET HAD NO FINGERNAILS LEFT. NOR DID Jean. On the same day that they got word the USS *Lubbock* was en route to Hilo, two letters arrived in the mail. One from Parker's mother, Elise, and one from Parker himself. It was only the third letter from Parker since he'd shipped out from Pearl Harbor. She felt a bout of hyperventilation coming on and dropped the other mail on the driveway. She gripped one envelope in each hand.

Where is Jean?

She forced herself to check the dates. The letter from Mrs. Elise Stone was dated March 20, Parker's March 12.

Trade winds had ramped up in the past few days, bending the trees sideways. *Iwo Jima has no trees.* Beneath her feet, the grass felt springy and soft. *Iwo Jima has no grass.* She made it to the patio and fell back on the *pune'e*, clutching both letters to her chest. A lizard watched from above with bulging eyes. She could see two eggs on each side of its spine, and wondered if Iwo Jima had any life on it at all.

Jean came out, letting the screen door slam behind her. "Anything?" One look at Violet and she froze. "What is it?"

Violet held up both letters. "One from his mom and one from him."

Jean shuffled over and joined her, letting her head fall back in the mound of cushions. "You haven't opened them?"

"Which one do I open first?"

"Let me see." Jean scanned both envelopes. "Maybe she wants to let you know he is okay."

"Parker told me if anything happened, his mother would write."

His envelope was crinkled and thin. His mother's was sealed with wax. Both felt heavier than a truckload of coconuts. She worked out the dates in her head. Parker could have still had time to write. And then die. Mail delivery was surprisingly fast in this day and age.

Please, God.

Violet remembered that first day on the porch when Zach had shown up unexpectedly. Parker stood outside. The man with silver eyes. Back then, he meant nothing to her. She thought about the telegram in the newspaper. Small black words. She felt dizzy.

Why has his mom written?

The passage of time seemed to change with the wind, gusting and then still as stone. If Parker was alive, she needed to know *this very second*; yet if he was dead, then what? Maybe it all boiled down to *acceptance*. Once again. Acceptance that life was far from fair, but if you followed love instead of fear, you would come out ahead. No matter what.

Oh, how I love him.

Jean took charge. "Listen, he has to be alive. They all do. I say open the one from him."

Perhaps if she remained motionless, nothing would change. But willing things not to happen was never enough. Violet's hands trembled. "It would be easier not to open either of them."

Jean avoided her eyes. "I'm here, when you're ready."

Her mind worked out a solution on its own. "I'll open his, and you open the other one." She handed Jean the letter. "At the same time."

Through the side of her eye, she caught movement, and noticed Ella was standing in the doorway, barefoot. No doubt wondering why her mother's face had lost all blood.

"Honey, go outside and check on the chickens."

Ella did not move. Her eyes scoured the letters in their hands. "Why do you look funny?"

"Letters from the boys." She and Jean both held them up. "Just a bit anxious. Go on. I'll be out in a minute."

Looking unconvinced, Ella skipped away across the lanai and down the front steps, singing a Japanese song.

Violet held the envelope to her nose. Traces of diesel and ash. Steadying her fingers was trouble, but she opened it without tearing the paper. The usual neat writing had been replaced by shaky scribbles. The words were all over the place.

Dear Violet,

I hope this letter finds you well, and pray that it reaches you before any other news. You see, there was a mix-up involving me missing from the hospital ship. I had a concussion and left without telling anyone. Maybe I was dumb to go back to the island. But what else could I have done when my brothers were still valiantly fighting, inch by inch, to gain hold. Now I've gone and gotten myself shot through the bicep. I'm not going to lie. There's a nasty infection and the doc is talking about losing the arm. I will try to write more when this fever passes. Did you know that I sneaked on deck and watched our favorite star last night? Trustworthy, even in the ugliest of times.

Always,
Parker

Lost in his words, she temporarily forgot about the other letter. When she looked up, she saw that Jean had turned the same color as a bedsheet.

Violet thrust his letter in her face. "Oh, dear. It was a mistake, honey."

Jean grabbed it, and once she'd finished reading, she let out the sigh of a lifetime. "Talk about the worst kind of blunder. His poor mother. That letter had me fooled."

"Someone owes her an apology."

When they had first sat down, clouds dotted the sky. Now rain hissed around them and Ella tore in from the yard. Maybe it was imagination, or wishing, but Ella looked rounder in places that before were just bone. All this took place in the span of a couple of minutes. But it seemed more like hours. And what of the infection? She'd read about a new form of drug called antibiotic being tested by the military. Couldn't they try that on Parker?

She patted the spot next to her for Ella. "Sounds like they're coming home, sweetie. Maybe not in one piece, but alive."

Four days later, news spread around town that a navy ship had docked at Pearl Harbor the previous night. Violet and Ella were walking up the steps from school when the phone rang. She tossed aside her purse and papers and dashed through the door, racing to answer before the caller hung up.

The connection crackled and a woman's voice came across. "Is there a Violet Iverson in the house?"

Her heart pounded. "Speaking."

"This is Wilma from Tripler Army Medical Center. I have a young man here, been pestering me to call you. Normally we don't do this. Hang on a sec."

Violet thought she heard the cord stretch and metal clattering in the background. She reminded her lungs to breathe.

"Violet?" His voice sounded far away, and yet more solid than the island under her feet.

All those prayers have somehow gotten through.

"Parker, is that you?"

"We made it, Violet. We're home."

There was so much blue in the sky.

Epilogue

I KNOW IT'S ABSURD, BUT I BELIEVE IN THE power of people loving you. While it didn't work for my papa, because everything happened so fast and we didn't have enough time to pray, I think it worked for Parker and Zach. Hearing they survived was like taking a huge breath after being held underwater for five minutes. Or like a hot bath on a cold night. Only, multiplied by a hundred.

After Mama got the call that he was still alive but in grave danger of losing his arm, we ramped up our positive thinking. Jean organized a get-well campaign and we all wrote cards and drew pictures for his hospital room. Umi and I even made him origami flowers, since we couldn't send real ones. He told Mama being in the hospital was worse than being in battle. I tried to imagine losing an arm, but couldn't. According to the newspapers, soldiers were losing more than just their arms. Bayonets were one thing, but cannonballs another. They ripped men in half.

But enough about that. Mama wanted to hop the first ship to Honolulu, but she had school to teach. Not only that but the nurse said no visitors. Parker was too sick. My fingernails were bit down raw, but I had the sense that he would live. Don't ask me how—I just *knew* he'd get better. He survived this far. I can't say the same for Mama, who crossed her arms and said she refused to lose another man. It was simply impossible. Her lip quivered when she said it and she broke down in tears. On a Sunday, she even went to church with Setsuko to talk to God.

After three weeks and loads of fretting, we got the call that we could come visit. "Looks like I get to keep my arm," he said, "and I'm sure going to need both so I can hug you and Ella tight. And I won't let go, so you better be ready." We danced around the kitchen after that, and Mama arranged for one week off. Luckily, Mr. Nakata found a substitute teacher. I think he would do anything to make Mama happy after all she'd been through. Anyone would.

Signs of spring showed up everywhere in Honoka'a. The plovers arrived back from wherever they flew off to, skies turned sunny, and *lilikoi* grew fat on the vine. Beaches were still blockaded, but something happened on that Island X that changed the feeling around here. There was talk that we might actually win the war and it would finally end. People's faces changed, weird as it may sound, and there were a lot more smiles going on.

Mama and I boarded the steamer down at Kawaihae. The *Lehua*, she was called. A very long and tall ship that seemed impossible to float. The water was clear and flat and colored like the sky. You could see the coral and yellow fish darting around as we went out to sea. When I stuck my tongue out, I tasted salt. Mama looked beautiful in her finest yellow dress. Setsuko had sewn me one to match. We held hands as we watched the Big Island get smaller and smaller and finally fall into the ocean. I felt so happy, I wanted to cry.

I think Mama was crying.

Then she said something I will never forget. "Ella, remember, you always have a choice in life. Even in the worst of circumstances, when all seems lost and the world is going down the tubes around you, surround yourself with love and everything will turn out all right."

I don't know about you, but it's how I plan to live.

★ ★ ★ ★ ★

Acknowledgments

THOUGH THIS NOVEL AND ITS CHARACTERS were formed from my imagination, Camp Tarawa and the soldiers who lived there were very real.

War never leaves you. I know this because my grandfather, Herman Larsgaard, was the high school principal in Honoka'a during World War II, and my grandmother, Helen, was a teacher. While many people left for the safety of the mainland, my grandparents stayed. They housed many of the marines on weekends and holidays, and they soon became close friends. When those soldiers left, it tore my grandmother apart. The only consolation was in knowing that she played a role in improving their lives before they shipped out to Saipan and Iwo Jima. I can still see the twinkle in her eye and hear the soft lilt of her voice telling me about the day she drove up Kawaihae Road with a lion breathing down her neck, or how she almost got shot simply for walking down the street at night. She was the real storyteller.

A book is never written in a vacuum, and I owe heartfelt thanks to my mother, Diane McFaull, a young girl when Pearl Harbor was bombed; my uncle Billy Larsgaard; my father, Douglas Ackerman; and dear friend Marilyn Carlsmith, who all provided me with rich details about wartime Hawaii as well as a lifetime of support.

Also, to Elizabeth Bernstein; my agent, Elaine Spencer; and my editor, Ann Leslie Tuttle, for their wisdom, guidance and brilliant editing skills, which truly made all the difference.

I've pored over numerous accounts from soldiers stationed here, where many of my ideas sprang from, and found an article in the *Waimea Gazette* titled "Waimea Remembers Camp Tarawa," written by Gordon Bryson, to be particularly helpful. Kathy Painton at the Camp Tarawa Foundation and Dr. Billy Bergin also took the time to meet with me and "talk story," for which I am grateful.

To my first reader, Mary Smolenski; my forest walking friends, Jennifer Freitas, Mahealani Holzman and Leesa Robertson; my fellow author and cheerleader, Lilly Barels; my number one fan, Mia Kresser; and my love, Todd Clark—a big, warm mahalo.

Aloha,
Sara Ackerman
AckermanBooks.com